ELLE RIVERS

Cover Design by Haya In Designs

Edited by Kasey Kubica, Basic Behemoth Edits

Proofread by Mae Peredo, Wildwood Author Services

 Created with Vellum

A Note from Elle

This novel contains scenes some might find upsetting. This book contains explicit spice and verbal and physical violence from a sibling, both past and present. A character also has migraines that affect their daily life, and one happens on page.

If you come across a potential trigger not mentioned here, please email me at elle@ellerivers.com.

For every "weird" girl who grew up finding peace in books, trying to please people who didn't deserve you—this one's for you. I hope you find someone who treats you like Levi treats Amy.

Playlist

Apple — Charlie XCX
Close To You — Gracie Abrams
Late Night Talking — Harry Styles
Safe and Sound — Capital Cities
Rather Be — Clean Bandit
Espresso — Sabrina Carpenter
Birds of a Feather — Billie Eilish
Juno — Sabrina Carpenter
The Perfect Pair — beabadoobee
Anti-Hero — Taylor Swift
Secrets — OneRepublic
Daylight — Taylor Swift
Karma — Taylor Swift
La La La — Naughty Boy, Sam Smith
my tears ricochet — Taylor Swift

Prologue

My parents went all out for this party.

All out might not even be enough to describe it. Maybe over-the-top would have been a better term.

There were balloons on every available surface. The cake ordered had its own zip code and was second in size only to the massive banner hanging on the wall behind the table.

I was pretty sure this thing was bigger than our graduation, which was only a year ago. All of my family had flown in for this, as well as most of our former high school classmates. They all wanted to see the Willard twins celebrate getting one year older.

Well, *twin*.

"Happy birthday, Calvin!" my parents called as he walked through the door.

Everyone else followed. I'd walked in a few minutes ago and had a few people stop to congratulate me, but it was obvious who all of this was for.

Calvin was the golden child, the one Mom and Dad poured all of their energy into. He thrived whenever all of their attention was focused on him, and I did okay fading into the background.

His straight As, endless girlfriends, and vibrant social life spoke for themselves. I was doing fine just getting on the honor roll. But having a social life? Impossible.

Earlier, I'd asked Mom if this party was for *him* or for us. She insisted that we were both being celebrated. She even showed me that my name was on the cake.

Under Calvin's, of course.

But it was nice that I was even on it.

"And Amy!" Mom added, pointing over to me. Eyes turned, and I had to resist the urge to look away from Calvin's near glare when his head swiveled with the rest.

The attention didn't last, though, because Calvin insisted we cut the cake. I wasn't sure if I was relieved or disappointed to have been passed over so quickly.

I didn't do well with attention, especially when it was taken from Calvin. Neither did he. My brother was as prone to jealous rages as he was at being perfect in all other aspects of his life.

Mom and Dad told me it was best that they focus on him to keep the peace.

I tried to be okay with it. And I would be.

I had my one friend, Ava, who I'd even invited here today. I met her on the first day of college, and I'd always kept my brother's identity a secret, determined to have a friend of my own. I was pretty sure she liked me now and would stick by my side rather than run to Calvin's as everyone else had.

The fact that she'd even come to the party without me having to mention Calvin's name spoke volumes.

That had never happened before, but I desperately hoped it would continue.

She arrived right after my shout-out, eyes wide as she searched for me. I waved her over, ready to introduce her to everyone I knew.

"Hey," she said quietly. "Happy birthday. I got you a card."

"Thank you," I said, opening it immediately. She'd signed it with a happy face and her name.

And had addressed it only to me.

I looked up at her, about to ask if she'd like to meet my little sister, who was heading over to us as we spoke.

But her eyes were on the crowd.

"I also got your brother one," she said. "Where is he?"

A lump formed in my throat.

"You know I have a brother?"

"Everyone does. He's famous, which means you are too. In a way."

Now I had a sinking feeling in my stomach too.

Was his card nicer than mine? Would she linger longer when she gave it to him?

No. She was *my* friend. I met her first. She met *me* first. She wouldn't do that to me.

"He's in the center of the room. He got cake already."

She nodded and went to search for him.

I tried not to feel bitter as I joined at the back of the line of people to get my slice, waiting for the majority to get theirs instead of rushing with the crowd.

"Did they really make you wait in line for your own birthday cake?" my younger sister, Emma, asked. She'd been an accidental third child. Both Mom and Dad were content to give all of their attention to Calvin, and sometimes me. When she came along, they were done with the parenting thing, giving her free rein to do what she wanted.

Emma wasn't a bad kid, but she was a newly minted angsty teenager. I'd done a lot of the childcare for her even when I'd been far too young to. At first, she'd blamed me for that, refusing my help in any kind of way. Then that anger had shifted to Mom and Dad.

She blamed them for everything these days.

"I didn't want to go up there anyway." I shrugged. She rolled her eyes and cut the line, loudly proclaiming that she was getting the birthday girl a slice of her own cake. I blushed and pulled her aside, waving off the glares of the other people in line. "You didn't have to do that."

"And yet, I did. Here you go," she said as I grabbed the plate and fork, taking a big bite. "Fair warning, it's chocolate."

I grimaced when the flavor hit my tongue. "Damn. I could have sworn I asked for half vanilla."

"They probably forgot. Like they always do with you."

"Or they handed you the wrong piece. It's fine. I don't hate chocolate that much."

"You absolutely do."

I took another bite to prove her wrong, keeping my face straight as I chewed.

"You're too nice," she said.

"And you're too angry," I replied. "I'm fine, Emma. All I wanna do is have a relaxed birthday party."

"Where's your friend?"

"She had a card for Calvin."

"*Oh.* And she hasn't come back yet?"

"She will."

An uncomfortable silence settled over us, and I put down my fork, unable to stomach any more chocolate.

"Can I at least have the rest of the cake?"

I wordlessly handed her the plate, eyes searching for water to cleanse my palate. She told me she was going back to her room to hide out from all the noise. I'd probably be following her soon.

After grabbing a glass of water, I gulped it down until the taste of chocolate was only barely there and took a deep breath. The kitchen was quiet in the way the rest of the house wasn't, even though I could hear the party going on in the living room.

Sometimes, being home felt like being the photographer of an event. I was the outsider, always slightly weird and quiet, while Calvin charmed anyone he was around. I thought it would get better in the anonymity of college, but he chose the same school as me and ruled things there too. He went to every party and kept his grade point average up. Whenever people said hello to me, they would follow it up by asking how or where my twin was.

I *wasn't* jealous. He deserved it. But it would be nice if someone noticed me for a change.

"There you are." A voice broke the relative silence. "I've been looking for you everywhere."

I paused with the glass halfway up to my lips. That was a *man's* voice. Not just any man's, but one who definitely should not be here.

Levi Hensen was the one person Calvin could *not* charm. They'd met in high school when Calvin was on the wrestling team with him. Levi was the top performer, and Calvin had tried desperately to catch up. When it didn't work, Calvin threw a hissy fit, demanding Levi take extra time to train him.

And Levi said no.

That was the start of the decline between the two of them. Things only grew colder ever since. I never talked to Levi since he was always in the popular crowd. I wasn't even aware he knew my name, especially since he was busy conquering the college we all went to.

Calvin had always said he wanted to take Levi down a peg and even followed him to my college to do so. So far, Levi was as vicious as he was smart. He challenged Calvin in every way and then beat him at his own game.

"I think you have the wrong person," I said. "I'm Amy, Calvin's sister."

"I know."

"And most people don't look for me."

"That's a shame."

I stared at him, his words not computing. "Is this a joke or something?"

"The only joke here is your twin brother, but he's not in the room right now, and I couldn't care less about him."

"How did you get invited to his party?"

5

"I thought the party was for the both of you."

"It is, but he's the star of the show and had control of the guest list."

Levi leaned against the counter. "If you must know, he invited me to show off."

"And you're okay with that?"

"Not really, especially since it's also your birthday and no one seems to be lining up to talk to you."

"You don't know me. I don't *want* people lining up."

"How about just *one* person?" he asked.

"And who might that be?"

"Me. Happy birthday, Amy Willard."

His voice curled around my name, making my skin erupt in gooseflesh. "T-thanks."

"You're welcome. Can I ask how you're spending your nineteenth birthday?"

"Mostly here. And then I'll pick a book for my book club on Monday."

"You have the one that meets at the library every week, right?"

"I do. How did you know?"

"I tried to book one of the study rooms once, but they were all taken at the time. Mostly by people doing homework, though the one you were in was very lively. Everyone seemed to be having fun."

"You probably caught us when we were reading a really good book. We've been told to quiet down a few times. Sorry you couldn't reserve the room, though."

"It's not a problem. It made me finally realize there was another, far better Willard at our school."

"Just because I'm not annoying to you doesn't make me better."

"I'll be the judge of that."

His eyes were on me. *Only* me. It did unfair things to my brain.

I wasn't one to get much attention, especially not from men. If I did, they all wanted to get through me to Calvin.

I hadn't gotten a gift for my birthday, but maybe whatever god above had decided to swoop in and give me *this* instead.

"D-do you want something to drink?" I asked. "We have water, soda. Alcohol, for some reason . . ."

"Just water, thanks."

My face was on fire as I got him what he asked for. I watched as he took the glass and drank the whole thing in one go.

How had I never realized he was good-looking? He was practically Adonis, with a symmetrical, chiseled face and dimples to die for. His dark brown hair was longer than I remembered but was casually pushed back on his head. His blue-green eyes were striking against his dark lashes.

I gulped, hoping I didn't blow this. The last thing I'd expected for today was to be living in my very own meet-cute.

"What book are you reading right now?" he asked.

"You want to know what kind of books I'm reading?"

"Of course I do. How many have you torn through by now, a hundred?"

According to Goodreads, I'd done that this year alone. "Yeah, something like that."

He tilted his head, a corner of his mouth quirking. "So, you have to be reading something right now, right?"

"I am. It's about a woman who's a wallflower. She meets this ridiculously hot guy—"

"Seems a little autobiographical, does it not?"

"What do you mean?"

He gestured between the two of us.

"Well, it could be. But the hot guy kinda breaks her heart after getting her pregnant, so I hope not."

Levi laughed and shook his head. His cheeks turned red, and I realized this was the first time I'd seen him embarrassed. "I should have let you finish your sentence. Is that sort of thing normal in romance books?"

"Some of them. This one is about groveling."

"And what's that?"

"Where the guy messes up and has to make it up to her." I couldn't resist my smile. "It's one of my favorite tropes."

"Did you know that your face lights up when discussing books?"

A flush of heat spread from my cheeks to my toes. "I . . . didn't. I guess I don't talk to many people about them."

"What about your book club?"

"I let others talk about their books. And there aren't any guys in there anyway."

"What book is it?" he asked. "I'll read it, even if only to prove that guys can like romance books."

I had to take a shaky breath before I told him the name of it. He took out his phone and ordered it without a second thought.

"That was quite possibly the hottest thing I've ever seen," I said.

He looked up, raising an eyebrow. "Really?"

"Yes. Definitely. Questions followed by conviction. Super attractive."

"Hopefully, I'll be half as hot as you are."

My eyes moved to the mirror in the hallway that was just barely in my field of view. Mom checked her hair in it every morning. I did sometimes.

With my curly hair, which usually was frizzier than anything, I didn't always look great. Tonight, I'd put more effort into my appearance for my birthday. Still, even with the makeup, I'd say I was more pretty than hot.

"Are you sure you have the right person?" I asked, eyes sliding back to Levi.

"Very sure."

"I . . . You . . . Do you want to go to my room?"

∽∽∽∽

My room was occupied. When I saw a flash of a bare ass, I slammed the door shut.

Technically, it wasn't my room anymore since I went off to college. Mom was desperate for a guest space, and since Emma existed and Calvin needed a game room, we were out of space despite our massive house. The second I moved into the dorm, everything I'd left behind was put in a storage room so Mom could let guests sleep here.

Still, I used it whenever I was staying at home, and the plan was for me to sleep in the house tonight. Shouldn't I have first dibs on bringing a guy there?

"Sorry," I said. "Seems like someone got to it first."

"There has to be somewhere else in this house that's free," he said. He gestured to the hallway. "One of these closed doors has to have somewhere private."

"One of them is my little sister's, and Calvin's room is off-limits, but his game one—"

"He has a gaming room too?"

"He asked for one a while ago. No one says no to him."

A shadow crossed over Levi's face and he grabbed my hand. "Sounds like that's where we'll find privacy. Lead the way."

I opened the door to the room at the back of the house. A massive TV sat on the wall with a couch in front of it. As with everything, there were no decorations adorning the white walls. Calvin liked to say that he didn't have time to decorate since he had such a full social life.

"I don't know what kinds of games Calvin has or if he'd ever *let* us play."

"Who cares about games? I want to get to know you."

While I gaped like a fish, Levi led me to the couch. I didn't think I'd ever sat on it since Dad got it two years ago.

I felt like a rebel tonight.

"Tell me about yourself."

"Well, if you know about Calvin, you know a lot about me. I was born in Nashville, we went to the same schools—"

"I don't care about the stuff you share with *him*. I want to know *you*. Like how you got this scar." His hand grazed the bottom of my lip where a barely perceptible sliver of white cut through my skin.

"I fell face-first down the playground stairs."

I was pushed by Calvin, but Levi already hated him enough. No need to say that out loud.

"Those things are dangerous."

"It's okay. I learned how fun reading was while recovering."

And I learned that it was the one thing my brother couldn't care less about.

Levi smiled softly, moving his finger from my lip and using his palm to prop up his head as he looked at me.

"So what about you? Admittedly, I didn't pay much attention to you."

"Why not?"

"People who see Calvin first don't really look twice at me." I shrugged. "You have my attention now, though."

He huffed out a laugh. "I'm a guy who sees through people's shit. Calvin has a habit of throwing fits when things don't go his way."

"He was like that when he was a toddler too."

"It must have been hard. As an only child, I can't imagine sibling rivalry."

"It's not much of a rivalry when Calvin gets whatever he wants."

"He doesn't get *everything* he wants," Levi said.

And it was true. When it came to the man in front of me, he was immune to whatever Calvin pulled over everyone else.

"Your hair is so curly." Levi tucked a strand behind my ear. "I love it."

"You should see me when I first wake up. It's not that cute then."

His eyebrow crept up to his hairline. "Are you offering?"

"I, uh . . . I have no idea." My entire body was on fire. "I didn't mean to, but I wouldn't say no."

I wanted to kiss him, but I had no idea how to ask for that. Did I lean in? Did I wait for *him* to lean in? I was so out of the loop with socializing that it wasn't funny.

Luckily for me, Levi took the lead. He wasted no time pressing his lips onto mine, silencing all of my thoughts.

Just like in my books, the world melted away. I wasn't at my brother's party, wishing someone would notice me. I had a guy whose only focus was on me.

I heard Levi suck in a sharp breath of air as his hands moved across my cheeks. His thumb caressed them, probably smearing the light dusting of makeup I had on. He leaned in, his body pressing closer to mine as his tongue brushed across my bottom lip. He smelled good. Every inch of him against my skin was nice.

This was electric. Perfection.

Nothing could ruin this moment.

"What the *fuck*?"

I had spoken too soon.

Slowly, I moved away from Levi toward the figure in the door.

Calvin stood, arms crossed and brows pinched as he surveyed the two of us.

"Wh-what are you doing here?" I asked.

"What am *I* doing here? This is *my* room."

"Technically, it's your game room, and someone was in mine."

And then I saw who he was with. Thick glasses. Wide eyes.

Ava.

He was holding her hand, obviously bringing her in here to do God knows what.

Damn it. She'd been charmed by him too.

But Calvin's jaw hung open, and he didn't stop to think twice about who he was with. He was more worried about who *I* was with. "You're kissing Levi Hensen, and *that's* what you say to me?"

"I . . . Is there something else to say? You're with my friend too."

He rolled his eyes, clearly seeing me as a lost cause, and his gaze fell to Levi.

"And *you*. I invite you to show off my party, and you get revenge by kissing my sister?"

Levi's smile was so different from the ones he had been giving me that it made me do a double take. "What, does it bother you?"

Calvin *did* look bothered as he glared and crossed his arms over his chest. "There is no limit to what you would do to piss me off."

Levi only shrugged.

Whatever joy I felt dissipated into a cloud of smoke. He . . . *what*?

Suddenly, it all made sense. Levi and Calvin's odd competition had reached a boiling point, and now I was involved.

I was collateral in their fight.

God, I was an idiot. How did I not see this coming? There was never a time when Calvin and I were in the same place and I was the one who got the attention.

Hurt bloomed in my chest and spread to every corner of me, started by Ava being with Calvin, and brought to the forefront of my mind by Levi's words.

But I wouldn't cry—not in front of everyone who had hurt me.

"I should have never invited you," Calvin said. "You can't handle seeing me do well."

"And *you*—" Levi started, but I'd heard enough.

I stood. "Excuse me."

Levi turned to me. "Wait—"

I didn't give him a chance to say anything else. I brushed past Calvin and headed outside, fishing my phone out of my pocket.

The only place I wanted to be was the one where someone would listen to me cry. I had one person in my life who fit the bill.

Gram.

GRAM PULLED up alongside me as I walked down the road, my arms crossed to keep myself warm in the cool spring air. Her gray hair was in a braid today, and she was so tall even when sitting that the top of her head brushed the roof of the tiny Toyota she drove.

"What are you doing a mile away from home?"

"I didn't want anyone to find me," I said. "I'm pretty sure some of the neighbors are scarred, though. They all saw me crying, and I am *not* a pretty crier."

"Crying is no way to spend your nineteenth birthday," she said. "What did Calvin do this time?"

"He didn't do anything. Well, nothing more than what I'm used to." I wiped my face. "Mom and Dad tried to make the party equal."

She raised one brow.

"*Tried.* It was a guy who did this."

"A man, huh? Typical. I know how they are." And she did. Gram had been through her fair share of heartbreak. Her first husband had left her the second she found out she was pregnant, and others seemed to disappoint her when things got real. It had started with her first love, a man who she never liked to speak of, and only got worse from there.

She always told me that romance was never like the books, but I held out hope.

I was wrong.

"You know that guy that Calvin hates?"

"There are many."

"Everyone likes Calvin."

"I'm sure that's what he thinks," she said. I would never know why Calvin didn't have the same relationship with Gram that I did. We were all close when we were younger, but Gram had gotten this way once he pulled away from me and excelled at everything. "So what did this guy do?"

"He made a move on me to piss off Calvin."

"He *what*?" Her eyes narrowed and her brow pulled low. "I should go back there and—"

"No," I said quickly. "I don't wanna be anywhere near the party. I just want to spend what's left of my birthday trying to feel better. I didn't even get a cake that I liked."

"Did they get chocolate again?"

"Yes." I sighed.

"All right, then. I know our next stop."

She took me to the store where she let me pick out whatever cake I wanted. We drove back to her house in the historical part of Nashville where we got into comfy pajamas and lounged on the couch. I wanted to enjoy my cake, especially since Gram had found a vanilla one with cream cheese icing, but I picked at it sullenly.

"Should I go get Emma?" she asked. "She can hang out with us too."

"No, she's probably in her room on the phone with her friends."

"What can I do to help?"

"I just feel so stupid," I said. "How long do I have to feel this way?"

"You're not dumb. *He* is for doing this to you. It took me a long time to learn that lesson."

"From Mom's dad?"

"No," she said. "From Albert. My first love."

Her eyes drifted to the nearby window, going vacant like they always did when she mentioned the past.

"We don't have to talk about it."

"We should," she replied. "Because it would help you."

"I don't know if anything would help."

"Amy, I need you to know you're not alone in this." She reached over to pat my hand. "Women, time and time again, have been hurt by those they love. Especially ones they trusted."

"Like you have?"

"Unfortunately, yes. In many ways."

"At least this wasn't as big of a deal. It was just a kiss."

"But it hit you where it hurts. I know you like to pretend Calvin doesn't bother you, but it's okay if he does."

"Everyone loves him. I'm just . . . different."

"And that's what I love about you," she said. "You're like me when I was your age. And I don't want to see you lose your spark because of some man's revenge tactic."

"I won't. I refuse to. I'll be okay."

"Good. Now eat your cake. We can watch whatever movie you want."

"What about a romance?"

"You want to watch *that* after tonight?"

"Fiction is easier. Everyone gets a happy ending there. I know it's not the same in real life."

"It's not." She turned on the TV. "But it's okay to pretend for a while."

As she put on the movie, the hurt that settled over me lifted and I finally felt like myself again.

I was dozing off when Gram's hand landed on my cheek.

"Do you want to stay here tonight or go home?" she asked as the clock struck midnight.

"I *am* home," I said sleepily.

She gave me a soft smile and ruffled my hair. "I'll make up the guest room bed, then."

∞∞∞

STRESS ALWAYS TOOK a toll on me, more so than I wanted to admit. A few days later, when my next book club meeting came around, I couldn't shake the pounding in my head and there was no way for me to lead the discussion.

But me being me, I tried to join anyway, but the library lights nearly made my head explode and I couldn't focus on the book at all.

"Amy, it's okay if you go home," one of my fellow members said. I was in so much pain I didn't even know *who* it was.

"I want to be here."

"But you obviously have a migraine," she said. "No one expects you to push through something this bad. It's just book club."

My heart lurched. I wanted to be here more than anything. I didn't want to deal with the pain that popped into my life whenever it decided to wreck my plans.

"I'll be back next week."

"Of course," she said. "And this time, I'll lead."

She sounded excited about it, and I wondered if she would be better at this than me and eventually try to take over the book club. Calvin would have.

"Okay," I said, despite my disappointment. "I'll see you next week."

It took all of my energy to stand and make my way out the door. As it shut behind me, I heard her continue on as if I hadn't even been there.

The drums in my head reminded me that I didn't need to be focusing on what was happening now that I was gone. I needed to get home.

I walked numbly through the aisles of the library, face down to avoid the fluorescent lighting. I didn't notice someone in front of me until I collided with them.

"I'm sorry," they said immediately. "Wait, Amy?"

I rubbed my forehead. I couldn't deal with anyone needing me at the moment, even with someone who had one hell of a nice voice.

"Yes, but you'll have to leave a message." I jerked a thumb behind me, hoping it was in the direction of the club. "I'm out for the day."

I rushed past whoever it was before they could say anything. Nausea joined the party and I was glad I left when I did. The last thing I needed was to add public throwing up to the list of reasons why I was the lesser twin.

IT WAS the next weekend before I could climb out of bed and get my life back together.

Becks had led the meeting last week, and she'd also sent me a get-well card with a lengthy note telling me about how her dad also had migraines and how he handled them. A few of the members had emailed me telling me to get better, and also that Becks had done an incredible job leading the meeting and that she could take over any time. I wanted to be jealous that she'd done so well in my absence, but she was so nice that I couldn't. All I could do was plan the next meeting and hope that I wasn't a disappointment in comparison.

When it came around, physically, I was feeling better. Mentally, not so much. I was a ball of nerves, wondering if people even wanted me to lead the group. That only grew when Becks found me at the beginning of the meeting.

"Hey! Feeling better?" she asked.

"Yes, thank you for the card."

"I hope you can go to the doctor about it," she said. "I knew when I saw you that it was serious."

"And I heard you did a great job last week."

"It was nothing. We all still missed you."

I wasn't sure if she was placating me or not.

Becks was a good person. I'd thought about trying to befriend her a few times, but Ava's hand in Calvin's was still fresh on my mind, and I didn't know if I could bear getting close to someone else only for them to ultimately choose him in the end.

"Oh, and before I forget." She pulled out a note. "Someone dropped this off for you."

"A book club member?" I asked.

"No, someone else."

"Did you get a name?"

She shook her head. "Sorry. I figured he was leaving something weird. I mean, a *guy* interested in a romance-only book club? Kinda creepy."

I held my hand out and took the letter. "I'll handle it, thank you, Becks."

I made it to a table before I opened it.

> Hi, Amy. I read the book you recommended me, and I really liked it. I'd love to talk more about it, among other things. I have an app we could use.

I SQUINTED at the name at the bottom of the page. It was only one letter.

"V," I said to myself. "Weird name."

I thought back to what had happened with my migraine. I *had* run into someone, though I never looked them in the face. I remembered them talking to me, but nothing else. Had I recommended a book to them?

Becks might have had an issue with a guy joining a book club, but I didn't. I was happy to talk about books with him, and I pulled up the app he recommended.

I sent him a friend request, which was accepted immediately. Once it was, I typed up a message.

> Hi! I'd love to talk about the book. Quick question, though, what book was it? I've had a wild few weeks between a complete asshole ruining my birthday and then the subsequent emotional breakdown, so I barely remember anything.

> Next week we read something in a similar vein. You should show up! Becks might have come across a little weird about a guy joining, but I won't be!

V TYPED. Stopped. And then started again.

> V

> Hi, Amy. I might just keep this between you and me for now. It's nice to be able to talk with you.

Chapter One

NINE YEARS LATER

IT TOOK me two years to learn to appreciate the quiet of my house. After Gram's passing, I struggled with how empty it felt, especially after the courts evened out the will dispute by giving Calvin all the furniture. For a time, I resented the feeling of emptiness.

Now, I didn't mind it too much.

Over time, I'd used my meager earnings to fill the house with vintage furniture again. I had a dining room table, a couch, and a few side tables taking up space. It wasn't everything I wanted, but it was enough to make my house feel close enough to home that I didn't feel sad every time I woke up.

Lately, my life had been so monotonous that it was close to boring. I had my usual morning routine of coffee, work, and then living vicariously through either reading or watching my neighbors through my windows. My newest yet closest friend, Lily, helped ease it ever since I met her, but I couldn't help but wonder if this was how my life was going to be until the end of time.

I worked a boring job at my family's company, and they didn't have anything for me to do. The weather was cold, so the neighbor-hood was quieter than usual, and most days, I was trying to find a book to read by noon to carry me through my shift that ended at five.

And this day was proving to be the same as all of the rest.

I checked my email one last time before pulling out my current book. It was like all the others I'd read, but there was something about watching two people fall in love that made me smile every time. I knew it wasn't real—Gram's ghost would haunt me if I believed it for a moment—but the escape was something I desperately needed.

After ten minutes, I'd made it to an adorable first-kiss scene when a message popped up on my phone.

V

> I'm never reading fantasy again. Rohanda's mom just came back to life and then DIED AGAIN. Cruel. Why are you making me read this?

I laughed and quickly typed out a reply.

> BECAUSE I need someone to talk to about it. The only other person I know LOVES fantasy, and I can't exactly tell her that this was nightmare inducing.

> So you chose me???

> You're brave enough for it.

> I am ... but I'll hold this against you for the rest of our friendship. This has a happy ending, right? If it doesn't, we may need to reevaluate things ...

> Just kidding. I'll forgive you if you give me an actual happy rec after this.

My friendship with V defied all odds, yet it was one of my greatest treasures. He didn't get bored of me, even when I had to hand over the book club to Becks because of my health or when the first messaging app we were using announced that they were shutting down.

Both times, V had suggested a solution rather than to drop me. The first was that we talked about books whenever I could, even though he didn't know health was the reason I was too busy for it. And he'd also suggested we move to Discord instead of paying a subscription fee.

I still had the letter V had given me, stored with the very few things in my house that I'd kept for years.

Back in college, I'd always hoped that he would show up to one of my weekly sessions, but he never did. I'd always told him he was welcome, but I was pretty sure Becks had done some damage. She was fun with all of the women in the group, but obviously her thoughts had leaked out into her actions when V had met her in person.

Over time, I figured out that it was best that he didn't come in person. About half the time, people joined the club to hear more about my brother, not to read books. And if I lost V to Calvin like I did everyone else, I knew that was something I wouldn't recover from.

I knew within the first week that V was special. And he stayed special, even to this day.

> I'll do whatever to earn your forgiveness.

> Actually, your forgiveness is coming early. It's getting romantic now.

I wanted to tell him that Lily had written this, and why it shifted so much near the end. When she had been forced into a contract to marry someone, her writing had been dark and twisted. Then, as she connected with her husband, she added more and more romance to get to the happy ending her series, *The Fair Originals*, had.

But Lily closely guarded her identity since her parents would try to take away her success if they found out how much they'd inspired the series. And while I didn't think V could be connected to that life in any way, it would be my luck if he was.

> The ending is so worth it.

I managed to do some of my actual job for a few more minutes before I got another message. I looked at my phone, eager to see what he said.

Instead, it was a message from Dad.

As much as I liked to think it was directed at me, I knew it was copied and pasted and sent to everyone who wanted to attend their parties. Most were in Calvin's honor, and this was no different.

DAD

> Come and celebrate Calvin's promotion to CEO! On his birthday no less! My retirement is now fully effective.

I rolled my eyes. My relationship with Calvin had only soured after Gram died.

The first will I found had given him the house, which made no sense because she'd insisted she would leave it to *me*. I later found a handwritten one that matched what she'd told me and I changed the date. I kept the old one in memory of what I'd done, but I *needed* somewhere to live. In true Calvin fashion, he took me to probate court to settle the dispute.

Somehow, I'd won.

Calvin didn't take it well when he didn't get what he wanted. Everyone in the family suspected that I'd forged the will, and Calvin didn't hesitate to remind me that I didn't deserve the house. To be fair, according to the latest will and in the eyes of the law, I didn't. But I'd spent my childhood here. I couldn't bear to let it get sold off to a stranger and leave me homeless. And that was exactly what Calvin planned to do.

These days, the only communication between Calvin and me was either corporate emails sent to everyone or invitations to his increasingly glamorous parties.

I usually tried not to go. After everything went south, I'd hoped he wouldn't invite me, but Calvin had a bad habit of inviting those he didn't like in order to show off his successes, including his own twin. He knew I didn't have a lot of money. But this was the only job I could get, considering my last name was on the company sign.

> Hey. I can't make it tonight. I have some plans with friends.

The response was immediate.

> Then invite them too. Everyone should be there.

That was the last thing I'd do. I trusted Lily with my life, but I wanted her nowhere near Calvin. I still thought about Ava's betrayal years later. I couldn't do it again. It was hard for me to even befriend Lily, but I took the chance since Calvin and I never saw each other these days.

And after what her parents did to her, I wasn't even sure she would like Calvin.

The more realistic ending would be that she would put him into one of her books and murder him. Hell, she'd even write another fantasy book just to do that. But after losing too many people to him, it wasn't a risk I was willing to take.

I switched the text chain to Emma. We talked far more than Calvin and I did, and I was the only one she came to for advice.

> Are you going to the BS party tonight?

EMMA

I wasn't told there was one.

Oh wait. There's the invitation. Ummm, no. I'm not driving four hours to see Calvin get his proverbial dick sucked by everyone.

Is there no other way to describe that?

Happy birthday, by the way. I would be there, but I have to work to support myself.

Same. It's the worst.

I went back to my computer and blinked in shock when I saw an invitation for a meeting starting in two minutes.

Since when was I included in such short-notice meetings? Maybe they were finally switching me onto a different team so I would have something to do. I would miss my reading time, but even I felt bad about being paid to do nothing—no matter how low it was.

I grabbed my phone and checked my appearance, eyes going wide when I saw how frizzy my curls had gotten. I shoved it into a ponytail and tried to tame the flyaways.

I joined the meeting one minute later.

Immediately, I wanted to leave.

My brother's face was the first thing I saw, along with the Nashville skyline. Calvin had a fancy high-rise, and his meeting background was so perfect it looked fake, but I knew his office overlooked the city and was so well lit that it was picturesque.

When his eyes met mine, I paled. Why was he on this? He never talked to me directly during work hours.

"Amy," the HR representative started. I scrambled to look for her name and found it at the bottom of the screen.

"Hi, Cora. What can I do for you?"

"This will be a short meeting. Unfortunately, I'm afraid there isn't much you can do for us at this time. We're letting you go."

An awkward laugh escaped me. "I'm sorry, what?"

My eyes flicked to Calvin, who was typing something, undoubtedly getting other work done. I knew he was still mad about the house, but he'd perfected treating me with painful indifference.

"Due to a decreasing workload, we have had to make some difficult decisions—"

"I'm the CEO's daughter," I said. "You can't fire me."

This time, Calvin spoke. "Technically, you're the CEO's *sister* now. And I need to play fair. Dad kept you on despite you having nothing to do, but we have shareholders to answer to and your salary is losing us money."

"B-but you could transfer me."

"Do you have an HR degree that I'm unaware of or something else useful? Last I checked, you got your degree in English."

"It's still a degree."

"It's not enough. You're the one with the least amount of work. You have to be let go. It's *fair*."

I heard his words, but I didn't believe them.

He didn't have a lick of guilt on his face, and I knew there was nothing I could do to get him to change his mind. Our parents would be on his side. HR was literally on this call. I was getting fired.

"O-okay. Is there any severance?"

"I consider the last few months you were employed without doing anything as severance. As of today, you will be paid out for your last paycheck, and your health insurance coverage will end."

"Shouldn't it go to the last of the month?"

"It will not."

Fuck. I had medicine I *needed* to be on, and it had been over six months since I last saw my specialist. According to their policy, I was due for a visit. I hadn't planned it yet since it was expensive, even with insurance, but without it, I was fucked.

"What about extending it past my last day? Cobra, I think it is?"

"Cobra benefits and your package are expensive," Cora said grimly. And then she said a number that was more than quadruple the amount of my current premium.

Oh, I was *double fucked*.

This was the worst-case scenario. Not only was being without health insurance going to make my medication impossible to get, but I also had way too many bills to count. Owning an old house had expenses, and my only option was to take out loans to be able to fix it up when something went wrong. Not only that, I had expensive land taxes and day-to-day bills.

I *needed* a job.

And it had already been nearly impossible to get *this* one.

"Calvin," I said softly. "You know what this will do to me."

"Maybe you shouldn't have pursued homeownership, Amy." His voice was cold and calculated. "It's obviously too much for you to handle."

Cora cut in to tell me to turn in my stuff by the end of the day, and that she was sorry to see me go.

I was in a state of shock. I had no idea what I was going to do, and the hurt festering in my chest was worse than when Levi Hensen kissed me to get back at my brother. Sure, technically, I'd screwed Calvin over by getting the house, but he was a *millionaire*. He didn't need it. He'd bought his mansion when he was twenty-one with the help of Dad.

After my screen cut to black, my breath turned shaky. Numbly, I packed my laptop into a box and then sat on my couch.

I had *no* idea how I was going to get out of this kind of trouble.

Chapter Two

AFTER DROPPING off my stuff to the receptionist at Calvin's stupid office, I came home and immediately went back outside. My other neighbor, Mr. Buford, was an old man with mobility issues, and I often helped him with his garden. I took out my frustrations on the dried weeds I had neglected to get to.

Mr. Buford was one of the few people who had lived here since the neighborhood was built. He bought his home for a meager $25,000 and had lived in it ever since. He'd always been kind to me, and in return, I worked on the things that he didn't need to worry about. As a man in his eighties, the last thing he needed to be doing was getting on his hands and knees. I was halfway through pulling them up when his front door opened.

"Amy, is that you?" he asked in his shaky voice. His cane hit the ground as he walked to the edge of the porch. "What are you doing out here in the middle of the day?"

"Enjoying the sunlight," I replied, leaning back on my heels. "It's keeping me warm."

That, and the rage I felt.

Mr. Buford's wrinkled face formed a frown. "You're never out at this hour."

"You know me. I have to change it up a bit. I was getting bored doing the same thing every day."

I refused to burden him with my problems. One time, when a pipe burst under my house, he offered to pay for it. *Him.* He had countless doctor's appointments and medical bills. He was only on Medicare, which didn't pay for everything. And most older adults, he had a limited, fixed income.

"Is something wrong with the house?"

"The house is great," I replied. "Nothing's wrong."

"Are you sure?" He raised one eyebrow.

"How is *your* house?" I asked back. "Everything good?"

"I know what you're doing. You're putting the attention on me."

"Yep. You can't leave me hanging now."

"My house is good as always. She's sturdy."

"And so is mine."

"Let me get you some coffee, at least. That'll make me feel better."

He ambled inside, and I had half a mind to tell him not to worry about it, but he clung to his independence, always making me coffee himself even though I had some at home. If I was lucky enough to reach his age, I wouldn't want people doing everything for me either.

I pulled out more weeds, banishing all thoughts of Calvin from my mind. I was determined to give my full attention to the kind man next door. The second I tried that, however, it hit me that I might not be his neighbor for much longer. If I couldn't figure out how to get money, I was going to lose the house—the very thing I'd worked so hard for.

Mr. Buford came out minutes later with a steaming cup of coffee in his hand. In the chilly, late-winter air, it was exactly what I needed. I stood and climbed onto the porch. "Thank you," I said.

"I even put in cream and sugar, though I don't know how you can ruin perfectly good coffee with that stuff."

"Not everyone can tolerate bitterness like you can." I took a sip of the delicious liquid. Mr. Buford never put in enough for my taste, but it was still good on such a cold day. My cheeks were ice, and I'd regret my last-second choice when I finally retreated home.

"How are you, Amy?" he asked slowly. "I know there's something on your mind."

"Just life," I said. "I think things will be changing."

"They always do, even when we don't want them to."

I sighed and took a long drink. "This isn't going to be a good change."

"Do you need help?"

I shook my head. "I don't think this is a thing you can help with. This is a consequence of my own actions. I'll deal with it."

"I can't imagine you doing something so bad that you'd get into trouble."

"I find ways." *Like forging a will.*

The caffeine was starting to hit my system and I knew my priority needed to be finding a job. "I should go," I said. "I'm sorry I can't stay longer but—"

"You have things to do," he said. "I get it."

"I'll be by tomorrow?"

"Not if it means you get in trouble," he said. "But I'd welcome you anyway."

I gave him one last smile and handed him the mug back before going inside. My expression dropped the second I was alone.

I hated the idea of finding a job. Not only did I have no filter, but I hated the idea of sucking up to someone just so they'd employ me. It was why I'd struggled so much to land anything and then had to come crying to Dad to get employment.

Now, I was on my own.

That was the thing about me: I didn't have connections. Not in the business world, at least. I knew people, some of whom liked me, but I wasn't good at crafting connections with people I needed something from. I liked talking to them because I *liked* them.

31

Calvin was the one who was good at the rest.

But I didn't have a choice. It wasn't like I was going to magically find money somewhere. The only well-off people in my life were my parents and Calvin, and they'd been very strict on sharing. Even when Emma had gotten into a wreck last year, they didn't help her replace her car.

And they wouldn't help me here either.

On my phone, I looked up any and all jobs. Some paid way too low or expected me to travel to the office. Neither were great, but the office positions at least had the potential of a livable wage, so I applied to them all.

After finishing more applications than I could count, I saw a familiar black car pulling into a nearby driveway.

And that was Lily.

I trusted Lily as much as I trusted V. Maybe more, considering I knew her full name. I needed to get her opinion of this, and if I were lucky, maybe her husband, Sebastian, would have a job for me.

"Hey!" I called as I jogged over. She jumped and turned, looking startled for only a second until her eyes landed on me.

"God," she said, letting out a sigh, "you sound like a photographer when you're excited."

With how low-key she liked to be, I couldn't imagine the version of her who had once been a famous Instagram model, especially now that she'd shed her entire look.

"Except I'm less annoying."

"You do spy on me."

"I've gotten so much better about that," I said. "Are you free, or will you be spending the rest of the day writing?"

She rubbed her eyes. "I just finished the longest writing session at the coffee shop. There's no way I can do more."

"Then I can distract you in the form of friendship. And news."

"Good news?"

I winced. "Not really."

She raised an eyebrow. "Come on inside. Now I *need* to know."

Lily and Sebastian's house had been tastefully remodeled. There were pops of color on the walls, and the floors had been refinished with a beautiful dark stain. If I were able to keep my house, I'd use hers as an inspiration.

"What happened?" Lily asked as she unloaded her bag onto the table. Her laptop, which she used to write all of her incredible novels, came out first, followed by her planner and other things.

"Calvin took over the company and fired me."

She paused and blinked. "In one day?"

"He's an overachiever. And he's still mad about the house thing."

"Poor guy. He can't build his pool with the family inheritance." She faked a pout. "You can find something else, right?"

"I have no idea. I'm trying but . . . I don't know. Is Sebastian hiring?"

"For his department? Probably not. He sticks to a smaller team these days. But maybe the company is. I can ask."

"That would be great," I replied. "Where does he work again?"

"It's called Leviathan," she said.

The name sounded familiar, though I wasn't sure why. I didn't need to harp on it. A job was a job, no matter how much I dreaded it.

"I'll owe him one if he saves my ass. Does he like it there?"

"Much more than working for his dad. He has a decent work-life balance these days."

I tried to sound excited, but it was hard to when I hated working. I wished I had a life like Lily's, where she had passive income and had free time that people with day jobs could only dream of. I knew she worked hard on her writing, and she'd had more than her fair share when her parents were still forcing her into modeling, but she had her happy ending now.

And I wanted that too.

But my life was all in books. My dating experience had been through apps and hadn't led to any sort of connection besides a night of sometimes good, but most of the time boring, sex. Thankfully, I had Lily now, so I supported her in every way I could, including reading her books and supporting her as she renewed her vows to Sebastian. I loved her the only way I could—all the way.

"Wanna play video games until Sebastian gets home? I desperately need to think about something else."

"Um, of course." She gave me a bright smile. "What else would I do with my free time?"

"Glad I left my Nintendo Switch here. Mario Kart, or shall we continue our Stardew Valley save?"

"I'm in the mood to be a farmer today," she said. "I'll get us a few snacks."

"I FEEL like I should marry Sebastian purely because he shares my husband's name," Lily said four hours later. She was following the in-game character with the same name as he walked to the beach.

"But he doesn't give the vibe that real-life Sebastian has."

"You're just saying that because you want to marry game-Sebastian."

"I do, but also, have you seen Harvey? He's way better suited to you."

"I like his glasses," she said as she changed course to do something else. "But you've played this before. Shouldn't you want to marry someone new?"

"Like who? Elliot? He's too poetic."

"Who is that again?"

"You thought he was a girl when we first started playing."

"*Oh!* Yeah, he's wrong too. The men in this game leave something to be desired."

"It's too realistic," I muttered. "Sebastian at least has a motorcycle."

"I keep thinking you're talking about *my* Sebastian."

"Did he *have* to be named that?"

"Ask his dad. Oh, wait. Don't. He's a dick."

I huffed out a laugh. "Fine, I won't marry a man with the same name as your husband. I'm going for one of the ladies this time. Abigail?"

"She's cute."

"When in doubt about men, go for the women. It works out for most not-straight people."

"Amy," a male voice said. "Nice to see you again."

I paused the game and turned to Sebastian, who'd just gotten home from work.

"Oh, hey," I said with an awkward laugh. "I realize that without context, that didn't make sense."

"I'm used to it," he replied, shaking his head. "I have a habit of only overhearing the weird things you say."

"And always when you get home too. What a welcome."

He laughed, but then his eyes turned to Lily, and she was all he saw. I didn't blame him. If I were into women, I'd do the same thing. Ever since Lily had begun living for herself and not her parents, she was ethereal.

I looked away as she stood to kiss him. The last thing I needed was to let my loneliness show on my face.

"But Amy does have a reason she's here," Lily said after a moment.

"Isn't socializing a good enough reason?" he asked.

"Always, but I do have something to ask of you." I rubbed the back of my neck. "I may need a job."

"Oh," he said. "What happened to yours?"

35

"My brother took over and fired me," I said. "I promise I'll work hard, though, and I'm willing to go into the office too."

The thought actually made my skin crawl, but I didn't let it show.

"I don't have any open spots on my team, but I wouldn't want to be your boss anyway."

"I'm not *that* bad."

"It's only because we're *friends*. I don't want anyone to think I treat you differently or that it was a favor."

"This *is* kind of a favor, though."

"I'll try to get you an interview. I can't guarantee you'll get hired, but it'll get you in the door."

"Could you also throw in some interview tips too?" I said weakly. "I think I'll need all the help I can get."

"Yes, of course. Let me see what I can find."

"See?" Lily added with a smile. "It'll all work out."

"Hopefully, it will. Thanks, Sebastian. You're a godsend." I checked my phone, hoping to see other interviews somehow lined up, but all I saw was a message from V. When I looked back up, I saw Lily and Sebastian getting closer to talk about their days, and I turned off the TV. "I should probably let you two have your night. I'll talk to you tomorrow?"

Sebastian blinked like he'd forgotten I was there. "Yeah. I'll let you know if I find something."

I thanked them once again before leaving. When it was just me in the cool air, I let out a long breath.

My stress was going to leak into every part of my life. It was a bitterness I couldn't stop. The same thing had happened when I was fighting for the house. Everything ground to a halt. I didn't even read until I knew I had a place to live.

V

All right. I'm done with The Fair Originals. Not bad. Very gory. What are we reading next?

I let out a sigh before answering.

> No idea. Honestly, my life is a bit of a dumpster fire right now. I don't know if I'll be in the headspace to read. I know we don't talk about this stuff, but I don't want to disappear like I did a few years ago.

V hadn't been too happy when I did that, and I promised I would let him know if something was going wrong. It was still weird, though, considering we only talked about books.

Is everything okay?

> Not really. Hopefully, it will be, but a lot is up in the air.

What can I do?

A warm feeling spread through me. V had no idea how hot it was to me that he'd asked that simple question. But conviction was always attractive in my book.

> Nothing at the moment. I'll talk more about it if it gets super dire. Right now, I'm just stressed. It's hard to read anything new when I'm like this.

What about an old favorite? It worked for me when my dad passed.

I considered it. Biting my lip, I reached for the one I'd been reading many years ago, the one I'd apparently recommended to V somehow.

> I'll give it a shot. Thanks, V.

I'm here for you always.

Chapter Three

SEBASTIAN REALLY WAS a god among men. I was sure Lily already knew that, but I didn't realize it until he landed me an interview within a week at Leviathan.

Of course, I didn't have an outfit, which meant I had to scour Lily's closet for something that would work. She didn't have anything professional either, but she had more regular-length tops than crop tops, making her closet a far better choice. I wound up with a pair of her slacks and a nicer-looking blouse. I didn't look like myself when I walked through the doors, but I highly doubted they'd want to employ the real me.

"Stay calm," Sebastian said. "The person who's interviewing you is nice, from what I've heard. Just mention your successes and strengths and find one weakness that is accurate but not too bad."

He was repeating all the things he'd already told me a few days before. I hated to admit it, but I needed the reminder.

"Right. I can do all of those things."

I definitely could *not*. Had I done anything good at my last job? Sure, I got things done and never missed a deadline, but the most I could remember was getting an entire book read in a meeting.

"And take a few deep breaths. There's no need to panic."

"It's not like the future of my homeownership counts on this or anything." I still tried to listen. I got a few breaths in before we exited the elevator. "Out of curiosity, you won't get fired or anything if I bomb this, right?"

"How bad are we talking?"

That didn't make me feel better. "You know what? I'll just sit and wait, and everything will be okay."

Sebastian nodded, but his brows pinched together. I had a feeling he didn't have any more confidence than I did about this situation. "I'll wait with you and give you an introduction," he said.

"I'll tell Lily you were extra nice to me." I gave him what I hoped was a warm smile and pulled out my phone to message V.

> Okay. I'm about to try and fix all of my problems here in a bit. Hopefully, I don't mess it up.

V

You couldn't mess up anything you tried to do.

> HA. I appreciate the kindness, but I need to be realistic.

Then we'll be realistic. You're smart, Amy. Even if you mess this up, you'll figure out a way to make someone laugh about it and still get whatever you need.

And before you ask me how I know how smart you are, I'm going to direct you to the notes of the last five-book series we read where you caught plot holes I didn't even think to see.

> You know my follow-up questions too well.

I do. And if we're sticking to being realistic,
then you need to know there's a difference
between realism and pessimism.

Fine. I'll give you that one. But there's also a
difference between realism and optimism.

We're two sides of the same coin.

I locked my phone and tried to calm down, but V's kind words did more for me than I wanted to admit. My entire body felt warm, like it was glowing under the compliments he'd just fed me. I'd never met the guy in person, but if he could do this to me through a phone, what could he do if he were in front of me?

"I-is there somewhere I can get some water?"

"In the break room, but don't be too long," he replied. "Sally will want to meet you any second."

I wasted no time following Sebastian's quick directions to the break room. I asked him to hang behind in case he needed to make an excuse for my temporary absence.

"Okay, Amy," I said to myself, pacing in front of the sink. "There's a lot riding on this, so you have to lock it in. No being weird. You need to land this job. This is *not* the time to talk about dicks, romance books, or anything in between. Be *professional*."

I was about to take a breath when I heard something fall. I yelped and turned, hoping whoever was in here was wearing head-phones and laughing at a video on their phone, which they'd just dropped on the table.

But I quickly realized things were *much* worse.

I had done my best not to think of Levi Hensen ever since I'd discovered he'd used me to piss off Calvin. It didn't always work, especially the nights when I would lie awake and think of him. Still, after college, I doubted I would ever see him again.

Yet, here I was, staring into his blue-green eyes while I gaped like a fish.

Levi had the same Adonis-like face, but now his hair reached past the nape of his neck. It was effortlessly brushed back on his head.

But what was he doing here? He had his own company, right?

That was when it hit me.

Levi.

Leviathan.

Shit.

Levi was taking a break from running a huge company by watching something on his phone, which was now in front of him on the table. He was staring at me as if he wasn't sure I was real. His eyes were wide, his jaw ticked. I didn't even blame him. He'd just caught me talking to myself like a weirdo, after all.

"U-uh, wow. Nice company you have here." I tucked a curl behind my ear. "Really impressive. I bet you're really good at pretending you didn't hear things. Like what I just said. A-anyway, I should get going before I make this worse for myself."

I went to make a run for it and hoped that I hadn't ruined my chances, but his hand clamped down on my wrist.

"Amy Willard."

This felt charged in a way I didn't know how to explain. His eyes were intense like he was trying to gauge my entire life story from one look alone.

Or maybe he was trying to work out how he could use me again.

I might have read a lot of romance novels, but I wasn't going to get bamboozled by Levi's pretty face again.

Still, if he were here and this was *his* company, I couldn't be as mean as I wanted to be.

I laughed awkwardly. "That's me. Here for a job interview."

"A job interview," he repeated.

"Yes. I hear the company has good benefits, probably because of your leadership."

"You're being very nice considering how we left things."

My eyes narrowed. Why bring it up? Plenty of people lived long lives running from their problems. I could too, if I got enough money to pay my bills while doing so.

"That's all in the past," I said slowly. It didn't sound very convincing.

A tilt of Levi's head told me he wasn't convinced either. "Are you sure about that?"

"Very sure. I can prove it in my job interview, which I really need to be getting to." I tried to tug my hand out of his grip, but it tightened.

"Did you know this was my company?"

I gritted my teeth. "No. A friend works here, and he got me an interview."

"*He?*"

"Yes. He. I can have friends of all genders." My eyes finally met his. "Even assholes, apparently."

He raised an eyebrow.

"Not you," I rushed to say. "Other assholes?"

"What job are you interviewing for?"

"The receptionist position. I promise I'm much better around people who didn't ruin my birthday."

"I'm sure you are," he said. "But I don't think that listing is a good fit for you."

Shit. "No, wait. I can prove that I'd be good at it. Levi, I seriously *need* this job. Please don't kick me out before I can interview for it."

He held up a hand and I shut my mouth, embarrassed that I'd practically *begged* for this already. "I wasn't kicking you out. I have an idea of a better fit."

"And what's that?"

"Come to lunch with me and we can discuss it."

"Lunch?" I repeated slowly.

"That's what I said."

"Why would I—" I stopped myself before I could offend him more and pushed down my annoyance.

"Why would you what?"

It was like he was testing me, and I was so close to failing.

"I don't go to lunch with random guys."

"I'm not a random guy. I've known you for years."

"And of those ten years, there was only about an hour where you were nice to me, and it was to fuck over my brother. So pardon me if I don't trust you."

"You don't trust me, yet you want to work at my company?"

Damn it. He had a point.

I didn't want to see him more than I had to, but if I *worked* for him, I would be in his presence for forty hours a week.

Did I like that idea?

No.

But did I care about keeping my house?

Yes.

"I'm . . . considering going with you, but let's make one thing clear. We are *not* talking about the shitty thing you did on my nineteenth birthday."

"You mean the stuff that's in the past?"

"Yes. If we want it to stay in the past, you don't bring it up."

"Fine. We'll catch up and discuss the perfect position for you."

Of all the people to run into. . . why did it have to be him? Maybe whatever god was out there hated me after all. "Okay. Lunch. Where to?"

Chapter Four

WHEN WE LEFT the break room, the first person I saw was Sebastian.

"Hey, we need to get to . . ." He trailed off when he saw who was with me and he stood up straighter. "Levi, hey."

"I hear Amy here has an interview for a receptionist position, but I want to talk with her first. Will you speak with Sally for me and tell her to move the interview to this afternoon?"

Sebastian blinked. "I can do that."

"Good. Come on, Amy."

Levi walked ahead, but I looked at Sebastian with wide eyes. "He better not be a secret murderer," I hissed.

"No, he's not. At least, I don't think he is."

"Let's hope not, because I'm going to lunch with him." I threw up my hands.

"Amy," Sebastian began, "he is the *CEO*. He's like my boss's boss's boss. Be careful."

"I'll do my best. Which is . . . mediocre at best. Wish me luck?"

"I don't know if that's gonna be enough."

I blew out a long breath. "If I get murdered, tell Lily I love her."

I ran to catch up to Levi before he could get too far ahead of me, and I found him waiting by the front desk.

"How do you know Sebastian?" he asked as we walked to the elevator.

"He's my neighbor. And the friend who got me this interview. Why? Are you jealous?"

Levi didn't answer, though I knew there was no reason for him to be. He didn't feel anything for me. Only for my brother, and those were angry-murder feelings.

"Not quite. But I do know he's married."

"Yeah, married guys aren't my taste. Neither are ones my best friend is into either. I'd rather fuck a frog."

His eyebrow raised again. "Isn't that what you told yourself not to say?"

Inwardly, I cursed. "Yep. But I feel very compelled to make it clear that I would never."

He pressed the button to the elevator.

"So, where should I meet you at?" I asked.

"I figured I was driving."

I shook my head. Be alone in a car with him? I might as well sign away my life if he were truly a killer. "You don't have to do that."

"I invited you out. It's polite of me to. Besides, anywhere around here doesn't have a lot of parking."

I didn't need to be reminded. Parking became impossible the closer one got to the city center. Anything free was either full or a tiny spot next to the road. And considering parallel parking was impossible for me to comprehend, I knew that wouldn't be an option. When I'd gotten here, I'd won the lottery purely by finding a garage that was free to park in.

Where we were eating, I might not be as lucky.

"Okay, fine." My survival skills must have been near zero. "You can drive. But that still doesn't answer the question of where we're going."

"Wherever you want," he said.

"I don't think the places I frequent are the kinds of restaurants you're used to."

One corner of his mouth tugged into a smile. "Try me."

If I got any joy out of the day, it would be seeing Levi struggle to deal with a busy mom-and-pop place that I loved.

"Mas Tacos Por Favor in East Nashville," I said as we walked into the lobby.

"What you want is what you get," he said.

I smiled to myself, wondering what he was going to do when he saw that this was a literal hole-in-the-wall and not a nice restaurant.

We entered the parking garage and he unlocked an Audi that was worth more than all of my previous cars combined.

"Nice car," I remarked. I got in carefully and told myself to brush off after eating. I would never live it down if I ruined something so pretty. "How many souls did you steal to get it?"

"None. I bought it like other people do. With money."

"Ah, yes. The thing we must have in order to live. How could I forget?" I looked out the window as he pulled into traffic, biting at my lip. It was easy to let my anger get the best of me, but I *needed* this job, no matter how much I was going to hate it. Sebastian was my only connection who worked full-time, unless I begged my favorite coffee shop for a barista gig.

It didn't take long to get to the eastern side of Nashville. Since it was the middle of a workday, the restaurant was somewhat slower than I was used to seeing, which meant it was easy to park on one of the nearby roads.

Levi found a spot a block away and parallel parked with ease.

He was hot *and* could drive? It was unfair.

I thought he was done surprising me, but then he got out of the car and walked around to my side. His hand landed on the door handle and opened it for me.

"Uh, what?"

"Can I not be a gentleman?"

"You can, but . . ." I trailed off. I had no idea what to do in the face of Levi being nice to me. It sent a warm feeling into my chest for all of one moment before the memories of *why* he was being nice hit me again.

I didn't need to let my guard down like I had nine years ago. That much was for sure.

I had no idea where their little rivalry was these days, but Levi had pulled ahead with his company. If Calvin still cared, and I knew he probably did, then he would be trying to catch up as the new CEO. They weren't in the exact same field, considering Levi worked in mental health and Calvin in hospital care, but it was under the same umbrella.

And that meant Levi would come for *me* again. He had the perfect opportunity to, considering I also needed something.

He's not being nice to you for you. It's who your brother is.

My little mantra made it easier for me to look him in the eye while I got out of the car.

A silence settled over us as we walked to the restaurant.

"So, what do you think about the place I picked?" I asked as we walked inside.

"It's one of my favorite restaurants."

"Seriously?"

"Dispel your assumptions, Amy. It'll make this easier."

I blinked in shock, but his answering smile told me he enjoyed my surprise. I immediately wiped it off my face.

"Thanks," I said. "But you're not allowed to say anything else to me until there's an order in for at least three tacos."

"Understood." He gestured for me to go ahead, and I ordered everything I wanted. If he invited me out, he was footing the bill. After ordering the tacos and an elote, he paid, and I looked forward to eating my favorite foods without the guilt of spending money raining down on me.

Hopefully, by the end of this, I'd have a job, and I wouldn't have to worry about my financial situation anymore.

We found a small table near the window and sat. Mas Tacos was the cozy kind of place where there wasn't space between a person and their guest. If their food wasn't so good, then I would have chosen somewhere else.

"Can I speak to you now?" he asked.

"It depends on what you have to say."

I should have said not to talk to me until we got our food. I wasn't fully in business mode, and I didn't know how to turn on the side of me that could get this job. I'd already misstepped way too many times while talking to Levi. I didn't need to do it again. If Mom and Dad were here, they would tell me this was exactly why I was fired.

"How did you find this place?" he asked.

"I used to come here during high school with my gram."

"What was she like?"

My heart panged. "Isn't this a little personal for an interview?"

"This isn't an interview. This is lunch."

"You're my potential new boss. Of course this is an interview."

His mouth formed a slanted smile. "How about we make an agreement. Everything said at this table is off-the-record. Deal?"

"Is this one of those interview manipulation tactics where you try to catch me off guard and then see what kind of person I truly am?"

"No."

Did I believe him? Probably not.

But whatever filter I did have was hanging by a thread, and his welcome dismissal of it was easy to accept.

"Fine, but I'm hunting you down if I don't get a job."

"I assure you, I have nothing to do with the job hiring process. Except where I asked for your interview to be rescheduled."

"You better not be lying."

"I promise I'm not."

I eyed him up and down, taking in all the ways he'd changed over the years. He had thick-rimmed glasses now, which only brought out how bright his eyes were. That, coupled with his dark hair, made him even more unfairly attractive.

"Since when did you decide to go for the Clark Kent look?"

He blinked. "What?"

"You're now hot in a nerdy way. You used to just be hot."

His eyebrows rose and I could have sworn I saw his neck turn red in the dim lighting. "You took 'off-the-record' seriously."

"I absolutely did."

"I sometimes wear contacts, but they get uncomfortable, especially since I spend a lot of my day looking at a screen."

"Well, it works for you."

"Am I allowed to be as unhinged as you, or is this just a one-way thing?"

I narrowed my eyes. "Say what you want, but you're on thin ice."

"Your curls are stunning these days. They were always alluring before, but now . . ." He cleared his throat. "Now they're perfect."

A warm feeling spread through my body, concentrated in my cheeks. That was way nicer than I expected. "I eventually figured out how to take care of them. I just have to spend hours on it after I shower."

And I'd gone all out for today. For good reason, apparently.

"It's working for you."

"It takes dedication . . . which coincidentally, makes me a great employee." Internally, I cringed at how thick I was laying this on. But hey, I was desperate.

"Any discussions about work are off the table."

"Then I'm a great employee off the table too. And on it. You could put me on whatever table you want."

Another eyebrow raised. "Did you mean for that to sound sexual?"

"No. Did it?"

"A little."

"Okay, no more table talk. Or bed talk. Or sex talk."

He laughed, and I wasn't sure if it was *at* me or *with* me. "I thought you already had that rule."

"Sometimes I forget them."

I waited for his subtle jab that those kinds of things did *not* make me a good employee. Thankfully, that never came.

"How have you been, Amy?" he asked, folding his hands on the table.

My immediate answer would have been not great. My life was on the brink of falling apart in a way it never had before. I lost a lot of time curled in bed with debilitating pain, which was going to get worse now that my health insurance was going away, and my doctor wouldn't refill my needed prescriptions without an appointment.

But even I knew that when people asked how I had been, they wanted a palatable answer.

"Good," I replied. "I'd ask how you've been, but—" I gestured to his nice clothes and badge for his own company. "—I'd say you have it all figured out."

"There are a few things I haven't figured out," he replied. "But thank you for the vote of confidence."

"You definitely need it, I'm guessing."

He laughed again. "Sometimes more than others. Now let's get back to you. Good was the most basic answer you can give."

"I don't think you want the real one."

"Try me."

The food arrived, giving me blessed seconds to decide if I wanted to open this can of worms. Levi seemed so innocent across from me that it would be easy to open up again, just like it had been the first time.

Fuck it, I decided. It wasn't like there was anything else for me to lose.

"My brother fired me recently from the family company. He

51

might have had some valid reasons, but now I'm at risk of losing my house, and I'm honestly anxious about it."

Levi had lifted one of the tacos and paused as I spoke. "Does your family usually do those kinds of things to each other?"

"Kinda. It started when I got the house in the first place. Technically, I stole it from him, but Calvin has *everything*, and I don't know why Gram left it to him in her will." I blew out a frustrated breath. I'd never know now that she was gone. "Anyway, I don't want to lose the one thing I have of Gram, so I need a job. And technically, anything will pay me more than my last job did."

"How much were you paid?" he asked. When I told him, his jaw dropped. "That's *criminally* low."

I shrugged. "My degree wasn't in a useful field. Apparently, the English language is dead."

"There are many people on my staff who have an English degree and make more than that."

"Yeah, but it was easier to take the shit salary and do nothing all day." My eyes widened as I realized what I said. "Not that I would do that at your company, I mean."

"This lunch is still off-the-record."

"And I'm still going to shoot my shot. Calvin treats every day like a business opportunity. Maybe I should . . . be more like him." I couldn't help the grimace that escaped me at the thought of being more like my twin.

"You wear every emotion on your face."

"Shut up," I said, taking a bite of my avocado taco. I was distracted momentarily by the incredible flavor on my tongue. God, could I be a professional food taster and earn a living? Could I do anything else but be trapped in an office forever?

"Most people have that same reaction when eating here," he said.

"I find that good food makes me forget my problems, even if only for a second."

"Would you have problems if you got a job here?"

"I should say no, right?"

"You should say whatever you want."

Another bite of taco gave me the bravery to say the truth. "Honestly? I hate working. It's not for me. I'd rather be in the garden or reading all day, like a housewife with a super-hot husband. But considering my dating history is as abysmal as my bank account, I don't see that happening anytime soon, so here I am."

His chewing stilled again. "That's what you truly want?"

"You asked for honesty, and you don't get to judge me."

He shook his head. "I'm not judging you. I'm only thinking."

"About what?"

"About how to give you exactly what you want."

"There's no job in your office that's like that, and it's okay. I'm fine doing what I need to."

"I wasn't talking about a *job*," he said. "I had something very different in mind."

"And what's that?"

He put down his food and brushed off his hands—a casual move that didn't match the shocking words he said next.

"Marry me, Amy. And I can make all of your problems go away."

Chapter Five

IN THE FACE of a ridiculous proposal, I did what any other woman would.

I laughed my ass off.

There was no way he was serious. Men didn't just *propose* to women out of nowhere. Marriages of convenience were only in books, and I was definitely not living in a book.

Between wiping the tears from my eyes, I said, "Good one."

"I'm serious."

"No, you're not. First of all, you wouldn't be getting anything out of this deal other than being married to *me*, and I assure you that while I'm a hilarious and entertaining companion—that's not enough."

"I have a reason."

"Oh, really?" I shook my head to clear any remaining mirth. "I can only think of *one*, and it's not one I'm interested in marrying you for."

"And what's my reason?"

"Calvin. You two have a weird dick-measuring contest going on, and he just got promoted."

His lips pursed. "It's been years."

"Has it? You started a healthcare company when you could have done anything else. And you're climbing to the top of the food chain in the industry faster than anyone has ever seen before. If it were anyone else, I would think it was ambition, but this is how you two have always been. Enemies vying for the position at the top."

"Is there anything I can say to change your mind?" He leaned forward, his eyes on me. I could have said yes, but I was *not* getting played by the man again.

Gram would roll over in her grave.

"There is literally nothing."

"Fine." The words were low, hard. "You caught me."

"Thank you for admitting the truth."

A shadow crossed his face, one that cleared the second I saw it. As much as he wanted to pretend he had other reasons, one mention of Calvin took him to a dark place.

"So he *is* still a pain in your ass."

"Always," he muttered. "He never lets go of anything, does he?"

"He absolutely does not. My lack of employment is the perfect example."

"And aren't you mad about that?"

"Of course I'm mad—"

"And what better way to piss him off than to marry someone he hates?" He waved his hand as if it were that simple, and yet I could see his shoulders were still tense.

"I—why is this your first option?"

"Go big or go home. If I'm going to piss off Calvin, I want to make him *mad*."

"Has he done something to you? Other than just being annoying."

"He did something to *you*."

"That's not a good enough reason for all of this. I'm not stupid."

Levi let out a long breath. "Fine. If you must know . . . He's poaching customers."

"How?"

"Expensive and slanderous ads about mental health care."

"From a hospital?"

"Last year, the company bought an inpatient facility. He's trying to say that therapy doesn't work, so people should go straight to more expensive care."

"The policy his own company offers doesn't cover inpatient stays," I said. "And he's pushing for that?"

"He's not a good man, Amy. And he's trying to get doctors my company employs on his side. I was going to handle it by letting him burn himself out, but now I have another idea." His eyes landed on me.

"You both are doing all of this because of your little high school thing?"

"After college, I was content to never think about it again, but he keeps pushing."

"Really?"

"Would you put it past him?"

No. I wouldn't. "So I'm your ploy to make him madder? He's not going to stop."

"He missteps when he's angry, and if he takes an ad too far, it backfires on him. It's in both of our interests to make him as miserable as possible."

"With marriage? I don't think that's a normal thing people do."

"I wasn't under the impression that you were *normal*."

That shut me up. He was right about that one. "So we get married, and I get a job?"

"We get married, and you get more than enough to live off of. No job needed."

"And what about when you have your revenge and you're done with me? I still need income at the end of the day."

"We'll sign a prenup that makes sure you don't have to work for a long time."

"I thought prenups kept me from taking all of your money."

"They're really agreements on how to split assets after divorce. We can do what we want to." He shrugged nonchalantly.

"And how long are we doing this for?"

"Do we have to put an expiration date on it?"

"Don't you want to?"

"I'm not worried about it. We can do this however long we need to."

I shouldn't have been shocked that he would be willing to do this for a long time. While he said he was content to let go of his rivalry with Calvin, he'd also spent years still in it. Even if it wasn't by choice, he was a patient man.

"Fine. If we're throwing all logic out the door, why not time too? No limit on how long this charade can go on for."

My heart raced. Marriage, *really*? God, Lily would kill me. I couldn't get married to a guy for money. Didn't that go against a rule of love somewhere?

Since when do you follow rules?

Levi's words played through my mind and they hit me hard. When I'd met Lily and she told me she'd gotten married for the same reasons, I told her I would do it too. Of course, she was offered a million dollars and I had a feeling Levi would not give me that much, but still.

This *would* solve my problems, at least temporarily. I was on the cusp of something I desperately wanted.

He leaned forward. "You want to say yes. I can see it."

"It's still a huge decision. It's *marriage*. Don't you have a girl-friend or something that would be against this?"

"I don't date, so no."

"I find that hard to believe."

"Just like I find it hard to believe you're still single. It's like we were waiting for this moment."

"For revenge on Calvin."

He blinked as if he'd forgotten the whole reason we were doing this. "Yes, of course."

I pressed my lips together. My appetite was gone, a true testament to how frazzled I was. "Can I think about it?" I asked. "Or is this a one-time offer?"

"You can think about it," he replied. "I have nothing but time."

"Good. I need to get the best friend's seal of approval. You know, normal girl things." I grabbed my purse. "We should get back to the office."

"I'll give you a ride, but I need you to promise me one thing first."

"Please don't be weird and ask for a kiss."

He laughed again. "No, it's not that. I need to know that you *are* thinking of this. You're not going home to simply figure out how to say no."

"Are you kidding? You're offering me money in exchange for my hand in marriage. I *am* thinking about it, but this is just . . . It's *a lot*. And I need to be sure you're not weird."

"They do say interviews go two ways. You still have yours later."

"You're inviting me to snoop?"

"I have nothing to hide."

"Everyone has something to hide," I replied, raising an eyebrow.

A shadow flickered over his face, giving me confirmation that there was something else. We weren't close enough for me to ask, but it was the reminder that I needed that he wasn't as open as he said he was.

And I had digging to do.

I FAKED my way through the interview. Half of my answers were lies and the other half were embellishments. Since I wasn't sure about what I would do with Levi, I knew I couldn't bomb this, but I was also so distracted that I couldn't think straight.

While I never had a plan for my life, getting proposed to as revenge on my brother had never come up. I could understand why Levi would want to piss off Calvin. After all, I wasn't his biggest fan either, but this was off the deep end in a way even I couldn't comprehend.

I didn't have a lot of expectations for my love life, but this certainly wasn't it. Gram had drilled her past into me, and I would have been happy to have temporary happiness with someone. But as time went on and my options dwindled, even that seemed impossible.

Sally asked her last question and finally opened up the floor for me to talk. My chest loosened as I could finally unleash the burning thing on my mind.

"So, what do you think of Levi?"

Sally slowly blinked. "Our CEO?"

"Yes. He seems . . . interesting. But the company is as good as its leadership, right?"

"I suppose that's true. In a leadership sense, he's good. He's present when he needs to be and opens the door up for us to talk to him about anything. I quite like working here, and the benefits make it even better."

Benefits. I needed to ask Levi about that if I decided to go through with this.

"And what about personally?"

Now, her eyebrows raised. I silently prayed that she would give in and give me the gossip. I, for one, *loved* to spill the beans about everything in my life. But some people didn't.

But then her lips curved into a smile and she leaned in—the universal gossiping pose.

"I mean, we all would like to know him *personally*, if you know what I mean."

My eyebrows raised. "Really?"

"He's so cute, and he's got that sweet personality that everyone dreams of marrying. That being said, his nights are *never* free. Either he has a girlfriend or he's got a *very* active nightlife."

"Oh," I said, my shoulders slumping.

"Don't get your hopes up with that one. He's good to look at, but he's far too much of a playboy, and he never dates his employees."

Which meant I probably wasn't getting this job if I went forward with the marriage.

"So he's a good person, just . . . busy."

"Exactly."

I nodded. Hearing that he wasn't a total dick helped, but it didn't make my decision easier.

I thanked Sally for her time before leaving the office. I let out a long breath once I was in the lobby.

"How did it go?" Sebastian asked.

"How long were you waiting?"

"Only a few minutes. I was keeping track of you loosely. And considering you were supposed to leave hours ago, I'm curious."

I glanced around, taking in the massive open floor plan filled with offices and cubicles to be sure Levi wasn't lurking somewhere. I didn't find him, but that didn't mean I was in the clear.

"This is not the conversation we should have here," I said.

Sebastian raised an eyebrow. "That bad?"

"No. That wild. When you get off work, I'll tell you everything. But if you'll excuse me, I need to go find your wife and panic for a bit."

"I'm about to leave now, actually. Can I join in on the panic?"

"Of course." I rubbed my brow. "You better be ready for the weirdest shit that you've ever heard. Well, maybe it's not the weirdest. But it's *close*."

Chapter Six

Levi's harebrained idea made less and less sense the closer I got to home, and by the time both Lily's and Sebastian's cars were in the driveway, I desperately needed advice.

"Are you ready for me?" I asked the second Lily opened the door. "Because I can't hold it in anymore."

"What happened?" she asked.

Sebastian was in more comfortable clothes and sitting on the couch. When he saw me, he leaned in with a raised brow. "We can start with the fact that Levi took her out to lunch and moved her interview back."

"Wait, as in a date?"

"No, it was a lunch to discuss the prospect of marrying me."

"No need for sarcasm," Sebastian said with a huff of awkward laughter. "Whatever happened, you can tell us."

"I *am* telling you what happened. That's it."

They both looked at me blankly.

"What?" I asked.

"I'm waiting for the punch line."

"There isn't one. I know Levi from high school. He proposed to me at lunch."

"Proposed like . . . marriage?" Lily eventually asked.

"Yes."

"Why?"

"Levi hates Calvin. That's why."

"And getting married is the only option to do this?"

"He said go big or go home, and I *did* say I wish I could be a housewife with a hot, rich husband."

"I thought we were done with weird conversations about marriage," Sebastian said as he rubbed his eyes. "Seriously. How many times can this happen?"

"At least it's not *your* marriage this time."

"She's right," Lily said, crossing her arms. She considered what to say for a long time. "What are you thinking about telling him?"

"Shouldn't the answer be no?" Sebastian asked.

"If that's what she wants, then yes. But we haven't heard what she's thinking."

"I want to not lose my house."

"Listen, you know how I feel about marriages for a purpose," she admitted. "And you know how bad it was for us."

"Even if the benefits are good?"

"They don't look as shiny when you're in it, trust me."

"It *can* still work out," Sebastian added. "But it's not easy."

"I'm not looking for this to work out. It's for money. Trust me, I *know* Levi. We have a history."

"You do?"

"He once used me to piss off Calvin by kissing me."

"That's . . ." Sebastian frowned. "That's not like him."

"It was nine years ago." I shrugged. "But he's known to hate Calvin. It's not that I blame him but . . . I can't fall for him. I know what it leads to. Not every fake marriage ends up in a relationship."

Even if theirs had worked out well for them.

"Well, at least she's realistic." Lily turned to Sebastian.

"Besides, how much time would we even spend together? He runs a company, and according to Sally, he has busy nights."

"He says he spends it relaxing," Sebastian said.

"There are many ways to relax," I replied pointedly.

"If you're thinking that he has a lot of women he spends his nights with," Lily added, "then that's not a good sign for marriage."

"It's a marriage for money."

"Sure, but it eats at you."

My lips twisted. When Sebastian and Lily had been in their arranged marriage, Lily spent many years thinking he was in love with his assistant. When I'd first met her in person, she'd nearly hit me with her car because she was leaving her house in a jealous rage.

But I *knew* Levi would do something like this. I'd been burned before, so I would go into this knowing what was going to happen.

"So you think this is a bad idea?" I asked.

"Normally, I'd say yes. But he *is* offering to solve your problems without you working. And I refuse to outright say no and risk alienating you if you decide to do it," Lily said.

Lily's friend, Jessie, had done just that. She'd been so forceful in trying to tell Lily not to go through with the marriage that it broke them in the end.

"I appreciate it. But you could tell me not to and I wouldn't hold it against you."

She tilted her head as she thought about it. "I probably wouldn't do it, but I get how desperate one can feel when they don't have options. And *you're* the one calling the shots here, so it's different than a contracted marriage like Sebastian and I had. You could say no to anything if you wanted to, so that changes things."

"And Sebastian?"

"I . . . agree with my wife," he said. "This seems like an easy way out, and as far as I know, Levi isn't a bad guy."

"I disagree there," I replied.

"He's not a bad guy in the ways *I* know him, and even if he is, you're going in prepared."

"I really expected you guys to be more shocked about this."

"Oh, we *are* shocked," Lily said. "But you need advice, and we can process how unhinged this is later."

"It's so wild that you could probably write a book about it. I'll need it when I don't get my own happy ending."

"Don't say that. You could meet the one during this whole thing."

"Who would I meet? Because it's not the guy marrying me for revenge."

"No, but someone else could walk into a coffee shop while you're there one day."

"I admire how positive you are since you and Sebastian ended up together."

"It'll happen to you too. And maybe you can help me write that book."

"I don't think I know enough words to write my own book. In fact, sometimes I feel like I don't know how to read, and that I've just memorized words."

"Is that a thing?" Sebastian asked.

"Wait, that's from a show you told me to watch . . . What's the name?"

"New Girl," I said. "You watched it?"

"Some of it. I use it as a palate cleanser between episodes of *House of the Dragon*."

I winced. "I don't know how you can stomach that."

"I'm just special," she said.

And with Sebastian's smile at her, I knew he thought the same thing. I watched the two of them gaze at each other, locked in their own little world. I couldn't help but linger on Lily's words.

Maybe I would find my person soon.

But first, I had to decide on what to do with Levi's proposal.

I didn't like the idea of revenge, and as I walked home later, I was going back and forth on whether or not to say yes.

As I lay down and drifted off not long after, I asked the

universe to give me a sign, something to tell me what to do. And whatever it gave me, I would follow it.

It was an ungodly hour in the morning when the sound of an excavator backing up woke me up. I groaned and rubbed my eyes. In my neighborhood, we didn't hear *that* sound unless a house had been sold to be bulldozed or someone had something really bad happening. I wanted to know about either of those options.

As I slowly got up, I knew the chances of demolition were low. Though Nashville was rich with development, our neighborhood had an unspoken rule not to sell to investors. This was the one place where things felt like old Nashville, and all of us wanted to keep it that way.

Whatever happened in other neighborhoods was none of my business. I knew that we needed more homes to accommodate the influx of people, but seeing a perfectly good place get torn down in favor of cookie-cutter homes was hard. I'd rather expand instead of changing existing neighborhoods. There was no perfect solution, but removing history seemed harsh when people wanted to move here for the charm.

The excavator was pulling up to the house across the street. That property had been for sale for a while, and I wondered if they'd finally sold it and the new owners were making repairs.

I threw on a robe, curious as to what needed to be done. As far as I knew, it was in good shape.

But if some major thing went wrong in a nearby house that was the same age as mine, I needed to start to save money in case it happened to me.

I walked across the street, spotting a note on the door. The workers didn't bother me as I walked closer, but then, when I saw what was on it, my jaw dropped.

Demolition scheduled.

No. No way. That house was perfectly livable! Why would it get demolished?

"It's so frustrating when things don't go your way," a voice said. For a second, I thought I had to be dreaming, but then I turned and saw Calvin smirking at me from the road, and I quickly realized I was living in a nightmare.

"What the fuck are you doing here?"

"Like my new house?" He turned to the home. "Well, *house* is a strong word. It's an antique. But it'll be a very nice new home once I'm done. I had to offer an extraordinary amount of money for the dump and fast-track the permits to get it torn down so quickly, but it was worth seeing your face."

I had to stare at him to process all of the *bullshit* he'd just told me.

"My . . . Calvin, what the hell? You're tearing down a house for revenge?"

"I'm investing in real estate. The neighborhood could use some work."

My jaw dropped. "Are you serious? Aren't you busy enough being a CEO?"

"I am, but this is a personal project."

"A personal—Calvin, get a *life*. Go hang out with your hundreds of friends."

"Why would I do that when this is way more fun?"

I knew Calvin was a dick and threw fits to get his way, but I never knew it had gotten this bad. Apparently, gaining power had only added to his big head.

"So you didn't get Gram's house. It doesn't mean you can ruin other things."

"That house was mine, Amy. I know it, and so did you. I don't know whose dick you sucked in the probate court—"

"Calvin!" I hissed.

"But I won't forget what you took from me. It took a bit for Dad to retire and for one of the losers in this neighborhood to put a house up for sale, but it's all coming together. And when you can't pay your bills, I'll tear Gram's down too."

My chest heaved. I wasn't going to let him get away with this, and I knew the one thing I could say to wipe that stupid smirk off of his face.

"I guess you're not getting invited to my wedding, then."

And it worked. Calvin blinked and frowned. "*You're* getting married?"

"Don't act so surprised. I'm a catch. And I guess I have you to thank, considering you're the one who led me to him."

"Who is it?" he asked slowly.

"He's the CEO of your rival company, a nerdy showboat, *and* kinda rich. But you know him as Levi Hensen."

I only got one second of a shocked look from Calvin before he shook his head. "You're bluffing. You don't even have a ring."

"It's getting sized. I have tiny hands."

"You don't even know him."

"I do, actually. And it only brought us closer when you fired me. He now hates you again. Congratulations."

"He would never go for you."

There was a nugget of truth to that, no matter how much I wished there wasn't. Ultimately, he only needed me for revenge, and he'd never thought twice about me other than that.

Calvin caught on to my pain just like he always did—with that shit-eating grin of his.

"I'll be waiting eagerly to see pictures."

"You will."

"Sure. Sure. Hell, if you do, let me see your registry. I'll buy the most expensive item."

"He's rich, asshole. He can get me whatever he wants."

"Which is why I don't think he'd ever be into *you*. Nice try, though."

"You're a jerk."

"And you're a loser. I don't have time to argue with you about who's worse. I need to get back to my work as a real estate mogul. How many houses do you think can fit on this property? Five?"

He laughed as I sputtered, and molten rage filled every inch of my body.

"Why would you do this to me?" I asked. "All of this over a house?"

"Yes, Amy. And like all of your other failures, you brought this on *yourself*."

There it was again, the bit of truth in his statement. I'd be lying if I said I didn't lay awake at night and wonder if I did the right thing forging that will.

I knew how Calvin was. And I went up against him anyway.

But still, did I deserve all of this? Did the gorgeous house that could have gone to a family deserve to be torn down?

No. And I was mad about it.

I could see why Levi would want to fuck this man up, even if it meant getting married to me.

And as I watched him drive away in his fancy sports car, I realized I'd gotten my sign from the universe, and it was time to make my decision.

Chapter Seven

I REALIZED FAR TOO late that when someone proposed, it was best to have their number.

The last thing I wanted to do was go back downtown to his office, but I had no other way to contact him, save for having Sebastian do it. I'd asked, but he'd gone green in the face at intervening between me and his boss at all, so I quickly rescinded the question before he could force himself to say yes.

After Calvin had finished harassing me, I headed to Levi's office. I parked, snuck in behind someone else heading into the elevator, and was stopped by his assistant outside his office.

"Hi," I said. "I'm a . . . close friend of Levi's. Can I talk to him?"

"Sorry," the receptionist said with an apologetic expression, "he's in meetings until one."

"Oh, uh, can I wait?"

She raised her eyebrows and looked at her watch. "It's only nine."

"I don't mind. I have nothing better to do."

She blinked but then put a kind smile on her face. "Then, yes. You can wait. Do you need water or anything?"

"No, thanks."

I walked over to a seat and made myself comfortable, but I knew I wouldn't be able to focus on reading for a good while. Instead, I took out my phone and typed a message to V.

> About to do something wild. Really in character for me.

V

How wild is wild?

I chewed on my lip. V and I didn't talk about our personal lives ever since he dodged questions on it. I didn't want to push too hard and run him off.

> Very. I can't even tell you because it'll open up a million questions.

Now I really need to know.

> I'm just solving some problems in my life. The only issue is that I have time to kill, and I'm panicking. Any advice?

Stay calm and levelheaded.

> You do know who you're talking to, right?

I do, but whatever opportunity you have happened for a reason. You earned it.

More like my asshole brother earned it, but it was close enough. I leaned my head back, trying to take calming breaths. It was too bad I was shit at it. My leg bounced nervously, and I knew I needed a distraction. So I replied to V.

> Now I just need to wait. Who I need to talk to is
> busy until one, and I'm waiting outside of his
> office. Hopefully, I'll be able to read the time
> away.

I got my Kindle out and forced my eyes to look at the pages. My focus was terrible, but I was able to find a rhythm for a few minutes.

But then a door opened and I looked up.

Levi's eyes found me instantly. I looked down at my Kindle and saw that only a few minutes had passed.

"Oh!" his receptionist said. "Need a bathroom break during all of these meetings?"

His eyes were only on me. "Amy," he said. "What are you doing here?"

"I was hoping we could talk about yesterday, but you're busy for a bit. We can talk about it when you're done with your meetings."

"They're canceled." His voice was firm, and I swore they echoed through the office.

His receptionist's jaw dropped. "But it's with the president of operations. He doesn't cancel."

"He did this time. I'm suddenly free."

"*What?*" His assistant sounded floored, but Levi wasn't paying attention to her.

His eyes were only on me. "Come on, Amy. Let's go talk in my office."

His assistant looked between the two of us like she was getting the hottest gossip of her life, and I knew most of the office would hear about this in minutes.

"Did your meetings really get canceled?" I asked as the door closed.

"What, do you think something else happened?"

"Your assistant seemed pretty shocked."

"If you're meaning to insinuate that I saw a message that you were waiting and then ditched everything, you'd *definitely* be wrong."

"Oh, would I?"

"You would. I canceled like a gentleman."

"*You* did it? Why?"

"I can't keep someone important waiting." He gestured to the extra chair in his office and I slowly sat, brain fizzling from what I was witnessing.

I'd never found this man more attractive.

"You're really good at words, did you know that?"

"I passed English with flying colors."

"I bet you did," I muttered.

"What can I do for you, Amy?"

Correction: He *could* get more attractive, and he just did, but I pushed past it.

"I-I have something to talk to you about."

One eyebrow raised. "Yes?"

"Some things have come up . . . and I'd like to accept your proposal."

"What came up?" he asked.

"Does it matter?"

"If I'm going to be your husband, then it does."

If I'm going to be your husband. The thought filled me with an energy I couldn't name. Was it nervousness? Or pleasure at hearing that I was going to be someone's *something*?

"Nice line," I said. "Did you steal that from a romance book?"

"I might have taken some inspiration. But that was all me. Are you gonna tell me what happened now?"

"It's nothing big. Just my brother being an ass. He bought one of the houses on my street and plans to tear it down."

"When did this happen?"

"Today. It was one of the main reasons I decided to do this. Maybe you should thank him."

His face darkened. "I will *not* be doing that. Where do you live again?"

I told him my address and the crease between his brows deepened. "I'm pretty sure about half of the homes there are registered as historical."

"The people who don't mind the historical society are registered. Some either didn't have the money or didn't want to have the oversight."

"Was it condemned?"

"No. This is purely a revenge decision on my brother's end. It's so sad. The house is in good shape and a family could totally live there."

Levi's lips pursed and he glanced at me before looking back down at his laptop.

"Have some work to do? I can come back."

"No, stay. This will just take a second."

I didn't say anything as he quickly typed something, but I did feel worse for showing up unannounced.

"All done?" I asked when he finally closed his laptop.

"For now, yes. You have my undivided attention."

"Good, because we need to talk about how to fake a marriage, which is a sentence I never thought would come out of my mouth."

Levi smiled and then leaned back in his chair. "You know what they say about lies: every good one has a nugget of truth to them."

"And what's our nugget of truth? It's not like you love me or anything."

"Right," he said after an awkward moment of silence. "I meant that we would go through with it like a normal marriage. We start with a ring and have a wedding. Do all the things normal couples would do."

"Not *all* of the things," I reminded. "But yes. That makes sense. You pick out a cheap ring and then we elope. Problem solved."

"The problem is *not* solved. I have a few things I want to do differently."

"If you're going to suggest something weird, like the Romanian tradition of kidnapping the bride for ransom, I'm gonna have to pass."

He laughed. "Nothing like that."

"Then what changes do you want?"

"We're not picking out a cheap ring or eloping. If we're doing this, then we're doing it right. And my wife gets exactly what she wants."

My wife.

The word was so shocking, all I could do was say, "O-okay."

Oh, fuck. Apparently, being called his wife made any arguments flee my brain. This was not good for my resolve *not* to get caught up in this man.

Don't trust him. He'll only let you down.

I could hear Gram's voice in my mind and I steeled myself. I could have fun looking at rings and not trust him.

Easy enough.

"Good," he said as he got up and put on his jacket. "We can get started now. Let's go ring shopping."

"What, now?" I asked. "Don't you have work to do?"

"I told you my meetings were canceled."

"But I'm sure you have other things on your list."

"Not anything more important than you."

I only had a second to ponder what the fuck was going on before Levi opened the door and I scrambled to follow him. I could tell his employees had eyes on us, and I couldn't bear to look at any of them.

"This is . . . Am I dreaming right now?"

"You're not."

"Then what the fuck is happening?"

"Go big or go home," he said as we got into the elevator. "And I don't think I want to be home right now."

He was on a mission, all of my questioning falling on deaf ears. I followed until we got to the parking garage. Then I broke out into a run to get between him and his car so he would fucking listen to me.

"Levi." I put a hand on his chest. I tried to ignore the way my heart sputtered when his eyes met mine. "You don't have to do this."

"I want to."

"That . . . *What*?"

"I know you're not used to people doing things for you, but you seem to like conviction. So get in the car."

The shock of him knowing me way too well almost made me listen.

"First of all, I don't follow orders."

"Should I tack a 'please' on at the end?"

I ignored him. "And second of all, have you lost your mind? This is a *fake* marriage. You don't have to buy me a ring or do anything other than show up to say some vows."

"It needs to be real for everyone else," he said. "Now, are you gonna keep asking questions or are you getting in the car?"

He leaned close and I froze. What was he about to do? Kiss me?

And then the door to his car opened.

"For the record, I'm getting in the car only because it's the natural next step of this conversation. Not because you told me to."

"Whatever makes you feel better."

What would make me feel better was some distance between us, though, when I was in the car, I was still baffled beyond measure.

We pulled out into the streets of downtown Nashville, and I marveled at the big buildings that had popped up over the last decade. It was better than thinking about how close Levi had been only a few minutes ago.

As a local, I didn't spend much time in downtown. None of us did. The most interesting things, other than the Ryman and concert venues, were all outside of it. Downtown Nashville didn't even have a bookstore, for crying out loud.

And as time went on, the look of the city scenery changed. More high-rises had been built to accommodate the new growth, and slowly, the city I knew had disappeared.

I had mixed feelings about it. On one hand, I was happy people were seeing Nashville for what it was, but on the other, I wished I could see the old skyline in person one last time.

"Your employees must hate driving in," I muttered.

"Some don't mind it," he replied. "A lot live in the nearby area, though. The ones in the suburbs can work remotely if they ask."

"Really? Most places prefer for their employees to be in the office these days."

"Luckily, you won't have to worry about that in your role. That's one hundred percent remote."

"What? Being your fake wife?"

He smiled. "Exactly."

I blew out a breath.

"By the way, you'll need to get used to referring to yourself as my *wife*. Not my fake one. We have to make sure it looks real."

"And what does that entail?"

"Spending time together."

"You could ignore me."

"I won't do that."

"So this means I have to deal with you all the time? Great." I rolled my eyes, wondering if sarcasm would get me out of this odd dream I'd found myself in.

"You'll adjust."

I bit my lip. That was exactly what I was afraid of.

We rode in silence the rest of the way to the jewelry store. I expected to go to a big chain and get the cheapest sparkly thing we could find.

But when we pulled up to a jeweler in the fanciest part of town, I realized I'd miscalculated.

"Levi?" I asked slowly. "Why are we here?"

"To find a ring."

"What about something middle of the line? Fancy, but not so fancy that I'd have to sell my soul to get it."

"You keep forgetting that money buys things."

"Money that I don't have. So for me, it would be either selling my soul or my body."

With a laugh, he got out of the car and once again opened the door for me.

"I have functioning arms, you know."

"And yet I'll still open the door for you."

Damn it. That was such a good line that I didn't have anything to say back.

He was too good at this.

The rings inside were worth more than Gram's and my life savings, if I had to guess.

They didn't have a price, but the number of glittery diamonds told me they couldn't be cheap.

I was careful to avoid any vases that I could knock over and put me in a lifetime of debt.

Some of the diamonds were so big one could skate on them and were attached to a white-gold ring. It hurt if I looked at them for too long.

I didn't realize Levi had been talking to an employee until both of them were looking at me expectantly.

"I'm sorry, what did you say?" I asked.

"What's your style, hun?" the saleswoman asked.

That was a loaded question. My style was fickle, brought in by either the season or whatever mood I was in. Sometimes, I had a floral phase that lasted for weeks. Other times, I lived in leggings and T-shirts until the inspiration to dress nicer hit me.

I was pretty sure a wedding ring was supposed to encompass all of that, but I had no idea how. The only wedding ring I liked had been Gram's. It was a golden band with a marquise diamond. Simple but elegant.

I didn't have any other leads.

"Do you have anything that's gold?"

She blinked. "Most of this is gold."

"I mean the gold kind."

"Yellow gold?" Levi asked.

"Yeah, that. I'm not in the habit of letting people spend thousands on me, so I'm figuring things out as I go here."

"That's okay," she said with a smile, but a glance at Levi made me wonder if she was thinking how the hell I landed a guy like him. "We have a few different styles in yellow gold. Classic, vintage—"

"That one, vintage." It was the only thing that felt right.

She took us to a different corner of the store. Looking at these rings was a totally different experience. Some were yellow-gold bands with diamonds. Some had different-colored gemstones and intricate patterns. My eyes lingered on each one. Any of these could come home with me and I'd be happy.

"What's the cheapest one?" I asked.

"No," Levi said, shaking his head. "We're not going for the cheapest. Which one do you *like*?"

"I like *all* of them. Seriously, it doesn't have to be fancy or anything."

He gave me a flat look. "Then I'll pick one for you to try. I saw something in the Woodland collection. It's an emerald-and-diamond set."

I opened my mouth to tell him I liked the vintage but closed it when I remembered that this wasn't real. As long as I could tolerate the ring, I could wear it while being married. Still, I longingly looked back down at the vintage and Levi pointed out the one he liked. I wished one stood out to me more.

"Okay, here it is!" The saleswoman sounded more excited than I felt as she pulled it out. "I think this one is gorgeous."

I pressed my lips together and told myself to stay positive as my eyes finally fell on what she was handing me.

And immediately, my jaw dropped. There were two rings, one with a large round emerald and a halo of gold and diamonds that made it look almost like a flower. The second one was an intricate weave of gold vines with tiny matching emeralds mixed within.

"Holy shit," I said, placing it on my ring finger, noticing how it brightened up the skin of my hand.

This was the one. It would have been the one even if I'd been getting married for real.

"Since when were you good at picking out rings?" I asked.

Levi laughed. "Since it was you I was picking it out for."

My eyes widened. There was no way he could know me that well, but then the saleswoman clapped her hands together and cooed, "*Aw*." And I knew this wasn't for me. It was practice for our fake marriage.

"You know what they say," I replied as I gazed at the beautiful ring on my hand, "the bigger the rock, the shorter the marriage."

"That's average sized at best, and I don't think that will be a problem for us."

Of course it wouldn't. This was fake, after all. I tried to remind myself of that, even as he stepped closer and put an arm around me.

I turned to the saleswoman, trying to play off the comment. "He's a good one."

"You two are just so cute," she said. "I live for moments like these."

"It's safe to say that's the one," Levi replied.

I put on a smile, but my thoughts were getting away from me. Would I find one as good as this when I really got married? Could I convince Levi to somehow give it to me so I could reuse it if I finally found someone?

These thoughts bounced around my head until the saleswoman rung us up. When I saw how many digits were on the screen, my stomach sank.

"Levi," I said lowly, grabbing his arm. "Are you sure about this?"

He turned to me with a smile. "Surer than anything else."

AFTER THE RING was sent off for resizing, I desperately needed to be somewhere that *wasn't* fancy, which was how we ended up at Prince's Hot Chicken.

I loved bringing people here. I loved to suffer with spicy food, and it usually broke any barriers whatever person I was with had. This time, though, I just craved the familiar burn.

We were at a different location on the south side of Nashville. I'd been to them all, and each of them had the same flavorful chicken I'd come to know and love. I remembered when I brought Lily to the original location, and she'd been horrified when she saw how spicy my chicken was.

In the boom of Nashville's housing market, I was happy to see that Prince's grew in the same way everything else had. This location was more spacious and even had live music on the weekends.

"I'll have the extra-hot breast quarter."

I was sure the woman at the front had heard people fly too close to the sun with their hot chicken. "We don't do refunds if it's too hot."

"It's fine. I know what I'm getting into."

"I'll do the same," Levi added.

"Oh, that's—" I tried to warn him, but he put his card down before I could say anything else.

Oh well. It was his funeral, after all. I knew about his little competitive streak, but seeing it was totally different.

Hopefully, he learned his lesson.

"You do realize that they're serious about the no refund thing, right?" I asked.

"Do I look like I care about the price of one meal?"

I shrugged. "Some rich people are penny-pinchers. Though after how much money you blew on a ring for a *fake* marriage, I shouldn't be surprised."

"Took the words right out of my mouth."

"Still, when they say it's hot, they mean it."

"I like spicy food."

"Hot chicken is on another level."

"I'm sure I'll survive."

"I'm just saying. Most people start with the mild and work their way up."

"Is that what you did?"

"No, I jumped straight into the hot and regretted everything. It's taken years to get where I am now. Years and tears."

"If you cry while you eat this, I won't judge."

"If *you* cry while you eat this, I definitely *will* judge."

He laughed as we filled our drinks. We sat in the corner.

"All right, so we have a ring," I said lowly. "All we need is a dress and to go to the courthouse."

"We're not going to the courthouse," he said. "I said we weren't eloping earlier and I meant it. We're having a wedding."

"*Why?*"

"My family would kill me if they knew I went to the courthouse. They've been waiting for me to finally settle down for years."

My eyebrows raised. "So you *do* have more reasons to do this."

"Maybe I do." He shrugged. "I love my family, but they can be overbearing, especially when I've not been serious about anyone."

"And why haven't you?"

"I haven't met the right person yet." He looked at me and I shook my head.

"It's not me. You're way too normal for me. And you have a revenge streak."

"*You* have a revenge streak."

"Exactly. We can't both have one or else the world might end."

He shook his head but didn't argue. "The world would also end if my mom or stepmom found out I didn't invite them to the wedding."

"Invite them to the courthouse."

"That's even worse. They're gonna want pictures and food and a whole party."

"This little scheme is getting more and more expensive."

"You'll see why I'm not worried about it when you have access to my bank account."

My cheeks flamed. "Levi, you can't just say things like that."

"Why not?"

"B-because you could get robbed."

"No one's around."

"And it's gauche to talk about money. Even *I* know that."

"Not when you're about to be my wife. Besides, you wanted the money, right? It's why you're doing this."

"Well, yes, but it's temporary. I just need a break from working, and then when we divorce, I'll get back to it."

"You'll have enough money to not worry about it."

Would I? Once my health came into play, I would eat through any money way too quickly without insurance. The medicine I was on was ridiculously expensive. I'd tried the cheaper ones, but didn't have luck.

There was a limit to how much money a man would give someone pretending to be his wife.

"Speaking of things not to worry about, do you have health insurance? And as your wife, can I get on it?"

"Of course you can. We can add you after the wedding."

"And how long does that take?"

"Usually not long, but there's some paperwork to file, and the person that usually handles it is out on maternity leave, so maybe a few weeks. Do you need it for anything?"

A spike of anxiety made me sit up straighter. I didn't talk about my debilitating migraines with anyone. They were a thing I dealt with alone, and I highly doubted that Levi would want to marry me if he knew how sick I could get.

I would have to hope that I would get on his plan fast enough to get as much of my usual medicine as I could, and then when I was on my own, it would work out.

"I fall sometimes. I'd hate to have a broken leg from being clumsy and not have insurance."

He slowly nodded, but his eyes lingered as if he were trying to figure out the truth.

"Don't worry about it," I added with a laugh.

"I think this is one place where I'm also not good at taking orders. Why did you ask?"

Great. Now, I had to lie. "Maybe I'm a high fall risk. My house is old, and sometimes I find out about issues by falling through the floorboards."

"Really?"

"It was one time. I was fine, but I had to get the subfloors replaced, and it was not cheap." I shuddered. I was still paying off that particular credit card. "Owning an old house is expensive. And my gram did as much as she could, but things aren't perfect there."

"I'm telling you, you won't have to work after this."

"And I'm telling you that I have to." I played with my hands under the table as his eyes narrowed at me. But I wouldn't break. Not about this. I could still hear the way Mom, Dad, and Calvin always made my pain feel so insignificant. Like I was a burden no one would ever want to bear.

"We'll revisit this later. The food is coming."

And thank God for that. I smiled, thanked the waitstaff who brought it to us, and then turned my focus to my pain-inducing chicken.

I loved this place so much, but they were so inconsistent with the spice of the chicken that it was akin to gambling when picking out the same heat level. I liked to joke that whoever was in the kitchen hated everyone whenever they added extra spice to the dish. Today's chef must have had a vendetta against humanity.

I coughed when I took the first bite, yet it was still delicious. A lot of the hot chicken places in Nashville went for pain only, but Prince's always had delicious flavor behind the heat, and that's what made me come back for more.

"I'm fine," I muttered to Levi. "Just let me die."

"Do you want me to avenge you?"

"Yes. Make an entire movie franchise out of it. And make sure no one knows that I technically asked for this."

He laughed and ate a fry.

I'd love to say that my mouth eventually got numb to the heat, but it didn't. It only grew as I ate, and by the time I was halfway through, I was chugging water. Nothing could make me more hydrated than hot chicken.

I glanced at Levi, hoping he was in the same amount of pain that I was.

"What the—is it even affecting you?" I asked.

"It's hot, but not the hottest I've had."

I gaped at him. "*How?*"

Levi smiled. "My stepmom is from Thailand and makes traditional dishes. Not everything is spicy, but she adds it. One time I told her to make the hottest thing she could and she almost killed me."

"So you and your stepmom get along?"

"It was rough in the beginning, but now I love her to death. Her cooking has made me numb to a lot of other things, though."

"That's unfair. I wanted you to cry."

"You're crying enough for both of us."

I flipped him off and took another bite of chicken. He was right. Tears streamed down my face, and it was an insult that he wasn't crying with me.

I thought he would rub it in. Instead, he let out a quiet chuckle and took another bite.

"Back to the wedding—"

"I'm surprised you can even think of marrying me when I'm like this."

"You're still pretty even when you've obviously gotten chicken way too spicy and you're tearing up about it. At least you're having fun."

"I *am* having fun, damn it." I leaned my head on the table and suffered with the pain in my mouth. When it had subsided slightly, I looked up to find him still smiling at me. "No one will know about this. This will stay between you and me. Or I'll commit mariticide."

His eyebrows rose. "Mariticide, huh? You must really not like me to go there."

"Sometimes, like when you prove you can eat hot chicken without being bothered, I do hate you."

"Fair enough. But we have to get married first for you to do that. And we still need to plan the wedding."

I groaned. "I don't even know what's *next*."

"The dress."

"What, your family won't be impressed by me showing up in a white T-shirt?"

"Absolutely not, and I'm half tempted to go with you, or else you'll pick the cheapest thing on the rack."

"This may be fake, but I do believe in superstition. You're not seeing me before the wedding. I'll take Lily. Technically, she's picked out two wedding dresses, so she's basically a pro, and I'm sure she'd love not to be in the hot seat for once."

"Sebastian's wife, right?"

"Yep."

"I hear good things about her. Sebastian talks about her all the time."

"He better," I said.

Levi leaned forward. "Do you want *me* to talk about *you* all the time?"

"Only say the good things."

"Not that you bit off more than you can chew in hot chicken?"

"Oh, I can chew it. I just cry a little."

"I suppose that's true. But about the dress, you should have . . ."

He reached into his pocket and pulled out his credit card. He slid it across the table to me.

"What? Why?"

"For your dress and anything else you want."

"You're just handing me a credit card?"

"Yes."

"And I can do what I want with it?"

"Yes. Flowers. Chocolates. Anything."

My first thought was books. So many books.

Then I wondered if I could get my medicine with this. But I knew that it would be far too expensive. The pills alone were a few thousand dollars without insurance, and that didn't include the specialist visit—something I was overdue for—and that was just as pricey without insurance.

No. There was no way I was using his *credit card* for that. I would wait to be on insurance and pay for it myself.

"Do you have another idea for the card?" Levi asked, and I shook myself out of my thoughts.

"Some, but they're all fun. You might regret this."

"I don't think I will."

His phone rang and he pulled it from his pocket with a frown.

"Work calls, huh?" I asked.

"It's fine. I can—"

"No," I said firmly. "We've gotten through a lot of marriage talk today. Take me back to the office and I'll head home."

"I have time."

"And I know you're lying. Seriously, go do your job."

Levi's phone rang again, earning another glare from him.

But I didn't feel like I could monopolize him anymore. He'd already done way too much as far as fake fiancés went. I was fine to head home and scream about this in private.

"Fine," he said. "I suppose I should reschedule those meetings."

"You didn't even reschedule them? What kind of CEO are you?"

"The one who wants to spend time with his fiancée. Which we could do more of."

"I've stolen you enough for the day." I took the last bite of hot chicken and stood. "Let's get back to your office."

Levi frowned again and said something under his breath. I turned with a raised eyebrow. "Sorry, just planning for the future. But if you insist we head out, then let's go."

He ran to the bathroom before we headed out.

The drive was short. For once, traffic didn't slow us down, and I was ready to be alone in my car. Levi's phone continued to go off, though he forwent answering anything while in the car with me. Instead, we talked about wedding plans.

He pulled into the spot next to my car.

I got out, planning to go right to my own.

"Amy, wait."

I stilled and turned to him. "What's up?"

He walked over to me with one hand lifted.

"You still have hot-chicken hands."

"I washed them. I was . . ." He trailed off and I tilted my head.

"You were what?"

"I just wanted to—"

"Levi!" a voice called. "Funny seeing you here! I need to talk to you about who I'm—"

I turned to see Sally walking toward us. When her eyes met mine, she stopped in her tracks.

"Amy Willard?" she asked. Her gaze darted between us. Levi was close—too close, even.

I took a healthy step back. "H-hello."

"Levi, are you trying to steal one of my candidates?"

Silence stretched out between the three of us, and I looked up at the man I was marrying, silently asking how he was going to play this.

"I'm afraid she can't be hired," he said, and his arm came to rest around my shoulders. "She's gonna be my wife. We just picked out a ring."

Sally's jaw dropped, and I had to resist the urge to let the same thing happen to mine. "You two are together? Getting *married*?"

"Yes," I said. "Suprise?"

I looked at Levi with wide eyes, hoping he'd take the lead on this one. I had no idea what story we were going to go with, and I'd spent most of our lunch freaking out about how nice he was being that I didn't think to ask about our story as a fake couple.

"We've been together in secret for a while," he said. "And known each other since we were in high school. She didn't tell me that she needed a job, and I had to inform her that I would be happy to take care of anything she needs."

"I-I'm secretive about money sometimes," I said. "And I did hear your company was good."

"You're not working for me."

"Luckily, we talked it all out last night and at lunch today. That's when we decided we were ready to take the next step."

"I see," Sally said slowly, but then her face brightened. "She's who you spend your nights with. I don't know how you kept a straight face when I was telling you about your boyfriend!"

"He doesn't spend *every* night with me," I rushed to say.

"No, I do. She's just shy about it."

What was he doing? I was trying to give him an out. Why did we need to say he was that dedicated to me? He could still continue doing his other stuff on the side.

I pushed down the angry pang in my chest at the mere thought of anything else he could be doing. This was a fake marriage. I didn't need to get defensive about a man who was marrying me for revenge.

"Well, I, for one, am happy for you, but also sad because you would have fit in great here."

"I still could—" I began, but I was cut off by Levi.

"She still thinks I'm not going to take care of her. Isn't that hilarious?"

Sally smiled. "Very funny. Don't worry about anything, Amy. You've just hit the jackpot of men. Oh, we should have a party!"

"No need," I said immediately. "I'm not good about parties."

Levi's eyes cut to me, and for once, I knew exactly how he knew this little fact about me.

"Are you sure? We love to celebrate things."

"I'm not good with all of the attention."

"Come to the wedding, then," he said. "We can all celebrate."

I smiled, but it was tight. If people he knew came, then it was going to be a slog of listening to congratulations for him and not for me. I was used to it, being Calvin's sister and all, but I wanted to make it through our fake vows and get this over with, not prolong it.

"I'll invite a few of the ladies at the office and we'll take enough pictures for everyone."

That would have to do.

But then Sally turned to me. "But trust me, you're not getting off easy. Prepare for questions at the holiday parties later this year."

Perfect. I doubted we would even last that long. "I'll be ready," I lied, forcing a bright smile on my face.

But Levi's gaze was still on me, and judging by the intense look in his eyes, I had a feeling that I was *not*, in fact, ready for this at all.

v

Did everything work out the way you wanted it to?

> Surprisingly, yes. I didn't get to read very much, though. Not that I could focus on it anyway. I did go to the bookstore though and grabbed every book I'd been wanting. *picture*

Is your shelf big enough for all of those?

> Good point. My next order of business is a shelf.

I'm glad you could finally get the ones you wanted. You've had a long list that I was tempted to get for you anyway.

> That was WAY too long for any book club member to buy. Don't worry about it. I'm just glad I can display them finally. Things are looking up for once.

Good. As they should.

You deserve all the luck.

> I think you're right, but life doesn't agree. But we should probably put up personal talk and actually read. Book club rules, you know?

Understood. What's next?

I SUGGESTED one of the new ones I'd just bought and waited for his opinion on it. While he typed, I went back up to our conversation.

That was the closest we'd gotten to talking about our personal lives. Or the closest *I'd* gotten. Over the years, I'd learned a few things about him purely from things going on in his life, but I was silent on my own. He knew who I was, but over time, I wondered when he would ask about Calvin and make it about him.

So far, my brother had never come up.

And bringing the same person who outshined me in conversation with V was not something I wanted to do.

But still, I wondered if I should have told him that I was getting married.

Would it change anything?

V and I only read books together, never even discussing the option to meet. But I would be lying if I said I didn't consider what he looked like. If I didn't consider the idea of more . . .

I didn't know much about him, and he didn't know much about me. Hell, he could have been married years ago and I would've been none the wiser.

But should I be?

The thought followed me until I went to bed that night, and as I thought back to how long we'd been talking, I wondered if the guy I'd been looking for had been on Discord all along.

And if I was making a mistake not looking into more with him.

Chapter Eight

LILY WAS at my door bright and early to take me dress shopping. I tossed my hair into a messy bun as I opened the door.

"Ready to go?"

"Kinda." I gestured to my sweatshirt and leggings. "Should I dress up more than this?"

"You'll be getting in and out of clothes all day," she said, shaking her head. "Of course not."

"Good. I'm trying to make it a few more days before I wash my hair again. I'm way too tired to try and style it."

"It looks good in the bun," she said. "Better than mine. And look on the bright side, if we go now, we can get coffee."

"You said the magic word." I grabbed my purse and got into her car.

"Want to go to our normal place?" she asked.

"Yes. I *need* their red eye right about now."

"So, how is wedding planning going?" she asked as we pulled out of the driveway.

"I have a ring. It's . . . gorgeous."

"I need a picture."

I grabbed my phone and took it out. She gasped. "That's *so* unfair. My first ring was so ugly."

"It's woodland themed. He picked it out. I didn't even know I would like it."

"Now that you mention it, I could see you with that style. That, and vintage."

"You know me so well," I said. "But you have a reason to. I have no idea how he guessed that one."

"It could have been a lucky guess," she replied. "It doesn't have to mean anything."

"It probably doesn't," I admitted quietly, trying to curb my disappointment. She raised an eyebrow at me, but thankfully, we were pulling into the coffee shop.

"Let me get my order of caffeine before you judge me," I said.

"I'm not judging," she replied. "I just have questions."

The smell of coffee hit me as we walked in, and I wasted no time getting in line.

"I know what you're thinking. I shouldn't be putting too much stock in him knowing my style."

"I'd think the same thing, but I also think your lines are getting crossed, which I know you don't want."

"I don't," I replied. "He's just being so *nice*. This is what he was like when I talked to him in high school. He really seemed into me, and then Calvin came into the picture, and I realized what he was really after."

"And right now, Calvin isn't around."

"Exactly. But you should see him when I mention my brother. His whole demeanor changes."

"Remember that," she said. "Especially once you're walking down the aisle."

"Who's walking down the aisle?"

I jumped, realizing Lily and I were at the front of the line.

Riley was the manager and part owner of the shop. Despite her status, she often worked as a barista and helped out around the store. I liked her a lot, and I knew Lily did too. I'd talked to her ever since the shop opened, but as was my usual style, I kept her at arm's length and knew more about her life than she did mine.

I stared, wondering if I should tell her about my impending fake nuptials. She looked so curious with her slight smile and raised eyebrow, and I knew I couldn't lie to her.

"I am," I said. "But it's for money, not for love."

Lily turned to me. "Wow, immediately giving out the truth."

"I can't lie to the woman who makes the best coffee in Nashville," I hissed.

"Married for money, huh? Is this like the whole thing with Lily?"

"No," both of us said at the same time.

"My family isn't forcing me to do this or anything," I rushed to clarify. "I mean, one person is kinda the reason why, but I have a choice here."

"Which is more than I had," Lily added.

"And that's *below* the bare minimum," Riley told Lily. "So why marry him for money?"

"My brother fired me and is trying to ruin the neighborhood I live in, so I'm getting married to his enemy to prove a point."

"That's shocking but also really in character."

"I feel the same way," Lily said. "We're going wedding dress shopping today."

"*Fake* wedding dress shopping," I corrected.

"The vows might not be real, but the wedding itself absolutely is."

I bit my lip. I didn't need *real* anywhere close to this wedding. Even only in words.

"That sounds *so* fun. I wish I could join you two. Will you take pictures and show them to me?"

"Of course," I replied.

"When's the fake wedding?"

"I'm thinking in two weeks. We haven't set a date or anything, but his family is coming, plus his coworkers. Meanwhile, I'm probably gonna have an empty side of the aisle."

"I could come," she said. "And my family. If you're okay with my husband and two kids, that is."

"You'd come to my fake wedding? Er, real wedding with fake vows?"

"*I'm* coming to your real wedding with fake vows," Lily said. "It's gonna be fun, even if you're doing it for money."

"Which no one else knows about, by the way."

"I'll keep it a secret," Riley said. "I won't even tell my kids about it. They're the ones that would spill the beans."

"Then you're welcome to join."

"Where is it at?"

"Ah, I have no clue. We haven't talked about it yet."

"I had mine at Opryland," Riley said.

"The hotel?"

"Yeah." She pulled out her phone and showed me pictures of a gorgeous setup. "Oliver insisted we do exactly what I wanted."

"I bet Levi would like this."

"But what about what *you* like?" Riley asked.

"I always wanted my wedding to be at my house," I said. "It was my favorite place growing up."

"That would be nice," Lily replied. "You have a big backyard, and the guest list isn't huge."

"You should do it there, then," Riley urged.

I shook my head. "Levi said we were going big or going home. I doubt he would wanna do that since it's not glamorous."

"It's *your* wedding too." Riley pointed at me.

"And he's footing the bill, so he gets a say."

"At least offer it," Riley said. "Maybe he'll surprise you."

"I'll try."

"Report back what he says," Lily added. "Sebastian says he's a good guy, but the jury is still out for me."

"I want to hear it too," Riley said. "I never get to know anything about your life."

"It's because I read and watch *other* people. Their lives are more fun."

Riley hummed. "I can understand that logic. It's still wrong, though."

I opened my mouth to answer but Lily pointed out that there were people behind us. We quickly placed our order and paid so we could get out of their way, promising to tell Riley more later.

After we had coffee in hand, Lily drove me to the same place where she got her second wedding dress. It was a local business in a nearby town, and when I walked in, I saw so many dresses that my eyes popped out of their sockets.

"It's a lot," she said with a sheepish smile, "but all you have to do is tell the stylist what you like and she'll do the work."

A smiling woman greeted us and whisked me away to the dresses. She faltered when I told her that I would need my dress immediately, but she said they had some dresses in the back that they could sell same day and have altered to fit me.

But when we went to the back, I realized they weren't selling nearly as many as they had on the floor. My heart sank as I looked at them.

"Well, you were overwhelmed," Lily said, giving me a crooked smile. "Some of these are still pretty, though."

"They're so basic," I said with a sigh.

"None of these speak to you?"

"I shouldn't worry about what speaks to me," I muttered. "I should try on whatever looks like it will fit the best."

"I'm gonna repeat Riley's advice and say get what you like, not what's easiest."

I bit my lip and considered the dresses.

"I want something that matches my ring," I told her. "Something lacy and floral."

"Okay."

"And something that just screams *me*."

"Do you see anything like that here?"

"Not really."

Lily hummed. "Then let's find something that suits you somewhere else."

"We don't have to make this a big deal."

"We absolutely do. I know how awful it is to be in a wedding dress you hate, even if it's a fake one. I don't care what this is for. You're finding something that suits you. I have all day and am hopped-up on caffeine."

"Are you sure?"

"*Yes.* Now, let's hunt down the dress of your dreams. I have some ideas, but they might be a little out there."

"That's my favorite kind of idea."

Lily's smile grew. "What about a vintage wedding dress from a thrift store?"

"What are the odds that we'll find a thrift store with a wedding dress that I like?"

"Low, but we have time. Come on."

She grabbed my arm and dragged me out of the store. The first few places had very few dresses that suited me, yet we still found stuff to look at. The next was more of the same, and by that time, our coffees were empty and I was getting discouraged.

"If this place doesn't have anything," I said as we pulled up to the next shop, "then we go back to the bridal salon. I can't keep dragging you all over town."

"You're not dragging me anywhere if I'm having a good time," Lily replied as she opened the door. "Besides, the reviews called this shop eclectic and fun. That describes you."

But even those words weren't enough to describe the 70s color on every surface. My jaw dropped, and I could see myself buying all the furniture they had and finding a place for it in my house.

If only I could wear furniture as a wedding dress.

Lily took me to the back where all of the clothes were, and they had a decent selection of white gowns for brides.

"I think we hit the jackpot," Lily said.

And we had. All I saw was gorgeous lace and floral patterns. My eyes widened. "I'd wear every single one of these."

Lily flipped through the tags, trying to find a size. "I think this one will fit."

She pulled out a long-sleeved dress covered with intricate lace, the body of it flowing to the ground like a waterfall.

"Oh my god. It looks similar to Gram's dress."

Her smile was bright. "Want to try it on?"

The fitting room was nothing more than a broom closet, but I didn't care. I was focused on the feel of the dress in my hands, the way it stretched over my skin. It wasn't a perfect fit, but it could be altered.

The second I walked out of the dressing room and saw myself in the mirror, I actually felt like a bride.

A fraudulent one, but a bride nonetheless.

"Oh my God," Lily said. "That's gorgeous."

It was. I looked like Gram when she was getting married in the black-and-white photographs stashed in one of the closets at the house. My throat went dry at the sheer sight of me in the dress and tears welled in my eyes.

Lily caught it immediately. "Are those tears of joy?"

I slowly shook my head.

She stood and put an arm around my shoulders. "What's going on?"

"T-this is perfect," I said under my breath. "Too perfect for this."

"We could go back to the other place."

"But I *want* this one. It's . . . I can't just leave it here." I swiped at my eyes frustratedly. I wasn't an emotional person, but something about getting fake married to a man who only cared about getting revenge on my brother made me one.

Lily pursed her lips before squeezing my shoulders. "We can repurpose it for after the wedding. Then you could wear it every day and give it new life."

"Or I could renew it and give it to a bride in need."

"Yes. That too. You get to wear it and make it beautiful for a day, and then someone else can. We can do the same for everything with this wedding. Nothing goes to waste."

The thought made me feel better. "That's a good idea. This all just seems too . . . good."

"We'll see the cracks at the wedding," she said. "Not to be negative, but it shows eventually."

"I'll be thinking of more books to buy to make myself feel better."

"And you'll have so much more free time. You could go see Riley at the coffee shop."

"I could read as you write."

"See? Think positively about this. Don't forget the good things."

"Is that how you went through with things in the beginning with Sebastian?"

"Sometimes. Other times, I wrote terrible things about him, but you're going into this knowing what you're getting into. You aren't as naive as I was. And no matter what happens, I'm here for you."

I smiled at her gratefully before turning back to the mirror. "Okay. Then this is the one. The perfect dress for a fake wedding."

Chapter Nine

IN ALL OF THE PLANNING, I'd forgotten the most terrifying aspect.

I would have to tell Emma that I was getting married.

She and I didn't see each other that much these days, considering she was working her ass off to be able to afford life just like I was, but we still called to catch up.

And I knew she was going to lose it when she heard I was getting *married* to a man who'd hurt me all of those years ago.

With shaky hands, I picked up my phone. Though we hadn't hammered out the fine details, we did have a day in mind for the ceremony, and I knew I couldn't delay this anymore.

Not without her coming and making a scene of it.

"Hey," Emma said. She sounded like she was in a good mood. "Where've you been? I haven't heard from you in way too long."

"It's only been a week."

"Still, usually I'm the one doing something stupid and ghosting you while I do it."

"I'm not immune from being stupid."

"Oh yeah? Name one thing you've ever done that is worse than the time I accidentally flooded my apartment."

"I actually have one," I said with an awkward laugh. "I'm getting married in a week."

"What?" Emma said. "Are you being serious?"

"Very."

"How? *Who?*"

"Levi Hensen. We reconnected recently."

"You have to be pranking me right now because there is no way you're marrying *Levi Hensen*."

I closed my eyes. This was why I dreaded telling her. Rule number one of fake marriage was not to let too many people know it was fake. I loved my sister, but she wouldn't hesitate to snap at Calvin about me marrying someone because he was such a bad brother, especially when he invited her to one of his bullshit parties.

I'd already taken a risk with telling Riley, but Lily had trusted her enough to tell her about her books recently, and no one knew.

Emma wasn't like that.

I needed to do this without messing it up, and while I loved her, she was sometimes a loose cannon. Once it was over, she and I would have a laugh while I told her everything.

"They say love happens fast. And you know I'm a romantic."

"Sure, but not a get-married-in-a-week kind of romantic."

"I've been talking to Levi for a while, actually. We just decided to make it official for . . . other reasons."

Me not having money.

Levi hating Calvin.

Calvin trying to take the house again.

"Wait, you always have some secret guy you're messaging. Was that Levi?"

Oh, God. V. It was wrong on so many levels to use him for this, but he was the out I needed.

V was not Levi, and I had a feeling he wouldn't want to be associated with the guy who broke my heart, but I needed to cover my ass with my perceptive sister.

"Yeah, that was him."

"Huh," she said. "Did he apologize for that thing he did?"

No. "Yeah, of course he did. It was one of the first things we talked about."

"So is this like a shotgun wedding because you're pregnant or something?"

"No!" Being pregnant would have meant having sex, and I definitely didn't need to be imagining sleeping with Levi. "We just didn't want to wait any longer."

"And where is this wedding?"

"At Gram's house." I said it without thinking and regretted it the second it came out of my mouth. I hadn't talked to Levi about where we would get married, but he'd sent me a list of places he liked. And they were all way nicer than my house.

"Really?" she asked. "You did always want to have it in her backyard."

"Yeah. And my future husband is supportive. Because why wouldn't he be?"

"Exactly," she said. "Are you sure about this? You sound . . . weird."

See? Too perceptive.

"Yeah, I'm fine. Just stressed with wedding planning."

"You could have given yourself more time."

A half-strangled laugh escaped me. "Come on, it's me we're talking about."

"Fair enough. Plus, I get to see Levi in person and be sure his intentions are pure. I'll definitely be there."

"Really? Can you get it off work?"

"Let me worry about that."

"But you work retail."

"And I can still take time off for my sister's wedding. I'm not missing this."

I winced. I had hoped she would.

"Is our family invited?"

"Calvin's been an even bigger ass since he took over the company, so he isn't invited, but Mom and Dad are."

She hummed. "Good choice. I think Calvin shouldn't be invited to most things."

I opened my mouth to respond, but bit my tongue before the words could come out.

"Wait a second," she said. "You're being quiet. This is usually when you say he's a part of the family."

"I'm not his biggest fan right now, so I won't be doing that today."

"What did he do?"

"He fired me the day he became CEO."

"*What?*"

"Yep. Same day and everything."

"But it's the *family* company."

"Yep."

"Dad gave you that job."

"Apparently, he was in support of firing me too."

"That *dick*. Wait—is this why you're marrying Levi?"

"What? Why would I—"

"Health insurance, Amy. Are you marrying him for the health insurance?"

"Well, yes."

Mostly.

"That makes more sense. So you were seeing each other and this was the final straw?"

"Yep. That's exactly what happened."

"I get it. American healthcare is the reason a lot of people get married, actually. And *you* need it way more than others."

"Yeah," I said with a sigh. "I do. But can you keep the reason *why* I'm getting married out of it? The last thing I need is Mom and Dad telling Calvin."

"I'll try. Just keep me away from them at the wedding. Or maybe I'll stay away on principle. Either one sounds fun."

I rolled my eyes, but then they caught on movement outside. A car pulled into my driveway. It could have been someone turning around, but my house was too deep in the street for that.

I got up to look closer and recognized the car. It was Levi's.

"I need to go," I said. "My—" I nearly choked on the word. "—fiancé is arriving."

"Don't let me keep you," she said. "Hope you get laid tonight."

"*Emma!*"

"What? You deserve it! Have fun!" She was gone before I could sputter anything else.

Levi was now walking up the path, and I let out a groan and opened the door before he could knock. "What're you doing here?"

"I didn't even get a chance to knock."

"I keep an eye on everything," I said, crossing my arms. "Now, what do you need?"

"We have more wedding details to figure out," he said. "Namely, the venue. And I brought dinner to hopefully get you to talk about them."

I eyed the bag of food. "What did you bring?"

"Not hot chicken," he said. "It's just burgers from a food truck nearby."

"That does sound good." I opened the door wider. "Thank you for bringing food, by the way. I'm sorry I didn't answer your message about the venues. We'll figure it out tonight."

"I can only hold off my mom and stepmom for so long," he said as he walked in.

"It's a bit messy," I rushed to say as his eyes trailed over every inch of my space. It wasn't *that* bad, but this would not be how I would let a visitor see it. I was already aware that the old yellow paint and scuffed-up floors didn't make the house look the best, and the dishes on the dining room table and the notebooks filled with plans for the next week didn't help.

This time, I also had wedding decorations scattered throughout the house. Lily had given them to me, and I'd put them in a pile and told myself I would deal with it later.

But this was home. *My* home, and I was defensive of it.

"Come on, it's not that bad," Levi said. "This feels more like a home than my apartment does."

"Really?"

"There are some spaces that I can tell hold a lot of happy memories. This is one of them."

"This isn't even the best part," I replied. "You should see the backyard."

I grabbed a sweater hanging on the armrest of the couch and took him to the back deck.

The door squeaked open, revealing the huge backyard. With a flip of a switch, lights came on and illuminated the area. When I was a kid, I would pretend my wedding was happening out here, using a teddy bear as my groom.

Not as much had changed in my adult life as I had hoped it would.

"This is beautiful," he said.

"It's one of my favorite places. When Gram was alive, we'd have dinner out here when the weather was nice. I love it here more than my own room at my parents' house. It's why I . . ." I trailed off.

"It's why you can't lose it."

I looked at my feet and cleared my throat. "Exactly."

"Then I'm going to make sure you never do."

"It's always a risk when I pissed off Calvin so much," I said. "He got the house at first. I'll never know why, but he did."

"Were he and your grandmother close?"

"Not at all. They didn't really talk much. He had Mom and Dad, and I had her. Maybe she regretted it in the end and wanted to give something to him."

"He didn't deserve it," Levi said firmly.

I shrugged. "Still. It's his. And if he finds out, he could take it."

"You said you stole it from him. How?"

I perked up. "You remembered that?"

"It's not every day someone says they stole a house."

"It sounds cooler than it was." I lowered my voice as if someone could overhear. "I found a different, older version of Gram's will. It was written out that I would get the house and I . . . changed the date to be more recent."

Levi stared at me for a long time before speaking. "That's . . ."

"Terrible of me, I know."

"No, smart of you. He wouldn't have cared about the house."

"Exactly," I said.

"How long ago did you change the will?"

"Over two years now. He already took me to court for it." And I had the bills to prove it. I didn't know how I'd made it through probate court and won, but I didn't want to question it.

"Then you have two things in your favor. He took you to court and you won, and the statute of limitations has expired. It's two years."

I wanted to be relieved, but I was sure Calvin knew all of this.

And now he was buying and demolishing houses in my neighborhood to get it anyway.

"He'll find a way."

"Asshole," Levi muttered.

"Man, you still really hate the guy."

"I have my reasons."

"So do I, I suppose. Do you want to see the house he's getting demolished? We can go out to the front."

Getting away from the glow of the lights would be a good idea. I was *connecting* with Levi—which wouldn't end well for me.

"I'll see it later. I like talking here," he said. "Besides, I have something I need to talk to you about. I checked my credit card statement—"

My cheeks grew hot. "You told me to spend what I wanted."

"And I haven't seen you buy a dress yet. Only books and something from a thrift store."

"My dress? I got it."

"No, you didn't."

"It's from the thrift store."

Levi sighed. "I told you that you don't have to cut costs."

"I didn't. Lily and I went to a really nice place, but none of the things there were *me*. The one I found is incredible."

"And you're sure it's what you want?"

"Hang on, you're grilling me because I didn't spend *more*?"

"You should use the benefits of this marriage to their fullest potential."

"And I am. The pile of books on my bookshelf thanks you."

"So, you're happy?"

"Very."

"Good. Because that's all I want for you."

My cheeks flushed and I hoped he didn't notice in the dim lighting.

"You're really good at this fake-husband thing," I said with a laugh. "Did you take acting classes?"

"For ten years."

"Really?"

"No," he said as he chuckled. "I'm just doing what any man should do."

"And yet a lot don't."

"I'm not most men," he said. "I have no problem doing that."

Wow. His acting made my chest way too warm. He had a very bad habit of turning my snark into a way that made me blush.

I needed to get down to business anyway.

"T-there was a reason I didn't respond about the wedding venue," I said.

"And what was it?"

"I want to have it here," I replied. "In the backyard, actually. I could decorate it and make it really nice."

His eyebrow raised and my heart skipped a beat. I wanted it here, so much so that I didn't know what I would do if he said no.

"I've always pictured myself getting married here," I rushed to explain, "and I can't see myself doing this anywhere else. A-and it would make Calvin really mad. Like *so* mad that it's here, since he lost out on it—"

Levi's hand landed on my shoulder. "Amy, breathe."

"But—"

"We'll have the wedding here." The words came so easily, and my entire body loosened. "Whatever you want is what you'll get. And if this is it, then nothing would make me happier."

"I thought it would be too basic. You're this rich guy with probably very nice taste, and I want to have a wedding in my backyard."

"You forget that I like simpler things too. This is a gorgeous house and you're lucky to have it."

"Luck, and casual will forgery."

"You worked for it and we're going to enjoy it. The wedding is small anyway."

"Good, then I guess we can go back inside and eat. I think my relief is making me hungry."

"Before you go . . ." His hand, which had still been on my shoulder, slid down to my elbow. "I have one other thing to do."

"You do? And it can't be done inside?"

"Not really. This is your favorite place, right?"

"It is."

"Then indulge me for a second, okay?"

I nodded. He reached into his pocket and pulled out a ring box.

"Oh, is that—"

His finger landed on my lips, stealing my question. "Remember what I said about indulging me?"

I nodded slowly and kept my mouth shut.

Levi's eyes roamed over my face before he took a shaky breath.

I opened my mouth to tell him he didn't have to do whatever he was planning, but then he did something so shocking that I lost the ability to speak.

He got down on one knee and opened the box.

My heart stuttered and it felt like time slowed. The ethereal glow of the lights glittered both on the stunning ring and in the sea of his eyes.

"Amy Willard, will you do me the honor of marrying me?"

In that second, it all felt real. This wasn't a sham marriage—it was one between two people who wanted to be married. If I had been on the sidelines, I would be cheering us on.

But this was happening to *me*.

"W-why are you doing this?"

"You deserve a real proposal. No matter why we're marrying."

My throat closed up. He didn't have to do this—coming all the way over here and asking me to marry him. He could have given me the ring on the day of the marriage and moved on.

Lines were blurring, and for a moment, I imagined this was a real proposal.

I could only nod, then he stood and slid the engagement ring onto my finger.

It was a perfect fit.

Looking up at him, his smile was soft. This felt romantic in a way nothing else had. That was the only explanation for what I did next.

I kissed him.

No one had ever applauded me for my good decisions, yet here I was on my tiptoes with my lips pressed against his. He didn't move; he was completely stiff against me.

I pulled away with a sinking feeling in my gut.

"S-sorry," I muttered. "I thought . . . You said to indulge you."

What had I been thinking? That this was real? That we could kiss and it'd be fine? That he wanted *that* sort of indulgence?

"I did say that." His voice was low, and he tucked a strand of hair behind my ear. "And we need practice."

"W-what?"

"For the wedding day. We want it to look natural."

I had to clear my throat. "Yeah. We wouldn't want anything to go wrong."

His hand brushed the skin on my cheek. "Call me a perfectionist."

I could only nod and pull away.

At least he wasn't being rude about it.

Levi's hand moved to my chin and made me look at him again. "The problem is . . . I don't think that was enough practice."

I only had time to blink once in shock before his lips returned. At first, it was a light brush of a kiss, but then he pressed in harder. I sucked in a sharp breath when I finally returned the gesture.

He was just as incredible as he had been all of those years ago. Never staying still, his mouth worked against mine in a way I wanted in other places.

His hands moved to my hips and he pulled me close. The kiss could have lasted forever or for mere seconds. But just like when he'd been down on one knee proposing, time felt weird.

When he pulled away, his eyes were locked intensely on mine.

"Was that enough practice for you?"

I nodded, though my body begged for more.

I had just enough self-control to cut this now, it seemed. If I let it continue, then I'd take him to my room and let him do whatever he wanted to me, and that was a complication I didn't need in this fake marriage.

As hard as it was, I needed to keep my head on straight.

His hand traced my cheek. "One thing's for sure. We'll have the perfect wedding kiss."

Oh boy. I'm in more trouble than I thought.

"Yeah," I said, trying to sound as normal as possible. "The line of people getting into marriages for revenge will be coming to *us* for advice."

I stepped away to put some healthy distance between us.

"We should eat before the food gets colder than it already has."

Levi gestured for me to go ahead, and I tried to calm down as we walked.

I'd just *kissed* Levi. For no reason. Sure, I could say it was practice. Maybe he thought it was. But the reality was that he'd done something so sweet and romantic that I did it because I wanted to.

And that wasn't my best idea.

I mechanically sat at the table, grabbing the Styrofoam packaging and taking a bite. I didn't even taste the food. I was too busy replaying the kisses over and over in my head.

"I don't think I've ever seen you be so quiet." Levi's voice was soft, and when I finally looked up, his eyes were firmly on me.

I didn't want him to know how hard I was thinking about what had just happened, so it was time to divert. "As hard as it is to believe, I do think sometimes."

"Why would that be hard to believe?"

"Just an observation people usually make. I can be a little impulsive."

"That doesn't mean you're not thinking about things. You do what you want. A lot of people have secret agendas. It's nice that you don't."

Secret agendas. Like he had with Calvin? Sure, all of it was a secret. This was for revenge, after all. But he had to have other tricks up his sleeve, something he was going to do to make Calvin pay for what he'd done.

Levi always had in the past.

"You're quiet again," he commented.

"I have a lot on my mind," I replied. At his raise of an eyebrow, I added, "Planning a wedding in only two weeks is a whirlwind. And on top of that, I told my sister today."

"Was she mad?"

"Curious, but not mad. Why do you ask? Was your family angry?"

"They were."

"That'll be fun to deal with at the wedding. Hopefully, I can smooth it over and be normal enough—"

"You don't need to smooth anything over. The only reason they're mad is because they didn't get to meet you."

"Meet me? Why would they be mad about that?"

"They care about me. A lot. Especially after . . ." He trailed off and then shook his head. "I have a habit of making problems go away, and that includes any of mine. It drives them nuts. So when I suddenly announced that I have a fiancée, you can imagine how they reacted."

"Well, it *is* sort of shocking. But at least they care about you."

"I'm lucky to have them. And you will be too."

"They're only gonna know me for a little while. I'm not getting attached."

"We have no idea how long this thing will go on for, and judging by what Calvin is trying to do with Leviathan, it might be—"

"What's Calvin doing to your company? Other than stealing doctors and the ads."

Levi paused and his shoulders tensed. "It's . . . just that."

"Hm, try again. I can tell when people are lying."

"And I can tell that boring office talk doesn't interest you."

It was a good response, and if I hadn't just reminded myself about his possible secret agenda, maybe I would have taken it.

But if I didn't know how bad Calvin was making things for Levi, then I didn't know how bad the revenge could be. Or how swept up into it I would be this time.

"Anyway," he said pointedly, "I'm just trying to say that this doesn't have an end date."

"Nice diversion," I replied. "Consider it a wedding gift that I don't dig further."

"That's a nice gift." He took another bite.

I did the same, but I knew I wouldn't be letting this go. I wouldn't be caught like I had been all of those years ago. I *was* going to figure out what was happening with his company.

And then I'd figure out just how hurt I would be in the end.

LEVI LEFT after we finished the food. Once I was alone, I pulled out my phone and tried to think of a way to connect with his coworkers.

I despised the idea of social media, but I despised getting the wool pulled over my eyes even more. I made a quick profile using an old picture I had on my phone, and then found Levi, then his coworkers. I sent a friend request to the first one I could find, which was Sally, and then leaned back on my couch.

A few minutes later, I got a message from V.

V

I've been a bad book club member. I haven't read in a week.

Same. I can't focus on it. At least our reading slumps are the same?

One of us can see the positives. How are you?

I tapped on my phone, unsure of how much detail I should go into.

Oh, you know. Making bad decisions one at a time.

Can they really be that bad?

I don't see how they can be good. But I'm
doing it anyway.

Does what you're doing help you?

Yes. In the short-term. Maybe the long-term.
It's not that, honestly. It's that I'm gonna get
hurt in the end.

This could be the time it doesn't end that way.

I wish. But no. It's fine, though. I've dealt with it
once and I can deal with it again.

The only thing you deserve to be dealing with is
how good your life is. I'm sorry it hasn't turned
out that way.

It's okay. At least I met you in the end.

And that was true. I had a friend. I had *friends*. Even if this
thing with Levi blew up in my face, I'd have them.

I'm glad I met you too. I'll try to talk to you
more. I'm sorry I've been so MIA.

It's really fine. I have been too. We'll catch up
on all of it once life slows down.

And I almost couldn't wait for it. I wouldn't miss being broke,
but once this was over, maybe I should tell him we should meet in
person. I may not know what he looked like, but I knew how he
made me feel, and I wanted that in my life.

I *needed* it.

And the idea of finally getting to know my little pen pal made
all of this just a little more worth the heartbreak.

Because when it all ended in fire and pain, I would finally
invite V into my life.

Where he belonged.

Chapter Ten

BEFORE I KNEW IT, I was sitting in my bedroom having my makeup put on for my own fake wedding.

Lily was in front of me, her brow creased in concentration while she made me look wedding ready.

For someone who never wore makeup anymore, Lily was incredible at doing it. I hardly recognized myself in the mirror. My skin glowed and my blue eyes popped against the taupe eye shadow she'd applied. The fake lashes she'd delicately put on were uncomfortable but beautiful.

"It looks amazing," I said.

"It helps that your hair is also perfect. Good job on it."

"Thanks. It only took me a few hours. But at least it distracted me."

Lily paused as she put up her brushes. "How do you feel?"

"Nervous as fuck," I said, blowing out a breath.

"You're faring better than I did. You're not throwing up."

"Instead, I'll stress eat later when our food is delivered." Levi and I had agreed on something simple: barbeque. I thought he would go for something fancier, but he continued to surprise me.

"You'll do fine. After this, you can buy yourself all of the stress food you want."

"Right. The money. And the other benefits of being married."

"How did your parents take it?"

I winced. "No idea. I texted them and they didn't answer."

Her brows pulled together. "Really?"

"I have no idea if they'll be here. But they know about it."

"If they're like *that*, then it might be better if they're not."

I only shrugged and checked the time. "I have a few minutes before I'm supposed to walk down the aisle." My nerves came back tenfold. "Distract me."

Lily's eyes were wide. "Uh, *how*? You're literally getting fake—"

The door burst open, causing both of us to jump.

"There she is!" an accented voice said. A short woman with long black hair walked in. I hadn't seen her before, which meant she must have been here for Levi. "I can't believe my mess of a stepson is getting married and didn't let me meet his bride beforehand!"

The door opened again and a woman with graying, dark hair peeked in. Her eyes were covered, but she looked vaguely familiar. "You're dressed, right? I'm so sorry if you're not!"

"We're all women here," the other woman said, crossing her arms. "And yes, she's dressed. She looks like a princess!"

"Um, what's happening?" I asked.

"I'm Isra," the woman with black hair said, turning to me. "Levi's stepmom."

"And I'm Nancy." The other woman uncovered her eyes and I saw the same blue-green shade that Levi had. "His mother."

"We had to sneak around to find you. I can't believe he didn't let us meet you before the wedding! Where was he hiding you?"

I knew nothing about Levi's family, which was not going to bode well for this conversation.

"Um, maybe we can chat after the ceremony—" Both women turned to Lily with a frown, and she straightened. "Or not?"

"It's okay," I replied. "I'm just a bit overwhelmed. I might not be the best at conversation."

"It's okay," Nancy said with a smile. "I was a nervous wreck, though my marriage didn't work out."

"I was calm as a cucumber," Isra replies, crossing her arms. "But I also never get nervous."

"Wow, what's that like?" I asked.

"So, you're Amy," Nancy said with a smile. "The woman who finally got Levi to settle down."

"It's about time," Isra added.

"I am. Don't ask me how, but I did."

"He once said he was never getting married," Isra said. "I told him he would change his mind."

"No I told you so's on his wedding day," Nancy said. "That's for the day *after*."

"So, you're his mom and stepmom," Lily said. "And you two get along?"

Nancy waved her hand. "Oh, we're best friends these days."

"And she was the one who introduced me to his father," Isra added. "Then he died and we decided to join forces on raising Levi."

I straightened. I didn't know his dad had died.

But it was something I should know, considering I was marrying him.

"I'm glad you did. I know it affected him *so* much."

"Has he admitted it to you?" Nancy asked. "He never wants to show it to us."

"O-of course. I mean, I'm his fiancé."

"And yet he couldn't invite you for dinner!" Isra scoffed.

"It was a whirlwind, and I'm known for moving fast."

Isra hummed and Nancy looked so happy, I hated knowing I was lying. "Then you'll have to come over after your honeymoon."

"Oh yeah. We'll definitely do that."

"And the yard is so beautiful!" Nancy said, looking out the window. "It—"

She didn't finish her sentence as she continued staring outside.

Isra caught onto her change in demeanor and quickly joined her at her post.

"Is everything okay?" I asked. "Did the arch fall again? I can—"

"We'll deal with this," Isra announced. "You need to focus on looking beautiful."

"Even though you already are!" Nancy said.

Isra threw open the door and left. Nancy laughed nervously and followed.

"That was weird," I said.

"I thought they were nice."

"No, whatever's happening outside. Maybe I should look."

"You're already stressed," she said, grabbing my shoulder. "And you're about to walk down the aisle. You should take a second before you throw up like I did."

I sighed. I might not have felt like I was going to throw up, but my nerves were making my hands shake. "Fine. You might be right about this one."

"And one of your brows needs some help. Give me just a minute." She returned to working on my makeup as I tried to take deep breaths to stay calm.

It didn't work.

MY BACKYARD HAD BEEN TRANSFORMED into the perfect wedding oasis. Chairs lined a white aisle and flowers were every-where. The slightly warm weather was exactly what any bride would want for the occasion. Whatever had gone awry was fixed now, and everything was right as Lily and I had left it.

Lily was in front of me, and seated on my side of the aisle was Sebastian. Next to him, I saw Riley with a dark-haired man and two little ones.

And then my parents.

Mom glanced at me, but quickly looked away. By the set of her brow, she was *not* happy. She leaned over and whispered something to Dad, and I had a feeling she was mentioning my brother, who was noticeably *not* here.

Behind them, Emma snapped pictures on her phone as if it was the best day of her life.

At least someone was excited.

I reminded myself that this was *my* fake wedding and that my attention should be on the groom. I focused my gaze solely on Levi.

He was stunning in his suit and tie. His hair was slightly trimmed and he seemed to be playing the perfect husband, with only eyes for me.

But something was off. His lips were pursed and his hands were in tight fists at his sides.

My breath caught in my throat. What if he was regretting this?

When he saw me, some of the tension melted away, and he put on a show of a lifetime. He seemed nothing but happy to see me, but I hadn't forgotten the tension that had just been in his features.

What was running through his head?

As I walked down the aisle, I saw the way his eyes traced *every* inch of me. My entire body heated at his gaze. After my own parents' lukewarm response, this was a breath of fresh air.

I tried not to think about everyone's eyes on me, and I wondered if my family had been right the whole time. I didn't do well with attention and this was proof.

"*This* is the hundred-dollar dress?" Levi asked as I moved close to him.

I shrugged. I'd had it altered to fit me to a T, yet my skin itched, wondering if the people staring at me were finding something wrong with how I looked. "Does it look okay?"

"It doesn't just look okay. It's fucking stunning."

"Thanks," I said. His words meant more than I wanted to let on.

Our officiant cleared his throat, and I stepped into my position. Our vows were going to be short and to the point. We had agreed on something that represented joining lives, but I didn't care much for the words themselves, so Levi had taken care of it.

All I could do was half listen as the officiant spoke about love and happiness. I knew I might start crying if I looked out at the crowd.

"Amy." The officiant's words were soft, yet I jolted anyway. "Do you take Levi to be your lawfully wedded husband?"

I put what I hoped was a relaxed smile on my face and nodded. "I do."

"And do you take Amy to be your lawfully wedded wife?"

He didn't hesitate. "I do."

"Then I pronounce you husband and wife. You may now kiss the bride."

I leaned in, heart still skipping a beat as he got close. Our guests clapped, but my eyes were stuck on him. His lips pressed against mine and my brain whited out again, choosing to focus on one stupid sentence.

This is forever.

I pulled away and shook off the thought.

No, brain. This wasn't forever. This was a plan for revenge. I was tied to a man who only wanted me for my brother. There was nothing else.

But then he smiled so wide his eyes crinkled, and for one second, I could pretend that he wanted this.

That he wanted *me*.

And it was fake. No one wanted me. Not in the beginning, middle, or end of my story. I'd long since made peace with this fact of my life.

But I didn't realize how easy it would be to pretend that things were different.

Chapter Eleven

I DIDN'T THINK things could get worse, but then I saw Mom and Dad glaring at me, and my heart nearly stopped.

I had a grip on Levi's hand and it tightened the second I saw them.

And he noticed.

"What's wrong?" he asked.

"This is a lot of attention. Everyone's looking at me."

I could tell he didn't get it, and I didn't blame him. Half of it didn't make sense to *me*. I was prepared to force myself to deal with it, but then Levi tugged me away.

"Sorry, everyone. Need a second with my wife."

There was a sound of a wolf whistle, and I heard Nancy yell, "Isra, *no!*"

It almost made me laugh as I was pulled into the house.

While I was alone, I was able to catch my breath.

"T-thanks," I said.

"I can go back out there and distract them."

"No." I shook my head. "We need to be united."

"But you're stressed."

"I've been stressed for weeks. Just give me a second."

"Amy, this was supposed to help your stress."

"Yeah, but everyone looking at *me* . . ." I took a shaky breath. "I think my parents and Calvin were right."

His gaze shot to me. "What could they possibly have been *right* about?"

"They always told me I wasn't able to handle the attention Calvin got, and this is just proving to me that I can't. I had maybe twenty people's eyes on me and I had to hide out." I rubbed my forehead, frustrated with myself.

"Is it the twenty people, or is it your parents in the audience?"

Fuck. He was right. "I think it's the second one. And . . . everything else."

"This is not a normal event. It's fine that you're a little out of it."

"They looked mad."

"Probably because you look prettier than Calvin ever could."

"The term they'd use is handsome."

"Don't worry about them." Levi's voice was gentle, but my head fell into my hands, and I wasn't sure what to do. But then his hands came to my shoulders. "Be yourself. We'll kick them out the second they do anything."

"I *am* myself."

"Not the version I know." His hold on me loosened and he moved to grab my hand again.

I happily let him.

Everyone turned to look at us as we reemerged into the backyard, even my parents. Levi's hand squeezed mine, reminding me that I was okay.

Logically, I knew that we had to play the part, and this was a part of it, but I would take any source of comfort and deal with the consequences later.

Isra made it to us first.

"That was beautiful! The best planned wedding since my own."

"Does this mean you've forgiven me for not letting you meet her until now?" Levi asked.

Isra's smile fell. "No."

Levi let out a long sigh. "Amy, meet Isra. She's my—"

"Stepmom. I know. She already introduced herself."

"When?"

"I found her while she was getting dressed. Nancy joined me. Now you can't hide her anymore."

"Isra," he said, exasperated.

"For the record," Nancy said, having finally made her way to us, "I tried to stop her. Not very hard, but I did."

"They were nice," I replied. "And you did warn me about them."

"My reputation precedes me." Isra smiled, but then she looked at me. "Though I can see why you wanted to lock her down so quickly."

"Right?" Levi put a hand on my shoulder. "Just look at her. The dress alone is incredible."

I had to resist the urge to sputter awkwardly at the compliments. What did people *do* when they got so many?

"Thanks," I finally was able to say. "It's vintage, like most of my things."

"And this *house*," Isra started. "Finally, Levi can move out of that ugly apartment."

Levi's hand tightened on my shoulder. We hadn't talked about this. *Why* hadn't we talked about it?

The answer was obvious. We wouldn't be moving in together. Not for a fake marriage.

"Um, yeah. We're still figuring out who will move." All I needed to do was delay until Levi and I could get our shit together and communicate properly.

"It should be him, obviously. You own this home, right?"

"Yes."

"This is a *family* home. You don't raise kids in apartments, Levi. You know that."

"I do," he said. He sounded much calmer than I felt. "We'll figure it out."

She narrowed her eyes; I knew that wasn't a good answer. But before I could try and give her a better one, I caught sight of my parents again, still staring at me.

"Um, I should go talk to my mom and dad," I said. "Give me one second."

"Are you sure?" Nancy asked. "It's very fun here."

"They came all this way," I replied. "It's only polite to."

"Then I'm coming with you," Levi said, his hand sliding into mine. "We should do everything together, right?"

"He's a pro already." Isra leaned into Levi and added under her breath, "Try not to lose it this time."

"Like you wouldn't."

I looked between the two of them with a raised brow. What the hell were they talking about?

"Come on," Levi urged, tugging me away. "Let's get this over with."

"H-hey," I said when I walked up to them. "So glad you guys could make it."

Mom glared at Levi before turning to me. "Yes, sure."

"It could have been a better day," Dad muttered.

"My wife didn't want her brother here," Levi said firmly. "So he had to leave."

"Wait, what?" I asked. "What do you mean he had to leave?"

"Calvin wanted to celebrate you, and this man kicked him out." Mom said it like it was the worst thing to ever happen to her.

"I'm her husband," Levi reminded. "And he was going to start a problem. So I prevented that."

"But I didn't invite Calvin," I said. "Why would you bring him?"

I'd been clear when I told them about the wedding. My text

130

said Calvin and I weren't on good terms, but I still wanted them to join me.

And they just invited him anyway?

"Because he's your brother," Mom said.

"And I said no."

Levi's hand tightened on mine. "It's our wedding day. We can do what we want."

"I can't believe you're being so petty." Dad shook his head.

"He sent you a gift." She handed me a blue paper bag. I sifted through and only found a book inside.

How To Get Divorced.

"Is he serious?" Levi muttered.

"It's more than you deserve, considering you didn't invite him," Dad said.

"He *fired* me."

"He thought long and hard over that," Dad replied. "And he had my blessing."

"He bought the house across the street."

"Only because you wouldn't let him have the one he wanted. If you would give in, this wouldn't be so hard on you."

My anger and confidence faltered. I felt the same regret I usually did when I tried to put my foot down. I didn't know how, but my parents always could prove to me that everything that happened was because of *me* and never because of him.

"Like I said"—Levi's voice was low, showcasing a dangerous tone I'd never heard before— "it's our wedding day. And I'm gonna ask that you have your attention on my wife and not her brother. Otherwise, I'll ask you to leave as well."

Mom's jaw dropped. Dad frowned.

I never talked to them that way, and I could see Mom look at me as if asking if I was going to let my husband talk to them like this.

I knew I shouldn't, yet I was angry.

Just like Levi said, this was my *wedding day*. Yet they weren't trying to get to know the man who had his hand in mine, who I'd just joined my life to. They only cared about why Calvin wasn't here.

"It's my day," I said quietly.

Mom shook her head. "Until you treat us like family, we'll be elsewhere."

Was I treated like family when I was fired? When Calvin tried to demolish a house just because I got this one?

I watched them go without saying anything, fists clenched.

"Have they always been like that?"

"Usually when I give in, it's easier."

"You shouldn't have. I wasn't kidding when I said it was your day."

"For revenge, at least. I guess I can't be too mad when we're also doing this all for Calvin."

Levi turned, his rage now directed at me. "I'm *not* doing this for—"

"Amy!" Emma called. I turned to see her running over to us. I barely got to see her ever since she moved out of town. The last time I visited was when she wrecked her car and nearly broke her leg. Most of our talks had been on the phone or over text. I couldn't help but grin when I finally got to hug her in person.

"You made it," I said. "Thank you for coming on short notice."

"And miss your big day? You look so fucking amazing," she said. "Like Gram's old picture. Is that her dress?"

"No, Calvin sold that. I found this all on my own."

Emma's face fell when I mentioned Calvin. "You know he tried to show up, right?"

"I do. Mom and Dad tried to defend him, and Levi just told them to leave." I jerked my thumb toward the man behind me.

Emma finally turned to him. "I like you already. I'm Emma. You probably only remember Amy and Calvin, though."

"No, I remember you. Amy talks about you all the time."

"That's surprising. I was sure I'd annoyed her into never talking about me. Even to her fiancé."

"I like to reiterate how much of a pain in my ass you are," I added.

"Welcome to our wedding," he said. "There's only one rule, and it's that you don't mention Calvin."

"I already do that," she said. "And I have way more important things to do now, such as know everything about how you two reconnected."

"We may not have time for all of that today," I cut in. "We still have people to talk to and things to clean up."

And Levi and I needed to come up with a better story.

"Fine. But I'll have questions later."

"As you should," Levi said.

"And if you break her heart, I have no problem driving four hours to kick your ass."

"I'd welcome it."

Emma nodded slowly. "All right, you're not so bad. And you make my sister smile bigger than I've ever seen, so welcome to our fucked-up family."

I gazed across the crowd of people and landed on Riley and her family. They were casually hanging out, but I saw her perk up when my eyes met hers.

"Sorry to cut this short," I said. "But I think a few people are waiting."

"It's nice to finally see people waiting for *you* to talk to them," Emma said smugly. "But go ahead. Have fun. I'll find out *all* the details later."

And I knew she would. She'd either call me when I least expected it or drive the four hours to corner me.

Levi followed me over to where Riley was holding hands with a little girl with brown hair. Next to her was a taller man with black hair, who watched a baby barely old enough to toddle around the yard.

"Hi," I said. "Thank you for coming."

"I'm so glad we could be here. This is Oliver, my husband."

"Nice to meet you," Oliver said.

"And this is Zoe." She pointed to the little girl. "And Xavier."

Zoe waved, but Xavier was far too entertained by a dandelion to notice us.

"You didn't tell me your kids were *adorable*," I said, looking at the two of them.

"I think they are, but sometimes others disagree."

"Where are they? I'll talk some sense into them."

Riley laughed, but then her eyes slid to Levi.

"Oh! Right. I need to introduce you to my husband." I tugged him to my side. "Levi, this is Riley. I go to her coffee shop all the time."

"This wedding was *beautiful*," Riley said. "I can't believe how nice your backyard is."

"Lily helped transform it."

"But still. And you got to have your wedding here!"

"She gets what she wants," Levi said. "And I don't think there was a venue my stepmom could compliment more."

"She's a big believer in homeownership, huh?" I asked.

"Always has been."

"You guys look good together," Riley said. "All things considered."

Levi's smile fell as she winked, and I was sure he was going to ask, but then both Oliver and Riley noticed Xavier running to the road, and they darted after him.

We walked toward Sally, who was bouncing on the balls of her feet, but paused halfway there.

"What did she mean when she said all things considered?"

"I may have mentioned some specifics about our arrangement."

"She knows?"

"She, Sebastian, and Lily do. They're the two people I had the hardest time lying to, and Riley is good at keeping secrets."

"Secrets? Do you have more?"

Not that Riley knows.

"I'm talking other people's secrets that I also can't tell you that don't involve you."

Levi's brows knitted. "I'm not sure that makes sense."

"Lily has a thing she tells no one, okay? And Riley knows and keeps it a secret, and no one else does."

"Does Emma know?"

"About the secrets? Why would she?"

"About *us*."

"Oh. She knows money was a factor, but no. She would immediately go to Mom and Dad's house and kick their asses for putting me in this situation."

"Maybe she should."

"If they found out I married for revenge, I'll never live it down. You know how Calvin can be. I didn't want to risk it with her."

"I understand, but if anyone else knows, you have to tell me. Communication is key to any marriage."

"Even fake ones?"

"Especially fake ones," he said.

"All right, I can do that. You're completely caught up on who knows."

"Good," he said. "Now, let's go talk to Sally. I'm pretty sure the entire office signed a card and tried to hide it from me."

"It doesn't seem like they did a good job."

"They never do."

It took far longer to talk to everyone than I thought it would. Sally did have a very sweet card loaded with gift cards to local restaurants. She was so happy for us and showed us all the photos she took while I was walking down the aisle. After that, we caught up with Lily and Sebastian, where we all talked about how to take down everything.

I expected it to be just the four of us after people filtered out of the house, but Isra and Nancy insisted on staying to help put the leftover food up while we cleaned up all the decorations outside.

"I should probably go make sure they aren't going through your house," Levi said after a few minutes. "I love them, but I don't trust them alone together."

"We can finish up out here," I said. "Don't worry about it."

He nodded and started to walk away, but then turned. "Before I go, I need to ask the two of you, how did we do?"

"Do?" Lily asked.

"With faking a wedding."

"You know that we know?" Lily asked.

"I had to get it out of her, but yes. I do. I knew some people did. She told me she needed her friend's seal of approval."

"And we're the experts on fake marriage," Lily said.

"Wait, what?" Levi looked between them.

"Wow, we're really going there?" I asked Lily.

"Oh, did Levi not know?"

"Why would I tell the CEO of the company I work for that our parents sold us off together?" Sebastian asked. "It didn't come up!"

"Now I need to know," Levi said.

"It was dramatic," I told him. "When I met them, they basically hated each other."

"To be fair, I thought he was cheating."

"I wasn't!" Sebastian said. "It was a misunderstanding that went on far too long."

"You're lucky Sally isn't still here," Levi replied. "She'd love to hear this."

"I'd rather the office not know how much of an idiot I was in the past," Sebastian said with a sigh. "But if you want, I can give you the whole story sometime. As long as you keep it between us."

"I can keep secrets, and I definitely want the whole story," Levi replied. "But speaking of things I have to do, I should really check up on Isra. Who knows what she and Mom are doing."

"Have fun with that," I said, waving him off.

Lily waited until Levi was inside before turning to me.

"That went well," she said. "You sold it *so* well. Even Riley thought so. You're a good actor."

"Y-yeah," I said. "That was *definitely* all acting."

Lily looked up. "What does that mean?"

I checked behind me, making sure Levi and his family were inside. "I don't know. He was really nice today, and I found myself leaning on him a lot. Plus, he did a really good proposal, and—"

"I thought we said that there was no romance happening," Sebastian added as he moved the arch Levi and I had gotten married under.

"There shouldn't be, but he's kinda romantic?" I groaned after I said it. "Which he was the first time too. This is how he gets me every time, by being nice until he pulls the rug out from under me."

He exchanged a look with Lily before walking to the shed to drop off what was in his arms.

"What?" I asked.

"What if he *is* actually like this?" Lily's voice was gentle, yet her words hit hard.

"No, I'm not falling for it again. You weren't there when he confirmed he kissed me to piss off Calvin, and he's made it clear that all of this is to make my brother mad."

"You don't have to fall for him to admit that he's nice."

"That's the thing. If I do admit it, then I could forget that this isn't real. None of it is. It's for revenge, and he always has to be the best at that."

"But does it feel like revenge?"

"None of it does. That's the problem. When we practiced our kiss—"

"Hang on, you practiced that?" Lily's eyebrows rose.

"Yes."

"And?"

"It was good."

"But practicing is gonna lead to more confusion."

I rubbed my forehead. "I know, and I accept that I'm shooting myself in the foot here. Even if I say it's practice, I know he's doing it to make this perfect. But it feels nice, therefore, I'm getting confused."

"At least you're admitting it," she said as she threw things away.

"Will you still be there when I get my heart broken?"

"Of course I will."

"It would almost be easier if he was a bad actor, but he's definitely not."

"After he goes home tonight, you'll have some time to cool down. I think you'll need it."

"Amy!" Isra called out from the deck. I turned to see her waving. "Can you please come talk some sense into my stepson?"

"That's my cue."

"We'll finish up here and head home," Lily said, giving me a smile. "You've got this."

I gave her a quick hug before darting inside.

"Isra," Levi said, head in his hands, "don't bring Amy into this."

"She's your wife!" Isra exclaimed. "It's important that she's involved."

"What's going on?" I asked.

"He's telling me he's going *home*. On your *wedding night*!"

"I said I was packing up my stuff to come back a different day. We're tired, Isra."

"So?" she asked. "This is your first night together! It should be in the same house!"

"Mom, back me up here."

"Sorry, kiddo," Nancy said with a shrug. "I agree with her. I thought it was a given that you were staying here. Not packing up the second the wedding is over."

"I . . . I told you, I need to pack."

"I'm sorry, pack for what?" I asked.

"Moving in, obviously," Isra said with a laugh.

I made a noise between a gasp and a scoff. "I . . . That's moving a little fast, don't you think?"

"A little fast? We didn't even meet you until your wedding day! You're slowing down *now*?"

"No, Isra, I'm moving in." Levi rubbed his forehead. "It's just not tonight."

"With the way you were talking, you were here already!"

Levi looked at me with wide eyes, and it hit me that we were not going to get out of this without lying our asses off. He and I could talk about what the hell we were going to do later.

"He has *some* stuff here, but moving is a lot of work. We figured we'd get it all done in one go and he could go through his stuff."

Isra and Nancy glanced at each other, obviously considering what I said.

I glanced at Levi and wondered if I had gotten through to them.

"We'll pack up for you," Isra said. "Problem solved."

"But—"

"You two get rest and we'll take care of it!" Nancy clapped her hands together. "Think of it as a late wedding present."

"You guys don't need to—" Levi tried to say, but Isra cut him off.

"No! No excuses. Spend time with your wife! Not packing up! We're going there tonight."

"Tonight? But—"

"Actually, right now. No leaving! Enjoy your time together!"

Isra grabbed Nancy and marched out the door, leaving us alone.

"What just happened?" I asked numbly.

"My mom and stepmom happened," Levi said, scrubbing a hand over his face.

"What the hell are we gonna do? We can't move in together."

"We can't *not*. Why would we rush into getting married otherwise?"

"No, *no*." I crossed my arms over my chest. "This isn't happening. This house isn't even your style."

"I thought we established that I love your house."

"Yes, but not enough to *live* here. Why aren't you freaking out more?"

"I *am*, but I've been arguing with them about this for a while, and I knew this would come up eventually."

I closed my eyes, trying to think of a way out of this, but one of my damn fake eyelashes stabbed my eyeball, and that was the last straw.

"God, I have to get out of this fucking makeup, and then I can deal with this disaster."

I walked to the hallway bathroom and grabbed my face wash to scrub everything off.

"I could get a place nearby," Levi offered as I worked on it.

"And when Isra and Nancy show up, you just come over? They're packing up your stuff. They'll know if it's not here. And —*shit*, I forgot a towel."

I heard footsteps and then cloth touched my face. "I've got it," he said, gently wiping off the water. Once it was out of my eyes, I was left gazing at him with a terrifying realization.

If he moved in, I would fall for him.

"Be honest with me, will your mom and Isra know if you don't live here?"

"They'll figure it out eventually. They notice way too much."

I tried to put myself in their shoes, and I knew that if I saw two people rush to get married and then live separately, I would question it.

There was no way to sell this without him being in my house.

"Just stay in the guest room," I muttered. "I have space in there."

"Are you sure?"

"No, but this is the best option. But don't be surprised when you get bored of watching me sit around and read all day."

"Reading, huh?" His lips curled into a smile. "We have the same hobby."

"You read?"

"Every day."

I put a hand on my hip. "What do you read? Don't tell me it's business nonfiction books."

"Good guess, but no."

"Self-help."

"Wrong again."

"Thriller?"

"No."

"Mystery?"

"Do you want to keep making wild guesses, or would you just like me to tell you?"

"Please tell me. I'm on the edge of my proverbial seat."

"I read romance."

That was not the answer I expected. "You read . . . romance. Like the genre?"

"Yes."

"You—" I cut myself off, thinking of V. He always told me that most people were shocked when he told them his favorite genre purely because he wasn't a woman. I didn't want to fall into that. "Wow, okay. Didn't expect that."

"Most people don't."

"I mean, it's cool. You read whatever makes you happy. But out of curiosity, what makes you like it?"

"The happy ending. It's a reminder that no matter what happens, we all get there in the end."

I blinked as I remembered something similar V once said.

After losing someone in my family, I needed an escape where I knew things would be okay.

"It's my reason too," I said softly. "Real life sucks in that we don't always know how it'll end. What's your current read?"

"I have a few."

"Maybe we could start a book club."

He laughed. "Wouldn't that be fun?"

"No, seriously. I know another guy who likes books too. You two could meet up and talk about your experiences being guys who read romance."

"You talk to another guy, huh?"

I realized how it sounded, and that feeling of guilt hit me again. I knew I wasn't going to talk to V any differently while I was married to Levi, but the regret I felt for *not* doing it was hard to stomach.

And it made me feel worse.

"Not like *that*. Just about books."

"I figured it was something like that. I'm not worried."

"Good," I said, pushing past the heavy feeling in my chest. "He's just a friend anyway."

A friend I had a deep connection with. A friend I wished I'd asked more questions of.

I didn't even know if he would want to hear them. After all, he'd talked to me for nine years and never brought anything up. Maybe things would never change.

Clearing my throat, I stepped away from Levi, putting some

healthy distance between the two of us. I remembered that I needed to put sheets on the guest bed.

"All right, if you're staying, we have work to do," I said. "But the first thing on the list is getting me out of this dress."

"And you want me to do that?"

My words caught up to me. "*N-no!* I'll get *myself* out of the dress and then we'll get the guest room together. Get your mind out of the gutter."

"Stop saying things to put it there."

"Keep going, and you don't get a blanket. You'll be sleeping in the cold tonight."

Chapter Twelve

THE NEXT MORNING, I stumbled into the kitchen to start the coffee pot. Everything felt blurry. I wasn't sure what was a dream and what had actually happened the night before.

Either my mom had turned into the Wicked Witch of the West and flown off into the sunset or Levi had moved in.

This early in the morning, both seemed equally possible.

There were wedding decorations strewn on the floor, and my ring was on my finger, so we were definitely married.

I just hoped I was alone in my morning misery.

As the coffee brewed, I grabbed a glass bottle from the fridge just as I heard footsteps. I turned to see Levi gazing at me from the doorway, and I knew that my denial could no longer continue.

He was here.

"I know there's a lot going on," he said, "but it might be too early to be drinking."

I paused, looking at the glass bottle in my hands and then to him. "No, this isn't alcohol." I turned the label so he could see. "It's maple syrup."

"You're putting that in your coffee?"

"As opposed to what? Maple-*flavored* syrup?"

His brows knitted, but then he grabbed a mug. "Can I try it?"

"You could just think I'm weird and move on."

"I do think you're weird. But you're *my* type of weird, and I wanna join you."

I pressed my lips together and poured him some. He added coffee to his cup and took a sip.

"This is good."

"Right? It's the best way to have coffee."

"Did you sleep well?"

"Yep. Slept great. Like the dead." My voice was flat.

"You're in a great mood this morning," he said sarcastically as his eyes roamed over me again.

I did not look my best. I'd tossed and turned all night and didn't put my hair in a silk bonnet, which meant my curls were two times bigger than usual. I'd groaned when I got up and stuffed all of my mane into a bun.

At least Levi had the sense to not say anything.

"I always am before coffee," I muttered before finally taking a long sip.

"Mind if I have another cup?"

"Sure. What's mine is yours, or whatever people say about marriage. Though, if you finish the pot, you better make more."

"That I can agree to." He walked by me, eyes flicking down to my top and back up. I frowned and followed his line of sight.

That was when I realized that he could see right through the thin material to my nipples.

"Oh my God!" I yelled, covering myself with my arms.

"I didn't see anything!"

"Don't lie! You did!"

"Only a little, but I wasn't gonna mention it. I have self-control. I can be respectful."

"That doesn't mean I'm letting you see my nipples for free, buddy!" I yelled as I darted back to my room.

I threw on a T-shirt and leggings, determined never to show

146

Levi my breasts again. When I got back downstairs, he was sipping coffee and *not* looking me in the eye.

"So, are we talking about that or . . ."

"Nope," I replied. I waved my hands, wishing I was a master of hypnosis. "You never saw my boobs. You'll never think of it again."

"You're going to have to try harder if you want me to forget that."

"What happened to being respectful?"

He put up his hands. "Sorry, I'll be respectful now."

I glared as I grabbed my own cup of coffee.

"By the way, my mom and Isra will be here in fifteen minutes."

I nearly choked. "What? Why?"

"They're helping me move in. Neither of them do anything halfway."

"Why couldn't you have shitty parent figures like I do? Ones that don't care."

"Sorry to disappoint. I think they're happy that I'm not living alone and . . ." He trailed off. "That I have someone now."

"How mad will they be when this ends?"

"I'm trying not to think about that right now. I'll cross that bridge when we get to it."

Guilt that I wasn't expecting hit me. Isra and Nancy seemed so happy for their son, and this was all a farce. I thought it would be between Levi and me, but this was bringing them into it too.

"I'll go clear out a part of my closet," I said. "It'll look like we prepared."

I walked away without another word, going to my room and finally pulling out the clothes I'd meant to donate a long time ago. I had a bad habit of letting things sit, but luckily, this was pushing me to make progress.

I heard them walk in only minutes later, and I took my medicine before putting on a newlywed smile.

"Hi, guys!" I said as I saw them. "Come in and—" I paused when I looked out to the driveway. "Is that a moving truck?"

"Of course, we got everything." Isra said it like it was nothing.

"Not *us*," Nancy clarified. "I got some of the boys I work with to do the heavy lifting. Levi can do the rest."

Isra smiled widely. "And anything ugly can be thrown away."

"Hey!" Levi moved toward the front door, but Isra held up a hand to stop him.

"You're not bringing your ugly bachelor pad furniture into this gorgeous house!" she said as she pointed to him.

"Not all of it is ugly. I think most of it would fit in nicely."

Isra shook her head.

"I'm sure we can put it in storage," I offered.

"Do you know how long I've been waiting for him to find someone with taste? That furniture is gone now."

I glanced at Levi, who looked resigned. "Fine, we'll go through it all."

"Good. Now, is that coffee?"

"Yes, I made plenty. Go ahead."

"Don't worry, kiddo." Nancy patted her disgruntled son's cheek. "Some of it will work here."

"You guys didn't have to do all of this."

"You kept your marriage from us until the last second. We have to overcompensate now."

"I think it's nice," I said. "You guys really care a lot."

"Even when he keeps stuff from us," Isra said as she returned to the living room with a cup of coffee in hand. She took a sip and nodded. "This is good."

"Thanks. It's from a local shop down the road."

"Oh, shopping from local stores too?" Isra asked. "She's got good taste. I don't know why you hid her from us."

Levi let out a stilted laugh. "I just had to make her see I was worth her time. Now, can we go through my whole life that you've packed in the truck?"

"Come on," Nancy said, pulling him outside. "You two come with me and we'll decide what you all want together."

To say that my house looked lived-in by the time we were done was an understatement. Levi had nice stuff, things that I could have never afforded in my life, and instead of the bleak modern style I expected, a lot of it was used pieces that had either been meticulously cared for or colorful, restored things.

I thought it would take years for my home to feel like it did when Gram was alive. All I had to do was marry Levi, apparently.

Isra was a powerhouse. She had seemingly endless energy, even when Nancy and I had to take breaks. Between her and Levi, everything was unloaded and put up by the end of the night.

As we all worked together, it felt like we were a family. I hadn't experienced any adult figure in my life giving me this much attention, and it was hard to remember that, eventually, they would no longer be here. I was just borrowing their kindness, and it would be hard to give it back.

Levi ordered us food, and we sat around the dining room table to eat. He had an easy demeanor with both his mom and stepmom, in a similar way to what Calvin had with Mom and Dad. When we'd been moving things in, I'd been more talkative and helpful in finding places for it all, but now as everyone talked about their lives, I did the familiar thing and sank into the background as I ate.

I learned that Nancy worked as a paralegal downtown and Isra spent her days running groups at the Nashville library. Their lives seemed to be full and interesting. There wasn't much that I could contribute.

"Hang on a second," Isra said after discussing a teen group gone awry. "Amy got quiet."

I sat up straight and blinked. They'd noticed? "S-sorry, I was just listening to you all."

"We still want to hear from you," Nancy added. "Levi hasn't told us much about you."

"I'm afraid there isn't much to say."

Levi's eyes cut to me. His flat expression made me reconsider my words.

"Isn't much to say?" Isra scoffed. "How about how you got this beautiful house? What do you do in your free time? What conditioner do you use?"

"You really wanna know those things?"

"How else would we get to know you?" Nancy said it as if it were obvious, as if it were a no-brainer. To anyone else, it would be. But I wasn't used to anyone asking anything about me.

"O-okay," I started hesitantly. "I inherited this house from my grandmother. Kinda. It's a long story."

"I love long stories."

I bit my lip, glancing at Levi. He nodded for me to continue.

"So, I stole it from my brother, actually."

"I knew this woman was hiding a secret dark side!" Isra said. "I love it. But I have to ask *how*?"

"Don't give too many details," Nancy added. "She might actually try to steal a house."

"It was mostly luck. I found a handwritten will, changed the date to screw my brother out of the house, and here I am. But to be fair, he was gonna sell it for the money to build a pool at his own place, and I would've been homeless."

"Hang on a second," Isra added. "Is this the brother that came unannounced?"

"Yes."

"That your parents defended?"

"They . . . like him more than me. More than my sister too, though with her, they always said she was an accident and they didn't have time to raise another kid."

An uncomfortable silence settled over the table, as it always did when I mentioned my shit parents. I hated ruining good conversations like this. Other people were sad for me, but I'd lived with this so long that I'd been through the stages of grief a hundred times over. It was nothing to me anymore.

"Needless to say," Levi said, "I'll be making sure I treat her far better."

"No, *I* will," Isra snapped. "I cannot stand parents who treat their kids less than. If I can love my stepson as my own, what's their excuse?"

"Welcome to the family," Nancy said. "You'll never get rid of her now."

"It's okay," I replied. "I'm good at being alone."

"Not anymore!" Isra nearly exploded. "Oh, if I see them again . . ." She reverted to Thai, and I didn't know if even Google could translate it for me.

"I'm sorry your childhood wasn't the best," Nancy said. "Luckily, you've married into a good family now. Or at least I hope we are."

Levi watched his stepmom with a wince. "Once you get used to Isra, that is."

Eventually, Isra calmed down, but was still red in the face as she took her seat.

"When you get back from your honeymoon, we should get together again. Isra can cook for you."

"We can do it whenever," I replied. "I don't think we're going on a honeymoon."

"Nope," Levi cut in. "We're going."

"What?" I asked, nearly breaking my neck to turn to him. "But that's expensive, and this is . . . so last minute."

"But you're *married*," Isra reminded.

"She'll figure out the whole 'what's mine is hers' soon."

"You should convince her with the honeymoon," Isra said.

"I will. As soon as she tells me where she wants to go." His eyes met mine.

We hadn't talked about this, just like we hadn't talked about moving in together. But since Isra's and Nancy's eyes were on us, we would have to find a way to fake it. We would go silent for a bit and pretend we were traveling. That was a good plan.

But even fake honeymoons could have a nugget of truth to it, and I had one place I wanted to go.

"The mountains. The Appalachians."

"Really?" Isra asked. "Nowhere else?"

"I have good memories there. It's the last place Gram took me before she got sick, and sometimes it's nice to go back to those places. It makes me feel connected to her."

"Then that's where we're going," Levi said. "Any city?"

"Outside of Gatlinburg."

"Gatlinburg? Really?" Nancy's eyebrows raised.

"Yes," I answered immediately. "I know it's boring but—"

"One of these days you're gonna understand that *nothing* is boring," Levi said, his eyes still on me. "Not where you're involved."

"Oh, I know a cabin there!" Isra said with a bright smile. "I can reserve it for you."

"You all have done so much." I shook my head. "And you want to do more."

"*More* is one of my favorite words. And you'll *love* this cabin. Trust me."

Chapter Thirteen

DAYS LATER, we were headed to the mountains. Levi had ordered a debit card to his bank account with my name on it, and he'd been with me nearly every day except when he was at work.

I hadn't quite accepted my new roommate, but I couldn't complain, considering he was helping me pick up from the last-second wedding.

For once, my house was clean when I left it, and I was finding that I didn't mind the company. As time passed and we didn't find anything petty to argue over, I realized that we meshed well together. I read, he read. And instead of constantly asking for my attention, we were able to sit in the same room and do our own thing.

And the fact that I had the honeymoon to look forward to helped as well.

I got excited at the first sight of the vast forest and tall mountains. The moment the car started climbing in elevation, I was home.

It was late winter, nearing spring. This wasn't the best time to come, yet the Appalachians were still gorgeous, even when the trees were bare. They stood tall in the distance, making me feel surrounded in the safest way.

We pulled onto the Gatlinburg exit but continued heading up the mountain. We passed the tourist traps and all of the eateries I'd known since I was a kid. We'd spend some time in downtown, but not much. I wasn't here to shop; I was here to enjoy the mountains.

It probably wasn't the most romantic thing I could do, but after years of walking the same neighborhood and being too broke to see anything new, I was in the mood for adventure.

Isra had insisted on taking care of everything for the cabin, and I was too busy worrying about making my dwindling migraine medicine stretch to think too hard about where we would be staying.

But as we pulled up, I realized I should have given it more thought. This was a cabin, but it was an A-frame with one room.

"That . . . is small," I said.

"It could be bigger on the inside."

"I think that's reserved for sci-fi shows," I said. "We should have booked this ourselves."

I got out of the car, grabbed my suitcase, and stared at the tiny cottage with concern. Levi went first and entered the code Isra had given him. When we walked in, my jaw clenched when I saw only one bed, a bathroom, and a kitchenette.

"So . . . no privacy," I said.

"Nope."

"At least there's a door for the bathroom."

"I should have seen this coming," Levi muttered. "But she usually goes overboard and gets places way too big."

"Levi, she thinks we're married."

"She always got six-bedroom cabins anywhere we went. Since she said she knew this place, I thought . . ."

My eyes trailed to the bed and widened. "Oh, she *did* go overboard."

But in a very different way.

There were roses everywhere, along with a stack of porn DVDs and condoms.

"I'm gonna kill her."

"On one hand, I'm glad your stepmom is sex positive, but on the other, this is my nightmare."

Levi looked as horrified as I felt. As much as I would laugh about this if it were happening in my favorite book, this was not funny now.

All we had were open windows and a stall for a bathroom. To make things worse, there was a massive jetted tub out in the open with mirrors surrounding it.

The honeymoon special, I realized with horror.

"We can find something else," he said. "I'm sure there's some other hotel open."

Rubbing my temples, I tried to think of a way out of this.

But then I looked out the windows that dominated the entire front of the cabin. I hadn't even noticed it outside because I'd been far too horrified. But this? This was beyond my wildest dreams. I could see down the mountain and into the distance. When the sun set in a few hours, it was going to be gorgeous. Even now, we had a breathtaking view of the clouds in the sky. There were even windows on the other side too, where the back side of the cabin had a balcony, giving us a view of the sunrise in the morning.

"This is . . . Oh my God. Look at these views."

Levi turned and followed my line of sight. "That's why she picked this place."

"I'm staying," I said.

"You're what?"

"I'm staying here. You can find somewhere else if you want."

"Do you really think I'm leaving my wife to stay in a cabin on the mountain by herself?"

"I'd be fine."

"I don't care. We aren't testing that. What would you do if you saw a bear?"

"Probably the same thing I do with most crises in my life. Panic and hope it goes away."

"That's not a good bear plan."

"So, if you're staying, and I'm staying, then who's getting the bed?"

His eyes went to the queen-sized mattress and then back to me. "We could share it."

"But aren't you supposed to argue with me and offer to sleep on the couch?"

"What couch?" he asked. "And we all know how this ends. We'll share the bed."

"You know how this goes in romance novels, right? You'll wake up with a boner and then we'll have hot sex or something."

"I've already seen your boobs and had no problems keeping myself contained."

"Through a *top*, and we aren't talking about that! Levi, what if I feel your hard, velvet rod and get horny?"

"Do you have to call it that?"

"What would you prefer? Disco stick? Tunnel penetrator?"

"Dick? Or penis? The *normal* terms."

"You said you read romance novels."

"I do, but I close the book the second it's called a velvet rod. Can you imagine how disgusting velvet would be . . ." He trailed off. "Never mind."

"You're not supposed to take it literally."

"It's how my brain works."

"You're really imagining a real velvet co—"

"Let's put any talk about velvet and rods away, *please*." He shook his head and set down his bag. "But the point stands, if you're staying, I'm staying with you. Are you okay with that?"

"I'd be stuck in this tiny cabin any day. You're just a bonus. Or a downside. It depends on how you act for the next three days."

"I'll be on my best behavior."

"And I won't. I have many behaviors, but none of them are my best."

Levi chuckled, no evidence of surprise on his face. "I wouldn't expect anything else. Now, what's the first thing on your list of things to do?"

"First is dinner. Then I want to find whatever local bookstore is around here. And after, we can deal with the only-one-bed thing."

A WOMAN COULD GET USED to being spoiled. Or maybe that was just me. I usually avoided going out to eat, save for the special occasions when I'd find myself at a local eatery when I had the money. But the family business never paid me enough for luxuries, and I'd gone without for far too long.

The same didn't go for Levi. He told me to order whatever I wanted and I intended to take him up on it.

The restaurant was somewhere I would have never been able to afford going to on my own. It was a Gatlinburg staple nestled in a log cabin. I'd always wanted to come here for the massive plates of delicious food alone, but it was considered a fancier place. The staff was dressed up and each table had a candle and flowers lit on its surface. Years ago, it had been way out of Gram's and my budget. I couldn't imagine what it cost now.

We were put in a back corner that was quiet, and I found myself wishing I'd packed one of my nice dresses rather than only leggings and T-shirts.

"Oh my *God*," I said when I opened my menu and saw the prices.

"What?" he asked.

"Nothing." My voice was high. "Inflation is *wild*. Are you sure you don't want a burrito out of a taco truck?"

"I only find the best for my wife, especially on our honeymoon."

My cheeks heated as they always did when he called me *his wife*. He said it with such emphasis that it sounded so important to him. "You don't have to call me that when it's just the two of us."

"On the contrary," he said, "it's what you are. Just like I'm your husband."

"Yes, but I don't call you that."

"You should."

"I prefer realism. Right now, you're a pain in my ass."

"I'm also your husband, which you seem to be avoiding saying."

I rolled my eyes. "You've met me. I have no filter."

"Then say it. Right now. Call me your husband."

Was it possible for people to explode from embarrassment? "Y-you're my husband."

"Good," he said. "But it still seems like we need practice."

"Practice for what?"

"Being in love when we get back." He said it like it was obvious. "Isra's already asking if we're okay. Apparently, we still seem stiff around each other, and we need to iron that out before we run into Calvin."

"Right." I nodded shallowly. "So more flirting. And more practice. You're really dedicated to this, huh?"

"Perfection is my specialty."

Yes. It was. And it drove Calvin crazy. Me, on the other hand? I would bask in his attention as long as I could, because when it was just us, I could forget about Levi and Calvin's stupid rivalry. I could see a version of reality where he liked me.

Getting the chance to flirt with Levi would be fun. All of my flirting was found either in my imagination or on the page of a book. Real-life Amy was sorely out of practice.

Calvin would call it out the second he saw it, which further justified everything Levi had just brought up. Even if he didn't figure out that this marriage was for revenge, he'd find any hole in our story.

But I couldn't forget my conversation with Lily.

"It's not too much to ask you not to break my heart, is it?"

His eyes softened. "I'll do my best to *never* break your heart, Amy Willard."

I nodded, but I didn't know what he could do when he would eventually be done with this and I would be alone again. If I fully gave myself to our marriage, I would never want it to end.

I was distracted by the waiter coming to get our orders. Once we were done eating, we headed to our next destination: a bookstore.

When we walked in, I made a beeline for my favorite section.

Usually, I made these kinds of trips alone. If Lily was with me, she would linger in the romance section for a few minutes before disappearing into the fantasy one. This time, Levi went with me and immediately picked out a book from the shelf.

I reached for one with a blue cover that I'd seen before but couldn't place.

"Nope. Not that one." Levi took it out of my hands. "It doesn't have a happy ending."

"Wh—really?" I asked.

"Yes. One of them dies in the end, but the publisher decided to market it as romance. It got me good."

I looked back at it. That was where I remembered it from. V had read it years ago and warned me.

A lot of people must have read this and been shocked.

"Thanks for the warning, then," I mumbled and went for something else. It was obvious that Levi was well-versed in the section. There were a few that I wanted to read but they weren't available at the library yet, so I grabbed those and smiled up at him.

"Does being a good husband mean you'll buy me more books?"

He did a double take, his cheeks going pink. "Yes, of course."

I should have married for money a long time ago. Who cared what it did for my morals? Buy me books and I'd instantly fold.

We both had a stack of them by the time we walked back out to the car.

"Okay, so we've done what I wanted to," I said. "Is there anything you want out of this honeymoon?"

"I've never been here, so I have no idea what's fun."

"There's putt-putt golf. Shopping. Movies—"

"What about the SkyBridge?"

I froze. That hadn't been a thing when I came here last. But "sky" and "bridge" were two things I didn't love.

"Um, are you sure? There're other things."

"I like adventure. I can do it on my own if you're scared of heights."

I should have let him go by himself. I didn't do heights. Even hiking in the mountains, I knew I would avoid any cliffs too high up. Anything less than the solid ground beneath me was a one-way ticket to a panic attack.

But I wasn't about to admit that to him.

"No, I'll be fine. But what if it's busy?"

"Google says it's slower than usual."

Fuck.

"It's far away."

"It's not far at all. But if you don't want to—"

"No," I said, shaking my head. "No. I love the sky. And I love bridges. It sounds fun!"

160

$\infty\infty\infty$

IT WAS NOT fun at all. To get to the SkyBridge, we had to go up the Gatlinburg ski lift. Luckily, there were sturdy safety attachments, or at least they *looked* sturdy. I'd never let Gram convince me to go up. Letting my feet dangle above a mountain in the dark was the last thing I wanted to do.

Levi didn't seem bothered. He took pictures of the town's skyline, which was lit with color. Meanwhile, I had a death grip on the metal in front of me that kept me in my seat. I hated that I couldn't see below me.

"Are you okay?" Levi asked.

"Yep. Never better!" My voice came out far too loud, and I knew I sounded the furthest from normal.

His warm hand encased mine. "Amy. We don't have to do this."

"I'm fine."

His grip tightened. "I care more about you than seeing a bridge. We can go back down."

I didn't doubt he would, but I wouldn't ask him to. He'd done so much for me—too much, by my standards—and I wasn't going to chicken out on the *one* thing he seemed interested in.

"I hate heights," I said through gritted teeth. "But I'll be fine."

"Amy," he warned.

"We're almost there. The bridge won't be worse than this."

I had no idea what the bridge would be like, but his hand on mine made me *think* it would be okay. If he wasn't worried, then I shouldn't be either. The lift didn't stop when we reached the top of the mountain, and my heart was in my throat as we leaped off onto the solid ground below.

"Oh my God," I said, gulping in breaths of air. "I made it."

"You did. You were very brave."

I didn't realize that I was gripping his arm like a lifeline until that moment, and I let go of him immediately. "Sorry. I'm actually gonna be brave now."

"No need to on my account."

I shook my head and my eyes roamed the gift shop. Thankfully, we were in a warm front, so the top of the mountain wasn't snowy like it could have been any other time of the year. I was able to see the incredible view of the lights of Gatlinburg from the top of the mountain.

"I'm going over the bridge," he said. "You can wait here."

"What? I want to go."

"This is a bridge over a mountain. I don't think this is something you'll enjoy."

"But I want to!" It didn't make sense that I did. All I knew was that I didn't want him to see something like this without me. "Can I go?"

"Fine, but if you freak out—"

"You can make fun of me like I deserve."

"No, we'll turn back." His hand tightened. "Say the word, and we'll make sure you feel safe."

My mouth opened and closed, words failing me. It was such a simple thing to say, yet it shocked me speechless. All I could do was nod and let my hand fall into his.

I hated how much it felt like it *should* be there.

It wasn't a long walk over to the bridge. I told myself the whole time that it would be fine and I would be brave.

All of that flew out the window when I got near the edge.

"Holy shit," I said, grabbing Levi's hand again. "Okay, remember how I said I hated heights? That was an understatement. A major one, actually. I'm *terrified* of heights."

"I put that together." He sounded way too calm for someone who was not only way higher up than any human should be, but also having his hand crushed to death by his wife. "Should we go back?"

I looked down and my heart clenched, but I shook my head. "No. I want to do this."

"Are you sure?"

I could only nod.

"Okay, then we're doing this." He spun on his heel to face me, not the bridge. His other hand moved to mine. "Let's take the first step."

"I don't know if I can move."

"Look at me. Don't look down."

I did as I was told, my eyes meeting his. I took one step. "There's no one behind me, right?"

"Who cares about other people? This is about you and me." Levi pulled me to take another step.

I was now fully on the bridge, and I wanted nothing more than to peek over the edge to see the nothingness below.

"No," Levi said as if he could read my mind. "Only look at me, darling. I'm the only one here."

Our steps doubled and then tripled. Wind hit my face as Levi guided me further on. When gazing at him, falling to my death didn't seem so bad.

"And we're here. We're in the middle of the bridge. Next is the glass part, but—"

"I want to go. I want to do the whole thing."

He didn't miss a beat. "All right. Then keep looking at me."

We slowly moved over the transparent ground. It was terrifying, but Levi's hand was solid.

"I did it," I said.

"You did."

I slowly turned, seeing the entire skyline below. I could still feel the fear hitting like a ton of bricks, so I leaned into the one safe person I had.

With him near me, I could finally notice that the bridge was still lit in colorful holiday lights and that people were taking pictures of the scene around us.

"It's beautiful up here."

"Yes, it is."

I glanced over at him and found him looking at *me*.

"Don't miss out by making sure I'm okay."

"Trust me, darling. I'm not missing out on a thing."

My breath caught in my throat and I dragged my eyes away. *Darling*. I liked that nickname, and now that I wasn't terrified, I could register that he'd now called me that *twice*.

"We should get a photo," I said. "For Isra and Nancy."

Levi got out his phone and positioned it above us. His long arms could get both us and the skyline. I leaned into his warmth, smiling for the camera. I didn't expect it when he pressed a kiss to my hair.

This was intimate. This whole night had been, and I could already tell I was forgetting that this was fake.

Once the picture was captured, I stepped away. "I should get back before my bravery wanes. We still have to go down the ski lift."

"I'll come with you."

"You should stay and enjoy the view."

Levi's eyes were *still* on me. "Don't worry. I got all that I needed."

THANKFULLY, the ski lift wasn't as terrifying going down. I must have used up all of my available fear for the day because I enjoyed seeing everything below me.

As we got near the car, more of the adrenaline faded, and I finally felt the cold in my hands. It wasn't a frigid night, but the mountain air, coupled with the wind, had taken a toll on my body, and all I could think about was the jetted tub back at the cabin.

I wasn't sure if I could sneak a bath in while Levi was asleep, but I was willing to try.

"Where to next?" he asked.

"Back to the cabin. I need to warm up."

Our drive wasn't enough to fully get rid of the chill that had settled in my body, even though Levi turned up the heat in the car.

"So . . . you must be tired from all of that driving," I said as we pulled up.

He opened the door. "I'm fine. Did you have something else that you wanted to do?"

"No, of course not. I was just saying that if you wanted to call it an early night, I wouldn't blame you."

He paused, hand near the doorknob, and turned to me. "What are you planning?"

"I'm not planning anything. I'm being nice."

"You're heavily hinting that you want me to be asleep. And what for?"

"I don't have to tell you."

"Is it something embarrassing?"

"What could be embarrassing?"

"There *is* a stack of DVDs in there."

My jaw dropped. "Levi, *no*. That's not—I just want a bath!"

"A bath?"

"Yes. In the big tub in there? After being outside all day, it sounds nice. But I *definitely* don't want you to see me, so you should be asleep."

"But I'm not tired."

"And *you* aren't seeing anything. What happened to being a gentleman?"

"I *am* a gentleman. I'll get the bath started while you get ready. And when you're back, I'll turn around."

"And you won't bother me?"

"If that's what you want."

"That's a decent offer," I said. "But I don't know if I trust you."

"You trusted me enough to go on that sky bridge with me."

That was a good point. An unfairly good point.

And damn it, I also wanted a bath.

"Fine. But if you peek, I'm revisiting mariticide."

He put up his hands in mock defense and then opened the door. I walked into the warm room and eyed the bath excitedly.

"Go get changed. I'll have this ready for you."

Before I even had the bathroom door shut, the water was running. I couldn't help the small smile that bloomed on my face at him running a bath for me. I'd never let anyone get close enough to do something like this, even when I tried my hand at relationships.

And hearing the running water only proved to me that *action* was one of the sexiest things a guy could do.

I slowly peeled off my layers and grabbed at the cotton bathrobe on the back of the door. I wrapped it tightly around myself and walked back out.

"Okay, I'm—" I paused when I saw the bathtub. "Are those the rose petals from the bed?"

"They're fresh. Did you really think I'd give you old ones?"

"I thought you were just running water, not making a romantic scene."

I eyed the red rose petals floating in the water. Gentle bubbles simmered at the surface and the air smelled floral and sweet.

"It's our honeymoon, after all. And you deserve the utmost relaxation after being so brave."

I narrowed my eyes. "I can't tell if you're teasing me or not."

"Does it matter if you get a hot bath out of it?"

Not really. The cold had gotten into my bones and the smell of the bath was enough to soothe any of my stresses.

"All right. Turn around. This bath is so nice that I have to get in now."

Levi looked at me one last time before turning. I watched him for a good few seconds to make sure he stayed with his back to me before I took my robe off and settled into the steaming hot water.

I couldn't help the moan that escaped my mouth as I sunk into pure heaven. This was the greatest bath I'd ever had in my life.

I checked on him again, but all I could see was the hard line of his shoulder. He was more tense than he had been a second ago.

"Don't get too jealous. You can have a bath after me."

"A bath isn't what I need." His voice was low.

I let out a puff of air and looked around for a book to read. That was the only way I could relax and forget that my fake husband was *right there*.

Only, I couldn't see any. I sat up, crossed my arms over my boobs, and cursed when I saw the one I was after was sitting on the bed.

"What? Did I make the bath too hot?"

"No. I left my book on the bed."

"I'll grab it."

I sank low into the water. "You'll see."

"I'll cover my eyes and then go outside."

"Okay," I said quietly. "Thank you."

Levi crossed the room, grabbed the paperback, and walked it over to me. I dried one of my hands and reached for it, checking once again to be sure he was truly covering his eyes.

And he was, so much so that he completely missed my hand. His other one reached down to grab it, right when I reached up, but as the book was safe from the water, I realized his eyes were open and he stared right at me.

Naked me.

His breath stuttered and I was pretty sure mine did the same.

Heat spread throughout my body, the kind that had nothing to do with the bath. His eyes didn't leave any part of me and I wasn't sure if I wanted him to look away or gaze at me forever.

But I had to diffuse the silence somehow or I would explode.

"Should I take your silence as an insult, or are you in awe?"

Levi's throat worked and I realized I'd never seen him like this. "A-awe. Definitely awe."

Shit. He was supposed to go along with the joke. "I . . . You know, you were gonna have to see some of this anyway."

"I'm not sure if I'm seeing *enough*."

His voice was rough and I realized what he was propositioning. He wanted *more*.

And judging by the way my body reacted, I did too.

My heart thudded. I was *so* close to saying yes, but my last shred of sense told me that this was a terrible idea, one that would get me hurt in the end.

"I shouldn't." My voice was as thin as paper. "It would make things complicated."

Levi's lips pursed, but he took one step back. Then another.

And then he was outside.

"Fuck," I said the second I was alone. My skin still tingled with the memory of a touch I'd turned down, and while I knew it was *right*, I wasn't sure if it was what I *wanted*.

My eyes slipped closed. It was way too easy to imagine what could have happened.

He would have pulled me out of this bath and put me on the bed, his hands attached to the swell of my breasts. His mouth could have been anywhere, but I would have wanted it on mine, making that kiss on my back porch real all over again.

My hand slipped down my body before I could stop it.

Back in my fantasy, it was his hand caressing my wet flesh. He was the one circling my clit, expertly leading me to an orgasm. When I'd had one, two, three, or however many I wanted, he pulled out his cock and pressed it gently into me, making room for himself.

I let out a gasp as my hands did their best to replay what was going on behind my eyelids.

It was wrong to fantasize about this when I'd just turned him down, but I had to get my shit together. I was stuck with Levi for the next few days, and if I didn't want to lose my last shred of sanity and jump him the second we were alone again, I needed to work out this tension.

And what he didn't know wouldn't hurt him.

Back in my own little world, he was fucking me with powerful thrusts. The whole bed moved with us, and all I could feel was the way his cock brushed against my sensitive G-spot.

I sank lower in the water, body going lax as my pleasure grew.

More, I'd beg of him. *Give it all to me. Make me forget every other man.*

He'd growl and do just that, plunging into me with new tenacity.

My body arched, fingers deep inside of me, and the taut string of my pleasure snapped, sending me over the edge of an intense orgasm.

"Y-yes, Levi." I tried to keep my voice low, but the images flashing through me called *his* name, and I was powerless to stop it.

As the orgasm crested, I caught my breath and hoped that was enough to curb any desire I had going forward. But I could feel pressure simmering under my skin. My own fingers weren't enough.

I wanted *more.*

"Fuck, that was stupid," I muttered. I slowly stood and pulled the plug on the bathtub. I quickly grabbed for the robe and ran to the bathroom to get fully dressed before I had to face Levi again.

I threw on thick pajamas and then the other robe in the bathroom before I steeled myself to go outside.

"Hey," I said quietly. "I'm decent now."

"I'll be in in a second." He didn't turn to face me, and I darted inside to give him his space.

Was he mad that I turned him down? Should I have?

I bit my lip as I climbed into bed. Maybe this was complicated either way I looked at it.

Maybe faking a marriage was harder than I thought.

The door opened and he walked inside.

Our eyes finally met, and his carried all of the heat they had when he'd left the room. All I could do was gulp and sink under the covers.

Levi's footsteps were heavy as he went to his bag and then the bathroom, and I tried to think about what to say while he did whatever he needed to. When he came out, he was in a T-shirt and sweatpants, and the bed dipped under his weight.

"Amy," he began, "I . . ."

"I'm sorry," I said. "I just can't—I didn't want to . . ."

"You don't need to give me an explanation."

"But you've done so much for me, so if you wanted to—I mean if you're mad, then we can work something out."

"What?"

"I'm offering sex."

"Yeah, I figured that. I just don't know *why*."

"I've spent a lot of your money. And we're stuck on the honeymoon together so—"

"Stop. If you think I'm gonna do *anything* when you're not one hundred percent willing, then you're dead wrong. I want you to *want* me, not have sex with me because you think I want it or because you have to."

"Then why did you sound like you did when you came in?"

He was silent for a long time. "That's a me problem."

"Are you sure?"

"Yes, I am. How little do you think of me?"

"I don't think *little* of you. I just don't think I should have all of this without some sort of reward for you."

I couldn't look at him, and it was easier not to.

"I'm getting all the reward I need."

"But you can't be."

"Trust me, I am. You may not believe it, but this is exactly where I want to be. And maybe one day, when you believe my words, I'll tell you why."

"That doesn't make sense."

"I know it doesn't, darling. But one day it will. Then all of it will be easy to understand."

My eyes were wide. Was there some other thing he got out of this? Was there something I was missing?

Or did pissing off Calvin make him this happy?

"Go to sleep, Amy. Save figuring all of this out for tomorrow."

Levi's hand rested on my shoulder, his heat a reminder of what had happened in the bath.

Damn it. I wanted him, even if I didn't understand him.

But I was an *adult*. I wasn't going to let anything happen.

No matter how close he got.

Chapter Fourteen

LEVI WAS on his side of the bed and I was on mine when we fell asleep.

What I hadn't known was we wouldn't wake up that way.

As consciousness slowly roused me, I realized that there was a comfortable weighted blanket on me, one that was a little too good to be an inanimate object.

His arm was around my waist, holding me tightly to his chest. I wanted to be horrified or embarrassed, but the only thing on my mind was what I thought of last night as I touched myself.

I liked him. That much was for sure—and liking someone made me way hornier for them. I tried to push it out of my mind, but I was already seeing memories of the way his hair curled against his neck, the way his jaw clenched when he was thinking hard about something.

The way he *smelled*.

And the third thing was very much a problem because I was surrounded by it while in bed with him, and, God, was I horny.

Who knew getting married and being given everything you wanted would cause that? I sure as fuck didn't.

But I told myself the night before that nothing good could

come from sleeping with the man who only wanted me to enact revenge on my brother.

However, when I woke up, it was impossible to think that way.

Levi was *everywhere*. His torso was behind mine. Every inch of him was pressed against me.

And he was hard. Because of fucking course he was.

The second I felt it, I knew there was no way I was getting out of this with my pride intact.

I could feel every inch of him at this angle, and I knew right where I wanted him. My mind knew this was a bad idea, but my body had no such reservations.

Levi took in a deep breath. His hand trailed circles onto my stomach.

I was on fire. I knew I should move away, especially since he was waking up. I needed to get out of bed and put a healthy distance between the two of us.

But I could feel him. *All of him.* And it was way better than my fantasy had been.

I swallowed and slowly turned. Levi's hand stilled, and I wondered if he was as shocked as I was. I might have propositioned him last night, but I was sure we'd put that to bed.

And now it was morning.

"Are you awake?" I asked.

"Yes. I can—"

"Don't move," I ordered.

"But—"

"Please." I was begging, and I didn't feel ashamed. "I need you to touch me."

"Because you want to pay me back?"

"Because I need you to. Levi, I *can't.*"

His eyes grew dark and his hand felt steadier on my hip. "Didn't get it out of your system?"

"W-what?"

"Last night. When you came and said my name. Was it not enough?"

My breath stuttered. "You heard that?"

"I did, and it was so fucking hot."

"More like embarrassing. I'm so sorr—"

"Don't apologize." His voice was harder now, as was his grip on me. "Just let me give you the real thing and give me the chance to prove how good it can be."

Yep. That was all I needed to hear. "Y-yes, *please.*"

His arms tightened and his cock rubbed against me again. I let out a broken gasp. "Do you like that, darling?"

I nodded, mind fully on all of the things he could do to me in this bed. And I'd let him do it all.

"Let me touch you," he said. "You came on your hand. Let's make it even."

"Wouldn't it be even if you're the one who gets my hand?"

His lips ghosted over the shell of my ear. "I haven't had the pleasure of hearing every sound you make up close. I want that first."

"A-and if we do this, we won't make it weird?"

"No. We'll be perfectly normal. Better than that, even."

"Okay." I gasped as he pressed into my ass again. "Now, *please* touch me."

"That's what I was hoping you would say." His hand went under the band of my pajamas. "You should have worn the pajamas you had on our wedding night. The see-through ones."

"I thought it would be a problem if I did."

"That sight is *never* a problem. Only what I might do when I see you in them is."

His hand found my core, crushing against the wetness that was only for him. I gasped, my eyes fluttering shut, and leaned into him. His lips latched onto my neck, and my hands tangled through his dark hair, needing something to grab on to as he touched me.

Levi made leisurely movements, gently tracing my clit. It had been too long since someone else had touched me there, and my body sang for him.

In the depths of the night, I always wondered what it would have been like to sleep with him. At first, I told myself he would have been a selfish lover, only caring about himself. And I thought I was right, judging by how the night of our first kiss had gone.

But now I knew that I had been wrong. Without a shadow of a doubt. Pleasure curled into my nerves, making me arch into him as it built up.

"The noises you're making," he growled in my ear, "they're gonna drive me to an early grave."

"I-I can quiet down."

His teeth sunk into my neck, a warning. "Don't you fucking dare. You can drive me to that grave. Or to insanity. As long as I get *this*."

He punctuated his sentence with a press of his finger into my pussy, and I couldn't help but mewl.

"Fuck, do that again."

"Gladly."

His strokes changed. He traced a line from my clit down to my entrance, pressing in each time. I opened my legs for him, whining when his teeth found my neck again. My hips jerked, barreling me toward an orgasm that was going to change my life.

"*Levi*," I gasped. "Yes."

He kept up the torture, and my eyes closed as everything in me turned into white-hot pleasure. It filled my every cell, made my jaw hit the floor.

And quite possibly destroyed me.

I came down from my impossible high, still panting from the climb. I rolled to my back and Levi wasted no time capturing my lips with his.

But I wasn't done. I could still feel the memory of his cock pressing into my ass, and I knew without a doubt that it was his turn.

I was good at making guys come, too good at it. In my one-night stands, I usually got him off before he even tried with me, and once they were spent, I was an afterthought.

But Levi had taken care of me first, and I was going to make him feel as good as I had just seconds ago.

"Stand up," I said as I pulled away.

"But—"

"You're not giving me an orgasm like that without some reciprocation."

"I felt good making *you* feel good."

"I'm sure you did, but now it's time to be a good boy and do what I say."

"And what's that?"

"Stand the fuck up."

His eyes widened, but he did as I instructed.

I pulled my hair into a ponytail and sunk to my knees in front of him.

His arousal was visible from the outside of his sweatpants, and I wasted no time taking it into my grip.

"Amy, you don't—"

"Sh, I'm enjoying myself." I dragged down his pants, mouth watering when I saw my prize spring to life in front of me.

"But—"

"What happened to doing what I said? You'll have to remember it, because my mouth is about to be very busy."

Levi's eyes were intense on me. I waited a moment just in case this wasn't what he wanted before I covered the head of his cock with my mouth. He let out a rough groan, his hands coming to my head.

I worked the entire length of it, letting it hit the back of my throat.

"You're impossible, Amy."

What was impossible was how good this felt, even with just his fingers holding onto my ponytail. I loved sex, yet I hadn't enjoyed it like I was with him.

I listened to every one of his groans and moans as I sucked. His hands tightened on my head with every second that passed.

"I need to fuck your face," he said. "Please tell me I can."

I looked up, smiling around his thickness in my mouth, and nodded.

Levi lost all control. He slammed into me, letting loose as he pumped every last inch of his cock into my mouth. I loved the roughness, and I wondered what his hardness would feel like pounding into my pussy instead of my mouth.

It would be world-ending, just like my first orgasm was.

He sped up, and every muscle in my body tightened in anticipation for him to come. The first jet of it landed in the back of my throat, but then he pulled out, spilling the rest on my chest and on the top of my shirt.

Glad I brought an extra.

"That was . . ." He was still out of breath, but I interrupted.

"Next time, I swallow."

"But then I can't see my come all over you," he said. "And that's a sight worth seeing."

I looked down, and it *was* hot. "Still. You wasted my breakfast."

"After what you just did? You can get breakfast anywhere. No matter the price."

"I plan on taking you up on that. And then after, I want to hike up a mountain. Think you can handle that?"

"I can more than handle anything you throw at me." In contrast to his words, he flopped on the bed. "I'll just need a minute."

∞ ∞ ∞

Levi did, in fact, order what I wanted for breakfast, and after eating far too many of the greatest flapjacks Gatlinburg offered, we went to a hiking trail in the mountains. The second the sky was obscured with trees, I felt at home.

I loved my walks through the neighborhood, but I didn't realize how much I needed a new setting. Sure, there were trees in the city, but the majority of them had been chopped down over the years, slowly changing the sight lines of the neighborhood.

"It's a perfect day for a hike," I said. The air was cool and clear, and though there wasn't a lot of leaf color, evergreen trees surrounded us.

"The sign says there's a one mile or a four mile."

"I'm going on the four mile," I replied. "But if you can't go that long, then I won't judge."

"I can go plenty long," he replied. "You've seen that yourself."

"Dick health isn't connected to leg stamina," I said with a shrug. "Let's see if you can keep up with me."

The trail was covered with roots and rocks, some of which we had to climb on. I had the time of my life and felt challenged in a way walking on the side of the road never could. I was a kid on a playground again. But instead of metal and plastic below my feet, it was all the earth itself.

Levi kept up with me easily, seemingly never out of breath. A few times he offered a hand to help me get up and down trickier spots, which I accepted gratefully.

It was just us out here, and I found that I really liked it.

That was the thing with Levi. When we weren't talking about Calvin, things were great. He seemed like the kind of man I'd be very interested in if things were different. We were compatible in all of the ways, sex included, apparently.

But like everyone else in my life, he'd met my brother first, and that was all that mattered.

Sometimes Calvin being the favorite wore me down, and my walks were the way to process that. Levi seemed quiet, only telling me where to go and what roots to watch out for, so I had time to think about all the ways I hated my lot in life.

I stayed positive on the outside simply because there was nothing I could do to change the fact that people liked my brother more than me.

Inside, I let myself feel everything. Even the worst parts of it.

When Levi offered me help for a particularly tall rock, I took it, but he didn't let go.

"You got quiet."

"I get introspective on walks sometimes."

"Anything you wanna share?"

I didn't want to talk about Calvin and ruin this moment, but I also knew I couldn't lie. "Sometimes it feels like I got the short end of the stick with life."

His lips pursed. "Not anymore, darling. I promise you, things are gonna change."

Not for forever. The reminder bounced in my head but wouldn't leave my lips. If I said it out loud, it made it all the more real.

"We should be near the top," I said instead. "That'll put me in a better mood."

"Then come on." He didn't let go of my hand and stayed next to me as we finished the climb.

My eyes widened as I saw vast, open land dotted with fluffy white clouds and tall mountains. Even in the winter, evergreen trees made the landscape beautiful.

"Wow," was the only thing I could mutter.

"Smile," Levi said. I turned to him and realized he was taking a photo with his phone.

"Hey, at least let me fix my hair."

"Why would you cover something so beautiful?"

My hands, which were trying in vain to tame my curls, stilled. "They're a mess."

"And they're still beautiful."

My cheeks heated and I could only stare, unable to process him being too kind about something that I'd been told made me look bad ever since I was a kid.

Silence stretched over us, and eventually, he broke it.

"Besides, we need photos. Candid ones. Isra will ask."

Now *that* made sense. "Right. Okay. Take all the ones you need. Just try not to make me look ugly."

"I'm pretty sure that would be impossible."

He snapped a few more of me, us, and the skyline before we made the trek back down and headed to get lunch. I eventually had to excuse myself to the bathroom, and when I came out, I saw him scrolling through messages. A *lot* of messages.

"You reading through all of your conversations with your secret woman?" I teased as I sat.

He set his phone face down and sat up straighter.

"No. There's nothing."

I jerked back, all thoughts of teasing gone. That was a very telling reaction.

What I didn't know was what it meant. It could have been innocent—just something he didn't want me to see. Or it could be that he was talking to someone else.

I knew I was not the person he spent his nights with before. But I also trusted that he wouldn't cheat. Whatever he had before me was put on hold for the time being, and both of us knew it.

I wanted to tell him that he didn't have to do this, that he could keep whoever this person was as long as it didn't blow our cover.

But was that what I wanted?

We'd gotten physical, and while it didn't mean anything, it was something more than I expected. Could I live with myself if I wanted more and he was with someone else at the same time? Or would I make myself suffer even more than I already was?

"I . . . It's not what you think."

"Does it affect the marriage?"

"It won't."

I could see the ghost of Gram telling me this was how men were. She'd gone through this time and time again.

This was my reminder—one that I desperately needed.

"Then I'll pretend I didn't see it."

"Amy," he began, "I *promise*—"

"You don't have to promise anything."

It was better if he didn't.

I wouldn't get let down that way.

My eyes finally met his and I saw the look.

Guilt.

It would have gutted me had I not known Gram.

"*The first time I got my heart broken, he told me he regretted it the second he did it. He felt terrible. He* looked *terrible. And that's real life, Amy. People do bad things and they feel bad about them. But it doesn't make what they did right.*"

Levi hadn't cheated on me, but there was something else going on.

And whatever it was *needed* to be the thing that prevented me from falling for him.

"Let's finish up here," I said. "There's a drive-up vista point that I want to see, and then I need to sit in hot water to recover from that hike."

"You want another bath?"

Yeah, right. I wasn't letting last night happen again.

"No, a shower this time. I need to wash away all of the dirt and grime of the day."

And maybe I could wash away the feeling of regret too.

Chapter Fifteen

SEEING those messages was exactly what I needed. The next morning, I wasn't all over Levi, which meant I wasn't horny and about to make another mistake.

Getting thrown back into reality wasn't fun, but it was good for me. I felt more in control, more grounded than I had since this marriage started.

Levi had told me one day that this would all make sense, and he was right. It did now.

How did I forget about his busy nights? Why didn't I realize that someone had to be filling that time? They didn't just disappear into the ether. They were around.

I wondered what they talked about. If Levi was like this to me for a fake marriage, what was he like to someone he really wanted to be with?

It might not have been a woman. It might have been something else, but the *guilt* in his eyes told me it was something I wouldn't like.

I slowly got out of bed. My first stop was to my purse to take my medicine, but I groaned when I only saw one pill left. *Shit.* I knew I was running low, but finally seeing one left was scarier than

183

I wanted to admit. The medicine I took every day was key to preventing migraines, and going off of it wasn't advised.

Too many things were going wrong.

I turned to Levi, wondering if there was something he could do, but after the quiet awkwardness of our entire night, I couldn't ask him to shell out the thousands it would be for me to go to the doctor.

I took the last one and checked on my emergency stash. I had enough of that to prevent an oncoming one. All I could do was hope that my brain worked with me until I could get back on my usual medicine.

I put on a robe so I could go outside and think. The air was cool, but the view was worth it. And I needed the quiet time after spending so long in Levi's orbit.

For a long while, I sat in silence. Then I pulled out my phone and opened the chat with V.

> I think I was right about this one.

V

About what?

> That I was doing something stupid.

What happened?

> It's gonna go pretty deep into my personal life if I tell you, but I'll leave it at this. If there are signs not to trust someone, then don't.

What if you're reading the signs wrong?

I huffed out a laugh. "Yeah, what if."

> I doubt it. But at least I can kinda vent to you. I know you'd never make me feel like this.

V typed for a long time. Stopped. And then started again.

> I hope whatever this person did is simply a misunderstanding. It's hard for me to imagine anyone hurting you, because you don't deserve it.

His reply was too sweet. Just like he'd been this entire time.

> Do you ever wish we'd met a different way? Like we had classes together and became friends in person?

Every day.

> I know we have an unspoken rule against this, but maybe we COULD meet in person. There's no harm in it. You're probably the only guy I ever talk like this to.

I waited a few minutes for a response, but I didn't even see him start typing. My heart pounded in my ears, and I was desperate to know what he was thinking.

Then the door opened and I turned to see Levi had gotten up. He had two cups of steaming coffee, and I took mine gratefully. It melted some of the ice that had gathered in my chest.

"Hey," he started. "About yesterday."

Oh no. I didn't want to talk about this.

"I thought I said I didn't see anything. I'm basically blind, actually. Especially when it comes to catching people doing things." My tone was all wrong and my joke came out more bitter than I meant it to.

"We're married, though. And I wouldn't—"

"We're not married. Not really. This is for revenge with Calvin. So, it doesn't matter what I saw. I don't feel anything about it."

"I don't know if that's true."

I tapped my finger on my mug. He was right, but one thing

was true. I *shouldn't* feel this way. I knew what I was getting myself into. Seeing confirmation shouldn't hurt.

Just like V's lack of answer shouldn't have hurt either.

"This isn't . . . entirely your fault. It's been a rough few weeks. And I'm not acting in my best interest as usual, but this isn't your fault. It's not about you at this moment."

It was mostly true. Now, V's lack of answer was at the forefront of my mind.

"You could tell me, you know. Even if it wasn't me."

Some days, it felt like I was over all of the things that hurt me. It felt like the dull ache was reduced to nothingness and I was able to go on with my life.

But on days like this where I opened up and got no response, it all came flooding back.

"Just give me time."

I could hear his response even now. *We don't have a lot of that.*

But his hand threaded through mine as he sat in the empty seat next to me. "Take as much as you need."

I looked down at where he held onto me, and the pain lessened, replaced by the familiar dull throb I had carried through most of my life.

And after a few minutes, it was bearable again.

"Today's the last day we have the cabin, right?"

"Yes, but we could stay longer if we wanted to."

"Would your company be okay with that?"

"Probably not," he said with a sigh. "But they'd deal. What can they do, fire me?"

"I see CEOs step down all the time, though usually it's through illegal dealings. Hey, you're not secretly running a rich people's sex ring, right?"

His jaw dropped. "Absolutely not."

"Then, you'd probably be good, but for me . . ." I thought about how my risk of getting a migraine was higher now that I was out of my medicine. And then I thought about how being in Levi's orbit all the time made me act out in stupid ways.

I probably needed space too.

"We should head out," I said.

"Are you sure you don't want to stay longer?"

I thought about it but then shook my head. "No. I'm ready to be back in my home. I want to read in my own four walls, and you need to get back to your job before you get in trouble."

"The second one is a boring reason, but okay," he said. "Then let's head home."

He walked inside, leaving me out on the porch. I was about to get up and join him, but I checked my phone to see if V had answered.

And I was still left on read.

I WAS able to get some peace on the way back when I pulled out one of the books I'd purchased. Leaving reality soothed me in the same way Levi's hand had earlier. It was comforting to know books would still be there for me since I knew people wouldn't be.

But it went by too fast. I was almost done with it by the time we got back to Nashville. Traffic was so bad that I put it up to prevent motion sickness from all the stopping and going.

"Was it good?" Levi asked.

"The traffic?"

"No, the book. You seemed so focused on it. I was almost jealous that I was driving."

"You could have put on an audiobook."

"And when it got to a smut scene?"

"Then I would either die of embarrassment or listen too. It just depends on the kind of smut you were listening to."

A ghost of a smile crossed his face. "You sound better."

"Reading always helps," I replied. "And this was a good book."

"Can I borrow it after you?"

"Technically, you paid for it."

"It's yours. I'm not gonna take it without permission."

"But what about the saying what's mine is yours?"

"Maybe I want to be respectful. Books are special."

"That's a point in your favor," I said. "Books of mine are fine to read. As long as you don't damage them."

"What was it about?"

I glanced over at him. V leaving me on read was still on my mind, but I still didn't talk about books with other people. It felt like a betrayal.

But Levi looked *so* curious.

"It's about a woman who goes on a road trip with the wrong guy," I said. "It's hilarious, actually."

"Reading about a road trip on a road trip, huh?"

"This is a little more in-depth. They're going across the country."

"We could have. Or we still could. Say the word and I'll take you anywhere."

I was happy with where we went, but even if I wasn't, I didn't like to take long trips. I could never guarantee I would be able to enjoy them like others could, and I didn't want Levi, or anyone for that matter, to see me when I was at my worst. Being far away from home and getting a migraine would be terrible, and there would be no way to pretend to be normal.

"It's okay. I like the mountains close to home. And besides, I can tell the authors did the journey themselves. It's so detailed."

"And the romance?"

"The characters are being idiots, but I love that."

"Tell me more. I love it when they're dumb."

I did, going into detail about where they started out in their relationship and where they were at the seventy percent mark. Levi listened intently. If I had any doubts that he was a romance reader, they were gone now.

We pulled up to the house around midday. While being away from home was fun, I was more than glad to be where I knew.

When we got out, Levi waved at someone. "One of your neighbors is out."

He wasn't looking at the side of my house where Lily and Sebastian lived. Slowly, I turned and saw Mr. Buford was outside, watching us closely.

Shit. I'd never caught him up on everything.

I would have invited him to the wedding if he'd been outside at all over the last few weeks. I thought about leaving a note, but when I peered into his mailbox, it was full.

Almost like he hadn't been home.

"That's Mr. Buford," I said. "You go inside. I need to go talk to him."

"Is everything okay?" Levi asked.

"Yeah, everything is fine. I just haven't seen him in a while, and we have some things to catch up on."

I didn't give Levi the chance for any more questions. I ran over to Mr. Buford's house.

"Who is that?" he asked suspiciously.

"Hey," I said. "Nice day, right?"

"You're dodging the question, kid."

I winced. "Okay, but I just need to preface this by saying it all happened really fast and you were also mysteriously busy."

"What happened?" he asked, frowning.

"I got married."

His eyebrows rose. "To *who*? That guy on your porch?"

I turned to my house and saw that Levi was still outside watching us.

Damn it. If only he'd listened.

"A guy from my childhood. He's nice, and it was all kind of a whirlwind, really."

"I bet," he said. "Considering you were single last time I talked to you."

"We were keeping it a secret, but then we decided it wasn't worth it. You only live once, why wait?"

Mr. Buford's eyes were still narrowed. "Is he good to you?"

"He's very good to me."

"And does this mean you're moving?"

"After everything I went through to get this house, I'm not giving it up. He moved in with me."

Mr. Buford smiled. "That's what I was hoping for. I can't lose my favorite neighbor."

"And I can't lose my favorite garden to weed. I swear, yours grows back so fast."

"It's those damn invasive species. They multiply. When I bought this place, there weren't any. But someone *had* to bring them here."

"I'll get rid of them for you."

"This is why you're my favorite neighbor," he said with a smile. "Even if you get married and don't let me know."

"If you forgive me, I'll forgive you for not telling me where *you* were."

"Mandated family vacation for my health," he said. "My niece has been trying to be sure I don't rot away in my house."

"That's sweet of her."

"I had to go to the beach," he grumbled. "I hate the sun."

"Oh, poor you. Getting taken on a vacation with family."

"Keep that up and I won't make you coffee anymore."

I gasped. "That's so cruel."

LEVI HAD to go back to work the next day. Just as I suspected, CEOs were very busy and needed to do their jobs rather than stay on honeymoons all the time.

I stayed around the house and kept checking Discord to see if V had gotten back to me. My message remained the last one sent as the day went on. His silence was loud. Had I made a mistake with my suggestion?

Probably.

But could I take it back without looking like a total fool?

Definitely not.

I'd do it anyway.

It was four when I finally sent him something.

> Ignore my last message. Obviously, I wasn't thinking clearly. Want to hear my last read?

He answered so quickly that I wondered if he happened to have the app open already.

> V
>
> Sorry, I was busy with someone. I might be in and out for a bit again.

That wasn't a great answer, but at least he was being honest.

I tried not to think too hard about it, but I couldn't help it. I couldn't stop thinking about our interaction, or lack thereof, even while I watched for Levi to get home. He pulled into the driveway around six.

But then he didn't come inside. Instead, he sent a text.

> LEVI
>
> Hey, my car is in the driveway, but I have some plans tonight. Be back later.

I wanted to be over the many messages I saw, but him having *plans* right after I caught him looking at messages sent a stab of anger into my chest. What was he up to? Taking a woman to a bar? Going to her place?

The thought brought tears to my eyes.

I wasn't even *with* Levi. Not really anyway. I thought of Gram. How had she had her heart broken and survived it? How was she able to move on when someone who loved her hurt her?

There was no way that I loved Levi. But I liked him.

And this was eating me up inside. I couldn't sit with this feeling. I needed to see someone and talk this out.

Checking outside, I saw that Lily's car was there and asked if I could come over. Thankfully, she said yes.

"Where's Sebastian?" I asked as I walked in.

"He's getting groceries and he takes forever."

"How does it take him that long?"

"He finds grocery stores fun. He never was able to go when we worked under his dad."

"That's so cute."

We sat on her couch and ordered pizza. Once that was settled, she leaned toward me. "So, how was the honeymoon?"

Memories of how it ended flashed through my mind, but I shook them off. "Levi tried to kill me by dragging me on this bridge high up between the mountains."

"Do you have pictures?" I pulled out my phone, showing her everything Levi had sent me. "Wow. A lot of these are of you."

"He's good at pretending."

"Better than Sebastian was," she said. "You look happy in these. And somehow even better at pretending. Why?"

"It all started when we . . . kinda slept together."

"*What?* Why wouldn't you open this conversation with that?"

"Because I caught him talking to someone else later in the day. It may have been innocent, but he hid it."

"Okay," Lily said, shaking her head. "So you've kissed and slept together."

"The kiss was practice, but the other stuff . . . Can I blame it on the mountains?"

"I don't think they're responsible."

"Then it was a slip of my judgment. I told myself I wouldn't, but I think I forgot this is all revenge."

"And obviously he did too."

"Maybe he didn't. He could have just slept with me for revenge purposes."

"That would be gross on *many* levels."

"It would be, but who knows? He's hurt me before, and I let him do it again."

She stared at me, and I wondered if she was working out how to tell me how much of an idiot I was.

I wouldn't blame her if she did.

As I said it out loud, I could see that I was heading for one hell of a heartbreak. As much as I told myself I wasn't going to let it happen, I also knew that I liked him. I'd liked him since that first day when he seemed to choose me over Calvin. And now all of the gifts and appreciation were making it worse, and all I could do was be along for the ride.

But this was Lily, and above all else, Lily was so kind.

"Okay, so you're making some choices."

"I know they're not the best ones. And I know I'll only get myself hurt in the end."

"Yeah, kinda. Unless you have things wrong about Levi."

"I don't think I do."

"I thought I knew everything about Sebastian, and look at where that got me. We wasted four years of our lives on assumptions we made about each other."

"Yes, but I know Levi is using me for revenge. And maybe my mouth? He seemed to enjoy the blowjob."

Lily's eyes went wide and she was looking at the door. I turned, and my face flamed to see Sebastian had just walked in.

"What the hell did I just walk into?" he asked.

"Girl talk," she said. "I thought you'd take longer at the store."

"Maybe I should have. I'm going to the kitchen and putting headphones in. I do *not* want to know the rest of it."

"Are you sure?" I called. "I mean, you're kinda like a girl too."

"Nope!"

He was gone before I could say anything else.

"Why does this always happen to me?"

"To be fair, we always have weird conversations. Besides, I think it's funny."

I glanced in the direction of the kitchen one more time and then turned to Lily. "Now where were we?"

"Assumptions and how you might be wrong."

"I think I was telling you how right I was."

She pressed her lips together. "No, that's not true."

"It'll be fine. If I break my own heart, at least I should have money for ice cream."

"And you'll find someone better."

I thought of V, who I regretted not meeting in person, and sighed. "Yeah. I'm sure there is."

If he would only open up to me.

The pizza arrived not long after, and we all sat to eat. Sebastian got over his embarrassment and was able to look me in the eye by the end of the night, and we had a fun time.

I left at nine, expecting Levi to be home.

But he wasn't.

I could have gone to bed and let him come home whenever he wanted to, but I knew that if he *was* with a woman, there might be evidence. And as much as I wanted to pretend I was fine with him doing whatever he wanted, I knew I wasn't.

Sitting, I pulled out my phone and got comfortable. It was eleven before he came home.

"Oh, you're still up?" he asked, but his words were off.

I narrowed my eyes. "Are you drunk?"

"No." But then he hiccupped.

I frowned but kept my thoughts to myself. Just because I didn't like drinking didn't mean other people were the same way. At least he'd parked his car here before going out.

But *who* was he drinking with?

"Did you have fun, at least?" I asked as I got up to take his work bag from him.

"Yes, but whiskey was a poor choice."

"Maybe you should sleep it off."

"I definitely should," he said and stumbled in the direction of the guest room. I put a hand on his shoulder in case he tripped on one of the rugs. I checked his neck, hoping and praying I wouldn't find either lipstick or a hickey.

Thankfully, I didn't find either.

"You're so nice," he mumbled. "And so pretty. So fucking pretty."

Despite my annoyance, my cheeks heated. "It's good to know that when you're drunk, you're nice."

"How do people not see you, Amy? How do they only see your turdhead of a brother?"

I paused. "Did you just say turdhead?"

"Yes. It's what he is. A big, fat, fucking turd. And you're nothing like him."

"Thanks," I said quietly. They were words I needed to hear, and yet he wouldn't remember them in the morning. "Let's get you to bed before you come up with any other ideas of revenge for my turdhead of a brother."

"I don't like revenge," he said with a sigh. "I hate it, actually."

"Whatever you say," I hummed. As the only sober person in the room, I knew the truth. This was *all* for revenge, and when he was sober, he would remember that too.

"I wish Calvin would stop trying to ruin my business. I wish he didn't exist so we didn't have to deal with him," he said as we got to the guest room and he took off his shirt. I averted my eyes out of respect and ensured he made it into bed before shutting the door.

The words didn't hit me until I was alone.

Ruin his business? I knew Calvin was stealing physicians, but I didn't know it had gone that far.

And I knew my husband wouldn't tell me if I asked.

I hated secrets, and I hated that he hid things from me even more. If my brother was doing something to him, I needed to know. I needed to prepare for the fallout that I'd be in the middle of. That was how things always went when it came to Calvin.

And now that I knew there was more, it was time for me to try to figure out some of what he was doing.

Chapter Sixteen

THE NEXT MORNING, I put out water and ibuprofen for Levi before checking my mail. The house that Calvin planned to demolish was still standing tall across the street. I'd been keeping an eye on it, not sure why Calvin hadn't followed through. A more naive version of me would think that he was having second thoughts, but I knew him too well for that.

I'd been so busy with wedding planning and the subsequent honeymoon that I'd put the house's inevitable fate in the back of my mind, but now that things had slowed down, I was ready to investigate.

There was a note on the door that hadn't been there a week ago.

The driveway was empty, and my curiosity spiked. I had to see what it was about. Abandoning my mailbox, I walked over and got close to the front door.

Notice of historical significance. Demolition delayed.

I couldn't help but laugh. "That's what you deserve, asshole."

This was probably the one time the government actually helped someone instead of making things harder.

Well, they helped *me*. I'm sure Calvin wasn't happy with them.

I skipped back to the mailbox and grabbed everything. I was on top of the world. Nothing could bring me down.

It was then, of course, that I finally saw my mail.

Calvin and our parents had a bad habit of sending out fancy invites for the parties they held—if there was enough notice.

The one for Dad's retirement was tossed straight into the trash the second I got it but they always texted the night before as a reminder.

And this time, there was another, but it was from Calvin.

Calvin Willard is happy to announce that the stocks of the company have gone up. We're throwing a party to celebrate that as well as some recent changes to my life.

And I hear Amy is married. Unfortunately, I wasn't at the wedding. So we will be celebrating that too.

Calvin was always one step ahead, and I had no idea how he did it. I doubted he wanted to celebrate anything about my life at all, but him mentioning me by name brought my naivety back. What if he really was at the wedding for me? That would have been why Mom and Dad had been so angry at the ceremony. Maybe this was their olive branch.

There was a low chance. A very low one. But there *was* one.

I stuffed it in my back pocket to look into it later. Levi would want to go. After all, it was the perfect chance to show off our marriage and make Calvin mad, and we could change our plan if it really was him being nice.

Or be worse than usual when it all came crashing down.

Walking back into the house, I saw Levi was up and moving around.

"On a scale of one to ten, how hungover are you?" I asked as I walked into the kitchen.

"A one."

"Seriously?" My jaw dropped. "How is that fair?"

"I drank water the entire time. It's a trick I used in college."

"Smart. Did you have fun?"

"I did. I'm sorry for however I came in. Isra tells me I'm funny when I'm drunk, but I never know."

"You were respectful. You called Calvin a turdhead, though."

"Ah," he replied, mouth twisting. "Not my finest choice of words, but it's true."

I laughed and started a pot of coffee, trying to figure out my next move. I had a hundred things going on, but seeing Levi reminded me of what he'd said the night before, and that was the most important thing happening.

By the time the pot was mostly full, I had a rough idea of what I was going to do.

"So," I said as I poured us both a cup, "what's on the agenda today for the office?"

He raised a brow. "You're asking about my work? Is this a thing we'll talk about at the breakfast table?"

"I'm your wife. Shouldn't I? Besides, I almost worked there. I'm kinda curious what Sally thought of the wedding and if Sebastian is as good at his job as Lily says he is."

"Sebastian is a hard worker. Too hard of one, if you ask me. And Sally loved the wedding. She keeps asking when you'll come in."

Oh, *perfect*. Now I had a reason to pop in. "Oh, really? I didn't think I'd made that much of an impression."

"Come on, Amy. It's *you*. Of course you did."

I wanted to fall into the warmth of his words.

But I also wouldn't let myself.

I stepped away to gather my wits and pulled the invitation from my pocket. When I did, glitter broke off from it.

"Damn it," I muttered. "Use higher quality shit, Calvin."

"Why is your ass covered in glitter?"

"My dumb fucking brother."

"That's not . . . I really hope you have a better explanation than that."

"Oh my God." I rolled my eyes. "He sent this and I shoved it in my pocket. The glitter got everywhere. Who even uses glitter for this kind of invite to a party?"

I handed him the card and he read it over. "He's doing all of this for a party in a week over stocks?"

"Go big or go home, I guess. I personally wish he would stay home and leave us all the fuck alone."

"Two of us want that."

"I figured we'd go to piss him off. I should have known he'd find a way to make me mad first." I swiped at my butt. "I think these need to be washed. Hopefully it all comes out."

"They look good from my angle."

I glanced over at him, and true to his word, his eyes were on my backside. The second he realized I was looking, however, he averted his gaze.

That warm feeling was back and I couldn't stomp it away.

"No matter how good it might make my butt look, I can't leave a trail like Hansel and Gretel. Whoever would follow me would *not* be very friendly." I went up the stairs to change, which gave me a moment to get my head on straight.

When I came back down, Levi was dressed too.

"I'll be back on time tonight," he said. "See you later."

"See you," I replied, though it would be much earlier than he expected.

WORD about our marriage had obviously gotten around the office. I was let in without a bat of an eye and led right to Levi's shut door.

"Is he in another meeting?" I asked the receptionist.

"Yes. He's in a ton of them lately with everything that's going on."

Everything that's going on.

"Oh, yeah," I lied. "I can't imagine the stress he's under."

"There you are!" Sally said as she nearly jogged down the hallway. "I heard from the front desk that you were visiting. Here to see your husband?"

"Here to surprise him with lunch, but he's busy." I gestured to the door.

"Always is, unfortunately. Though I'm sure he'd cancel something for you. You could tell him she's here, Maisie."

"Interrupting the boss in a meeting is a bad call. He's so stressed today."

"He's not like your last boss," Sally said, shaking her head.

"I know, but I don't wanna get in trouble."

"I would never ask you to do that," I cut in. "But I have wanted to get to know my almost coworkers. Have either of you had lunch yet?"

"I haven't." Maisie sighed and rubbed her stomach. "I'm starving."

"Me either," Sally added. "There's a new barbecue place I've been dying to try."

"We should go there. My treat."

Sally clapped her hands together excitedly and Maisie perked up. Even though I was here to get information on Levi, I was glad to make their day a little brighter.

We were able to walk to the new place, and when I entered, I knew by the smell alone that this was going to be good.

"Damn," I said. "I wish I worked at Leviathan. I could have this every day."

"But you have Levi as a husband instead." Sally sighed dreamily. "I bet he's the best."

"He's great. A little tight-lipped about some things, though. Admittedly, I didn't know he was that stressed at work."

"I bet he wants to live in the honeymoon phase."

"Yeah," Maisie added. "He always says work stays at work. He really wants people to have a good work-life balance."

"Still, is what's going on bad?"

Sally and Maisie looked at each other. "It's not the end of the company bad," Sally said. "There's just someone who's trying to hurt Levi, and he's doing a good job of it."

"Let me guess," I said dryly. "He owns some hospitals."

"Yes, that's him. Calpert or something."

I laughed at the terrible version of my brother's name. "I bet that's it."

"I've never seen someone with a vendetta like this." Sally's smile was suddenly gone. "He's coming after people who work here exclusively. I already got a job offer for *double* my pay."

"Double?" I asked. "But that hospital pays way below what you guys do."

"According to their page, they do," Maisie said. "I guess this guy is giving special incentives to those who work for Levi."

My stomach churned. He wouldn't pay me a livable wage, but he would do it for revenge?

"Some people have taken the offers, and neither Levi nor I can blame them. In this day and age, money talks. But those of us who are loyal are just so shocked. It's so unprofessional."

"There should be laws on this kinda thing," Maisie added. "But there's not. Levi is mainly doing damage control."

"There has to be something. Calpert needs to get in trouble for this."

"He would deserve it," I said lowly. "But I know men like that. They never get what's coming to them. They find a way out."

Both women didn't seem happy with that answer. Maisie shook her head and Sally scoffed.

"Levi did tell me he's also going after the doctors that work here too," I said.

"And the nurses," Sally added. "He's stealing the whole business model and trying to pass it off as his own."

"Asshole." It was one thing to be in the direct line of fire of Calvin, but it was another to see him try to take down Levi's business. I'd done my research on it. Leviathan's method of providing care was the cheapest on the market, and it had helped countless people.

Why couldn't Calvin let things go? Why did he have to be such a dick?

"When did all of this start?" I asked.

"About six months ago. Though the poaching only got worse these last few weeks. We've gotten more messages than ever."

Right when I'd married Levi.

Calvin was upping the stakes, and it wouldn't be too long until I was in the middle of it again. Though hearing about this, I wasn't sure I cared. Maybe this would be the time that Calvin finally got what he deserved.

"A man like that doesn't need any more attention." Sally waved her hand. "I want to know about *you*."

"Right," I said. "No more work."

I tried to put it out of my mind, but I knew I would be talking to Levi later.

The three of us got in line, and I told them about the honeymoon and the time after. Both women loved to hear about it and were excited to see the pictures. By the time I had caught them up, the food had arrived, and the three of us talked about how amazing it was. We then shared all of our other favorite Nashville spots.

I'd almost forgotten the fact that Levi had chosen not to mention all of the things Calvin was doing to his company.

Almost.

When we were back in the four corners of the office, it all came back.

And by then, Levi was out of his meetings.

His office door was open and he was glaring at his computer. I knocked and he didn't even look up.

"I'll skip lunch today, Maisie."

"It's not your receptionist, unfortunately," I replied, and his gaze shot up.

"Amy? What are you doing here?"

"I wanted to see how things were going and had lunch with Sally and Maisie." I walked fully in and shut the door. "Funny. I hear Calvin is being more of a little shit than normal."

"They told you, didn't they?"

"Without much prompting, actually. Which is why I'm wondering why my husband didn't."

"You knew enough."

"He's *my* brother."

"And this is *my* business."

I blew out a frustrated breath. "I don't understand. This whole thing is about making Calvin mad. Why are you not telling me the full story of what he's doing?"

"It's like I said, you know enough."

"Obviously, I don't."

He let out a sigh, and dimly, I recognized that this might be the first time he was mad at me.

Good. I was mad at him too.

"So your answer was to ask my employees?"

"Let's get one thing straight. If I know there's something going on, I'm gonna figure it out." I pointed at him. "And then I'm gonna figure out why you didn't tell me. Is it because you're planning some sort of big revenge you know I won't like? Something life ruining?"

"Maybe it's that I don't want to make everything about your brother, Amy. Did you consider that?"

I blinked. "No, I didn't actually."

"You know more than anyone else that he doesn't stop. You're dealing with a lot from him already. You don't need any more."

He was . . . protecting me? Wow. That was new.

And it was sad that it was new.

"It still affects me, though."

"Not this time. I'm more worried about keeping my employees and going after him for stealing them."

"You have to have some big plan to get him back."

"Not really."

"But you married me as a part of it."

His eyes cut to me and then he looked back down at his laptop. "Yes . . . I did."

"You have to have something else, and when you do, it's gonna come back on me."

"I'm not gonna let that happen."

"But he'll still try, and I'd like a warning before he does. He knows that he can only do business stuff with you, but with me he can . . ." I trailed off. He could try *anything* with me. It had been years since he got physical, but that didn't mean he wouldn't again.

The scar on my face ached as a reminder of what he was capable of.

"He could do what, exactly?" Levi asked lowly.

"Bad things. Mean things. I can handle it, but you can't keep stuff from me."

"I can protect you."

"Yes, that's nice and all, but—"

"Amy," he said. "Let me do this for you."

"You've done a lot for me."

"And I'll do more. But you have to let me handle things."

I crossed my arms. I didn't want him to handle anything. At least not on his own, but I didn't know if I could turn him down. Had I been alone for so long that I didn't know how to hand things off anymore?

Did I trust Levi to handle them in the first place?

"Please," he added.

"Fine," I said, even though it went against the roiling feeling of my stomach. "I trust you to handle it, but can we meet in the middle here? If you do find some legal way to go after him, some way to make him look like the idiot, you have to tell me. I won't stop you, but I need to know."

"Yes, I'll do that."

It was something, at least. It didn't completely get rid of the feeling in my gut, but I would have to make do.

"What do you want for dinner?" I asked. "The least I can do is cook something, considering I came into your office and made you tell me what was going on."

"I'll handle dinner."

"But—"

"I'm fine," he said. "Trust me, I am."

I didn't know if I did. But he wanted to do it all, it seemed.

And I wasn't sure I was okay with letting him.

Chapter Seventeen

THE NEXT MORNING, my phone rang when the first tendrils of light broke through the curtains. I cursed. I'd done no work on figuring out how I felt about Levi's insistence on doing everything for me, and whatever telemarketer was bold enough to call me right now had to face my wrath.

But the voice on the line was *not* who I expected.

"Amy?" Emma's voice broke, and I froze. "I need help."

"What happened?" I asked as I tumbled out of bed. "Where are you?"

"I-I wanted to come visit you, but my car started smoking, and I'm on the side of the interstate by myself."

"Okay, first things first, call 911."

"I—is this serious enough?"

"Yes," I hissed. "Then send me your location. I'll be there as soon as I can." I found the closest shirt and threw it over my head and struggled into a pair of pants I picked up from the floor.

"Thank you," she said. A message came through and I saw it was her location. "I owe you one."

"You don't owe me anything. I'll be there as soon as I can."

I rushed down the stairs to gather my things.

"Amy?" Levi asked. I turned to see he'd followed me. "What's going on?"

"Emma. Car issues."

"Are you going to get her?"

"Yes," I said as I grabbed my keys.

"I'll go with you."

"No," I snapped. "I've got this."

His eyes went wide, and I paused. I knew I shouldn't have let the residual annoyance of him trying to handle everything get me like this, but this was *my* sister. And *I* would be going to get her.

"Let me help," he said.

"I've got this. Just go back to sleep."

"Amy," he began, but I was out the door before he could say anything else.

I started the car and backed out of the driveway, determined to get this done on my own. I got out of town as fast as I could, heading to where Emma was. It looked like she had made it about halfway to me before her car broke down, and I tried to shave off every second I could from the drive. I didn't usually speed, but I would break a lot of laws for my sister.

Levi called about halfway through.

"Listen, I'm sorry for leaving but—"

"Amy, it's fine. You're panicked about Emma."

Some of my annoyance melted as I remembered that Levi was trying to protect me, even if it wasn't what I wanted.

"She's my sister."

"Are you bringing her home tonight?"

Home. As in *our home*.

"I don't know," I said. "She usually wants to stay with me when something like this happens, but you're using the guest room."

"We can sleep together."

My jaw dropped. Was he seriously thinking of *sex* right now?

Sure, it had been a few days since the blowjob, but this was not the time. "Wh-what? No, we absolutely can't—"

"If Emma is staying, we need to be in the same room."

"Oh, *sleep*."

"Yes, to sleep. I wouldn't suggest the other thing while you're worried about Emma."

"S-sorry. I'm tense right now. I don't like hearing her that upset."

"I would be the same if it were Mom or Isra."

"I'm the only family who gives a shit about her. Neither Mom or Dad would get her."

"What do I need to do?"

I fought against the rising need to say *nothing*. I needed nothing.

Because that wasn't the truth.

"We need to clean out the guest room."

"I'll get it done. And I can stay home from work—"

"No, don't do that. She's my sister. I can handle this."

"And we're married. So if you need a break, I'll take over. I can miss a day in the office. And work from home."

"Emma probably won't be up to seeing anyone else. But I'll text you if I need you. As long as you're not in a meeting or busy."

"I'll know if you need me, no matter what's going on."

"What, do you have some special alert for me or something?"

"I do. I don't care what I'm doing. If it's you, I'll answer."

I swallowed around the ball of cotton that had formed in my throat. He would be here. He would *answer* when I called.

That was something most didn't give me.

So why didn't he fully tell me everything? Why was he hiding things?

"I'll keep that in mind." I checked the navigation. I still had a ways to go, but I was now in unfamiliar territory and needed to focus on the roads, not question my marriage. "I need to go. I'm close to Emma."

"Let me know how it goes, darling. Good luck."

When I hung up, I was still reeling from him calling me *darling* again. I didn't know feelings could be so mixed for one person. I was angry he didn't tell me things and wanted him to do more for me.

But I couldn't think about that. I had a sister to deal with.

Emma was on the side of the road when I found her, thankfully talking to a police officer. I pulled up and she was running to me the second I was out of the car.

"Thank God," she said, pulling me into a tight hug. "The car is still smoking, and they're saying it's not going to be fixable."

I surveyed the scene, eyes widening when I saw her Jeep surrounded by black smoke. Along with the police officer was a fire truck, and everyone was monitoring the car closely. The car must have ignited because the red paint was charred too. A tall man in a fireman's uniform walked over.

"Are you her sister?"

"I am," I replied. "Did you help her with . . . all of this?"

"We did. The car is, um . . ."

"Gone?" I asked. "Yeah, I figured it was when more of it was burned than not."

"We can tow it. Are you her ride?"

"Yeah, I'll take care of her."

He nodded, his eyes moving to Emma. "I hope you have a better day after this."

"Me too," she said miserably. He gave her a crooked smile before walking off.

"Are you okay?" I asked once we were alone.

"No," she muttered. "I thought I was gonna die. It was smoking and there were so many cars going full speed in the right lane."

My breath hitched. "I'm glad you're okay."

"Can we go to Gram's house?" she asked shyly. "I was coming to stay for a bit anyway, but now I *need* to be there."

"Of course you can."

"Will Levi be okay with it?"

"He already knows. Family is important."

She wiped at her nose and gave me a watery smile.

"Now, let's get out of here," I said. "I don't think you need to look at the car anymore."

"On the bright side," she said as we drove away, "we were overdue for some girl time."

"You're right. It's been months since you stayed at the house."

"And I can finally ask about your husband."

I winced. "Sure. But don't you need some time to decompress?"

"I'm fine now," she said.

I raised an eyebrow. "I seriously doubt you're fine."

She looked like she wanted to argue, but her face fell. "Maybe you're right."

"Don't worry, you can stay with us. Levi is moving his stuff from the guest room—"

"Why was his stuff in the guest room?"

Oh, *fuck*. Her arriving while Levi was in the guest room did *not* look good for us. I'd have to answer to that later, along with all the other things Emma would want to know.

"His stuff is just in there. It's not like he's sleeping in there or anything."

"I didn't assume he was, so why did you bring it up?"

"No reason!"

"Are you two not sleeping in the same room? Is this purely a marriage of convenience?"

"No, of course not!"

"It would make sense, especially since our asshole brother fired you. God, if you had to marry someone because of him, I'll go to his house myself—"

"Levi just snores!" I said desperately. "It's not . . . Who would marry someone for anything other than love?"

"Someone who needs it."

"Emma," I started. "Calm down with the questions. You just had something bad happen. Let's deal with one thing at a time."

That was the pot calling the kettle black, but if it worked, I could take being a hypocrite.

"I'm just gonna ask them later."

"We're both stressed," I said. "And I haven't even had coffee yet. Can't this wait?"

"Fine," she said. "You might be right. I can't believe my car did that."

"Was it acting up?"

"It overheated on the way to your wedding."

"*What?*" The words came out high as I struggled to understand why she wouldn't tell me.

"I didn't want to worry you! It was fine after."

"Obviously not!"

Emma frowned and crossed her arms. "You had enough on your plate, and you know Mom or Dad wouldn't help."

"But I don't need you to handle that for me. Don't you trust me?"

Silence rang out in the car. I wasn't even sure *why* I said it. Emma trusted me, but she still hid something from me.

And that was a pattern these days.

Emma wasn't the only reason for my frustration, but it took her doing something similar to Levi for me to finally see why I'd been so short with him trying to help.

I wanted him to trust me.

While I'd never had that many people to care about me enough to solve my problems, I was realizing I didn't want them to fix them *for me*. I was capable, even with my disability. I'd lived alone and made it all of these years just fine.

I couldn't deal with the stress or the anger of people hiding things from me, especially when they were doing it in my best interest. They didn't get to decide what that was.

Only I did.

And now that I was *married*, I knew I wanted this to be a partnership, not Levi swooping in to save me.

But this wasn't a true partnership, was it?

We were *fake married*.

"Of course I do," Emma said, bringing me out of my thoughts. "Why would I not? I just want to take care of you."

"Don't do it by hiding things from me. I swear, everyone treats me like I'm fragile—"

"Who else does?"

"No one." I said it too fast.

"Oh no, you can't get on me about honesty and hide things too."

"It's payback for you hiding the car."

"That's not how this works."

"Fine," I snapped. "Both you and Levi love to fix my problems and hide things. And it's pissing me off."

"I can see that," Emma said. "And . . . from my end, I just didn't want to be another burden on you."

"You're not."

"But you're my sister, not Mom or Dad, and you've done more for me than they have. It's wrong."

"It is. Our parents suck, but that doesn't mean we need to separate ourselves and hide things."

"But Mom and Dad already fucked up your wedding. I didn't want to add to it."

I sighed. "And that's on them. You wouldn't have ruined it. We could have figured out a solution together."

"You're right." She picked at the hem of her shirt. "I know you are. I should have told you."

"Thank you for admitting it," I said. "Let's get home and get coffee. Once you're settled in at the house, we can fix this mess."

"Yeah, that sounds good." She looked out the window. "Thank you for coming to get me, by the way."

"I'd do it anytime."

And it was true. Even if she didn't have Mom and Dad, she always had me.

WE GOT on the road and when we arrived at the house, Emma headed to the guest room to put away her stuff.

I flopped on the couch. I needed coffee and *soon*. But I didn't have the energy to make it, nor did I want my usual kind. Plus, I still had to deal with the dangerous mix of emotions swirling in my gut.

Out of habit, I pulled out my phone to text the one person I usually would when life got like this.

> Why do bad things always happen all together? I need a NAP.

v

> You've got this.

> You're not even gonna ask what's going on?

> I wasn't sure if I should. Sorry.

> No, I'm sorry. I shouldn't have mentioned us meeting up. I think it's making things weird.

> Trust me, it's not just you.

> What can we do to fix this?

I stared at my phone, eagerly awaiting his response. I was so focused that I didn't even notice Emma walking into the room.

"Wow, you really must be having an intense conversation over there."

I instantly locked my phone. "No, I was just staring into the abyss."

"Sure. The abyss that also happens to look a lot like a messaging app."

"It was nothing. Are you all unpacked? I thought that would take longer."

"I only meant to be here for a day or two. But now I have no idea." She threw her hands up. "I have a lot to figure out, apparently."

"We can do all that after coffee. Want to go to my favorite shop?"

"Absolutely. But I dread getting into another car."

"Luckily for you, we can walk."

I grabbed my purse and led her outside.

Spring was in the air, and it was only getting warmer as the sun beat down on the ground. In the nights and mornings, winter was trying to hang on. It only lost the battle in the day. Daffodils were already blossoming, and I knew the other spring flowers would soon follow. I loved the time when nature came alive from the quiet of winter.

It reminded me of Gram. Her garden would soon be filled with tulips, her favorite flower.

"So, how is being a rich wife going?"

"It's fun. I'm sure you saw how many books I bought."

"I did. And the house is looking good. I can't believe how fast you filled it up."

"That was mostly Levi. His mom and stepmom insisted they get all of the stuff from his apartment and moved it in the next day."

"So, that's all his?"

"His stepmom made him get rid of the ugly things."

She hummed. "And how are *other* things? Are you gonna talk to him about what you were upset about in the car?"

I should, but that kind of ask would mean admitting that I

wanted this to be closer to real. And I wasn't sure if that was something I was ready to say.

"I'll try," I said.

"Marriage is about communication."

"Can we get our coffee before you interrogate me more?" I asked.

"Fine, but you can't keep me away forever."

She walked up to the counter and I took a steadying breath to calm myself before following her.

"Can I get a red eye?" I ordered.

"Is that a good idea, considering your migraines?" Emma asked.

Today was the kind of day where I didn't care about my caffeine consumption. I was getting something that would wake me up, and that was all there was to it.

"I'm fine. Don't worry about it. What are you getting? I'll pay."

That got her to stop worrying about me. "I guess I can't question you too much since you have the money now. Can I get a vanilla latte?"

Without thinking, I pulled out Levi's card and handed it to the barista.

"Is that yours?"

"Mine is in the mail."

"So it's Levi's?"

"What, did you think he gave me an allowance?"

"Kinda. I didn't think he'd give you access to that much money."

"We're married. It's what married people do."

"Not all married people. He has to trust you for that."

"He does." Kind of. Not really, in some ways. But I definitely didn't need to tell her that.

I quickly paid and then turned to see if there were any free tables. I spotted Riley cleaning one in the corner.

I waved at her and was rewarded with one of her smiles.

"Hi," she said. "It's nice to see you in."

"I'm here showing my little sister Emma what's good in the city."

"I saw you at the wedding," she said. "You two look so much alike."

"Unfortunately," Emma said.

"So, how much do you know about this marriage?" Riley asked, looking between us.

"Hardly anything." Emma crossed her arms. "She just popped up engaged."

"Oh, interesting." Riley glanced at me, and I shook my head.

"I told her that I move fast," I added. "But we're happy."

"I didn't get to see your ring up close," Riley said, grabbing my hand. "This is *nice*."

"Nice and way too much. I told him he didn't have to go all out but he did."

"Rich, huh? I have one of those."

"Does everyone have a rich husband?" Emma asked. "Where's mine?"

"You could be a nanny for one like I was," Riley said.

"Or just marry someone out of nowhere," I added.

Emma turned to me. "Which I'm still reeling over."

"I also need to catch up," Riley said. "I bet a lot's happened since we last talked. You two looked *very* cute at the wedding."

"I get first dibs," Emma announced. "I've waited long enough."

"Spoken like a sister. I wish mine and I had that kind of relationship," Riley said. "But we're getting there. I'll leave you two to chat, but write down your damn number, Amy." She said it like a threat, handing me a napkin and a pen from her apron.

"Didn't Lily give it to you?"

"She wanted to be sure your privacy was respected, which is sweet, but I need to be able to contact you."

I laughed and wrote it down.

She gave me one last smile before walking away.

"Riley is so nice." Emma turned to me. "Why aren't you closer to her again?"

"She's closer to Lily."

"And?"

"*And* I don't want to encroach on that."

"But you three could be a dynamic trio," she replied. "There's always room for more friends."

"With my history?"

"Come on." Emma rolled her eyes. "You're walking sunshine. Not everyone will do what Ava did."

"I don't want to take the chance."

"But you're an adult now."

"I don't feel very adult-ish."

"You own a house."

"I was given it by Gram."

"And you have a car."

"You had one. You bought it yourself."

"And look at how that worked for me." She sighed. "I should have done more research on it, but it was so cheap."

"How long was it having issues?"

She winced. "Since I got it." I gave her a flat look. "I had a plan anyway. I was working doubles to save up for a new one. I just have to do it earlier now. And now, my amazingly adult sister can help me. Obviously I have bad taste in cars."

"I can try. Nashville is not a cheap place to buy a car."

"We could travel. Please? I'm so bad at this adulting thing."

I rubbed my forehead. I didn't have the patience to go on a hunt for a car. It had been miserable finding my little sedan.

"How much have you saved?"

She told me a decent amount, but it wasn't enough to buy one outright.

And she read my resulting wince like a book. "Is it too little?"

"Yeah. You could do a car note."

"I haven't built my credit yet."

"Okay, so that's out."

"What am I gonna *do*?" she moaned. "I needed that car to last longer."

I bit my lip and thought about it. My car was paid off since I'd gotten it at a good deal. It was one of the few things I *didn't* owe money on.

And I didn't need it as much as she did.

"You can take mine," I offered.

"What? But how will you get around?"

"Levi can drive me."

"No way am I taking your independence from you when you just got married. Never depend on a man." She sounded *so* much like Gram.

"I'm not depending on him *that* much."

"Still. You said you don't want him solving your problems."

"It'll be fine."

"I barely know this guy. And so do you. What if he changes?"

"He . . . won't."

"Really? You trust him that much?"

I thought about how he was out late two nights ago, and the person he'd been messaging.

"It's not a huge deal."

She raised her eyebrows. "That's not a direct answer."

"Emma," I begged. "You're more important."

"No," she hissed. "You have to stop with this. You matter."

"I know I do, but you do too. And you need it more."

"I'm still not taking your car. It's not an option. I'll figure something else out."

I frowned, wondering if there was a way to convince one of the most stubborn people I knew to accept my help.

And as she stared me down, I came up with nothing.

∽∽∽∞

I DIDN'T ALWAYS WATCH for Levi's car, but I wondered if he would leave work early in an attempt to help with Emma. He didn't need to. I had things handled, but he dropped everything whenever it came to me, and I didn't understand why.

He pulled in right at three. Emma noticed his arrival too.

"So, how do you greet your husband when he walks in?"

"With a kiss, like a normal person. But since you're here, I'll forgo it."

"Even though I find you kissing a man gross, don't stop on my account. You're newlyweds. Act like it."

"Emma," I hissed, but she raised an eyebrow and I realized what she was doing. She was seeing if she could find a hole in my story.

And I wasn't going to let that happen. When he walked in, I stood.

"Hi, darling," he said. "I hear we have a—"

I pulled him into a kiss before he could stop me. He froze for a moment before his hands came to rest on my back, pulling me closer.

When I moved away, he stared at me intensely.

"We do have a guest. But I couldn't skip my favorite thing to do every day."

"Right," he said slowly. Then he stepped away and turned to Emma. "It's good to see you again."

"You too," she said. "Sorry to cramp your style."

"You're not an imposition. I heard you had a rough morning." He turned to me. "And you too. Are you feeling better?"

Emma's eyes shot to me, as she usually did when someone mentioned my health.

"Did something happen I should know about?" she asked.

"I was worried about you. That's what he's asking about."

She narrowed her eyes. "Sure. Because worry never leads to anything more."

"I'm not the one who had the car issues today. Your day was far scarier." My voice came out louder than it needed to, but I couldn't let her keep talking about this. The last thing I wanted was for Levi to catch on and think I couldn't follow through with the revenge due to my health.

"You're changing the subject."

"And I thought you were hungry. We skipped lunch."

"That doesn't sound like a good idea," Levi said. "How about an early dinner?"

Emma's lips twisted and I knew she caught that I hadn't told Levi everything yet.

"Fine. Food is a good distraction."

"What are you feeling, Emma?"

"I was thinking about cooking."

"Since when do you cook?" I asked. She'd had a stint with it in high school, but she stopped after lighting the kitchen on fire.

"Since I've been practicing. I'm working on being a well-rounded adult."

"What do you want to make?" Levi asked.

"You have a grill, right? I have a hankering for burgers."

"Someone would have to go to the store," I said. "I don't think I have anything for that."

"I could go, if I could borrow a car. I have a secret ingredient."

"That worries me."

She waved me off. "You won't say that when you try the food."

"I'll take you to the store," Levi offered. "Amy can have a moment to relax while we go."

"And she needs to drink some water," Emma added. "You've had enough caffeine to kill a lesser person."

"I'm the one who's supposed to tell you what to do."

"Then take care of yourself so I don't have to." Emma stuck out her tongue.

"I second that," Levi said. "Please drink water, darling."

"Fine," I muttered. "Have fun at the store."

I did what I was told, and as I drank water, I realized that the stress *had* taken a toll on me. A distinct pressure built behind my eyes, which was not a good sign.

I pressed my palm against my forehead. I needed Emma to accept my damn car so she would be okay. Then everything would be fine.

But that would have to take convincing, so I sat after drinking water and read while I waited for them to return.

I was stuck trying to comprehend the same page for the tenth time when they walked through the door.

"So not only is chocolate banned, but so is red velvet, which is honestly the most tragic part of this," Emma said as she walked in.

"Have a fun trip?" I asked.

"I was just telling Levi here all about your birthday parties."

"Emma, why?"

"Because some were funny. And I needed to warn him never to get you chocolate. You've suffered with enough cake that you hate for a lifetime."

"And it's telling me that we need to make sure all of your future birthday parties are better," he added. "No more of you being ignored."

Emma nodded with a smile on her face.

"D-don't we have dinner to cook?"

"We can't be too hard on her. She'll explode." Emma laughed. "Now, time to go light the grill."

"Did your store run go well?" I asked Levi as Emma went to the back door.

"I think I got her to like me. All I did was say the things I liked about you."

"And you managed to do that the whole time you were gone?"

"Absolutely. It wasn't that hard." His lips pressed to my temple before he went to follow her, and I had to take a second to process before I did the same.

"You'll have to turn the gas on," I said as I got outside and saw Emma staring at the grill like it was a command center for a spacecraft.

"Got it," she said after turning the knob on the top of the gas can, then turned the burners on. "Now, how do you light this thing?"

"You press the button on the side."

She fumbled with it for a good minute. At that point, I knew we were headed for disaster.

"The gas has been on for a bit, maybe we should—"

"There it is!" she called, but the fire took off with too much gas. I recoiled and didn't realize Levi had jumped in front of me until I saw the wall of his back.

"How about you make the patties?" he offered. "I'll cook the burgers."

"Since when do they light up like that?"

"It happens when the gas is on for too long," I said with a wince. "Thankfully, it was clean, or we'd have a fire. *Again.*"

"Again?" Levi asked.

"Emma set my kitchen on fire once."

"It was an accident!" she defended. "I didn't know grease started fires. And I put it out."

"With the rag I gave you."

"Come on. You're making me look like an idiot in front of your husband! Aren't there any good memories you have?"

"I laughed my ass off while it happened."

"That's not helpful," she grumbled. "But since I start fires, I'll let Levi grill. But I'm still flavoring everything."

"And I'll help," I said.

"I can make patties!" Emma nearly screeched.

"Yes, but I'm here for moral support. And monitoring."

"So rude," she said as we walked into the kitchen. She grabbed the hamburger meat.

"What's this secret ingredient?"

"It's just onion soup mix," she said. "You don't think I made a bad impression, do you?"

"Oh no. He's heard me give myself a pep talk saying not to talk about dicks. You're fine."

"That actually makes me feel better." She gave me a small smile. "By the way, what's up with *you* not feeling good?"

"It was just the stress of the day."

"But you look off."

"I'm *fine*," I said. "It got better when I had some quiet time."

Or it was starting to.

"Okay," she said. "But if you get a migraine . . ."

"I'm okay," I replied. "Don't worry about it."

"What's Levi said about it?"

"Oh, um . . . He doesn't know."

"What? He's your *husband*."

"I thought you were worried about the kind of guy he was."

"And then I talked to him in the car. He cares about you, Amy. Like, a lot. And he would be here for you if you let him."

I wanted to tell her that there was no way he cared that much since this was fake, but I couldn't.

"I'll tell him soon. It's been hard when he's *also* trying to solve everything. I need to fix that first, then I can tell him."

"And if this headache turns into a migraine?"

"The headache's gone. Besides, I have other things to worry about. Like my sister not accepting my help."

"I stand by what I said." She pointed at me. "You're not giving up your car for me."

"We'll talk about that later."

"Seriously, there's nothing you can do to make me take it."

"Seems like my headache never left at all, then." I gave her a pointed look.

"Always happy to help," she replied as she stuck out her tongue at me.

She would always try to out-stubborn me. It had been like this for her whole life.

But I'd figure her out and get her to accept my help. I always did.

Chapter Eighteen

My headache stayed away, even when Emma nearly dropped the platter of burgers while walking back into the house.

Despite the mishaps along the way, everything tasted delicious and I was in a good mood by the time we cleaned up.

And then Emma brought out Uno.

"You do realize this is a dangerous game, right?"

"It's not as bad as Monopoly," Levi said. "Trust me, you don't wanna play Monopoly with my family."

"Emma and I could kill each other."

"But it's been a while since I was here long enough to ruin your life with cards," Emma said. "Please?"

"You're not gonna ruin my life. I'm gonna ruin *yours*."

We got out the cards and quickly realized that Emma and I weren't the problem. Levi was. After a few rounds, he hit Emma with a plus-four and she looked him in the eye and threatened to kill him. I then earned my own threats by stacking two draw-two cards that they'd thrown my way.

Levi followed that up with skipping me two times in a row.

"Get *fucked*," I said to him.

"Those are the words a husband always wants to hear from his wife," he said, and then put down another skip.

"Levi!"

"It's beautiful," Emma said. "You deserved that."

I glared as I put down a reverse card.

She then hit me with a plus-four.

"Emma!" I snapped. "How could you do this to me?"

"With no guilt or remorse."

The game continued on, up until I finally got Uno and dropped my last card.

"You all suck! I win!"

"I could have made you lose that game," Levi said. "But I didn't because I was nice."

"Thank you, but also, I won and will still rub it in your face."

"I wouldn't have it any other way."

"If I hadn't had the day from hell," Emma said with a yawn, "I'd ask for a rematch. But I need some fucking sleep."

"Cars blowing up will do that to you. It's almost like you need something *reliable*."

"Don't," she hissed before getting up. "Once I get eight hours of sleep, it's *over* for you." She made a cut motion across her throat as she headed to the guest room.

"I'll never hear the end of it if she does win," I said. "We'll have to team up. Just like we will for other things."

Levi raised an eyebrow. "Did you mean for that to sound sexual?"

My cheeks immediately lit on fire. "N-no! I meant about something else."

"So you want sex to stay off the table?" he asked.

"I'm not saying that! I'm saying I haven't thought about it. Well, I have but—"

His eyebrows raised higher.

"I'm gonna stop talking before I embarrass myself more."

"I think we should take your sister's advice and get some rest. We can talk about anything in the morning."

"Fine," I said. "Maybe I'm a little tired too."

"Come on, darling. Let's go to bed." He grabbed my hand and led me upstairs.

A bubble of nervousness hit me as I thought about sleeping in the same bed as him again, but exhaustion weighed me down. I'd narrowly avoided a headache tonight, but I knew I'd need sleep if I wanted to keep my good luck.

"I could sleep on the floor," I offered.

He turned to me with a flat expression. "You know we're not doing that. This isn't all that smaller than the bed on the honeymoon."

And yet, in a bed like that, I'd jumped his bones the second I felt his erection. I knew myself. I would do it again if given the chance.

I was doing good at not thinking about the incident with Levi except when I was in bed alone. But now I wasn't in bed alone. And he would be here with me.

"Once again, are you sure about this?" I asked.

"I'm very sure about this," he said. "We can be adults."

"Because that went so well for us last time."

"It went very well."

"You're only saying that because you got a blowjob."

"I believe you also benefitted from that."

My cheeks heated. I had, and it was something I couldn't manage to replicate on my own.

Damn him.

"We're sleeping," I said. "Just sleeping."

"Okay."

"No funny business."

"Understood."

I went to my dresser, only to pause. I didn't have much in the way of night clothes. Usually, I slept in my underwear or in nothing at all.

What I did have was . . . skimpy.

It had been a bit since I'd done my laundry, and all the shirts I could manage to sleep in were dirty. That left me with a thin, pink nightgown.

Not my best choice.

I grabbed it anyway and ran for the bathroom. When I put it on, I groaned. My nipples were visible again.

"So," I said, crossing my arms as I walked back into the bedroom. "We have the same problem as the first night you stayed here."

Levi's eyes slid to me and landed on my chest. Thankfully, most of it was covered.

"Is it a problem?"

"Shut up," I said, red in the face. I climbed under the fuzzy blanket to hide from him. "You're not gonna look."

"Too late."

"I hate you."

"Do you really?" he asked, but this time, his eyes were on mine.

"No, I don't. I'm just embarrassed."

"You have nothing to be embarrassed about."

I focused my gaze on the wall. "I'm not necessarily insecure, but I know I'm not like all the heroines in the romance books. I'm not a size zero. I have stretch marks on my thighs from puberty, and my hair is a ball of frizz half the time. And it's not like I let myself trust people to get in a relationship, so all I know is my family's indifference."

"First of all, when Isra finally saw you, she asked how I landed you."

"Oh, come on. I'm not out of your league."

"She saw me when I was in middle school. That's probably burned in her memory."

"She seems like the kind of lady who never forgets anything."

"But the point still stands. You're gorgeous, Amy. And if you could see yourself through my eyes, you'd know why I think that."

"Really?"

"I'd never lie to you."

"Thanks," I said with a small smile. "But I'm still not letting you see my boobs for free."

"I'd be willing to earn it if you want me to."

The words sent a thrill down my spine. I wanted more after the honeymoon. It wasn't in my best interest to, but I did.

"We'll see how you act tonight."

"I'll be on my best behavior. At least a version of it."

He leaned forward and captured my lips in a chaste kiss before he retreated to his side of the bed.

I WOKE up to a hand on my back, followed by an exhale somewhere above my head. It felt like the end of a pleasant dream, the kind where I wasn't alone.

Only this time, the dreamlike state of comfort was my reality.

My head was pillowed on his warm chest and my leg was hiked up onto his. Every inch of my torso pressed into him.

My breath caught in my throat as I tensed. The second I did, his hand moved up and down my back.

"It's fine, Amy. Don't worry about it."

"What happened?" I asked. "How did we end up here again?"

"You moved to my side sometime during the night."

"You could have pushed me away."

A low chuckle left his mouth. "No, I couldn't have."

My cheeks heated, and instead of thinking too hard about what he'd just said, I sat up. "Don't get too flattered. This is just the best side of the bed."

"Best side because I'm here or some other reason?"

"I—other reasons, of course!"

"You don't have to get embarrassed for flirting with me, Amy Hensen."

"I'm embarrassed for many—wait, Hensen? That's not my last name."

"It sounds better than your current one."

"Willard is a beautiful last name!"

"Not as pretty as your first with my last."

Oh, boy. I couldn't handle early morning Levi. He had no filter.

"Do they do name changes when it's a fake marriage?"

"The marriage is real on paper, so yes. They do."

I shook my head, taking stock of the heat in my body. Seeing him relaxing in my bed, with his loose T-shirt exposing a touch of his stomach, was too much. It was like the honeymoon all over again, except now I knew exactly how he could make me feel.

But anywhere except my bed felt cold, and I wasn't sure if I was ready to face that.

Then Levi pulled me back down.

"We can take a few minutes."

It was before coffee. That was the only explanation for the way my body curled into his and accepted my fate.

Or at least that was what I told myself.

But the addition of him in my bed made my room a dreadfully comforting place.

I closed my eyes, wondering what my life would be like if I woke up to this every day.

For one, I'd be far hornier. I could feel it now, moving through my body like liquid heat, making every part of me want him.

And two, it would hurt even worse when it all went wrong. Screwing my eyes shut, I tried to picture the pain I would be in when this all ended. If I thought about it enough, I could muster the bravery to get out of bed and move on with my day.

I thought of how he'd texted someone else on the honeymoon, how that secret could end us.

But I also remembered how good he'd made me feel on the honeymoon too.

Logic was at war with lust, and unfortunately, logic didn't usually win for me.

I wanted him, and the consequences were a future-Amy problem.

All thoughts of what could go wrong vanished. I leaned into him more and then looked up at him.

His eyes met mine and I wondered if this was doing the same thing to him. Did he wonder about what happened on the honeymoon? Or was it just me?

My gaze fell to his lips and the memory of what they'd felt like on me played back in my brain.

I needed that again, so before I could talk myself out of it, I reached over and kissed him.

Levi took in a sharp breath of air and his hand on my shoulder clamped down as if he wanted to keep me close.

Little did he know, I couldn't leave.

My palms slid down his chest and his other hand landed on my cheek. The kiss turned from chaste to more as I moved my lips against his. I took a chance and swiped my tongue against his bottom lip.

His resulting groan made him pull me closer and I hooked my leg over his lap and swung myself to where I was on top of him.

"What are you doing?" he asked as he pulled away.

"I don't know. I'm just doing what I want."

"And kissing me is what you want?"

"I could go for a lot more than that. And if we need a justification, I bet it would make us look—"

His hand covered my mouth. "I don't care about how it looks. Do you want me because you want this?"

"Y-yes."

"Then I'll do whatever you want."

His hand moved to my stomach, just under my breast. My nipples, already hard from the feel of him, now begged for attention. Slowly, he trailed upward until his palm encased the whole thing.

"Is this good?"

"So good." I gasped when he moved again.

"Do you know what these fucking nightgowns do to me?"

"I have an idea."

"I don't think you do." He rolled his hips up, pressing his hard cock into me. "Every day I've been tortured by the memory of the outline I saw."

"You can see the real things if you want to."

"*Fuck* yes." His other hand pulled at the spaghetti strap, revealing my top half to him. "They're gorgeous. Just like every inch of you."

I gasped as his mouth clamped over one, his hand going to the other. Every movement sent pleasure straight down to my clit.

God, this was going to ruin me for all men.

His tongue played with me, flicking over the hard bud and making me arch into him. I could only make pitiful gasps as I struggled to wrap my head around how good this felt.

He tortured my breast and then moved to the other. Each second, I was growing more and more desperate.

My clit needed attention and I uselessly moved against him, desperate for any kind of contact.

But then he rolled us over. The room spun and he landed on top of me.

I could feel him smile as he kissed his way down my stomach, pulling at the waist of my underwear. There was only a second between the cool air hitting my core and his mouth overtaking it, lapping up all the wetness that dripped out for him. I let out a sigh of relief as I opened myself wider.

He was as skilled with his tongue as he was with his hands, it seemed.

Levi must have remembered what I liked last time. His tongue drew circles around my sensitive clit and then dragged its way down to my entrance before pressing inside of me.

My fingers sank into his hair as my eyes closed.

Yes. This was what I needed. This feeling of climbing to impossible heights. There was no way I could regret this.

Levi kept up the pace as every muscle in my body tightened. I was a mess of gasps and muttered curses.

I had to cover my mouth to keep from yelling as I shuddered. A shock wave of pleasure erupted from my core, filling every inch of my body.

And when it finally subsided, he was *still* going.

My body responded in time. Pleasure faded and then built again. I arched into him to get a better angle, and this time, his mouth focused on my clit while his fingers dipped into my pussy.

"Yes, Levi. Just like that."

His finger hooked, earning a broken gasp from me.

When I came again, I swore I blacked out. The only thing I could feel was *perfection*. The world could have ended and I wouldn't have cared.

"Good?" he asked when I finally came back into myself.

"Yeah," I managed to say. "So fucking good."

Levi kissed his way back up my body before landing on my mouth. I tasted my own pleasure on his tongue and I knew I wanted to give him the same feeling.

My hands moved to his erection, giving it one pump. "Your turn," I said. I tried to turn us over so I could return the favor, but he pressed into me harder, keeping me in the same position. "Don't you want a blowjob again?"

"I want you to come again."

"But what about you?"

"I'll feel it when I'm inside of you."

My breath caught in my throat, but I nodded. This was now the one thing I wanted more than anything in the world. He took off his shorts and lined himself up with me, his mouth coming down to mine. He pressed at my opening, pushing in a half inch. I was so ready to feel him all the way and I was half tempted to tell him to get on with it.

"Amy!" Emma called. "Do you have any extra pads?"

Nothing was more of a buzzkill than that.

I let out a sigh. "She has immaculate timing."

"We'll finish this later," he said into my neck. I felt empty without him, but I got up anyway.

"I'll be right there," I called as I threw on a robe. Emma was waiting in the hallway, foot tapping nervously.

"Thank God. It's seriously an avalanche right now."

And that ruined my mood even further. "They're in the very back of the closet. Come on, I'll show you."

She followed me dutifully, but the pads were well hidden behind a stack of towels Levi had brought. Emma had to find a step stool just to get to it.

Once what she needed was in hand, she kicked me out to do her business and I headed downstairs. Levi was dressed in sweatpants and a sweatshirt, making coffee.

"I find it so hot that you make coffee for me."

"Hopefully, that's not the hottest thing I've done today." He pulled me close to him and pressed his lips to my temple. "Or what I'll do later."

I let out a giggle and stepped away to start cutting fruit for us all. If Emma was truly on her period, then she'd be hungry the second she came downstairs. Levi got started on some sausage.

Halfway through cutting up a carton of strawberries, I was proven right when she walked in and grabbed the bowl that was meant for all of us and sat at the table to eat.

"So, she's hungry, huh?" Levi asked as he handed me another. "Is that normal during this time of the month?"

"Yep. At least you weren't there during her *first* one. I thought she was gonna kill me."

After cutting enough for Levi and me to eat, we sat at the table while Emma furiously typed a message on her phone.

"Everything okay?" I asked. "Have a secret boyfriend I don't know about?"

"No," she huffed. "It's nothing."

Her phone chimed.

"Are you *sure* it's nothing?"

"Yep."

Then it rang.

She flipped it over only to push a button and then threw it back down. "Sorry about that. It's on silent now."

I raised an eyebrow. "Shouldn't you answer that?"

"It's just work. My boss is on my ass about coming in. Apparently, they're short-staffed. I was only expecting to stay here for a little while, so I told them I'd be heading back today."

"It sounds pretty serious."

"Amy, it's fine. I can't even *get* to work right now. They'll have to deal, even if he makes true to his threats to fire me."

I leaned back. "You could if you had a car."

"*Amy*," she hissed.

Levi watched me curiously, so I figured it was time to explain. "Since Emma needs a car, I keep telling her to take mine for the time being so she can get around."

"And you don't want to?"

"Of course not. You're nice and all, but I'm not taking away my sister's independence just so I can have my own. She worked hard for the car and paid it off. She gets to keep it."

"I at least live in a city with public transportation."

"Nashville's transit system sucks."

"But it still counts," I said. "You live in a small town with no other options. If one of us has to have a car, it needs to be you."

"You don't need to solve my problems."

"I'm not gonna force you into this, but we *need* to talk about it. And that's what we're doing."

"There's nothing to talk about. It's still a no."

"So the issue is that you don't want Amy to not have a way around, am I right?" Levi asked.

"Yes," Emma replied. "She doesn't have to give her car to me. I'll figure something else out."

"But—" I tried to say, but Levi held up his hand.

"I think you should take Amy's car."

Emma narrowed her eyes. "Of course *you* would say that."

"And I'll buy her a new one."

The table went silent.

"T-that's n-not necessary," I stammered.

"No, it is. You need a vehicle and so does your sister. The problem's solved."

"You're just gonna buy her a car?" Emma asked. "What kind of stipulations does that come with?"

"None." He said it like it was easy.

"And what happens if you get in a fight and she has to leave but your name is on the car?"

"The car will be completely hers. I won't put my name on it."

"I . . . You." Emma's glare grew more intense. "Are you usually this good at solving problems?"

"Most of the time. It helps that I have money."

I looked between Levi and Emma, trying to see if he was serious about this whole car thing. I'd get it if he only offered all of this to get Emma to see sense.

However, Emma wouldn't when she eventually found out.

"So I have no reason to avoid work?" she asked with a groan. "Thanks a lot."

"You're the one who likes small-town life," I said. "And if you wanna continue to live alone, you should probably not get fired."

"So I leave now? What if you need something today?"

"All I'm gonna do today is read and relax. Even if I *wanted* to go somewhere, I won't."

"I can also take her wherever she needs to go after work. And while I'm in the office, she can call an Uber if she's going somewhere in town."

"When you got married, you weren't supposed to choose someone as good at arguing as he is."

"We can keep going back and forth or you can call your boss back."

Emma flipped off Levi before grabbing her phone and disappearing into the other room.

"Thank you," I said. "You have no idea how much better it makes me feel that she's leaving with reliable transportation. Even if I've torn up the trunk with dirt."

"You're welcome," he replied. "Now, I do have to get ready for work. I have an early morning meeting that I can't miss."

"Go ahead. I'll clean up."

He pressed a kiss on my lips before leaving.

A few minutes later, Emma returned with her bag. "I was one more ignored call away from getting fired," she said. "They're desperate for someone to come in."

"Then get going. I'll be fine here."

"At least I feel better about the two of you. I mean, I see why it moved so fast."

I blinked. "You do?"

"Oh yeah. He's down bad." She gave me a hug. "And thank you. I hate that I have to leave early, for *work* of all things. But I owe you one. I owe you a lot, actually."

"I'll help you with anything."

"Don't forget about you," she said under her breath. "Seriously."

"Are you leaving?" Levi asked as he came downstairs. "I am too."

"Looks like we both have to work. Disgusting. Thanks for

letting me stay, though. You're nicer than a lot of the other brothers-in-law I've heard about."

"I try to be."

"Now, here are my keys." I threw them to her. "Be safe, please. Both of you."

"Call me if you need me." She gave me one last hug before leaving. Levi gave me a smile before following her out.

I cleaned up after breakfast, checking in once again to be sure my headache from the day before hadn't returned. Since I was off of my medicine, I knew that the odds of pain simply going away wasn't very possible.

Luckily, it seemed that I was in the clear.

I lounged on the couch and was reading a book when my phone jingled.

And it was a message from V.

I scrambled to open Discord.

> V
>
> I don't know. I hate to say this, but what if this has reached its natural end?

My heart sank.

> What do you mean?

> We've both been so busy. We hardly read anymore. And I would bet that both of us have people that we care about now.

> You have someone.

> I do. Don't you?

I wanted to tell him no, but that wasn't exactly true. I had Levi now, and I couldn't deny that he meant *something* to me.

I don't like endings. Especially when they're not happy ones.

I'm sorry, but I think we let this go too far for too long. We should focus on the people in our lives.

Okay. Thank you for reading with me.

It was one of my greatest pleasures.

I let out a long sigh and closed the app. Tears pinpricked my eyes, even though I knew he wasn't entirely wrong.

Still, I wished I knew who he was. I wished I'd asked more questions.

The mystery would haunt me.

I tried to put it out of my mind as I finished my book. When I was done, I wanted to tell someone about it, and for the first time, I found myself missing having a book club to talk to. It was so much easier to organize what I was thinking about the books when I was able to talk about it, and the sense of community was something I hadn't experienced since then. V had helped, but that was over now.

Levi got home at six, his phone glued to his ear.

"Yes, Mom, I'm gonna ask her." His voice was soft and he looked at me apologetically. "No, she likes you guys. I'm sure she'd love to. I'm home now, so I need to go."

He said his goodbyes and put his phone away.

"Sorry about that. Mom called to check in and asked if you wanted to go plant shopping with them tomorrow."

I shouldn't. I needed to rest to be sure a migraine didn't start.

But I *wanted* to.

"Yeah, of course I'll go." I plastered a smile on my face. "It should be fun."

"And after, we go car shopping."

"We're staying busy," I said with a laugh. "Great."

"I think what I'm more concerned with is whether or not we're finally alone in our house."

"I'm pretty sure we are. Other than the gnomes that steal my socks. Why?"

"Because it's time to pick up where we left off." His smile was devilish as he crossed the room and captured me with a searing kiss. My body lit up with sparks as I felt him *everywhere*. I'd almost forgotten about our missed opportunity this morning, but I was more than okay picking up where we left off.

"There's not enough room on this couch for all the things I want to do to you," he muttered.

I could picture all of the things he wanted to do to me, and if it was anything like what happened this morning, I would be in heaven again soon. "Then where should we move?"

As soon as I finished my sentence, I was up in the air, cradled in Levi's arms. He set me on the dining room table, tongue swirling in my mouth. Just a minute of kissing and my body was already revving up to be destroyed again. No one was around and no one could stop us. "Wait a second. The blinds aren't shut."

"I don't give a fuck. If anyone looks, they'll see a man pleasuring his wife."

My body hummed at the idea of that. I didn't think I'd ever be okay with leaving the blinds open while Levi was all over me.

But I'd do anything that he asked me to.

His hand touched my lower back, dragging every inch of my skin to be flush with his. My legs opened to accept him into my space. His tongue took over my mouth until he pulled away and tugged at the hem of my shirt.

"Do you know how long I've waited to do this? How long I've waited to have you all to myself?"

"Is this where you tell me no other woman was like me?"

"There were no other fucking women."

I could only let out a broken gasp as his mouth claimed my skin. I wanted to believe that. I wanted it so bad.

But the evidence didn't match.

My questioning didn't get to linger as his teeth nipped me, pulling me back into the moment.

I didn't understand how all logic could fly away whenever he was touching me, yet I would let it. I spent far too much time in my own head anyway.

"How do you wanna come?" he said against my skin. "On my hand or my cock?"

I wet my lips. "Good communication."

"Don't stall," he warned. "I *will* be getting you off, but I won't be waiting long."

"On your cock," I said. "I need it."

He hummed, and his hand slipped under the waistband of my pants. I thought he'd tug them off to fuck me, but instead, his hand touched my pussy.

"I'm pretty sure that's not your cock."

"Trust me, you'd know the difference." His finger pressed in. "I'm making sure you're ready first, darling."

I gasped as he hooked his finger, finding my G-spot with ease. His mouth returned to mine, swallowing my moans as they escaped.

I fought the urge to come, but his movements were too good, too perfect.

"L-Levi," I managed to say between gasps. "I'm gonna—"

"Do it. Come for me."

I whined as he buried his teeth into my bottom lip and he added another finger.

"B-but I thought—"

"Trust me, you'll do it again. And it'll be exactly how we want it." His thumb pressed onto my desperate clit. "Come, Amy. I want you to."

And I did. My head fell back and my body was encased in warm light. It was as euphoric as all of the other ones he gave me, and when my brain came back online, I wondered if this man ever could mess up in sex.

"Fuck me," I said, my voice breathy as if I'd climbed a mountain.

"Gladly." Levi's pants came off and I caught a glimpse of his hard cock. "But I need to grab a condom."

"Don't." I said it before thinking. "I-I mean, I have birth control literally implanted into my arm. And I don't have anything. I was tested, and it's been a while . . ." I trailed off before I could kill the mood with details of my inactive sex life.

"I don't have anything either," he said. "And I would *love*—" He stopped himself. "Are you sure?"

"Yes. More than anything."

He moved forward and *finally* pressed into me. If I thought his fingers were good, his cock was incredible. This time, as he sank inside, there was nothing to stop us. I panted as he stretched open every inch of me. I'd never felt this full in my life, and now I was glad I'd had that orgasm before he did this.

"My God," I managed to say.

"Are you okay?"

"More than okay. You need to move. *Please*."

He pulled all the way out of me before surging in again, eyes locked on mine. "Fuck, Amy. You feel even better than I imagined."

"You do too," I said, head tilting back again. He thrust into me, pushing the table fully into the corner while holding me as tightly as he could. His mouth locked onto mine.

If I could have talked, I would have screamed *yes* and *harder*.

Levi seemed to get the message without me saying it because his hips bucked into me, sending his cock to new depths. He fucked me hard, and I could feel myself gripping his cock as he continued.

I'd never come from just penetration, but I'd also never had anything like this before. As his tempo continued, my body tightened and rose in anticipation of a life-changing orgasm.

Then the table broke.

He caught me before I toppled to the ground.

"Oh my God. We wrecked the table."

"I don't care." He pushed me into the wall and my legs wrapped tightly around him. "We're fucking here."

"But the table—"

"I'll buy you a hundred tables, and we'll fuck on each and every one."

I opened my mouth to argue, but he thrust upward again, shutting off every thought I had.

The wall was hard and unforgiving and so was Levi. He continued his movements and my eyes closed to take in the pure perfection he was giving me.

It didn't take long for my body to remember where it was. I came with my head pressed against the wall and his name on my lips.

All I could manage was a scream that I hoped the neighbors couldn't hear.

"God-fucking-dammit, Amy. You're gonna make me come just from the sounds you make."

"Come in me," I begged. "I fucking need it."

I'd never let a guy do this, but when it was my husband, when it was *him*, it was all I could think about. His thrusts became erratic as his lips closed on the side of my neck. I fell back, spent body already building up again.

"I'm going to fill you with my come. And when it drips down your thighs, you'll think of me."

"My *God*, Levi."

"And then I'll do it again and again."

Just the idea of his words sent me over the edge. "L-Levi, I'm gonna come."

"Do it," he dared. "Come while I fill you."

I did exactly as I was told, and his cock jerked inside of me. I may have slept with other people before, but he was the first to do this.

And I wondered if he would be the last.

"That was . . . I don't know if I have words."

"We'll be doing it a hundred more times," he replied. "Maybe a thousand."

And in the afterglow of the best sex I'd ever had, I believed it.

Levi deposited me on the couch before returning with a rag. After I'd been thoroughly cleaned and given fresh pajamas, we laid down in my bed.

And as I drifted off, I wondered if anything could ruin this moment.

That was my first mistake.

Chapter Nineteen

WHEN I WOKE up with a symphony of misery in my head, I knew my day was fucked. I couldn't move, or else I'd start crying, and as Levi got up, all I could do was pretend I was sleeping in while he got ready for work.

Cymbals crashed in my head and every beat of my heart sent pulsating pain to every part of my skull.

This was a migraine, and a bad one at that.

It had been a long time since I'd had one with no medicine. When I was younger, more than half of my time was spent either with one or recovering from one. I was never functioning at one hundred percent.

And I had a feeling I wouldn't be this time either.

A part of my brain was shut off, too busy dealing with the agony. When I finally heard the front door shut, tears gathered in my eyes as I dragged myself out of bed to find over-the-counter medicine.

It probably wouldn't work, but it was worth a shot. I was clinging to the hope that this was a normal headache, even as all the signs pointed in the other direction.

I took that and drank water before closing every curtain in my room and falling back in bed. After an hour of no relief, I was *fucked*.

Both Nancy and Isra wanted to go plant shopping today. Levi had already texted me trying to solidify the plans and I *couldn't*.

There was no hope that he wasn't going to see me like this, but I couldn't work out what to say. All I could do was take in one breath after another and hope it abated in any capacity.

Tears leaked out of my closed eyes. I didn't want to disappoint them. I didn't want Levi to come home and wonder what the hell was wrong and why I hadn't answered him all day.

I didn't want him to see me like this and wonder if I was even worth it.

By the evening, I wondered if I could afford an ambulance. I knew that it would be expensive, but the hospital could give me *some* sense of relief so I could think. I'd made it through pain like this before, but I hoped I would never have to again since I was so religious about taking medicine.

Well, I was until Calvin blew up my life.

All Levi had talked about was wanting to have sex again. He probably would want that tonight after car shopping, and I wished I was able to do all of it. Unfortunately, I wasn't as reliable as I wanted to be. I'd managed to deal over the years, but even now, a migraine would ruin any plans I had.

And in the haze of pain, there was no time for grieving that. There was only misery, both emotional and physical.

An unsung benefit of living alone was that no one had to witness my darkest moments. I'd gotten good at taking care of myself when these migraines hit. So good that I kept a trash can next to me in case I threw up.

I had no idea what time it was when the front door opened, but I knew there was no faking being okay. My only hope was to pretend to be asleep.

"Hey," he said. "Are you napping?"

I couldn't get an answer out and he turned on the lamp next to the bed.

All I could do was yelp in pain as the light turned the migraine up to ten.

"Turn it off," I begged. "Please, no light."

Immediately it was shut off. Even talking had pounded on my head, and I curled into myself. God, I wished I had medicine. I could have caught this right when it started and it would have been okay.

"Amy," Levi said. Dimly, I was aware of how panicked he sounded. "What's going on?"

"I'll be fine." I curled in tighter on myself. "I'm just not well right now."

But I'd not felt one this bad since the first one when I was a teenager.

"You're not fine," he said, his fingers touching my forehead. I let out a hiss of pain and shied away. His hand jerked back.

"Just leave me. I'll get over it eventually."

"What's going on?" he asked. "Please tell me."

"M-migraine. It's bad."

"On a scale of one to ten."

"Nine," I said without hesitation.

"We're going to the hospital," he replied immediately.

"No," I begged. "I can't afford it."

"I don't care about money."

I opened my mouth to respond, but another wave of pain was sent my way, and all I could do was bear it.

By the time the wave subsided, Levi had left. I laid in the darkness, wondering if he was gone for good. Maybe he went to dinner without me.

But he was back before I could finish the thought.

"Put this over your forehead. We're leaving now."

"But—"

"No arguing." His voice was soft yet filled with an unrelenting tension I hadn't heard. "We're going to the hospital. And that's final. Cover your eyes. I'm carrying you to the car myself."

He was going to regret this the second he saw the hospital bill. I'd gone once when I had insurance and I was still paying it off now.

But the idea of *any* medicine was enough to let him lift me up. I now had a thing to look forward to, a light at the end of the tunnel. I kept my eyes closed as he put me into the car and we sped through Nashville.

Time always moved funny when I was in pain, but it felt like we were at the ER way too fast.

My pain was worse, and the car didn't help. The second he parked the car and I opened the door, I threw up. I hadn't eaten anything, but my stomach wouldn't stop roiling.

"I'm sorry," I mumbled. "I know I must be so gross right now."

"Amy, you're sick. Very sick. Don't apologize for a single thing."

The lights of the hospital were awful, and all I could do was sit in a corner while I pressed the washcloth to my eyes. I resisted the urge to throw up again while Levi handled talking to the front desk.

"Come on," he said. "We're going back now."

"Wh-what? Shouldn't we have to wait?"

"When my wife is sick? You're not waiting for a single fucking thing. Come on."

"L-Levi, seriously. We could just go home. This is gonna be *so* expensive."

"We're seeing a doctor *now*, Amy," he snapped. "I won't accept no for an answer."

Fuck. He was mad. And I didn't blame him. He didn't know what was going on, and now I'd ignored him all day, possibly subjecting him to questions from Isra and Nancy, and ruining the other tentative things we'd wanted to do. I hated that I had bad days.

And that it often made people angry.

Lily was good at tolerating the times when I would go quiet. She was so busy with writing and creating her own worlds that I doubted she noticed. But she'd always been such a relaxed friend. Before I met her, people weren't so chill.

It was why I kept my migraines to myself. Usually, no one needed to know because the medicine worked so well, but I'd flown too close to the sun. I'd gotten too comfortable with not having them and then let one sneak up on me.

And now I'd pay the consequences.

I let him lead me to the back room while my eyes stayed glued to the floor. I nearly fell into the chair and hoped that they would move faster so I could get relief and apologize to Levi.

"And who is this?" the nurse asked as she took my vitals.

"Husband," I replied. It was all I could say.

"Are you okay with him being here?"

I gave a thumbs-up, unable to nod. He might as well know the full story.

"Your blood pressure is high," the nurse said.

"It usually is when I get one this bad."

"Are you on any medicine?"

"Beta blockers . . . but I ran out of those a few days ago."

Levi's eyes shot to me.

"Why didn't you get a refill?" the nurse asked.

"My doctor's office needed to see me in person and I don't have insurance."

"Ah, I understand." A silence settled over the room, as it always did whenever I was at the doctor and mentioned how little money I had. The nurse couldn't do anything about how expensive health care was in America, and I didn't blame her anyway. Just like everything else, I sometimes had to go without.

"That won't be a problem again," Levi muttered. I winced at

the sound. His anger was only growing, and I could imagine what he was thinking right now.

Do you know how mad Isra is because of this?

You should have warned me.

Ugh. It wasn't going to be easy.

"Dr. Spinel will be in here momentarily. I hope you feel better."

Once she was gone, silence settled on us again.

"I'm sorry," I said. Levi only looked at me, his jaw ticked. "I'm sorry I didn't answer earlier."

His entire posture was a rigid line, and I looked back at the ground, putting my head in my hands.

Thankfully, the doctor came in right after.

"Ah, there she is. And here is the husband. I heard from the front desk that you were quite worried in the lobby."

"I haven't seen her like this."

"Migraines this severe are very worrying." Dr. Spinel turned to me. "How long have you had them?"

"Half of my life," I said.

"And what would you rate the pain?"

"A nine."

"Have you ever had one this severe?"

"Yes, a long time ago."

"Do you have any other medicine?"

"I usually have pills for when they start . . . but I'm out of that too."

"You'll need to see your regular doctor after this," he said. "But we can give you an injection and some of your beta blockers for now."

"However little you can give me. I still don't have insurance, so—"

"Don't listen to her," Levi cut in. "Give her as much as you can, and I'll make sure she goes to her doctor."

Dr. Spinel nodded. "Will do."

"Levi," I tried. "You can't—"

"Don't tell me what I can and can't do with my money, Amy."

I could have sunk down into the floor. The doctor looked between us like a bomb was about to go off.

"Now, some things for when you recover: no coffee, and try to eat after this."

"Yeah," I grunted.

"Let me go get the injection."

He didn't waste time, a welcome departure from how my other ER visits went. The pain of the shot was nothing compared to the pain in my head, and he also gave me oral medicine. I checked my watch. I would need to get some food in my system as soon as possible. Then I could pass out in my room and be mostly okay for Levi to yell at me before he went to work in the morning.

"Don't forget to avoid stress," Dr. Spinel added.

I winced. "Yeah, I'll do my best."

Levi glared and I looked away. I had a feeling whatever would happen next would be the very thing Dr. Spinel warned me to avoid, but hey, I'd disappointed Levi enough today. I deserved it.

We left, and Levi took me to the pharmacist. Once I had all of my medicine, he also stopped to get me food. I took the beta blockers and slowly ate the donut he got me. I could still feel the nausea, but it wasn't as bad.

When we got home, I was feeling a little better. The medicine Dr. Spinel gave me worked way better than anything over the counter.

"The medicine is kicking in," I told Levi. "I'm gonna go to bed now, and you could try to take Isra and your mom to dinner to salvage the night."

He slowly turned to me, eyes narrowed. "Do you think I'm going to *dinner* after that?"

"Um, yes? You have things to do."

"I walked in to my wife nearly passed out in her room. Do you think I give a fuck about anything else?"

"I'm fine," I said.

"You're pale and you look . . ."

I winced. My hair was a mess, as it usually was when I didn't have the energy to take care of it.

"I look bad. I get it, but it's mostly the hair. I bet if I styled it, you wouldn't even notice my paleness. If it had been just a little less intense, I could have—"

"Do you always have this little regard for yourself, or is this something you're reserving only for me?"

My jaw dropped. "I . . . I take care of myself."

"You were out of your medicine."

"Levi, a thirty-day supply of *one* of them costs more than two thousand dollars out of pocket. I can't . . . Yes, I made cuts, but I had to."

"You have all the money you could need."

"But—"

"Amy, what do I have to say to get you to understand, you didn't *need* to make cuts. You're not out of money."

"Have you seen my bank account?"

"Have you seen mine? I'm rich and you have access to—"

"And when has that helped me?" I snapped. "I grew up with money, Levi. And it meant nothing, because you know what happens when I get sick? People tell me to get over it. I'm supposed to be happy-go-lucky. It's the one thing I *can* be after . . . after everything. This ruins me every fucking time."

"It doesn't ruin you."

"Yes, it does. Do you know how much debt I have because of nights like tonight? I have over ten grand in medical bills because of what insurance didn't cover. My parents were obligated to pay for anything before I turned eighteen—and I still never hear the end of that—but anything from eighteen until now? All mine. And even after ten years of paying it down, I've barely made a dent."

And that was the truth, the one I didn't want anyone to know. That I was a burden, even when I didn't want to be.

My eyes fell to the floor. I felt terrible. There were things I wanted to do today. Things *Levi* wanted to do too. And as usual, it all fell apart because I didn't want him to know about my condition. I wanted him to think I was fine.

And it blew up in my face.

"Let me get something straight"—his voice was barely controlled— "your family saw you like that and they complained about having to pay for you to feel better? And then let the bills pile up on you the second they could? And then offered you a job barely over the poverty level?"

"They would have offered more if I hadn't gone to school for English."

"*What?* Amy, stop. Just fucking listen to me for a second. Yes, you can't control if you have a chronic disease, but it makes you no less of a person."

I swiped at my face, trying to will away the tears gathering in my eyes. "They're a burden. One I can't get away from. One that you're *mad* at."

Levi's head jerked toward me, his brow pulling low. He opened his mouth to speak, but my heart skipped a beat and I talked over him.

"I'll go lay down and get more rest," I offered. "I'll take my medicine every day and you won't be bothered again."

I turned to go to my room. By the time I came out again, I would be fine and this would all be a memory.

But his hand latched onto my wrist.

"Do you really think I'm mad because you're a burden, Amy?" His voice was dangerously low.

"Is there any other reason you'd be mad?"

He let out a humorless laugh. "I was fucking *terrified*, actually. Terrified that something was going on that I didn't know about. Terrified that this could have health repercussions and there was nothing I could do. I didn't know about the migraines and then I came in and turned the fucking lights on—" He stopped and let out a harsh breath. "And you think I'm upset because I'm inconvenienced?"

"They are an inconvenience. That's just a fact. You had things to do—"

"And what about *you*? You were the one in pain. I care about that, Amy. I don't give a shit about anything else when you're hurting. And then to find out you needed your medicine and you were just going without? That kills me. You're my wife now, and if you need anything, I'm gonna get it for you. Why is that so hard for you to believe?"

"B-because that's not how things work."

"They work that way now. Unlike the idiots who came before me, I care, Amy."

Tears gathered in my eyes, and I squeezed them shut and turned away. I didn't want to cry, not when I was the one who'd screwed up.

"Amy," Levi said gently. "What's going on? Is the pain coming back?"

"N-no," I managed to say. "I'm now at the part where I cry like a baby. I fucking hate this. I feel terrible for all of it, and I feel even worse physically. I just . . . I want to be *normal*. I don't want to live this way."

"I know, darling." His voice was soft, and for some reason, it made me sadder.

"And I hate that I need people after these damn things because the only person I had is gone and my family doesn't care. God, was it too much to ask for a hug when I was sick?"

"Absolutely not," he said. "It's never too much to ask for a hug anytime from your family. When Dad died, I wouldn't have made it without Mom being there. Or Isra. Or . . ." He trailed off. "Or my friends. And I can't imagine what it's like to have migraines and do it alone."

"It's better that way. If I do it alone, then no one can leave when they see me like this."

"Did you think I would leave?"

"Y-yes."

"Amy, *no*. I would never leave because you got sick."

"But it's gonna happen again. It always will."

"And next time I'll know how to help you. And every single time after that."

More tears fell. He wanted to help *more*?

"Can I touch you now?" he asked. "Please tell me I can."

"I don't . . . I don't want sex—"

His eyes went wide. "God, no. I just wanna hug you."

"Oh" was all I could say.

"Please?" he repeated. His voice was on the brink of desperation, like he needed this.

And I did too.

"Yeah, you can."

He let out a breath of relief and pulled me into him. I could hear his fast heartbeat with the way he pressed me into his chest. I closed my eyes.

A desire I'd had for years was finally coming true and it made a different kind of tears brim in my eyes. I didn't want to admit it, but I needed this. I needed someone to be here, to take just a pound of the burden off of my shoulders so I could breathe for a minute.

"We can wait until I'm finally on your insurance to—"

"I'll have you retroactively added. But I'll pay millions out of pocket. You're going to your specialist tomorrow."

"They're usually booked up."

"I'll call, and I'm getting you in. You're getting taken care of, darling."

"Thank you," I managed to say. "For everything."

"I'd do that and more. Anytime and any day."

My hands gripped his shirt. I didn't know why he was doing all

257

of this for me, but I knew I couldn't tell him to stop. I would take every second of this care and attention up until he decided he was done.

"I want to sleep next to you tonight. I won't touch you without permission, but I want to be there in case you need me."

"And if I don't need you?"

"Then I get to be next to you anyway."

Chapter Twenty

WHEN I OPENED my eyes the next morning, I felt more like myself. I knew not to go back to normal activity, for I'd done that many times before and wound up right where I'd started.

But the relief was palpable.

Levi's arm was slung around me loosely, keeping me close. I could only stare at him for a second and take in all he'd done in the last twenty-four hours. He wasn't going anywhere. He helped me through my migraine.

And I'd gotten him all wrong.

If he truly didn't care, he would have let me suffer. There was no one else watching, meaning he truly did it for *me*.

He may have hated Calvin, but at least a part of him cared about me. I wasn't sure which one he felt more strongly about, but I could hold on to the fact that I didn't mean nothing to him.

My mouth was dry and I was sticky in all the wrong ways. I slowly got up and went to get water and take a shower. I even had the energy to make decaf coffee.

I sat on the couch, determined to take it easy for the day. I opened my Kindle to read for a while, and found myself lost in my book. I had to take breaks to give my eyes a rest, but I was lucky that this one had retreated so quickly.

After getting to a scene that made me smile, I flipped to Discord to tell V about it out of habit.

But then I stopped when I saw the message where we'd said goodbye. I wanted to tell him about my book, about my *life*, but I knew I couldn't go against his wishes.

I sighed and closed my phone, losing all motivation to read. Instead, I slowly moved to open my blinds, wincing when I saw the bright weather.

Spring had officially sprung, and despite my lingering pain, I wanted to be out in it.

I went outside, feeling the sun on my skin. The porch was one of my favorite places to sit and I loved watching things after I'd been down-and-out for a few days. The house Calvin bought still had the note on the door and Mr. Buford was outside dumping mulch on the ground.

Wait a second.

"What are you doing?" I called over to him. "Aren't you supposed to leave the gardening to me?"

"And what, sit inside all day? I'm old, but I'm not completely decrepit."

"Let me help."

"Your hair is in a *towel*. I've got this."

I blew out a breath. "Fine."

Levi would kill me if I did anything physical anyway.

"Thank you," he said. "You know, I saw your husband's fancy car speed out of here yesterday. Is everything okay?"

I cringed. At least he hadn't seen him carrying me to it.

"Everything is fine. Nothing to worry about."

"You don't like to talk about yourself, huh?"

"Other people are more interesting."

"But friendships work two ways. I talk about me. You talk

about you. I've known you for two years, and I think it's your turn."

"He just had something to take care of."

It was nowhere near the full story, but it was more than I'd usually give, and Mr. Buford knew that.

"It seemed like he was in a rush . . . like it was an emergency."

"It kinda was, but not really. My life wasn't in danger or anything."

"So it was you?"

"Yes, but I'm fine. Levi was there and handled it. I'm lucky to have a guy like him."

"Good men are rare."

I huffed out a laugh. "You're telling me. When Gram was alive, she would tell me about the guys from her youth. She had multiple men break her heart. And then her husband was . . ." I paused when I saw Mr. Buford had stopped weeding. "Sorry, I can leave you to your work."

"No, please don't." He slowly turned to me. "You just don't mention her much."

"My gram?"

"Yes. It's nice to hear about someone so important to you."

"She was more than important to me," I said, rubbing my head. "Did you know her?"

"Of course I did. I lived next to her for fifty years. I didn't get to talk to her as much as I wanted to. She didn't like me very much."

"Why wouldn't she like you? You're so nice."

"I was an idiot young boy. And she was smart enough to stay away. You're seeing the much more mature side of me."

"It might not have been you. After getting burned so many times, she hated men as a whole."

"I'm happy to hear that you don't have the same fate. But if *any* boy does what happened to your gram, tell me. I'll make sure it doesn't happen again."

I imagined Mr. Buford swinging his cane at Levi's head and laughed. "That would be a sight."

He huffed a chuckle of his own before he turned back to his garden. His hands were still and he let out a sigh. "All right, my hip is telling me I've had enough." He moved to get up and I grabbed his arm to help him. He tried to wave me away.

"How can you tell me to ask for help when you won't?"

"Do as I say not as I do," he said. "That's my motto for life. Have a good day, kid. Hope you feel better."

He ambled away, and I slowly headed back into the house, eager to refill my coffee cup and return to reading. As I walked in, Levi came around the corner, eyes wide.

"Hey," I said. "Everything okay?"

His eyes landed on me and he made a beeline, stopping right in front of me. "I woke up and you were gone, so I . . ." He gently grabbed my shoulders. "How are you feeling?"

"Mostly back to normal," I said. "I got up and made coffee and read a bit."

He let out a sigh of relief and his shoulders slumped. "Thank God. But you didn't drink too much caffeine, right?"

"It's decaf. I have a bag of it in the back of the pantry. In fact, I'd barely consider this coffee, but it helps the cravings."

"Good. The last thing we need is for you to overdo it before you see your specialist. I called them right when I woke up."

"Did they tell you they were booked?"

"They tried to. But I got you an appointment anyway. It's at eleven."

"Okay, thank you." I picked up my phone. "I guess I need to download the Uber app."

He turned to me, face twisted in confusion. "Why would you need to do that?"

"I don't have a car."

"I'm driving you."

"You can't skip work for this."

"I'm the boss. I can do what I want. Work can wait while I make you breakfast and take you to the doctor."

"B-but—"

"Besides, Sally would kill me if I came in. Expect a delivery of flowers anytime now. She said she used the company card to get you something, and I have a feeling she went overboard."

I WAS STILL on the upswing even after the doctor's appointment where I got the lecture of my life, which was made better by the massive flower delivery from Sally. Levi made sure I took all of my medicine before we even got back home, and I planned on pulling out my Kindle and ignoring the world for a few hours.

But there was another car in the driveway when we pulled in.

"Shit," Levi muttered. "I'll get rid of them."

"Who are you getting rid of?" I asked.

"That's Isra and Nancy. When they didn't hear from you all day and I canceled last night, I told them you weren't feeling well, and now they're probably here to make sure we're eating."

"Really? They weren't mad about what happened?"

"Absolutely not. They're more worried about you. They've been texting me all day."

"R-really?"

"Yes. Just give me five minutes."

I grabbed his wrist before he could move. "We can't kick them out if they're checking on me."

"We can if you don't feel up to seeing them."

"I've done a lot more feeling a lot worse." His eyes narrowed in a silent warning. "And I *want* to see them," I quickly added. "I feel terrible that I couldn't go plant shopping."

That proved to be a better answer. "Fine. But if you get

stressed out at all, I'm sending them away. I love Isra, but she can be a lot."

"I come from nothing," I said with a sad shrug. "So a lot is kinda nice."

Levi looked back over at me, a frown etched onto his face. After a second of staring into my soul, he got out of the car. I tried to open the door, but he locked it with the key fob.

"What the—"

I stopped my complaining when he walked around to open the door for me.

"Did you really just do that?"

"You wouldn't have let me any other way," he replied.

My cheeks heated as he offered his hand. What was I going to do with this man?

"There you are!" Isra called. "I was about to look up how to break into a locked house!"

"Not so loud," Levi said gently. "She's still recovering."

"Sorry."

"We brought you food," Nancy offered. "We can either drop it off or stay."

"If you let us stay," Isra added, "I'll clean for you."

"Don't sound so desperate," Nancy hissed.

"What? I only have you for company. Can I not hope for more?"

Nancy's eyes narrowed marginally. "You *like* spending time with me."

"You guys can stay," I said as I unlocked the door with a smile. "No cleaning needed."

"I think we'll still clean," Isra said. "Whatever happened terrified poor Levi. It must have been bad."

I winced. "It was more like I had a lapse in my communication. My life was never in danger or anything."

"It doesn't have to be in danger for it to be serious," Nancy reminded.

My gaze fell to my feet. "Maybe." I pointed to the food in her hands. "I'll take that and heat it up."

She turned from me with a raised eyebrow. "I know how to use an oven."

"If you think we're letting you do a thing, you're wrong," Isra warned. "Come on, Nancy. Let's start the food before she tries to show us around."

"You might as well sit on the couch," Levi told me. "They're not letting you do a thing."

"But they're guests."

"And you were sick." His hands landed on my shoulders and he gently coaxed me to sit. "They said you were a part of the family, so you'll have to get used to them running around your house like they own the place."

I let out a long sigh and leaned back, arms crossed tightly over my chest. "This feels weird."

"We're done," Nancy said, walking back in. "Now, how about you tell us what you need and we do it for you?"

"That's gonna be an uphill battle," Levi said. "She's very stubborn about accepting help."

Isra crossed her arms, and I wondered if I was about to get *another* lecture.

"Nothing needs to be done. I've been handling my brain lighting itself on fire for over ten years. I can keep my life running while it does."

Isra looked bewildered. "Brain lighting itself on fire," she repeated. "Is that an English phrase I haven't heard yet?"

"It's her trying to make light of what happened," Levi grumbled.

"They're migraines," I said. "Just migraines."

"*Just?*" Nancy asked. "Good Lord, honey. Those things are terrible."

"And this one was a nine," Levi added.

"Okay, okay. I was out of my medicine and I should have

handled being out of my medicine differently. No one needs to gang up on Amy anymore."

"You remind me of who I was before I realized people were there for me," Isra said pointedly. "There's no pride in doing it alone. Only loneliness."

"That's the thing. No one *wanted* to before."

"What's your parents' address again? I . . . need to know . . . for *science*."

"They're hopeless," Levi said. "Trust me, I've met them."

"You're probably the best thing to come out of that, then," Nancy said.

"My sister is pretty cool too."

"We'll have to meet her."

"I don't know," Levi said. "Isra and Emma might burn down the world."

"Then I *definitely* should meet her," Isra said.

I glanced over at Levi, unable to help the intrusive thought that popped into my head. Would he be around for long enough for all of that to happen? Or would he get bored?

Levi wound his hand through mine. It wasn't an answer, but it made me feel better.

"So *what* are we going to do the next time you get sick?" Isra asked.

"Take my medicine."

"Yes. And call your family."

"They mean them," Levi explained.

"But you guys don't have to do that."

"You're part of the family now," Nancy said it like it was obvious.

"And our family takes care of each other," Isra added. "Even when we drive each other crazy."

"Don't I know it." Nancy rolled her eyes and Isra elbowed her.

I didn't know what else to say other than a heartfelt thank you.

"You're welcome. Now, can I have permission to sort your books? They're just thrown on the shelves!"

"Oh, sorry. I haven't had time to organize them."

Isra rubbed her hands together. "Don't apologize. Just let me at them."

I gestured for her to go ahead and she hurried into the den where I kept my books. But as she disappeared, her head peeked back out.

"Levi, I need you to come and help me."

"With what? Smut levels?"

"Sure, yeah. Whatever that is. Just come over here."

Levi glanced at me before following his stepmom with a sigh.

"Are they gonna be okay?" I asked. "I get the vibe that Isra can sometimes press Levi's buttons. And I've already done that enough for a lifetime."

"Isra and Levi get along when it matters. And you shouldn't be worrying about anything. You're resting."

"I'm a pro at worrying, just like the rest of my generation."

"You don't need to. Levi is a fixer. Let him help you."

And I had, but now that I was back to myself, I already was back to where I started. Yes, I wanted his help. But I wanted to help him too.

"I'm gonna check on them anyway." I stood. "And at the very least, I can tell Isra which shelf is which."

I made it to the den before Nancy could stop me, and I wasn't prepared for what I saw. Isra stood close to Levi, her arms crossed. I thought they were fighting, but then I heard her speak softer than I thought possible.

"You're allowed to be upset, kid. At least in front of me. And don't try to tell me you're fine again. I know you're not."

"I thought the days of me coming home to someone in pain were over," he said lowly. "I guess they're not."

"Why she didn't tell you is between you two, but I hope you'll tell her what it meant to you."

"It doesn't matter."

"Come on—"

"She needs me. That's what I care about."

"Levi, *no*. When your dad died, you jumped in to help Nancy and me. More than any child should."

"I was an adult."

"You were *our* child. We should have been there for you."

"You were grieving."

"And so were you. When did you take time to do that?"

"I did it privately. With . . ." His eyes moved toward the door, as if he were about to look out into the distance. They landed on me instead. "Amy." He stepped away from Isra. "Is everything okay?"

"I . . . I was just checking in on everyone."

"You don't need to do that. You should be resting."

Isra's previous words rang out: *You jumped in.*

And he was jumping in now.

"I'm good. I feel better than ever, actually."

"Do you?"

Do you? I wanted to ask back, but I had a feeling I knew what he would say. Instead of starting a fight in front of his family, I smiled. "I think the food is ready. Should we all eat?"

Chapter Twenty-One

I TOOK my time getting up the next morning. Levi slept next to me the night before, but he wasn't there now, and I assumed he'd gone back to work. He needed to, especially considering he ran an entire company. But I didn't mind. Him not being here would make it easier to figure out what to say to him, would allow me to wonder if this was how things were now—him sleeping next to me every night just like we were a real couple.

But as I walked downstairs, I found him making breakfast.

"Good morning," he said. "How are you feeling?"

"Fine. The same as last night. I think it's over."

"You still need to take it easy. I figured we could watch movies all day and try to relax."

"We? Shouldn't you be leaving for work?"

"I can take another day off."

"Can you? Don't you need to be working on how to deal with everything Calvin is doing?"

He paused, but then he shook it off. "You don't need to worry about any of that."

I crossed my arms. "I'll tell you what I told Nancy. I'm a pro at worrying."

"So am I. And I want to be sure you're okay."

"I can take care of myself. You can take care of you."

Levi's eyes cut to me, and for a second, I saw his jaw tic.

And I knew that I'd stepped on a nerve.

But as soon as I saw it, it was gone.

"I know my limits," he said. His words were choppy, the only evidence of his irritation.

"Really? Do you?"

"Do *you*?" he parroted back at me.

Damn it. I'd wanted to ask him the same thing last night.

"Yes, I do."

He huffed out a humorless laugh. "The last few days have been a *great* example of that."

I wanted to be mad. I really did, but I knew he wasn't wrong. "Okay, fair. I pushed myself too far. Which means I also know when people are pushing themselves too far. Have you had time to process what happened?"

He blew out a breath. "Isra talked to you."

"No, I heard Isra talking to you. And she's right. You need to—"

"I know what I need," he snapped. "And I've got it. That's not your job."

"I'm your wife, aren't I?" I snapped back. "And don't even give me the 'this is fake' excuse. You sleep in my bed. You live with me. And yet I don't feel like your real wife."

"How could you still not feel like this is real?" Now he was mad. Really mad. I'd never seen him this way, chest heaving, face set in a glare—I was tempted to back off. But no. I'd held onto this for long enough. "I've done *everything*—"

"For me, yes! But you never let me do anything for *you*. It's all about me, and *fuck*, I don't want that."

"Why would you not want that?"

"Because if this is real, then I want to be *partners*. Not just someone you save. I want your help, yes. But I also want to help *you*, and you keep pushing me away when I know you need me, and that tells me you don't trust me."

"I trust you."

"Then open up to me!" I exploded. "I've been here waiting for you to."

The anger melted off of his face as my words *finally* sank in. "I —I didn't know you cared."

"I spend nearly all of my time with you. Why wouldn't I care?"

"I figured you saw me as who I was nine years ago, not who I am now."

What happened nine years ago was my reminder that I couldn't get too deep into this. And yet I'd slowly forgotten it as Levi had done more and more *for* me instead of *against* me.

"It was a long time ago," I said slowly. "And if you're serious about this . . . about *me*, then you have to give me something. Anything."

"I'll give you whatever you want."

"Then it needs to be *you*. Even the parts you try to hide."

He ran a hand through his hair. "I don't see why you'd want that."

"Telling me to trust you is hard. You're asking me to put my faith in you and I want the same in return."

His eyes met mine. "I didn't think of it that way."

"Did you really think this was going to be you doing everything for me?"

"Honestly, yes."

I shook my head. "Maybe someone else would want that, but I don't. So, please open up to me."

He started to speak but then stopped. "I . . . don't think I know how to."

"I can help with that. First, we're gonna talk about how this felt for *you*. That's where we start."

"But it happened to *you*."

"Come on, Levi. We're married. We've been joking about the

phrase 'what's mine is yours and yours is mine,' but there's a nugget of truth in that. I'm sure you felt some of the stress too. And I'm okay. I really am. I've recovered. So, it's time to give you space to feel how you do."

Levi's hand landed on the counter and he drummed a nervous beat as he worked out what to say. I waited, but he only seemed to grow more conflicted.

"Come on." I walked over to him and grabbed his hand to lead him to the couch.

"I have something in the toaster."

"That can wait. We're talking about this." I sat next to him. "Isra mentioned that this meant something to you."

He turned to me. "You heard that?"

"I did. And I heard how you dodged everything she was trying to say."

"I didn't want to worry her."

"Yeah, that seems to be a theme with you," I said dryly. "Now, why did you not want to open up to her?"

"Isra and I butt heads a lot, but it's because we're similar. Too similar. We try to fix things when they go wrong. When Dad died . . ." He trailed off.

"You can tell me," I urged.

"I . . . I think it was her breaking point. And Mom's. I'd never seen them like that, so I stepped in. I handled the funeral and all of it. I think both of them feel bad, but especially her. She's been trying to make up for it ever since. But they didn't do anything wrong."

"So when did you deal with it? Or did you deal with it at all?"

"I read. And I thought about what I read. Sure, it wasn't direct, but it was nice to be reminded that people can die and things would be okay. And I *am* okay. I did eventually process Dad's death. And I had someone to help me."

"A friend?"

"Yeah. They were key to it."

"Do you still have this friend?"

He thought about it, and I wondered if any of his friends did what Ava did to me. "I wasn't sure for a bit, but I think I do."

"You could talk to them if you wanted. About this. It doesn't have to be me."

"I want it to be," he said.

"Then tell me. Even about the parts I messed up."

"It's not . . . I don't want you to feel worse than you already do."

"I'm a big girl. I can handle when I screw up."

He sighed. Was I going to have to pry more? But then he *finally* spoke. "That's not the first time I've come home to someone being *very* sick. Dad knew about his cancer before he told any of us. And I didn't find out until I came home to find him passed out in his room."

My breath hitched. "Levi, I—"

"Just let me finish. If I don't, I don't know if I'll ever say it."

I nodded and gestured for him to continue.

"You didn't know, but I can't help but wonder *why* you didn't tell me. Or why Dad didn't. I've spent my entire life wanting to fix things for people, and yet they never trust me. If I could take back everything I've done to start over, I would. Because obviously, I got it wrong somewhere."

"Levi, no." I leaned forward and grabbed his hand. "Even if you did start over, no one is perfect. We hurt each other and make a mess of things . . . just like I did when I didn't tell you about the migraines. I should have. A marriage is no place for secrets."

He opened his mouth to say something, but I stopped him.

"It's my turn to talk for a bit because there's so much I need to say." I took a shaky breath. "My choice had to do with *me*. My reasons for not telling you were my own insecurities. I felt like you wouldn't want to do this once you knew, and I was wrong. I'm sorry."

"It's fine."

"We can call it many things, but fine isn't one of them. I fucked up and I own up to it, okay?"

"It's not like I don't understand your point of view. If I grew up with a family like yours . . . I'd be in the same position."

"It wasn't all that bad," I said.

Levi gave me a doubtful look. "Are you sure about that?"

"I had Gram," I reminded him. "She's the one who got me to the doctor. She took all of this very seriously and she wanted me to as well. Now that she's gone . . . I think I'm forgetting some of the lessons she wanted me to learn."

"I understand. Dad was always on me for fixing things too much, and yet here I am."

"We might need to remind ourselves."

"We can be a team," I said. "I can remind you if you do the same for me."

"And that's what you want? With me?"

Gram's lessons were still fresh on my mind, and her biggest one was trust. She'd told me never to trust someone unless I was one hundred percent sure they wouldn't hurt me.

And there were still things I needed to talk to Levi about. There were still questions.

But I *wanted* this.

"Yes," I said. "Do you?"

"More than anything."

A CALL from Sally was ultimately what made Levi go back to work, despite him insisting he wanted to stay at home with me. Apparently, one of their best workers had interviewed with Calvin, and wanted to offer more intel on what my brother was offering.

Levi offered to still stay home, but I told him he should handle it and we could talk later.

He made me promise to call him if I started to feel any worse.

I wasn't worried about it. The plan was to take it easy, and I did exactly that. I was able to finally style my curls and look more presentable, then I sat on the couch with a book while my hair dried.

At noon, I was trying to figure out if I should have lunch when my phone rang and Emma's name flashed on the screen.

"My God," she said when I answered. "Having a reliable car is a lifesaver when you live in the middle of nowhere."

"I'm glad you have one," I said.

"But I'll give it back if Levi didn't hold up his end of the agreement," she said. "Did he?"

"Not yet."

"See, I knew he was lying—"

"Not because he didn't want to, but because we got a little busy."

"With?"

I blew out a breath. Levi's and his family's concern was a reminder of how much I didn't talk about my issues.

And Emma didn't deserve that.

"The ER. I had another bad migraine."

"Oh, shit," she said. "I knew you seemed a little off."

"It might have been one of the worst I've ever had. I was completely out of my medicine and—"

"Why were you out of your medicine?" she cut in.

"Is there any chance you could *not* grill me on this? Trust me, I've heard so many lectures about this that I can't take any more."

"I'll do my best. What happened?"

"I ran out after Calvin fired me, and I wasn't on Levi's insurance yet."

"But don't health benefits last for bit? Like the rest of the month?"

"Not when Calvin is the one making the decision."

"That *dick*!" she snapped. "Fuck, I hate him."

"I do too," I said. "And I made some pretty bad choices. When Levi walked in, he was pretty freaked out."

"Did this happen before or after you told him?"

"Before," I admitted with a wince.

"*No*. Amy, I told you to—"

"I know! But it all happened so fast. And to make matters worse, I found out this was a recurring thing for him. His dad did this same thing with his cancer diagnosis."

I heard Emma suck in a breath. "Seriously?"

"Yeah. Not my finest moment."

"How bad was the fight?"

"Actually . . . He wasn't as mad as I deserved. Especially since he's about to get a massive ER bill after this."

"Why are you worried about money? You married a rich guy!"

"Even if he's rich, it doesn't mean he wants to spend that much money on me."

"I wish I was in front of you so I could smack you. Amy, *come on*."

"Mom and Dad were nearly as rich as he is, and they still fucking complained."

"And they're shitty people. They wanted to spend their time and money on their worst kid."

"I know," I said miserably. "Levi said the same thing."

"And do you have a reason to not believe him?"

"Not that he's given me."

"But the ones Mom and Dad gave you?"

"You saw how they acted."

"And I wanted to kick them in the shins, but I had a feeling you would hate that."

"It didn't occur to me that life could be different until . . . Levi. He's offered to solve every single one of my problems, and I can't help but wait until the other shoe drops and he's gone."

"Please. That's not gonna happen."

"And how do you know that?"

"Amy, you're married to a guy who's obsessed with you. When I went to the store with him, he wouldn't shut up about you. I get that you're protecting yourself or whatever, but it sounds like it's an excuse to keep him at arm's length instead of giving yourself the happy ending you deserve."

"He only talked about me?"

"Yes. And he lit up like a kid at Christmas as he did so. It was so cute that it made me want to throw up."

"I'm being dumb, aren't I?"

"Very."

"And somehow you're the smart one."

"I had years of you guiding me to get me to this moment. Don't worry, in a few weeks I'll do something else stupid and you'll have to save my ass. Besides, this is the first time you've gotten close to someone. You're bound to have a hard time. Your emotions are all tangled up in this."

"I really underestimated how hard it would be."

"I think he's a good guy, though. Doesn't that count for something?"

It did. Emma didn't see the good in people. My entire life, she told me that our family sucked, or my one-night stands weren't good enough for me, even for one night of sex.

"One of these days you'll see yourself as others do. You could ask that woman you had at the wedding."

"You mean Lily?"

"The one with the brown hair and freckles? She seemed nice."

"She is," I said.

"I bet she'd back me up. If she doesn't, then she sucks."

"She doesn't suck." My eye caught on the window, where the very person I was talking about was walking up. "She's actually coming over right now."

"Good. You should hang out with her. I need to go into work anyway."

I told her goodbye and opened the front door.

"Hey," I said to Lily. "How are you?"

"With me? Everything is fine. But I haven't seen you on your walks for a while."

"You notice my walks?"

She put a hand on her hip. "You're the one who taught me how fun observing people in the neighborhood is."

"I didn't know you'd use it against me so fast."

"I'm not using anything against you. I'm merely curious."

"Everything is fine now," I said.

"But it wasn't fine before?"

"There's been a lot. You could come in and catch up."

"I was gonna walk to the coffee shop since it finally warmed up. We could include Riley in this catch-up."

I looked at the weather outside. The birds were chirping and more flowers were starting to bloom. I'd missed so much while being inside.

"I want to, but I might need to take it slow. A part of what happened was me getting sick."

"You got sick?" Lily's eyes grew wide. "We can drive if you want to."

"No, it's such a nice day. I'll be fine as long as we're patient."

"I can do that. And if it's too much, I'll come back and get my car."

THE WARM SMELL of coffee hit my nose, and I was relieved to see Riley standing behind the counter. We must have come at a good time because, for once, there wasn't a line to the door.

"Hey, you two," Riley said when she saw us. "I was beginning to wonder when I'd see the both of you again."

"I'm taking a break from writing so I don't burn out," Lily said. "But I finally got Amy out of the house, so this is a special occasion."

"And it's not too busy, so I can finally hear what's going on with you and Levi."

"You can also hear about my last life event."

"You had *another*?" Riley asked.

"Does going to the ER count as a life event?"

Both women's eyes grew wide.

"What?" Lily asked first. "When the hell were you in the ER?"

"Are you okay?" Riley added. "Do you need anything?"

"No, I'm okay now. I was only there for a few hours two days ago for a migraine. I'll just probably need decaf today. Too much caffeine might bring it back."

"Is that why your car has been gone?" Lily asked.

"Um, no. I gave that to my sister, but that was before."

"So, a lot's happened. But the migraine—was it your first one?"

"No, it wasn't. I tend to keep them to myself since it used to bother people that I had them."

"Shouldn't it bother *you* the most since you have them?" Riley asked.

"My family kinda sucks," I said. "I'm trying to unlearn it since I feel terrible that Levi found out the way he did, but it's hard."

"Oh," they both said at the same time.

"On that note," Lily added after a while, "I hope you're ready for me to be really annoying. If you disappear, I'm checking in on you."

"I'm back on my medicine, so hopefully it'll lessen them."

"And I'll be watching your caffeine intake too," Riley said. "One a day. Maybe two if I'm feeling nice."

"Come on, guys. You don't have to worry too much about me."

"We're your friends," Lily said. "Does this have something to do with Calvin?"

"Who's Calvin?" Riley asked.

"My brother." I rolled my eyes. "I don't know if you saw it, but he tried to show up at the wedding . . ."

"I saw some drama, but I was dealing with a meltdown from my youngest," she replied. "Was he not invited or something?"

"No, he wasn't. But neither he nor my parents listen. Still, a lot of people think he's the better of the two of us. A lot of people use me to get to him."

"First of all, that's terrible. And second, what makes him better exactly?" Riley asked.

"He's popular. Rich. Everyone loves him."

"Everyone?" she countered. "How good of a person is he?"

"He's terrible."

"Does he have a good sense of humor?"

"Not really."

"And does he have any *close* friends?"

"I don't know. I personally don't wanna get close enough to find out."

Riley wrinkled her nose. "Then he's fake. And definitely not better."

"Someone tell my parents that."

"Parents sometimes pick a favorite," Riley said. "My mom did, and it definitely wasn't me. Thankfully, she came around, but I'm lucky. And even so, it did a lot of damage. The kind that I tried to hide."

"I could see you doing that," Lily said.

"Don't let your brother make you feel like you're not enough. Or walk all over you."

"She doesn't always let him walk all over her." Lily turned to me. "You wanna tell her about the house?"

"Oh yeah, I stole a house from him."

"What?"

"He got it in my gram's will and he didn't deserve to have it," I said. "He was gonna sell it to have the money to build a pool at his place."

"I need this whole story," Riley said. "But just from what I'm hearing, I'd rather have you as a friend."

"Me too," Lily added.

"Both of you are the first."

"Then you were around shitty people," Lily said. "You were *so* friendly when we met. I didn't even think you would want to know me because I'm nowhere in your sphere of niceness. You were friends with Riley first."

"Friends is a strong word."

"I wanted to be friends," Riley said. "I figured you had too many, though. You're so fun."

My cheeks heated. That's how people saw me?

Damn it. Emma was right. When I told her, she would never let me live it down.

"I guess I didn't know that."

"Do I have explicit permission to force you into friendship?" Riley asked. "I'll do it."

"I'll help," Lily added.

I couldn't help but laugh. "You totally do. You have my number."

"You're either gonna regret this or love this," Riley said. "But I'll start by giving you decaf for free."

"You don't have to—"

"I owe you a wedding present *and* a you-were-sick present. Shut the fuck up and let me do something for you."

"Yes, ma'am."

"It's so nice to be talking to adults," she said as she stepped to the side to grab coffee. "I can't say fuck when I'm talking to my kids."

She handed me the cup and deflated when she looked behind us. I did the same and saw a line had formed.

"I'll talk to you later," I offered with a bright smile.

"Life sucks when you have to do your job," she muttered.

Lily grabbed my arm and led me to a table.

"Okay, so what have we learned today?" she asked.

"That my self-esteem sucks and it's my parents' fault?"

"And?"

"That I have friends?"

"Good. You're learning."

"I'm trying. Having Levi there really showed me that I need help in those moments. When Calvin fired me, I ran out of my medicine and didn't see a way to get it. Levi made it happen."

"You said you were back on it. Why did you go off of it?"

"Without insurance, it's over two grand. And that's just one of them."

"I would have paid for it," she said immediately.

"What?"

"I have enough money saved up."

"But I don't know if I could pay you back."

"*Oh no*, I'm out a little bit of money but my friend gets to feel okay? That's *so* terrible."

"Still, it's a lot to ask of someone. Would you ever ask that of me?"

Lily blew out a breath. "Okay, good point. But you'd do it."

"Yes."

"And I would do the same for you."

"You *also* have a good point."

"Why haven't you told anyone?"

"It's hard for me to talk about the things I don't like about my life. I wanna be happy-go-lucky all the time, but I can't be. Sometimes, I'm holed up in bed with pain so bad I can't move. It's annoying for both me and the people around me."

"But you can't do anything about it. And I know for a fact that I care about you. I can help."

I smiled at her. "I'm getting it. I promise. It's weird to actually have friends."

"I know," she replied. "But we're gonna make it work. Plus, your fake husband seems to help you."

"I don't know if it's fake anymore."

"Oh . . . interesting."

"You don't sound shocked."

"I'm not. You kept saying you weren't gonna fall for him, but it honestly sounded like you were trying to convince yourself more than you were trying to convince me."

I rubbed my neck. "You caught that, huh?"

"Yep. Though, I still don't know the details, and you better start spilling. And then prepare to tell Riley again once she's done with that line."

"IT'S *MARCH*," Lily panted as we walked back to the house. "How is it so hot?"

"This is insulting," I said. "Where did this heat come from?"

She shook her head. When we'd left my house, there was still a cool breeze wafting through the air that made the trek there easy. We'd stayed at the café until later in the afternoon while catching up, which allowed the sun to bake the roads.

"Note to self," Lily said, "we drive next time, even if it feels nice when we leave."

"I'm on strict bed rest," I replied. "So I'm gonna get some water before I give myself another headache."

"You better!" she said, and with a wave, she disappeared into her own house. I walked into mine and got the biggest glass I could find. I was chugging it when the front door opened.

Levi's eyes found me immediately.

"What are you doing back?" I asked. "It's not even five."

"And what are you doing looking like you just worked out?"

Busted.

"That's the weather's fault. Lily and I took a walk to the coffee shop. It was fine on the way there, but it got so hot on the way back. I'm chugging this to be sure I don't get a headache."

"Amy . . ."

"I'm okay!" I insisted. "Seriously. I feel normal. And I took my medicine today. Everything is fine. Besides, you didn't answer my question."

"I wanted to check on you and be sure you weren't overdoing it."

"Ah. Well. I *tried* not to. The sun betrayed me. Besides, I have to go back to normal living eventually. I know this was scary for you, but this wasn't my first rodeo."

"It wasn't, but I'm not all that sure you have your own best interests in mind."

"I did have a massive migraine that landed me in the hospital to prove that I was wrong. I'm listening now, I promise. I don't need you to get all overprotective of me."

His shoulders slumped. "You know why I'm doing it, right?"

"Because you have a crush on me and I'm the light of your life?"

"You sound like you're joking, but that's actually the reason. I want to take care of you."

"And you have. But I wanted to spend time with Lily and feel a little normal."

"Did it help?"

"Yes. And I got some surprisingly good advice from Emma when she called."

"What did she call about?"

"She was checking in to see if you got me the car, and I told her about the migraine and stalled her. I'll have to get a rental after this so she doesn't force me to take my old car back."

"Why would you need a rental? We're still getting you whatever you want."

"Are you serious, a whole-ass car?"

"As opposed to what, a half-ass car?"

"I—you know what I mean. That's expensive, and with the medical bills—"

"Stop worrying about all of that. I'm paying for it all."

God, I needed to message Riley and see if her rich husband did this same thing. I had no idea how to respond.

But I did want a new car.

"Fine. Thank you."

"Are you listening to me now?"

"Only when I want to. What's my budget?"

"No budget."

"What? Come on, you have to have something. Give me a number."

"There isn't one. You're getting what you want. So tell me what it is."

"An SUV is fine. I just want space for gardening. It can be used—"

"It won't be."

"But it *could* be. Then again, there's one I've always liked the look of."

"Tell me what it is. A Volvo? A Mercedes?"

"It's a Toyota."

"Seriously?" he asked.

"Don't make fun of me. I like what I like, and that's practical. Besides, have you *seen* car prices?"

He pulled out his phone and looked it up. When I saw way too many tens of thousands, I said, "See? That's *so* much."

"Amy, this is nothing. What color do you want?"

"C-color? Why?"

"I'm finding one for you."

"There's a gray that looks kinda green. I always do a double take when I see it."

"Got it," he said. "We'll go to get it tomorrow."

"Are you su—" He gave me a flat look. "Okay, sorry. We're going tomorrow."

"Good girl," he replied. "Now, take your water and sit."

"Why? Do you have big plans?"

"We're gonna relax," he replied. "And maybe read."

That sounded like the perfect plan, one that I couldn't wait to get started on.

Chapter Twenty-Two

"IF ANYTHING IS GONNA GIVE me a migraine," I muttered to Levi, "it's this damn car dealership."

"Not funny," he replied.

"I finally have someone who knows everything and I can't even joke about my disability?"

He huffed out a laugh. "You can after I've had five to ten business days to process the trauma you put me through."

"We live in fast times. Get with the program."

"You're ridiculous."

"But you like me."

His hand threaded through mine. "That I do."

Levi wasn't going to have me join him at the dealership after working the morning in the office, but my being here made it easier to put the car in my name. It should have been a simple transaction, yet we had to wait way too long as salespeople tried to get us into a more expensive car.

One look at it told me that I had what I wanted. I didn't consider myself very picky, but this car had features I could only dream of. It was the highest trim with floor liners for all of the gardening I was about to do. The second I got behind the wheel, it felt like mine.

"I could pretend to have a migraine to get us outta here faster."

"I don't think it'll work," he said. "They should be getting the paperwork ready."

Levi was right, and thankfully, we were able to sign and leave soon after. I couldn't help the excitement that hit me as I drove in something that was *mine*.

On the way to get an early dinner, I called Emma to tell her that Levi had held up his end of the deal and that she had no reason to worry. We talked until I pulled up beside Levi's car at the restaurant.

After eating, I was still feeling good about life, but when I got home, I received a text from Calvin.

CALVIN

Are you coming to my party? It starts soon.

It's the only way I get to celebrate your wedding, after all.

"You're gonna have to work on your parking in the driveway," Levi said. "You're used to smaller cars."

"Ah, yeah. Probably."

He turned to me. "What's wrong? And don't say it's nothing."

I wanted to, but his call out made me rethink my choices. "Calvin just sent a reminder about his dumb party."

"The stock price one?" he asked before rolling his eyes. "And, of course, it's because of this damn mental health thing he's pushing."

"So then we have plans tonight. We need to go."

"You just recovered from a migraine. There's no way we're going."

"I'm over it. I can easily go." At his answering glare, I added,

"The whole point of this was to piss off Calvin and we've not done very much to accomplish that. I'll be fine."

"You keep saying that, but I don't think you know what fine means. Migraines take days to recover from."

"Levi," I said as we entered the house. "I truly am okay. The medicine I'm on is very effective and getting back on it so quickly helped. But if I feel anything in my head, I'll tell you, okay?"

"Will you really?"

"*Yes.* But you've said Calvin is hurting your business, and you just spent days taking care of me. Let me do this one thing for you."

He sighed but nodded. "Fine. But only if you're honest with me."

"I promise I will be."

"Do you still have the invitation?"

"Yeah, I think I threw it in my mail sorter." I grabbed it and handed it over.

"It says it's at five. Does this man ever work?"

"And yet you're here."

"I'm here because I had to help my wife. Trust me, I have plenty of things I need to do when I get back tomorrow."

"Like find a way to make him look bad for poaching your employees?"

"I can't believe what he's doing is even legal," Levi muttered. "But no. I have a connection with a talent agency and I'm making sure my benefits are as good as his. Even though he's offering things he can't afford. I'm working on expanding to rural areas right now on top of everything else."

"Rural areas. I remember something about that when I was asleep in meetings."

He laughed. "They're underserved. Very much so."

"Then it sounds good. And you know what's even better? You telling me these things."

"I'm really surprised you care, considering how little you liked your parents' company."

"I disliked it because they steamrolled me. You're not doing that." I checked the time. "I would talk longer, but I do need to get dressed. At least I already did my hair."

I had quite a few cute things, but one of my favorites was a dress with lemons on it. It had a fitted waist and made my curves look even better than they usually did. I'd yet to have a place to wear it, and Levi told me to wear something nice, so I threw it on and did my makeup while Levi grabbed a dress shirt and slacks and got changed in the bathroom.

Levi waited in the living room in his new outfit and watched me as I walked down the stairs.

He froze. "You look . . ."

"Is it too much?"

"I was gonna say incredible."

"I've had this dress forever and—"

He crossed the room and pulled me into his arms. "And you'll have to wear it more often. This is my favorite thing you've ever worn."

"What about my wedding dress?"

"Ah. Well. I suppose this is a close second." He looked down. "Maybe it takes the number one spot. I can't tell."

A giggle escaped me and I grabbed my purse. "You'll have all night to figure it out, I guess. Ready to go?"

"More than anything."

Going to Calvin's house always solidified my confusion on why he wanted Gram's so bad. And why she had given it to him in the first place. To say he had a mansion wasn't enough. He had more than that, all sprawled out on perfectly mowed land. Cars were parked on the grass and people were everywhere, reminding me just how many people he'd gotten in his corner over the years.

I took a shaky breath. I was dreading how poorly this could go. I was dreading even seeing Levi and Calvin in the same room, because when my brother wasn't present, it was easier to pretend that Levi was here for *me* and no one else.

When we got out of the car, I felt like I couldn't move.

Then a hand grabbed mine.

"Say the word and we'll leave."

I shook my head. "We have people to piss off."

"I don't give a fuck. You're my wife and you come first."

I loved it when he called me his wife, but I also hated it. Deep down, I knew more than anything that I wanted to be someone's *something*. Whether it be wife or a friend, or even a partner. For far too long, everything was about Calvin, and I wanted Levi to be *mine*.

But all roads led to Calvin in the end. This had been the way of the world for so long that I didn't feel sad about it anymore. It was only a fact of life. I was not as important as my brother.

Still, Levi's hand helped as we walked through the front door.

We waded through the people, all there for him. Did other people throw a party like this over rising stocks? I had no clue.

"Son of a bitch," Levi muttered. "He has five of my practitioners here."

Levi was looking at a group of guys huddled in the corner, all talking among themselves. I hadn't seen him look this irritated in a while. It was a sore reminder of his competitiveness, no matter what he had said previously.

"We should go say hi. I bet they wouldn't expect to see you here."

"Are you sure?"

"Yeah. In this group of people, there's no one that I'd like to talk to more." I followed him through the crowd. I smiled and waved as if I knew his former employees. "Hi! It's nice to see you! Have you met my husband, Levi?"

Levi took over, calling them each by their names. He plastered on an easygoing smile and asked about their personal lives. I did my best to play the happy wife while he schmoozed.

But then I saw a flash of brown hair and a familiar face.

Ava was staring at me from within the crowd.

Calvin was nowhere to be found, and I wondered if she'd been left in the dust while he found other people. A wad of cotton formed in my mouth. I knew that feeling better than anyone else.

"Excuse me," I said, patting Levi's shoulder. "I'll be right back."

His hand on my waist gripped me tighter. "What's wrong?"

"Nothing," I said. "I saw an old friend in the crowd. I wanna say hi."

He nodded and let me go, and I moved in Ava's direction.

She walked off and into the kitchen, head hung low. I followed her.

"Hey," I said. "Enjoying the party?"

She turned. "Are *you*?"

"Kinda. It's a lot of business talk. Is Calvin not hanging out with you?"

"It's fine. I got *all* of him this morning."

I cringed. I did *not* need to know that.

"So, are you two dating?" I asked.

"Of course. I couldn't believe when he contacted me a few weeks ago. I thought he'd forgotten about me."

He probably had. Until I got married to his enemy.

Calvin knew that Ava was my friend first. And he'd gone after her anyway, just like he always did. I didn't want to pop Ava's bubble, but I didn't want to leave her in the dark either.

"That's funny," I said. "That's right when I announced my engagement."

"Oh yeah. Levi, right? Kind of a bold move, going after an enemy like that."

"He's not *my* enemy."

"Sure, but there's a history there. You really hurt Calvin's feelings."

I blinked. "I wasn't aware that I had to consider his feelings when choosing a partner."

"I know you don't want to. Leave it to Amy to make it all about her." She walked to the doorway and glanced at Levi. "Seems you're in familiar territory. He's over there talking business without a second thought about you. There's not even a chair for you."

I followed her line of sight; Levi *did* seem focused on his conversation. He'd found a seat, the only one open, chatting away with the clients Calvin was trying to steal.

"Are you trying to make me feel bad?"

"It's pretty easy to," she said with a smile. "You have so many insecurities."

That familiar feeling of rage flooded me. She used to be my friend. Why would she want to pick at all of my insecurities? Why couldn't she simply *be my friend*?

"I don't have any insecurities."

"We'll see if that's true the longer he ignores you."

"You have no idea what our marriage is like."

"Oh yeah? I bet it's quiet. He works all the time and you're left at home by yourself. I can tell by the bags under your eyes that you had one of those headaches of yours. And I have a feeling he didn't even notice."

I laughed. Everything she said was wrong. I shrugged. "If that makes you feel better."

"Calvin tells me how jealous you are. About how you'll do anything to pull ahead. And marrying Levi? We both know it's not because you love him. You might love his money, though."

I wasn't going to let her make me feel bad about my marriage. Not after everything Levi and I had been through.

"You know, I was hoping to catch up with you, but your conversation skills suck. I'm gonna go to where I'm actually appreciated."

"So you're just gonna stand by his side like a good little wife?"

"No. You might have missed it, but my *favorite* seat is open."

I brushed by her and walked right to my husband. And without another word, I plopped myself right into his lap.

Levi didn't miss a beat. His hand curled onto my hip, pulling me closer.

"Hi, darling." His voice was low and warm. "To what do I owe the pleasure?"

"I missed you," I said loud enough for everyone to hear, but I leaned in and lowered my voice. "And my former friend Ava is here."

"Is this all for show?"

"Well, it *is* a comfortable seat."

"It's always open for you."

His hand tightened on my hip and I turned to everyone and asked what I'd missed.

The conversation between Levi and his clients went well, and I smiled whenever they laughed. Eventually, we moved to one of the other rooms to let someone else have the one chair, yet Levi's arm was still slung around me no matter where we went.

"I got one of them to send me the offer letter they received," Levi said once we'd broken from the group. "I didn't think I could do that. They seemed to only want attention."

"And the free food."

"Is this what he does? Charms people with these parties?"

"It's not just the parties. People have always been drawn to Calvin. He makes them feel what they want, and ultimately, he gets what he wants. It's how it works."

"Flattery doesn't work on everyone."

"Does it not?" I asked. "He gets all the attention."

Levi opened his mouth to argue, but we were interrupted by cheers for the man of the house. Calvin came out, all smiles, as he saw everyone.

It dropped when he saw us.

I excused myself to get a drink, Levi following me. Calvin found us not long after.

"Hi," he said, looking in between the two of us as Levi slid an arm around me. "There's the happy couple. I can't believe I missed the wedding."

"I can," Levi said. "Considering I told you to leave."

He shrugged as if it were water under the bridge, but his eyes zeroed in on Levi. "Always good to see you. Tell me, did it get any better after I left?"

Levi's arm tightened. "It was perfect after you were gone."

"You'll have to send me photos. Gram's old shack doesn't usually clean up that well."

"It's not a shack," I hissed, "it's a house."

"It's something. I bet there are far nicer things that could fit on that land, don't you think?"

"No. Families and memories are enough."

"You're so . . . hopeful." Calvin turned to Levi. "Is that what you saw in my dear sister? I can't really think of anything else that would bring you two together."

I gripped my water cup tighter. "Damn. You're really choosing to be an ass tonight. I thought a part of this party was for the wedding."

"It was on the invitation. I can't help it that people came only for me."

"For all your success, right?" I asked. "How's your real estate business venture going, then?"

I smirked when he frowned. I couldn't wait to see Levi's face when he found out that they'd been shut down.

"I've hit a snag with the government, but I'll get it sorted soon enough. It's just a temporary pause."

"Such a shame that the city cares about historic homes and stopped demolition," Levi said.

"Yes, it's—wait, how did you know?"

I could have asked the same question. I told him about the

house— not the delay in demolition. Then my brain slowly caught up. Maybe he walked by the house and saw it. *Duh.*

"When my wife told me, I was shocked that they'd tear it down, considering the historical significance. I called the city to double-check and they said they didn't have the required permits." Levi took a sip of his drink. "Odd."

Calvin's eyes grew wide. "You called them on me?"

"Just out of curiosity. You know how it is. But they tend to look closer once they know you're trying to fly under the radar. I hope you have everything under control and didn't do anything unsavory to get that house."

Calvin's jaw ticked at Levi's thinly veiled threat. He was good at this.

And as much as I wanted to revel in Calvin's annoyance, a prickle of discomfort made its way up my spine. Sure, getting him mad was the goal, but good things didn't happen to me when Calvin was like this. Usually, he made my life a living hell.

"We should let you say hello to your other guests," I said, grabbing Levi's arm. "Don't worry, we'll entertain ourselves."

I dragged my husband away to the hallway where I took a deep breath. "What's going on?" His hand touched my elbow. "Do we need to leave?"

"I forgot how scary Calvin can be when he's angry. Sorry, I'll be up for more revenge in a second."

"Scary? Has he done anything to you?" Levi's voice was low and dangerous. It made my skin tingle.

"He just finds a way to make me miserable, mostly. Like with trying to tear down that house and firing me. Apparently, it makes me nervous when I purposefully test him."

"Whatever he does, we'll handle together, okay?" His hand moved to my chin and he tilted my head up to look at him. "And if he hurts you, then he deals with *me*."

"Levi, there you are. I've been looking for you everywhere." We both turned to see one of Levi's practitioners coming down the hallway. "I wanted to discuss some business with you. Do you have a second?"

"I was talking to my wife about something."

"It's okay," I said. "I'm fine. It sounds important."

Levi frowned. "But—"

"Seriously, it's fine. I'll be outside, okay?" I walked off before he argued any further. I didn't know what he was doing talking to me when he had so many other things to deal with.

When I got out into the fresh air, I could breathe better. I was on my own, and through the glass door, I could see everything that was going on. If Levi needed me, I'd know.

I had a few blissful minutes alone before the door opened and the last person I expected walked out.

"Ava," I said. "Still alone?"

Her eyes were devoid of any kindness. I didn't have a doubt that she was back to make me feel even worse.

"Is your husband done with you again?"

"He has some business to talk about. He's a CEO, after all."

"I find that the right CEO always has time for those around them." She flicked her hair over her shoulder. "Mine always makes time for me."

"That's great."

"He's so sweet. Attentive too. He sent me the biggest bouquet of flowers at work. What did Levi get for you again?"

"Books, mostly."

"Oh, interesting." She waved her hand. "Cute, if that's your thing."

"I think I see Calvin in there. Don't you wanna go talk to him?" At her shrug, something in me snapped. "Unless he sent you out here for me."

Ava rolled her eyes. "Obviously, he didn't. You think he's obsessed with you."

"That she does. She always thinks everything has to do with her."

That wasn't the voice I wanted to hear. Chills broke out over my skin and I turned to see Calvin had joined us. He threw a casual arm around Ava and pulled her close.

"Hi, babe." She smiled and pulled him into a frankly gross kiss that I had to look away from.

"What are you doing out here, Amy?" Calvin asked.

"Just wanted some air."

"Or did you want to look at my empty yard? The pool would have been long open if you'd let me have my way."

Oh, *come on*. Was he still on about this? "I'm sure you'll find a way to get your pool. Stocks are up."

Ava scoffed. "You do realize it's the principle, right?"

"You do realize that your little boyfriend has money, right? I mean, look at this house. It's so big it's ridiculous. I got Gram's old 'shack,' as you called it. There's no reason for us to be fighting over this."

His eyes narrowed. "You took what's mine."

"And you have everything else," I snapped. "Let it go."

"Like you let it go? You married Levi to get under my skin."

"What?" I asked, voice high. "No, I didn't."

"You know what? That sounds like something she'd do," Ava said, rolling her eyes.

"Just like he found you to make me jealous?" I said to her. "Do you really think he found you just because he missed you? He did it right when I got engaged."

Ava stiffened. "You don't know anything."

"It's just perfect timing."

"Just like your marriage," Calvin added. "Ava, go inside. It's time for me to talk to my sister alone."

I thought she would fight him on it, but all Ava did was nod and leave us. I didn't realize how much I didn't want to be alone with Calvin until I was. My heart stuttered as I faced him down.

"Right when I *finally* get everything, you have to ruin it. I don't know how you found him, but I don't buy your little love story. I know he only cares about making me mad, and he'll never care about you."

"And if you're wrong?"

"Oh, I'm not. I know how you work." He stepped closer, now in my face. "You always have to have something from me because you can't accept that you're second best."

"You think I don't know that?"

"Not enough, apparently. Because you're still in my way. And I will stop at *nothing* to be sure you get what you deserve."

Something about his voice, the dark tone of it, the way he glared, sent me back to when we were kids, when he would push me down the playground stairs for interrupting him or yell at me for being in the way.

Back then, he'd just been a kid. Now, he had *power*. He'd taken away my job and my health insurance. He was trying to ruin my neighborhood.

And my *life*.

What else was he capable of? What would he do if he found the few people I cherished? The ones who liked me for me?

"Who the fuck do you think you're talking to?" A hand clamped around my arm, pulling me away from Calvin's too-close position in front of me. Levi's voice was angry and when I turned to him, my breath caught. His eyes were narrowed, his chest puffed up. He looked like he was one word away from punching Calvin.

He was this mad *for me*.

And while it shouldn't have, it filled me with a warm feeling that someone cared enough to get this angry for me.

"I think I'm talking to my little sister."

"Actually, you're talking to my *wife*. And I don't tolerate your bullshit like everyone else does."

"You're really getting defensive over *her*? You do realize who you married, right?"

"I'm very aware of who I married. The only person fucking lost is *you*, so let's clear a few things up. Amy is my *wife*, and I'm in love with her. If I ever catch you intimidating her like that again, I'll show you exactly what a weak little bitch you are. Do I make myself clear?"

"T-this isn't wrestling in freshman year anymore."

"I'm always up for a rematch, Calvin. Especially when you mess with someone I love."

"You can't touch me."

"Can I not? Remember, Calvin, it took one call for me to shut down your little revenge tactic on your sister, and you cut all control you had on her when you fired her. And I'll be sure you can't do anything else to her."

"And when you're done with her?"

"You'll be waiting a long fucking time for that."

Calvin's eyes widened and then his anger returned.

I didn't have time to feel anything about Levi's declaration. All I knew was that my fear was back and my stomach was roiling with unease.

"W-we should go," I said, grabbing Levi's arm. "I think I've hit my limit of drama."

Levi turned to me, his expression softening the second his eyes met mine. "Okay," he said. "Lead the way."

"What, you're just leaving?" Calvin demanded.

"Yes," I said. "I just wanna go home."

"And where is that? His fancy penthouse in downtown?"

"I'm selling that," Levi said. "I'd much rather have the beautiful four square Amy lives in. I hear it has a lot of . . . history for this family."

Levi grabbed my hand and led me away, leaving Calvin sputtering after us.

"THAT WAS A DUMPSTER FIRE . . . in a bomb . . . in hell," I said as we drove away.

"It could have gone worse."

"How?"

"I could have not held back."

"That was you *not* holding back?"

"Amy, think about what I saw," he said. "I saw him crowding you while you looked one step away from crying."

"And?"

"*And?*" he snapped. "That's all I needed. He doesn't get to talk to you like that."

"I hate to tell you this, but he's always been like that."

"That's why you got nervous, isn't it? Because he corners you?"

"That's the least of what he's done."

"Excuse me?"

"He was worse when we were kids. He would push me down in the playground—"

"Wait, is that where you got the scar?"

"W-what?"

"You said you got the scar on your lip from falling down in a playground."

"I told you that *nine years ago.*"

"And I remembered. Did he do that to you?"

"Well, *yes,* but—"

Levi pulled the car off the road and we came to a jerky stop. His knuckles were white on the steering wheel.

"That *fucking* asshole."

"It's not a—"

"Don't tell me it's not a big deal. It is. To me."

I could only stare. Mom and Dad hadn't been this protective when they found out. All they asked was what I did to deserve it.

What did that say about them?

"We were kids. He stopped doing that in adulthood."

"You covered for him."

"I was told I shouldn't have antagonized him."

"So he got away with it?" he hissed as he turned to me.

"He always does. They never see what he does as wrong, and all I've ever been is in the way."

"You're *not* in the way. You're a person too. You're more than that."

"To who?"

"To me."

That did unfair things to my heart. Levi had proven time and time again that he cared, yet it was still so shocking every time.

"You know he's an asshole, right?" Levi's words pulled me out of my thoughts. "That this isn't how life should be?"

"I know it's wrong," I whispered. "If I saw Lily getting treated the way I did, I would be on her side. But inside of me there's still that little girl who thinks it's all my fault. No matter how old I get, she's still there, begging to be loved by the people who are supposed to love her. And sometimes she wins. And I go home thinking things will be different."

"But they never are."

"No. They aren't. Calvin is possibly the worst person I've ever met. And so are my parents because they enable him."

"I should have kicked his ass in wrestling more."

"That wouldn't have changed anything, but it would have been fun to see. Thankfully, he moved on to more . . . manipulative practices."

"Thankfully?"

"When I kept my mouth shut, it was easier. But him not getting the house made him worse than ever. Especially when the court ruled in my favor."

"You needed the house."

"I did. But I still feel bad."

"You have *nothing* to feel bad for."

"You can feel guilt and be right," I said. "And that's how it is for me."

"What you experienced tonight is not how it's going to be anymore. I'm done letting him hurt you."

"You can't always be here."

"I can always be a call away. I'm telling you right now, if you need me, I'll be there."

"And what if . . . this doesn't last? If things change and you don't want this anymore?"

"That's not gonna happen."

"How do you know?"

He opened his mouth and shut it, obviously unsure of what to say. I prepared myself to hear him correct himself and tell me he would only be here for the time we had.

"Because I like you. And I want to keep liking you. Is that so hard to believe?"

"Kinda. Most people use me as a stepping stone to get to Calvin. Ava did. And when she had him, I was dust."

"Is Ava the woman you went after?"

"She was a friend from a long time ago, but then she was his girlfriend. And she is again. For now. I think he did it right when we got married."

"He found your old friend just because we got married? Do you know how sad that is?"

"I mean, you married me for revenge."

"It was *not* just for that." His voice was so sharp that it made me pause.

"But that's what you said."

"That was the reason you'd believe."

"You *hate* him. Anyone can see it."

"Yes, but I don't care about the revenge part of it."

"Then what do you care about?"

"You."

My eyes grew wide.

"Since when?"

"You wouldn't believe me if I told you."

"It has to be after the honeymoon. Or maybe *just* before, but—"

Levi cut me off with a laugh. "When you're ready to know the truth, let me know."

"And until then?"

"I'll be doing what I have this entire time: proving you wrong. About us. About Calvin. All of it."

I swallowed. "That's what you've been doing this whole time?"

A slow smile spread on Levi's face. "Yes. Glad you finally caught up."

Chapter Twenty-Three

FOR TWO WEEKS, things were good. Levi always woke up first to make coffee and breakfast. I would soon follow to take my medicine, and we would sit at the new dining room table to talk about our plans for the day. He would tell me about everything that was going on in the office, and I would either tell him what book to read or talk about what outside project I was working on that day.

And when we went to bed, he would always kiss me good night before holding me as I fell asleep.

Things were good. Nearly *too* good.

But there were cracks in our happy little marriage.

Despite us sharing a bed, Levi never seemed interested in anything more than holding me. Before the migraine, there was no space between us. Now, it was like he was trying not to awaken the horny side of me every time I woke up next to him.

I wasn't sure if he was giving me space to make a move or if he was afraid that somehow fucking me against the wall was the cause of my migraine, but either way, I didn't know how to ask him about it.

If he told me he was simply giving me space, that was one

thing. If he turned me down, I might not be able to recover from that.

I knew chronic conditions weren't sexy. But I had never let a guy see me like that. I was terrified of the repercussions.

It wasn't the only off-limits topic we had. Since the party, Levi hadn't mentioned Calvin once and changed the topic when I tried to. It wasn't like I loved talking about my brother, but I knew something was coming. Calvin wouldn't take what I'd done lying down, and he would retaliate eventually.

And I wasn't sure if either of us were prepared.

Despite the holes in our communication, I still didn't want to lose any of what I had. I kept telling myself that we would be fine, but I was slowly remembering the other things I didn't know about.

One of which came up whenever he looked at his phone.

Most of the time, he would tell me who it was he was talking to, but there was that one time on the honeymoon that stood out to me.

And I didn't know if he'd ever tell me who it was.

It was a normal morning when I saw Levi checking his phone and the familiar feeling of uncertainty overwhelmed me again. I'd been busy sipping on his perfect coffee when I saw it, and whatever peace I felt fell to the ground when I saw his focus was purely on his device.

At first, I let him have his time. But then he *kept* talking to whoever this was and I had to know.

"What's going on over there?" I asked. "I've never seen you that into your phone at breakfast."

"I'm currently trying to contain the storm that is my stepmother. And as usual, she's not giving up."

"Isra? What, is she trying to fix something that you don't want fixed?"

His sigh was a clear answer and he slid his phone over to me.

ISRA

You can't ignore me about this. I have a right to
have her number!

LEVI

And so you can send twenty messages to her
like you do me?

I won't send twenty if she responds.

I'll ask her some other time. She said she wants
to relax today and I'm not taking that from her
by letting you blow up her phone.

Ooh, so protective. This horny honeymoon
phase is getting old!

Horny honeymoon phase? Is this why you
didn't text me in the group chat?

I will remain undiluted.

And I will bother you until you listen to me.

Isra. Migraines. If she says she needs to relax,
she needs to relax.

Let her tell me that herself!

"Uh, wow. Is all of this really because she wants my number?"

"Yes. And you can see how she is."

"But I don't mind it."

Levi sighed. "Not you too."

"When I said I needed to relax, I just meant I need to not kneel
in the garden or else I'd lose my ability to walk. I don't mind
talking to her, and you don't have to be so protective."

"I'm trying to take what you say seriously."

"And I'm trying to clarify it. Isn't the whole thing about
marriage communication? I'm fine to talk to her. If it's too much,
I can block her number."

"That will not stop her."

"Good thing I have a protective husband here to help if I need it."

"Fine," he said with a sigh. "Take her number from my phone. I'm gonna go get ready for work."

He left the unlocked phone with me.

Did he really trust me this much? I could easily swipe to other apps and see if he was talking to anyone else.

And I *wanted* to. It would answer so many questions.

But it was also a betrayal of trust.

I refused to do that, but I knew I had to ask him about it eventually. And I needed to do it *soon*.

After grabbing Isra's number, I opened a text chain.

> Hi, Isra, it's Amy. Got your number from Levi's phone.

ISRA

> FINALLY. How are you feeling?

> I'm good. Sore from working in the garden but that's my own fault.

> Too sore to go plant shopping? There's a place up north of Nashville that's a whole GREENHOUSE. I've been looking for something for us girls to do and Nancy and I are off today.

> I'm NEVER too sore to look at plants.

> Ooh, we can take my new car!

> Ah, a gift from Levi. Finally, he has some place to spend his money. I'll gather Nancy and be over in an hour.

"Please tell me she's being nice to you," Levi said.

"She's being more than nice. She just asked how I was and invited me plant shopping."

"That's what she wanted? She wouldn't tell me what it was."

"She did say it was girl time. And you're not a girl."

"She usually drags Mom into all of this. I'm happy she has someone else to hang out with too. You should go if you feel up to it."

"I was going either way. And I get to show off my new car."

He walked over and pressed a kiss to my lips before grabbing his phone. "Have fun and let me know what you find."

"It might not be enough to fit in a single frame."

"I expect nothing different."

BY THE TIME Isra and Nancy pulled in, Levi had left for work and I had found a pair of overalls in the back of my closet to put on. Nancy was in a similar state of casual dress while Isra was in her usual blouse and jeans.

"You both look like construction workers!" Isra said as she looked at us.

"I plan to be covered in dirt by the end of this," I said. "And these are so cute!"

"Isra just likes to look nice wherever she goes."

"It's only Americans who wear pajamas out in the streets!"

"I assure you," I said, "I'd never sleep in this."

"I bet you sleep with nothing on."

"Isra!" Nancy scolded.

"Not true, but also these things are so difficult to pee in. I'd need a diaper."

Isra laughed while Nancy shook her head. I locked up the house and showed off the new car.

"Isn't it nice?" I asked. "It's even got floor liners for dirt."

"And Levi bought you this?" Nancy asked. "Usually, he buys things that are . . . fancier."

"Way *too* fancy, if you ask me." Isra crossed her arms.

"Yes. He said I could get what I wanted. And this was it. He said it was cheap, but it was literally more than I've ever spent on any of my cars."

"He likes the fancy brands," Nancy explained. "But I like these kinds myself. They're more practical."

"You let him buy you that Volvo," Isra said, shaking her head.

"Like I was gonna say no."

I laughed at their antics and made sure both of them had space in the car before we set out. Isra and Nancy squabbled for the front seat, reminding me of how Emma and I used to be.

The drive took nearly an hour. When I saw the size of the grounds, however, I knew it had been worth it.

I usually went to local greenhouses for my plants, but when I was low on money, I had to choose from the big box store sales to make sure I could afford my second favorite hobby.

Now, I didn't have to worry about it, and it was nice to be somewhere that I could feasibly run into the owner and strike up a conversation.

Nancy was a keeper of houseplants, so much so that Isra said that she was in danger of clogging up the walkways with all of her greenery. Isra told her not to get any more, but by the time we were done with the indoor section, she had five.

"I can't believe you have more plants than Amy does," Isra griped. "This whole day was for her!"

"Wait until I see the fruits and vegetables," I replied. "Then I'll catch up."

And I did. As soon as I saw tomatoes and peppers, I loaded up on them. I already had a few planted, but I hadn't gone to get a huge load like this.

After just a few minutes, I had an entire cart full, and Nancy was teasing Isra about saying I hadn't gotten enough.

"Glad you got a bigger car," Isra said as we loaded up. "But we still have to put some next to Nancy to get home."

"I can't believe you're making me sit in the back," Nancy complained. "With my car sickness!"

"Mine is worse! And I won rock paper scissors."

I laughed as I loaded everything up. My legs were still tired, but I knew I could push through to get it all done.

"Hang on a second!" Isra said. "Hand me that pot. You're sore."

"I'll be fine."

She hit me with a look so much like Levi's that I had to remind myself they weren't actually related.

"Never mind," I said, handing it to her. "You win."

"As I usually do."

It was easier with her help, and when we set off, I was in a good mood. I hadn't had a day like this in a long time. I could see Isra and Nancy being a part of my circle, especially since they were so easy to be around.

And for someone whose circle had gotten way too small, it was nice to talk to more people.

"So, we've been meaning to ask," Nancy began, "how are things after the migraine?"

"Did he actually talk to you, or is he still pretending everything is fine?" Isra asked.

"First of all, I overheard you calling him out on that."

"I thought so."

"And yes, I made him talk it out. And told him if he wants me to open up, he needs to do the same. We're partners."

"I'm *so* glad he met you," Nancy said, grabbing my shoulder. "We were worried he'd never settle down!"

"Never settle down?" I asked with a laugh. "I'm sure he'd find someone eventually."

"We were worried. For a while, he only cared about that little rival he had in high school and college. I can't remember his name, but they were at each other's throats."

"Was it Calvin?" I asked.

"Yep, that's it!" Nancy said with a laugh. "He was working himself way too hard then. I'm glad he grew out of it."

"Um, yeah. He did. He still hates the guy, though."

"Have you heard about him?"

"He's my brother."

The car lapsed into silence before Isra laughed. "That's the way to win a rivalry, then!"

Nancy chuckled too, but I could only manage a smile. Thoughts of revenge floated in my mind, and though Levi had told me that wasn't what this was for, hearing his family make ties to it made me wonder.

"It makes sense, though," Isra added. "I kept asking when he would settle down, but he said he was waiting for one woman. That must have been you."

"It's so cute!" Nancy added.

"Y-yeah. Cute."

My grip on the steering wheel tightened. I'd momentarily forgotten that he had been texting someone else.

All of my happiness came crashing down. If he'd told his family years ago that he was waiting on one woman, then it had to be the one he had sent all of those messages to on the honeymoon.

I knew he wasn't cheating. He spent too much time with me to, but what it did tell me was that I was his second choice.

And that seemed to be the story of my life.

What if she changed her mind and chose him? Would he leave me for the one he waited for? What if he regretted choosing me in the end, especially if my migraines got bad again?

"I'm happy to see him happy," Nancy was saying, unaware of my internal freak-out. "It's what we were waiting for after all. I kept telling him to give up on her and go after someone else, but he was right to wait."

"Yeah," I said, trying to seem okay. "I bet it was."

I DISTRACTED myself in the garden for the rest of the day, but what Nancy and Isra had told me in the car weighed heavily on me. I needed to ask him who the other woman was. I needed to know for sure what he'd wanted the last nine years while we'd been apart.

Levi got home at five, and I was still in the garden when his car door shut. I leaned back on my heels, taking a shaky breath before he found me.

"I thought you were taking a break from gardening," he said only moments later.

My legs didn't feel the soreness anymore. I was too busy thinking about what I'd learned in the car.

"I've got too many plants for me to take a break."

"I can see that now, but I was waiting for a text all day. Did something happen while you were gone?"

"Nothing bad," I said. "Let me go wash my hands."

I took my time getting the dirt out from under my nails while trying to figure out what to say.

"So, what did my mom and Isra say?" he asked while I dried my hands. "I can have a talk with them if they upset you."

"No need. They were great."

"But something's bothering you. What is it?"

I could have spent forever delaying, but I needed to know, and I'd put it off long enough.

"Something was mentioned in the car . . . about you never settling down because you were waiting on one woman." I lifted a shoulder. "It made me do a lot of thinking."

His eyes widened. "Oh."

He looked down, but I could see guilt in every inch of him. My heart ached in response.

"On our honeymoon, I did see something. A lot of messages, actually. Was it her? Is that why you didn't want me to see it?"

"Amy, it's not what you think."

"It's a yes or no question, Levi. I can handle either answer."

"Yes."

I gave one jerky nod. Inside, my heart was crushed.

"Can I explain now?" His voice was gentle, and I knew that this meant bad news.

Could I handle the explanation?

I knew that this had to be how Gram felt when her heart was broken, only this was nowhere near what she went through. How did she pick up and carry on? How did she continue to be kind with all of this pain weighing her down?

"Amy," Levi's voice cut through my thoughts. "I know you're thinking the worst right now, and it's not that."

"How can it not be bad? You have someone else—"

"There is no one else." His voice was firm. "Let's be clear about that."

"But you just said there was."

"There. Is. No. One. Else. This is a misunderstanding."

"What am I misunderstanding?"

"It was you, Amy. It was always you."

"It can't be me."

"And that's where you're wrong."

"Well, you couldn't be waiting for me. What about when you were out late drinking?"

"Mr. Buford introduced himself to me. I was with him."

I blinked. *That's* who he had been with?

"Still, it has to be someone else."

"And why couldn't it be you?"

"Because we talked *once*. You may have liked me, but that's not enough to fall for someone. And you obviously were messaging her, because I saw you. And I don't get why you'd lie and make it seem about me when I saw it with my own two eyes."

"I'm not lying. I'm just terrified of what you'll say when you figure it out."

"Figure *what* out?"

"Do you remember what you saw? Do you remember what app it was on?"

At first, I shook my head, but I knew it wasn't a text. It could have been anything, but it looked familiar, like something I used.

"Wait a second, it looked like Discord."

"Yes, it was."

"And you're saying it was always me so . . ." I trailed off. Messages through Discord.

And he was scrolling through a lot of them.

Suddenly, I was back in college, reading a note from someone who knew who I was.

But I didn't know him.

"V," I said slowly. "The only person I ever talked to through Discord was a guy named V."

He didn't look shocked. "I know."

"You *know*? How could you know? I only ever told Emma about him, but didn't even use his name."

"No one *told* me."

There was a painful, sinking feeling in my gut.

"You know because you *are* V, aren't you?"

He let out a long sigh as if he were preparing himself for war. "Yes. I am."

"I—*what*? But V was the guy I nearly bowled over when I was running to my dorm."

"That was me too." His brow creased. "I assumed you recognized me because you wouldn't look me in the eye."

"I had a migraine. The whole day was blurry." I couldn't look at him and I sank onto the couch. "But the letter was so vague. It was just about a book."

"If you knew it was me, you wouldn't want to talk to me. I figured I could explain eventually if I could just get you to talk. But then you called me, *Levi,* an asshole, so I figured any apology I had wouldn't work."

"Then why keep going?"

"I just wanted to talk to you, even if you didn't know who I was."

Everything rearranged itself in my mind to fit this new information. "So you lied? You were V the whole time and you didn't tell me?"

"When was I supposed to tell you?"

"When you *married* me, Levi. God, I trusted V. What was this? A joke?"

His eyes grew wide. "Why would you think that?"

"*You* were behind it. What, was it some guilt trip for what you did to me? Or was it to keep some sort of connection to Calvin?"

"And *that's* why I didn't tell you, because you would turn it into something I did because of *him* when I just honestly wanted to talk to you."

"That's how life is for me! Especially back then! Once people meet Calvin, I'm second best."

"You do know that's the power *you* give him, right? He's not special. He's not a god on earth. He's a jealous man who can't handle the word no."

"I don't give him power, he takes it."

"Then why bring him up?"

"You hate him! You always have, and you kissed me to get back at him."

"I *talked* to you to get back at him. The kiss only happened because I liked you."

"Then you should have worded it very differently."

"Yes, I should have. I should have done many things differently.

But I was just a man meeting the first woman I liked, and I didn't know what to do. I *never* know what to do around you because I'm too busy staring at you and wondering why the hell you're talking to me to have any logic, Amy. I'm tongue-tied around you, and you think it's all for a man I couldn't care less about."

"But you get mad whenever I mention him."

"I'm mad because he laid a hand on you. And I don't care if you were kids. He's a bully and he hurt my wife. That's more important than any of the petty things he did to *me*."

"But you said you were marrying me to piss off Calvin."

"I said it before and I'll say it again. That was the only reason you would believe. I could get down on my knees and tell you that every single second I'm with you feels like the best kind of torture, and you wouldn't hear it because you truly don't think it's true. And that *kills* me that he and your family twisted your reality so bad that you don't see what's right in front of you."

"Then what is my reality? You're telling me I can't see, but you've never told me what's really going on! You have my attention. Now *use* it."

"Fine. I pretended to be someone else named V because I would take anything I could get. I told myself I was fine with only messaging you, and then I wasn't. You walked into my business and I needed more. You need a husband? I'll be that. You need income? Take all of mine. I've lived off of messages and stolen moments, but then I had *you*. And I can't go back now. I want to be with you as *me*, and I would do anything to get you to see that."

I blinked. I didn't want to be obtuse. If he said I was missing something, then I would listen. But I didn't *understand*.

"When did you decide that I was worth all of this?"

"When I saw you smile for the first time. The first night I actually talked to you."

"The first *night*? Nine years ago?"

"Yes. Even then. From the first time I talked to you, you put a spell on me that I've never been able to shake. You think your brother steals everyone from you, but one look and you had me. You stole me from revenge. From anger. From *him*. And ever since, I waited for the nights I could read the book you were reading. Or talk to you through messages. And now I live for the things I get when we've finished dinner. Or sitting on the couch."

"*That's* what you were busy with? Reading the same books I was?"

"Yes. And when I read them, I could imagine it was you."

"So then you got more, and you *liked* it?"

"Am I really the only person who sees that?"

I wanted to open my mouth and scream *yes*. But it wasn't true. Riley said she would choose me. Lily too.

"O-okay, maybe you have me there. But I still don't get it."

"What don't you get?"

"Why did you break it off?" I asked slowly. "Between V and me."

"Because pieces of us were always going to be in those messages. And I knew if I kept on, it would only get worse. But I still didn't know how to tell you."

"I thought I'd lost my best friend."

"And I hoped I, *Levi*, meant more to you."

"I thought it was *fake*," I snapped. "I thought you were using me for Calvin."

"Damn it, *I know*. I know it was illogical. You only looked at me and saw your brother's enemy. I wanted you to see *me*. And V felt like a distraction for both of us."

"H-he—" I wanted to say he wasn't, but then I remembered the regret I felt for not getting to know him early in our marriage.

What must he have felt like, having me in front of him and not seeing him? How many times did I look through him in favor of a man in my phone?

I was *so* angry that I didn't know, but I also didn't know if I would have believed him if he told me before.

I would have made it about Calvin.

Damn it. He was right. How much power was I giving my brother without realizing it? How many times had I interrupted my own happiness by wondering what his next move was?

"Fuck, we made a mess of this."

"We did," he admitted.

This must have been how Lily felt when she figured out she had it wrong for four years. Nothing made sense. Yet *everything* did.

The pang in my temple was a dangerous reminder that I couldn't think too hard on this. I tried to rub it away.

"What's going on? Is it a migraine?"

"It could be the start of one," I said. "I'll go take the emergency stuff."

"Please," he urged. "I don't wanna stress you out."

"Is that another reason you didn't tell me?"

"After the migraine, yes."

I let out a sigh. "You can't treat me like I'm fragile. And keeping secrets makes it worse."

"I know. But you *just* had one, and I didn't . . . So much time had passed that I didn't know what to do."

"It's almost like when I kept my migraines from you for so long that I ended up in the hospital."

"Yeah. It was."

"I wondered why you forgave me so easily. You were hiding something of your own."

"That, and I can't stay mad at you."

I looked away, knowing I felt the same. Underneath my anger for him was a feeling of longing. I still cared about him more than anything. This one thing didn't undo all of the things he'd done for me, all of the times he'd saved me.

"Stay mad at me as long as you want," he said. "But go take your medicine and *rest*. I'll be in the guest room."

He walked away before I could stop him and I fell back on the couch, looking at the sky.

What would Gram have done if she were here? Would she have held on to her anger?

But she had been left before. Totally and completely left. What Levi did wasn't that bad. And deep down, I wondered if she regretted spending her life alone.

Would she tell me to be happy? Or would she tell me love isn't worth it?

Either way, I'd never get an answer. She was gone. And all of my questions were my own.

Chapter Twenty-Four

I WISHED I could have rested when I was supposed to, but all I could do was lay awake and think of everything that had happened.

Levi was V. He waited too long to tell me.

I was mad at him.

Yet, I also hurt him.

And despite all of this, I still missed him sleeping next to me.

We'd only been in the same room since my migraine, and I'd gotten used to that far too fast. I was used to listening to the sound of his breathing as I drifted off or feeling his warmth adding to my own.

I was frustrated with myself. I needed to sleep to process everything, but I also couldn't sleep because I kept thinking of other things to say.

Sighing, I swung my feet over the side of the bed and got up. It had to be early in the morning hours, and I was slowly giving up on sleep. I thought about going downstairs to read on the couch, but I knew that wasn't what I wanted.

My legs stopped me in front of Levi's bedroom door before I

knew it. My hand rested on the doorknob and I wondered if Gram was turning over in her grave. She always said to stay away from men who hurt you.

But I also hurt *him*.

Levi kept a secret, one he should have told me, but I was slowly realizing that he didn't have anyone else. If it was truly me and only me, it didn't change the fact that the lie was wrong. But I could move past it.

Just like he moved past me hiding my migraines.

I didn't know if I was an idiot or if this was how marriage worked. Was it a symphony of mistakes until you got it right?

Or was I careening into pain?

Apparently, I didn't care.

I wanted him anyway.

I gently pushed open the door and saw his form on the bed.

"Amy?" His head popped up, eyes on me. "What's wrong?"

My feet moved of their own accord. I walked to the bed and climbed in, pressing myself into his chest.

Levi's breath stuttered, but his arms wrapped around me instinctively.

"I can't sleep," I said.

"Me either," he replied. "I missed you too much."

"Same. I'm too used to you being around."

His body folded around me, pulling me impossibly closer— more so than we'd been in weeks.

"Why haven't you touched me since I had the migraine?"

"I've done nothing but touch you."

"I don't mean like that."

"Oh," he said. "I was waiting for you. I looked up the medicine you're on and saw all of the side effects. I didn't want you to think you had to worry about me, especially since you thought that I'd ask you for that when I was sick."

"You said you wanted to do it a thousand times. Why wait?"

"Because I want *you* to want it."

"I do. But after seeing me like that—"

"I still love you. For better or worse. That's what a marriage means."

I squeezed my eyes shut, emotion clogging up my throat. "Love, huh?"

"Yes, darling. I love you. Even when you're sick, and every second in between."

A single tear rolled down my cheek. I'd waited for this moment. I didn't know I had, but there was the truth. It was why I kept picking up books that could make me feel a mere fraction of what love could be.

And now I had it. I really had it.

"You were always here, huh?" I asked. "Right in front of me."

"Yes."

I saw it all through a new lens.

And old confusion finally cleared up. Everything from why he bought the ring to rushing me to the hospital made sense.

I finally understood.

And I wanted to move on, but I had one more question.

"There's no more secrets between us, right?"

"Not that I know of. But if I think of any, I'll tell you."

I nodded, but I still wondered what could be waiting out there.

"Wait, I thought of one."

"What is it?"

"I don't like tomatoes."

"What? But you said you would try my salsa when the plants grow."

"And I will, but I hate the vegetable."

"It's a fruit."

"That's a technicality."

"If that's your secret, then I guess I can live with it."

"I have more."

"What are they?"

"First, I knew you hated chocolate cake when Emma told me. You mentioned it all those years ago on your birthday."

I laughed. "She's gonna be so mad when she finds out. What's the other one?"

"I knew where Isra was picking for our honeymoon. And I let her do it."

"You did? Why?"

"I hoped I could be close to you," he said, his arms tightening. "And I was."

"You're sneaky," I said. "I have one this time."

"Yeah?"

"I think I might love you."

He froze. "Really?"

"Yeah. Is that life-changing?"

"Yes. But in the best kind of way."

"We have more to talk about tomorrow," I said as my eyes closed. "Don't think I'm letting you off easy. But I think I can fall asleep now."

Levi hummed and his breathing eventually relaxed. And I finally drifted off.

WAKING up in the guest room was disorienting. What was even worse was that I was alone. Slowly, I rolled over and felt the sheets next to me. They were cold, and I frowned as I checked the time. I sighed.

It was well past ten. Levi was probably at work, and while I knew his job was important, I needed to talk to him.

Slowly, I peeled myself out of bed and went downstairs. I didn't notice anything was off until the smell of food hit my nose.

Levi was in the kitchen cooking something, and I couldn't resist a sigh of relief.

"You're here," I said.

"Of course I am. We have business to finish. First thing is a groveling breakfast."

"You don't have *that* much to grovel for," I said, but then I saw the spread of bacon and hash browns on the stove. "I'll still take it."

I grabbed coffee while he plated my food. He went all out for this meal, and my stomach was ready to eat everything he had cooked.

We sat down at the dining room table and I opened my mouth to say something first, but he beat me to it.

"I should have told you sooner. I'm sorry."

"I get it," I replied. "Admittedly, I probably wouldn't have believed you about it at first. You were right about how much power Calvin has over me. I thought I was seeing things as they were, but I was seeing things how he wanted me to. I don't want to live like that anymore. Thank you for being patient."

"I get why you felt that way. It's important that you know that if anyone grew up like you did, they would feel the same."

"There's not only that," I said as I traced the patterns of the wood on the table. "Gram was pretty against love. And men in general."

"Why?"

"Her first husband left the moment she got pregnant with my mom. She would always tell me about red flags she missed before her husband left, and I never wanted to miss them myself."

"Did I have any?"

"How much you hated Calvin. At first, I thought it was that you wanted revenge. Then it was that you liked me but also hated him."

"I *do* hate him, but you're not a part of that."

"I think I hate him too. I can't be around him anymore."

"You're removing yourself from his power, which is exactly what he deserves."

I nodded, eyes catching on him. This was V in front of me, the man who I'd talked to for years, the one I'd shared every single book with. The man who read every single one of my suggestions.

"What are you thinking?"

"Remembering you're V. I have a feeling I'm gonna be seeing a lot of things differently," I said.

"Hopefully in a good way."

"Yes, definitely in a good way."

He gave me a smile before fully turning to me. "What's on the agenda today?"

"First things first, I'm gonna try to convince you that you don't have to take the day off work."

"And I'll stay home anyway. What's next?"

"I still have tomatoes to plant. Then I was thinking about reading once it gets too hot outside."

"Count me in," he said.

"You wanna work in the garden with me?"

"I'll do anything with you, even plant tomatoes."

"Planting is not the same as eating, thankfully. I think it'll be fun."

After breakfast, we went outside. It was starting to get warm, but the breeze kept us cool as we finished the garden. By the time the sun was high in the sky, both of us were covered in dirt and in need of a shower. I got in first and then lounged on my bed while Levi did the same.

I was in the middle of a spice scene that had my entire body warm when the door opened and Levi strolled in.

"What are you reading?" he asked.

On instinct, I threw down my Kindle. "Nothing. I was just . . ." I trailed off when I saw him *shirtless* of all things.

Was he trying to torture me?

"You were just what?" he prompted.

"R-reading a book."

"I gathered as much. *Which* book?" His eyes landed on my burning cheeks. "Judging by how red your face is, I'm guessing smut. Wanna tell me about it? Was it good?"

"We don't have to talk about it."

"We were in a book club for years. Of course we have to. I've personally been dying to talk more in person about books."

"Even when you were V, we avoided the topic of spicy scenes."

"I didn't want to talk about that kinda stuff when I knew who you were and you didn't know who I was. But now all of that is different."

I tapped the side of my Kindle and handed it over. I watched as his eyes widened for all of one second before he focused on reading.

"This is . . ."

"I know, right?" I grabbed the Kindle. "I need to cool down after that."

"Or," he said, leaning toward me, "we could make up for lost time."

I dropped the device, pulse kicking up. I didn't realize how much I'd wanted to do just that until it was finally being offered.

He walked close, his breath ghosting over my ear. "And I could make you feel like she did in the book."

I closed my eyes. She'd had four orgasms in the span of minutes, and I wasn't sure that was possible for me.

But I was more than willing to try.

"P-please."

That was all Levi needed to hear. He laid me back on the bed, lips grazing over my neck. My body was sensitive, a side effect of the weeks we'd gone without having sex while he was right next to me. I was more than ready to break that streak.

"How did that scene start?" Levi asked lowly. "Wasn't it with him leaving a hickey right here?"

He nipped the skin below my collarbone and I let out a whine. "Yes."

He did it again and I buried my fingers in his hair, trying to keep him close.

His attention moved to my nipples, which were desperate for attention. Levi had barely started and yet my body quickly built up the pleasure—that's how much I needed this.

"And then he finger-fucked her before going down on her." His hand moved downward. "Sound good to you?"

At the first brush of his hand, I knew I was a goner. "We're gonna have to deviate."

"Why's that?"

"Because I'm already close."

"This soon?"

"It's been a while, and I really need this."

"Then I'll give you what you need, but I'll never let you go this long without feeling good again."

His mouth closed over mine and his hand moved in the way I loved. I whined as my body heated as if I were in a microwave, then exploded with immense pleasure.

Everything was sensitive as I came down from my high, and I pulled Levi from his position until he was lying on his back.

"I'm pretty sure this wasn't in the book," he said.

"Fuck the book. I didn't get to do this last time, and you owe me."

I slid his sweatpants down his hips and took off my underwear before climbing on top of him. I knew I was wet for him already, but I took a moment to press my lips to him before slowly sliding down on his erect cock.

As I stretched for Levi, his hand tightened on my hip, guiding me farther down to take him in deeper. It was too good, yet I needed more.

My hips shamelessly ground down as he thrust up into me. My head fell back, jaw opening as I felt him *everywhere*.

I bounced on his lap, lost in a sea of perfection. I met every one of his thrusts with a jerk of my hips, my body reveling in each one of his movements. I panted, feeling ecstasy in every corner of my body.

"You've gotta stop," Levi said through gritted teeth. "Or I'll come."

"I'm so close," I said. "Please come in me. *Please.*"

"Fine, but we *will* be doing this later."

He went harder, making my eyes roll to the back of my head. I leaned forward, finding the right position.

Levi's mouth latched onto one of my breasts, sucking gently.

And that sent me tumbling over the edge. I moaned as every part of me lit up for the second time.

"Fuck." He bottomed out in me. His cock twitched as he came too, just in time.

For a second, both of us had to catch our breaths.

"You better be ready to never leave this bed."

"I'll go close the blinds for the night, and then we'll have round two."

His mouth covered mine before I got off of him, throwing on a robe and running downstairs.

I did my usual sweep of the house and closed the blinds as if I were heading to bed.

But as I glanced out the window, I saw Mr. Buford in his living room. He had a guest—an older woman I'd never seen before.

I knew he had people coming in and out. But he didn't offer up any information about it, so I figured it was none of my business. However, this time, whoever was over had one of his windows open to give him fresh air.

And I had a view inside his house.

Right in the view of the window was a large picture of Gram, there with all of his other family photos.

I stared at it for a very long time.

Why would my neighbor have a picture of Gram? He said he didn't know her that well, so how did he get that?

"Ready for round two?" Levi asked when I numbly walked back to my room.

"I . . . I don't know."

"What's wrong?"

"I think Mr. Buford knew Gram. Like *way* more than he said he did."

Chapter Twenty-Five

My hands shook as I walked up to Mr. Buford's door. It took convincing to get Levi to go to work considering this conversation, but he had an important meeting on his calendar that he couldn't move. I told him I'd have him on speed dial if something went wrong.

And as much as I enjoyed his support, Mr. Buford was *my* friend. I wanted to face this myself, even if I delayed doing so all morning while I tried to go over just what to say in my head. I'd never questioned him before, and I wasn't sure how to.

He opened the door seconds after I knocked.

"H-hey," I said.

He looked at me with those same kind, brown eyes.

"Here to garden? It's warm today. Are you sure you should be out in this?"

"It's only in the high seventies," I said. "And I'm actually here to talk to you. I need to ask you something."

"Yes?"

"Last night, you had someone over . . ."

"Oh yes, a niece of mine. She made me air out my place since it was such a nice night. I feel better."

"Right. You don't usually open your windows, but I happened to see that they were open and . . . Well, I saw a picture of Gram. *My* gram. In your house."

"Oh."

"She was on your wall. Like a family member."

Mr. Buford looked like a deer caught in headlights, but eventually, his shoulders slumped. "You should come inside. We have a lot to talk about."

The inside of his house was similar to mine, but pictures were everywhere. My eyes found the one of Gram immediately.

"Can I get you coffee?" he asked.

"I'm okay."

"Are you sure? I'm sure it'll be the last time you let me."

"Maybe not. Unless you tell me you're an axe murderer. In which case, I've probably gotten myself killed."

"No, it's nothing like that."

I frowned as I turned to the photo again. It was older, back when she was young.

"I love that photo of her," Mr. Buford said. "I took it myself."

"You did?"

"She'd just bought the house. I asked her if I could take her picture. That was how I met her."

"So you were friends."

He smiled. "She was more than that. So much more. I loved her."

I whirled to face him. "Are you my grandfather?"

There was no way he could be. That man had *left*, and with it, hardened Gram's heart. She'd already hated men before, but it made it worse.

If he'd been there the whole time, right under our noses, why didn't she say anything?

He shook his head. "Oh no. We were never married. I knew her long before that."

"And you loved her?"

"She was my first love. And I was hers."

My eyes widened. "Her first . . . You're the one she would never talk about."

"I'm not surprised she didn't talk about me. She grew more and more distrusting over the years, and I'm the reason why."

I stared at him, trying to remember anything Gram could have said about him. All I could remember was her rants about how she'd been let down, how no one stood by her side when she needed them.

And how she sometimes looked out the window when she said that.

"Wh-what happened?"

"I was stupid. So, so stupid. Her mama didn't like me very much. She said I was too rough for her girl. And I knew I was. So I sabotaged things. Like I always do. She asked me to marry her anyway, to defy her mama. But I knew she would be disowned if I did. I was told so."

"But she loved you."

"She did. But I couldn't be the reason she lost her family. Not without guilt."

"Guilt doesn't mean you're wrong."

He smiled sadly. "I wish I'd known that then. But I thought I had her best interests in mind. So, I did the one thing that would push her away. I found someone else."

Cold horror washed over me. "You cheated on her. That's *terrible*."

"It is. I regretted it the second I did it. And even more as her mama set her up with someone else. She invited me to the wedding to make me watch. I didn't go, but it was in the backyard. I saw it anyway. I deserved it."

"But Gram didn't stay with him," I said. "They were divorced before my mom was born."

"Yes. When I found out, I tried to make amends, but she told me the pain of losing me was worse than losing him. And to her, I was the worst husband of them all. Even if we were never married."

"So . . . what happened? You guys lived next to each other all of this time?"

He leaned on his cane. "Time softened some of it. We could talk without ripping each other's heads off near the end. I'd go so far as to say we were friends, at least, *I* considered *her* a friend. In the rare times we spoke, she told me about you a lot."

"What kinds of things did she say?"

"She was so scared when her daughter was choosing favorites. She said you were so happy and bright. And I told her never to let that light go out."

"You said that? About a kid you'd never met?"

"You were hers. That's all I needed to know. And once I met you, I saw it even more."

I bit my lip. I didn't know anyone else had been on my side. "I wish she'd told me."

"You would have never talked to me if you knew. And besides, you got one more thing from her. She loved to hide her mistakes. I was her biggest one."

I remembered the nights when Gram would tell me about her past and all the times her eyes slipped to the window. I assumed she was talking about my grandfather, the man she'd married. The pain in her eyes still shone brightly even all those years later and it had to be the one she seemed to hate the most.

Instead, it was Mr. Buford.

"You really fucked things up with her."

"I did. And sometimes I wonder if I ever really learned. I probably should have told you who I was, but I wanted some chance to get to know you without my past mistakes weighing me down. I knew it would happen eventually."

"You definitely should have," I said. "But . . . whether you were a mistake or not, you were hers too. It's nice to talk to someone who knows her."

He blinked. "What?"

"When she died, my family cared more about her house than they did her. And over time, I realized that my little sister only had a few memories of her. I had more, but no one to share them with."

"But I hurt your gram."

"Yes. But you've been here for me. If I give too much power to the past, then I miss out on good things in the present. I might not like what you did, but we can still be friends."

He stared at me, eyes shining. "You're something else, Amy. Now I see why she cared about you so much."

"Until the end, I guess." The words were muttered, and I regretted it as soon as I said it. Mr. Buford frowned.

"What do you mean by that?"

"It's just that . . ." I took a stabilizing breath. "Something happened in her will. Something changed that I didn't expect. You said she cared for me, but the house wasn't left to me. She chose my brother for that. Even when she said she would do otherwise."

I expected his eyes to widen, as everyone but Calvin's did when the will was announced. Instead, he gripped his cane tighter.

"She didn't *choose* him," he said firmly. "She wasn't your parents."

"Wait a second, you know what my parents did? You know what happened with the will?"

"Of course I do. I might have messed things up once, but I would never let anything happen to her. Even when each day felt like I was dying, my purpose was *her*. I saw her getting sick and I called her daughter."

"You *what*?"

"Your gram warned me about her. She said she didn't know why she was playing favorites and why she was drifting away over time, but I thought that she was the best option. And I was wrong. I kept tabs on everything, and I quickly saw how you and your little sister were never mentioned, yet your gram could only say good things about you both."

"That's because my brother was the favorite."

"*Of your parents*. Not your gram. And soon I understood why. When she got her diagnosis, I saw that brother of yours coming here. I had an odd feeling."

"I remember that. I thought he was making amends. I thought he was helping."

"He said he was. And I tried to get more information, but there was something about the way he talked about the house like it was a reparation that told me something was wrong. And it got worse when she went to the care facility that *he* paid for."

I remembered that. In light of Gram's sickness, I thought that we were all a family.

And then the will was read.

"I posed as her ex-husband to get in. She was so in and out of it that she let me. I always visited and only caught it when she mumbled about it. She wanted you to have the house, but he convinced her he could cover it financially and let you live there."

"I . . . He tricked her?"

"Yes."

"And said he would let me live here? He was lying. After she died, he wanted to sell the house for the money to build a *pool*."

"I had a feeling. And with how quickly she took a turn for the worse, she didn't pick up on his little scheme."

"He's such an ass," I said. "Why couldn't he let me have this one thing? Why did I have to steal the damn house just to get what Gram wanted for me?"

"Your brother is threatened by you."

"What? By me?"

"There're always those stories about little boys who push down the girls they're jealous of. I don't think he ever grew out of it. Your gram never liked him. He took that personally."

"I forged a version of the will, you know. Now I feel less bad for it."

"I know."

"H-how?"

"The probate court Calvin took you to, I watched it closely. I was going to testify. Until your brother threatened me and smashed my window."

"*What?*"

"He's not a kind man, Amy. He never was. I was awarded a restraining order against him, but they knew you forged the will and were going to give it to him unless someone knew her real wishes. I did, so I testified anyway, privately."

"You're the reason I got the house," I said, my voice faint as it all hit me.

"I am."

"You kept track of *everything*. Why?"

"That's the thing about love. It never leaves, even when you try to force it away. I lost the woman I loved, but I was able to help someone. *You.* I hoped that, even though she was slipping away, I could do *one* thing that would make her proud."

Overwhelming emotion hit me. "You didn't have to do any of that."

"But I did. And I was happy to."

"Thank you," I said against the cotton in my throat. Tears gathered in my eyes and I wiped them. "You literally saved me. I would have been homeless."

"It was the easiest thing to ever do, Amy. Helping you was one of the few things I don't regret."

"She would have been proud," I said. "I know she would have."

Mr. Buford gave me a sad smile. "I don't think she could have felt anything for me but hatred. And that's okay. I didn't do what I did for a reward. I did it because I wanted to."

"Still, you did it. God, I . . . I hate that she's gone. I wish you got your happy ending."

"Oh, Amy. I did. She's in everything. Those tulips that are blooming right now? She planted them all those years ago. I see her in those. I see her in bright days and in the stars at night. I see her in the places I can. And then I got the greatest gift of all."

"What was that?"

"I got to see her in *you*. Your smile pulled me through my grief. Your laugh made me laugh. And sometimes I wonder if she sent you as one last thing I didn't deserve. A second chance, if you will."

"But if she were here, maybe I could have given you that second chance."

He shook his head. "I don't need that. Just this is enough. I got to see you fall in love, Amy. With a man who deserves you. For me to see you be happy, to end up with someone you love, it's like I'm giving it to *her* too. She would want this for you. She would rest easy knowing you have what she wanted for you. Your *light*."

I wiped at my eyes again, which now steadily streamed tears. "You've done more for me than my own family, Mr. Buford. Do you know that?"

"I'm happy to do it. I never had grandkids of my own. I'm sure she'd have something smart to say about me stealing hers, but—"

"I think she'd thank you for being here when she couldn't."

"I'd like to believe that too."

"Thank you for testifying," I said. "You have no idea how much I owe you."

"The only thing I want for you is to live the way I didn't. Be happy, Amy. Find what you deserve. Don't linger in the pain of your past. It doesn't get you anywhere."

"I won't. I'm gonna be free of them. I'm done."

"Good. It's what you deserve. You have so much life, Amy. Spend every second of it with the people who see *you*."

"I will," I promised before pulling him into a tight hug, mind swirling with all of the things I'd just learned.

Mr. Buford knew Gram. He hurt Gram.

And he lost her.

I was still wiping at my eyes. I could see why Gram hated him. I would hate anyone who cheated on me too.

But he also stuck around and watched her to be sure she was okay. And then when she was gone, he did it for me.

If that wasn't love, then I wasn't sure what was.

"I hope you aren't too mad," he said when I pulled away.

"I'm not," I said. "You may have been wrong, but you've also been right too. Especially when it mattered."

"I tried. And I got the best neighbor out of it."

"And I'll continue to be. Gram may have planted tulips, but I'm adding lilies. You'll never forget me now."

"Oh, I won't. Now, get back home and enjoy the rest of your day. Don't think too hard about this."

"You know I will."

"Live in the moment. Be happy. And bring Levi over again. I enjoyed watching that boy get smashed."

"I think he enjoyed it too. He wasn't even hungover either."

"He stayed hydrated. He's a smart guy."

I smiled before telling him we'd be back soon, and then left to go home. When I shut the door, all of what I learned hit me again, as well as a renewed anger with Calvin for being such a piece of shit and manipulating Gram while she was sick.

I was shaken from mulling over my thoughts by a car pulling into the driveway. It wasn't Levi, but it was someone I knew.

"S-Sally?" I asked as she climbed out. "Is that you?"

"Amy? Thank God I have the right address. I need to speak with you."

"Why?"

"Because I think your husband is about to cheat on you."

My jaw dropped. "What? No way."

"I wouldn't think he was the type but a woman came in today.

A very beautiful woman. Nothing like you, of course, but she said she had to talk to him."

"Did she say who she was?"

"It started with an A. Arie . . . Alex . . ."

"Ava?" I asked slowly.

"That's it."

"What did she look like?"

Sally described a woman who could be none other than my former friend. And it hit me that *this* was Calvin's move after that party. This was how he wanted to hurt me.

He wanted to send someone to try and take my husband from me.

"She said she needed to talk with Levi about something. He let her in his office when she mentioned your brother, but she came out and told me to leave because they would be *busy*. All I could do was think of you. I had to warn you, so I found Levi's address. Well, his new one that he just changed everything to."

"That's . . . Levi wouldn't cheat on me."

"She seemed determined."

A text came to my phone and I pulled it out.

CALVIN

> Party right now at my place to celebrate a very good Friday. I have a feeling your husband will be staying at work later than usual, Amy, so you don't have plans.

"Fucker," I muttered.

"He might still be there. You could find out for sure."

I gritted my teeth, going over every option in my mind. It would be easy to run to Levi and let all of my insecurities fly. It would be easy to be angry at him for my brother's manipulation, even though I didn't know what he'd done.

But this was *Levi*, the man who carried me to the car when I was sick, the man who'd grown so much even when we were only virtual friends.

"No, I know exactly where I need to be. This was planned, Sally. This is a power play."

"It is?"

"Let's just say my brother is very unhappy with my marriage. And he's making it known by sending his girlfriend to try and seduce Levi."

"He would do that? What kind of brother is he?"

"A terrible one. He loves to remind me of my place. So I think it's time to remind him of *his*."

Sally didn't understand, and I'd explain it to her later when I thanked her for her warning.

But for now, it was time to turn this scenario on its head.

Calvin should have let me have my peace. He went too far this time, and now, I was coming for *his* power.

I was done waiting to see when he would break. It was time to make it happen myself.

As I PARKED in the grass next to way too many cars, I realized that this was the biggest party I'd seen in a while.

Perfect.

Mom was by the door, greeting each and every one of the guests. Her eyes widened when she saw me.

"Amy?" she asked. "I wasn't aware you were invited."

"Calvin reached out to me personally."

She put her hands on her hips. "I hope you're here to apologize."

"I'm here for something, that's for sure. Where's Calvin?"

She narrowed her eyes at me. "I don't like your tone. I suggest you change your attitude before apologizing."

I clenched my jaw. "It'll be hard to when Calvin's girlfriend is currently trying to seduce my husband."

"She's what? But why?"

"Oh, I don't know, to come between my marriage? To try and ruin my life? You seem to forget that Calvin has a track record of that."

"He would *never—*"

Huffing out a humorless laugh, I shook my head. "You willfully turn a blind eye to him, don't you? You think the sun shines out of his ass no matter what he does. God, there's no getting through to you."

Her jaw dropped. "Amy, pull it together. This is your brother's day and he deserves to be in the spotlight."

"He tricked your mother into giving him that house. You know that, right? He told her he would take care of me, and he *didn't.*"

She crossed her arms. "It's probably because you were never worth being taken care of."

"I'm worth a lot more than that," I said. "And it's sad that you don't see it."

"So, are you just here to start a fight?"

"I'm not starting anything. I'm ending it."

I turned away and went to the living room where everyone gathered around Calvin. He was laughing, enjoying every second of being the center of attention.

I grabbed a champagne glass and climbed onto the table.

"Can I have your attention, please?"

Everyone turned to find the source of the voice, including Calvin, whose expression morphed from his usual devil-may-care attitude to alarm.

I saw the fear on his face, and I knew it all too well.

I'd felt it my whole life.

"A lot of you don't know me, but I'm Amy, Calvin's twin. And I just want to say a big congratulations to my brother."

A few claps rang out in the crowd.

"He needs this," I said. "You know, when we were kids, he always used to push me down whenever I was getting the attention."

"Amy, get down." Calvin's voice was hard as he tried to make his way to me.

"Yes," Mom added. "Enough of this."

"No, no. Let me finish. It's about time that you got the attention you *deserved*." I raised a glass, and the crowd did the same, unaware of what I'd say next. "Anyway, when we were kids, I would be so jealous when people would flock to him. I just wanted a friend for myself. But you know what? I realized that he needs this. He can't function without it. When things don't go his way, Calvin struggles. He might do things like smash windows or manipulate someone who's dying. He also fires his sister and leaves her without health insurance when she has a chronic condition. You know, things like that."

The crowd was silent. I was sure I could have heard a pin drop from a mile away.

"So, please, for me, continue stroking his ego. You don't wanna see what he does when you stop."

Whispers broke out as I jumped down and headed for the door.

"Amy!" Dad yelled. "What the hell was that?"

"That was me finally saying what I should have for all of these years. You're welcome."

"I am *not* thanking you."

"Good. Neither am I. You and Mom have consistently chosen Calvin over me, and I'm tired of it. I have no interest in celebrating a spoiled man-child who can't handle the word no."

Dad went red in the face. "You're the only one causing a scene."

"Good. I deserve at least one. At least I won't be following up a funeral with a fucking court case."

"Y-your gram was wrong!" Dad snapped. "She never loved him like he deserved."

"Not loving people like they deserve runs in the family."

Calvin was making his way to me and I knew he wanted to get me alone. Pure rage was on his face, and he wouldn't let me get away with this.

And he wouldn't want an audience.

I darted out the door and into the side yard.

He caught up quickly.

"Amy! You don't get to run from me after doing what you just did."

I turned to him and flipped him off. "You deserved it!"

"And you deserved to get fired."

"Yeah, you know what? I did. And it led me to my husband, so thanks for that."

"Your husband who's spending his night with another woman."

"He's not gonna touch Ava."

"Really? He wouldn't be the first person to leave you when something better came along."

I laughed. "Like Gram did with you?"

Calvin's jaw dropped for a fraction of a second before his entire body hardened with anger. "How *fucking* dare you."

"Yeah, she hated you because you *suck*. She's the one person you couldn't make like you. You're fake, Calvin. You're fake and you're sad. People are gonna leave you because you're a shallow, self-absorbed asshole who only lives for revenge! And I bet you're terrified of the people who see you for what you are. Just like Gram did. And just like I do."

"I'm not scared of you."

"And I'm not scared of you either." That was a lie. I was terrified, but I could be that *and* annoy the hell out of him.

"You should be," he said through gritted teeth.

"Oh, what are you gonna do? Try and take my job again? Try and take my husband or my house? You *can't*."

I turned away with one last smirk, but his hand clasped my arm, pulling me back to him. His hand raised when I faced him again, and I saw it coming for me. I closed my eyes, knowing this was going to hurt.

And it fucking did. My ears rang. My vision went dark. And I was pretty sure I heard a chorus of gasps.

When I opened my eyes, I expected to see Calvin about to deliver another blow, but instead, he was pinned on the ground by the last person I expected.

"What did I fucking say about not touching my wife?"

Levi was *pissed*. More so than I'd ever seen him, and I knew he was about to undo my plan.

"Levi!" I said.

"What the fuck are you doing here?" Calvin ground out. "I had you busy."

"Because you sent a woman to try and seduce me?" he yelled. "Your little manipulation tactic was never gonna work. At first, I was mad, but now I think I'm gonna actually kill you."

Calvin struggled. It did nothing.

"Levi," I said as I tried to stand, but I was unsteady on my feet.

"Shit, darling." He was off of my brother and by my side in half a heartbeat. "Are you okay? I should have gotten here sooner, I—"

"It's fine."

Calvin laughed and got to his knees. "Is it? I finally got to land that hit on you that I've wanted to this whole time. You deserved that, Amy."

Levi growled and was about to go back to Calvin, but my grip on him tightened. "Stop," I said. "He wants you to fight him."

"But he—"

"He hit me." I leaned closer. "In front of everyone."

Levi finally turned to see a crowd had gathered in the yard. A few people were recording. Many had their jaws on the ground.

"Come on!" Calvin said as he got onto his feet. "I hit your wife! Aren't you gonna retaliate?"

"So you can spin yourself as a victim?" I asked. "I don't think so. For the first time, I defended myself and you showed your true colors. You don't get to tell a different story. All my life, you've threatened me, and now that I don't give a shit, you hit me for it." I wiped my nose and saw it was bleeding. "Fuck. You."

"You're never coming near her again," Levi said. "The next time I'll see you will be in court when I get a restraining order."

"It won't be your first," I added.

"Fuck you!" Calvin yelled. "I wish those stupid headaches you got killed you so I didn't have to deal with you anymore!"

The words were brutal. But so were the reactions around him.

"Oh my God!" a woman yelled. "That's your *sister*."

"He hit her too. I saw it!"

"Is this the man we want running a mental health clinic?"

I laughed. "Now everyone sees who you are. You can hate me all you want. But you deserved this." I grabbed Levi's hand and pulled him away. "Let's go."

"Are you okay to drive?" he asked.

"Good enough," I said. "The dizziness is better. Just let me get the car out of here before Calvin finds a bat."

"I hate every part of this," he said. "But that was very smart."

"Well, I needed one more stupid thing to add to my list. And it should be enough to get him out of our lives forever."

We got into our respective cars and I ignored all the shouts from Mom and Dad as they chased me down before driving away. The pain dulled into a throb, one that was nothing compared to the other pain I'd experienced all my life.

I'd finally seen the worst he could do.

And I handled it.

I was able to drive the entire way home. Mom and Dad's calls moved to my phone, but I didn't care to answer. Instead, I blocked both of their numbers.

They would tell me I deserved what happened to me. And I was done hearing it.

My car door opened and Levi leaned down. "Are you okay?"

"I'd take getting punched in the face over a migraine, honestly."

"Jesus," he said. "I'm cleaning you up. And then we're *never* doing anything like that again."

"Agreed. That was a once-in-a-lifetime thing."

"We're pressing charges, just so you know. He's not getting away with this."

"Of course we are. Why do you think I let him catch up to me in the yard?"

He huffed. "A genius idea. Still an idea I fucking hate."

I followed him inside where he got a wet rag to gently wipe at my face.

"So, how did being seduced go?"

He looked up. "You tell me. You're the only one who'll manage to do it."

"Fine. Then the attempted seduction."

"She tried to say she wanted to vent about Calvin. Then she took her jacket off to the ugliest and most revealing top I'd seen, and I kicked her out. And you need to know that I would *never*—"

"I know," I said. "But Sally didn't. She came to warn me."

"She did the right thing."

"Even though she works for you?"

"She had my wife's best interest in mind." He gently wiped again. "Even though you never seem to."

"Hey, short-term danger for long-term benefit. It's an investment."

"I never want to see that again, though. Do you understand me?"

"You won't. Hopefully, we can press for prison time, especially since it's not his first offense."

"I was gonna ask about that. What was the first restraining order he got?"

"Oh, I have a long story for you. One involving what I learned from Mr. Buford."

"I completely forgot you confronted him."

"And I learned a lot. Ready to hate Calvin more?"

"Who the fuck cares about him? I'm ready to hear about what *you* learned."

I laughed. It would take time to fully get used to the attention being on me.

But I would get used to it.

"I'll tell you everything, but first things first, I'm gonna go take my medicine. I feel a headache coming on."

"Then the conversation can wait. We have all the time in the world."

I pulled him into a tight, crushing hug. "And we won't waste it. We're getting our happy ending."

"Darling"—I could hear the smile in his voice— "I think we already have."

Epilogue

I WOKE up alone in my bed, which was unusual for me.

I frowned as I slowly got up. I threw on a robe—since I'd dozed off in nothing after another night of Levi rocking my world—and went to the kitchen. Levi was nowhere to be found and neither was his car.

One of our favorite things when we woke up was to have breakfast together. It was a tradition, even on the days he worked. And for him to be gone was worrying.

I turned to the coffee pot, which had freshly brewed liquid in it. I poured a cup and went to grab my phone to ask where the hell he was. But then I reached into the fridge and saw no maple syrup.

That was when Levi walked into the house with two massive bags in his arms.

"You better have had a good reason for leaving me in bed alone," I said as I closed the fridge.

"I was trying to make you coffee for when you woke up, but we were out of maple syrup, so I ran to get some."

"And these bags were for *just* maple syrup?"

"Yeah, about that." He put the bags on the counter. "You

know how I said there was no recipe you could make that would get me to like tomatoes?"

"Of course I do." I crossed my arms. "Are you about to admit you were wrong?"

He sighed. "The frittata you made was incredible, and the tomatoes that were ripening on the window sill are ready now. Can you make that again?"

"Only if you admit I'm amazing and right all of the time."

"You're amazing and right *most* of the time."

I glared. "Not what I asked for."

"Maybe these will make up for it." He pulled out a huge bouquet of flowers from the second bag.

My heart skipped a beat as it always did when he did something sweet like this.

"It kinda does. But you don't have to get flowers for me all the time. You just did last week."

"You're my wife. I have to make you smile somehow. And I'm making up for your entire life."

"You're not responsible for that."

"But I'll do it anyway."

Some days, I didn't know how to bask in my new life. Levi was attentive—more so than anyone I knew. The only close second were Isra and Nancy, who I grew closer to by the day. When I accepted that I deserved love, it was more difficult than I expected to let them in, but I worked hard at it. Now, the three of us had a group chat where I would tell them about my day.

Levi put the flowers in a vase as I worked on food and sipped on coffee. We'd fallen into an easy step since fully leaning into the marriage. As time went on, I was taking on DIY projects on the house and making it more like a home. I was determined to keep the charm, but Gram would have wanted me to make it mine.

It even extended to Mr. Buford's house. Levi had paid for a ramp since Mr. Buford was now in a wheelchair full-time. He'd fought the financial assistance, but both of us insisted, especially since he'd already been given the chair by a charity organization.

One that we'd started, of course.

But the changes also extended to the neighborhood.

The new family who lived in the old house across the street were in the midst of remodels too. They had two adorable kids who I often said hello to on my morning walks while they waited for their bus. Our little undisturbed corner of Nashville had stayed that way.

Calvin had to sell the house quickly to pay for court fees. After we'd pressed charges, he was removed as CEO, and his focus quickly moved to trying to fight going to jail for assault.

It didn't work. There were too many people with video evidence and I had the scar on my chin to prove his troubled past. Mom and Dad vowed to never speak to me again if I went through with sending him to jail.

I didn't care. I had no interest in talking to them.

They'd sold the family company too, and the new owners were *not* pursuing Levi's business anymore.

From the little I'd heard, Calvin had spent a few months in prison. Mom and Dad had pleaded to get him out on bail before his sentence was up, and at first, I'd been worried he would come after me. I got one letter in the mail from him, which Levi sent to the cops and put him back into jail for a few weeks, and he finally got the message.

I wished he was spending *more* time behind bars, a sentiment Levi shared, but him losing the company and a lot of his money was almost enough for me to be satisfied.

I was more focused on ensuring that my life was perfect.

I spent a lot of time with Lily, and Riley when I realized she was more than serious about befriending me. Lily and I had gone to trivia and karaoke nights at Riley's shop, and recently, we started hanging out outside of her work. She was busy with her two kids and husband, but she tried to make time for us.

I couldn't explain how happy I felt to have a group of people who liked *me*. Once my family could no longer ruin things, I was dedicated to working on my self-esteem and feeling like I was worth all of the greatness in the world. It took time, but I was finally coming around.

"Are you still meeting Lily for coffee?" Levi asked as we ate.

"She's showing me her newest book," I said with a smile. "I'm so pumped."

"Fantasy or romance?" he asked. "I love that your best friend is a writer, but she's brutal when she writes fantasy."

"Romance this time, which is why I'm extra excited. She's been working her ass off for the last year, and it's finally time for me to see the fruits of her labor."

After a few months of marriage, I'd asked Lily if she was willing to let Levi know about her life as a writer. She told me she was surprised I hadn't already told him.

His expression was priceless when he found out the author of the dark fantasy that still gave him nightmares was my best friend. I'd laughed until I nearly passed out, and he told me I wasn't allowed to keep secrets anymore until I reminded him that this one wasn't *my* secret to tell.

Once I showed him her new romance collection, it was far easier for him to see the genius that was my best friend.

"When is this one coming out? Maybe we can add it to the book club."

"Sooner than later," I replied. "I'd love to have her secretly there or something."

As time went on and I worried less about my family and more about living my life, I needed a book club of some sort to go to every week.

I'd told Levi, and while he and I often read the same books, I wanted to expand. I asked Riley if there was one that met at the coffee shop, and she told me I could start one. I wanted to, but I was still nervous about the breakthrough migraines I could get even when on my medicine. That was when Levi reminded me that we were a team now, and he could cover when I couldn't.

And I finally felt like I could run one again.

Sally and Maisie were our first members. Riley joined when she could, and Lily did when she had time. I'd even made new friends through our current members, and our number slowly grew.

"Have fun," he said. "And see if she'll give me a copy."

"I will," I replied. "But for now, this first copy is *mine*."

"I can't believe she gave you and Riley a copy, but not me."

"She's been oddly secretive about this one. She won't even tell me what it's about, and usually, she at least lets me beta read. Maybe this one has a cool twist."

He laughed and then got up to get ready, giving me one last lingering kiss as he left. I went to the coffee shop right after. Lily was waiting with a book in her hands.

"And here you go," she said with a smile.

"Do you have one for me too?" Riley asked, nearly running to the table.

"Duh."

"I won't be able to keep up with Amy here," Riley said, shaking her head. "But in a month, I'll have something for you."

"You have kids, so I understand." Lily put a hand on her stomach. It wasn't rounded yet, but I knew the truth.

"That'll be you soon," I replied.

"And I'm planning the shower." Riley rubbed her hands together. "Finally, I can plan something that isn't a kid's birthday party."

I laughed. "And I'll decorate."

Lily turned red, but I knew she and Sebastian were excited about the baby. It had taken them a while to get pregnant after agreeing to have kids, but now that it was happening, they were over the moon. I didn't know if kids were in my future, but Levi was happy to be with me either way.

After taking a long drink of coffee, I got to work reading. The book was incredible, but after a few chapters, I began to see a pattern.

"Hang on," I said as I put down the book. "A woman who lives in the shadow of a sibling? Is this based on me?"

She smiled. "Surprise."

"Are you serious? Is this why you wouldn't tell me anything about it?"

"She kept me in the dark too," Riley said. "Mostly. I figured it out after a while."

"What? I knew I wanted to see the look on your face when you found out. It's hilarious."

"It really is," Riley added.

"She's inspiring, isn't she?" Lily asked.

"A whole romance heroine based off of me. Are you trying to get this to be Levi's favorite book?"

"Absolutely," she said. "I even brought an extra copy for him too, so if you argue that you're not good enough, he has evidence on his shelf."

"First off, we share shelves, and second, I've been working on myself. I definitely deserve this. I'm the light of all of your fucking lives."

"She's got a whole book *and* self-esteem?" Riley said with a laugh. "She's unstoppable now."

"I always was. It took me getting you guys and Levi in my life to finally make me see it," I said, and it was true.

I once thought I was made to blend into the background. Now, I knew I was the main character of my own life, and I was more than happy to make sure it stayed that way.

Want more?

GET an epilogue exclusively from Levi's POV here!

Thank You

A novel is a labor of love. And I'm fortunate enough to be surrounded by a lot of it. To my husband, Josh; my best friend, Lizzie; and everyone else who helps me: You guys are the inspiration that feeds my work.

I wasn't sure about this book for a long time. I loved Amy in *Contractual Obligations*, and I didn't know if I could do her justice in her own story, but I had extra help in the form of an incredible alpha edit from Mae, which helped me get both Amy and Levi perfect.

And as usual, I need to give a massive thank-you to Kasey for copyediting this beast. I yapped A LOT in this book, and while I'm so happy I gave Amy time to grow, this was far more than I told you it would be when I started writing.

And to the readers, I hope you enjoyed reading *Ill Will* as much as I did writing it. I always wanted to continue in the world I built in *Contractual Obligations*, and you all made it possible.

About the Author

Elle Rivers writes fun romance books filled with real-world problems wrapped in beautiful, heartwarming happy endings. When not writing, she can be found speed-reading other authors' amazing romance novels, curling up next to any warm object she can find, or singing obnoxiously loud to Taylor Swift.

Elle was born and raised in Nashville, Tennessee, and she considers herself one of the few native Nashvillians who does not like country music. She has eight cats who fight for the spot on her lap, and eight chickens who couldn't care less about her unless she is bringing them food. She lives with her romance hero of a husband who endlessly supports her writing endeavors, and her son, who is the biggest, but most adorable, distraction.